The Messenger
Let There be Light

Kristin Osborne

Ukiyoto Publishing

All global publishing rights are held by

Ukiyoto Publishing

Published in 2023

Content Copyright © Kristin Osborne

ISBN 9789360495527

All rights reserved.

No part of this publication may be reproduced, transmitted, or stored in a retrieval system, in any form by any means, electronic, mechanical, photocopying, recording or otherwise, without the prior permission of the publisher.

The moral rights of the author have been asserted.

This is a work of fiction. Names, characters, businesses, places, events, locales, and incidents are either the products of the author's imagination or used in a fictitious manner. Any resemblance to actual persons, living or dead, or actual events is purely coincidental.

This book is sold subject to the condition that it shall not by way of trade or otherwise, be lent, resold, hired out or otherwise circulated, without the publisher's prior consent, in any form of binding or cover other than that in which it is published.

www.ukiyoto.com

Dedication

To the omnipotence (all mighty, infinite in power), omnipresence (present everywhere) and omniscience (knows everything at all times), everlasting Creator of the Universe.
His "Messenger", Archangel Saint Michael who is 'Unto like God'. And to all life forms and civilizations in the celestial wonders of the Universe.

Contents

'Sanctified'	1
'The Arcturians'	6
'Friendship In The Making'	12
'New Beginings'	20
'Space Odessey'	25
'The Bait And Switch'	32
'A Cosmic Universe'	41
'Divine Intervention'	47
'Ask And Receive'	55
'Inspiration And Hope'	62
'Ultimately'	73
'Embracing Change'	81
'Kindred Spirits'	89
'The Enchantment'	100
'Persuation'	105
'Synergy'	115
'The Universe'	122
'Covered By His Grace'	126
'Salvation'	143
'Compassion'	151
'The Pure In Heart'	154
'Victory In The Light'	160
Soul Mates	167
'Shameless'	185
'The Fabulous Five'	210
'Harmony'	233
Enlightenment	244
About the author	*256*

'Sanctified'

Peering out of her office window on the third floor of the Plantation under the attic which faces down a mile long driveway lined with hundreds of ancient Magnolia, Ash and Pecan trees that were planted in the 1600's with thousands of acres of crop and timber land. Kristin, the lady of the house notices a brand new Rolls Royce limousine driving towards the mansion.

Wearing a navy blue eyelet floor length sundress with her long blonde hair flowing down below her shoulders, she walks down the three flights of stairs to the first floor. Heads down the hallway to the servants entrance and steps out onto the kitchen landing staring at the limosuine emblazoned with a logo that says 'Criss Cross Properties LLC'.

Kristin walks up to the limosuine with curiosity. The back cabin window rolls down. A man wearing a custom tailored navy blue suit with a twinkle in his blue eyes, who reminds Kristin of George Clooney smiles at her affectionately.

The man says "My name is William Poindexter. We were just driving through town admiring the history of Gloucester and visiting old Plantations in the area. I have always wanted to see Eagle Point Plantation. The setting here is absolutely stunning. And so is the mansion" as he admires the waterfront view.

Kristin with a keen interest smiles and replies "Thank you Mr. Poindexter. It is a pleasure to meet you. The waterfront view is one of the reasons I fell in love with Eagle Point. Here is my business card should you like to schedule a tour of the mansion. That happens to be one of my specialties. I love showing her off with all of her grandeur and the glory that she once was".

Mr. Poindexter replies fondly admiring her sophistication, class and sensuality "Kristin-it is all my pleasure. Thank you for your kindness. I can only imagine what a show place that she was at one time. I will definately take you up on your offer Kristin. Have a blessed day" as he rolls up the window. Kristin waves goodbye smiling. The limousine drives by the barn then out through the main entrance.

Not recognizing his name or his business emblem, Kristin thinks nothing of it. She is ambushed with unwanted visitors here constantly. Mostly from decedents from the previous owners and distant relatives from the servants that once lived here. The Plantation is notorious for many reasons.

If she only knew that the few brief minutes with a man named William Poindexter would bring the most thrilling, life changing, everlasting sequence of events to her world, she might just not beleive it. And the story of Eagle Point Plantation carries on.

'Angels bring humans the power to transcend the limitations of space and time'. The setting is Eagle Point Plantation. A space odessey in itself where the human mind seeks the great unknown. A pre civil war Plantation built circa 1680 situated directly under the planet Mars which is 176.14 million miles away from Earth.

The Plantation, measuring a massive 12,000 sq. ft. filled with twelve bedrooms, nine bathrooms and fourteen fireplaces abandoned after the civil war. Surrounded by three miles of water frontage. Two island graveyards, has it's own airplane runway, and was established before Virginia was colonized.

And the walls in the house speak as if it is alive, filled with ancient history. The Plantation is the home of Kristin, a divorced mother of two and her son Ryan who is almost 23 years old and is on the spectrum. The setting at Eagle Point is spectacular, with unwarrented supernatural events that ever occured on planet Earth. Which have become Kristin's families reality in the midst of unchartered waters, situated not too far away from the Bermuda Triangle.

And Ryan, Kristin's son keeps prophesying that the year 2039 will be the greatest 'Coming of the Eternal Light' in the history of the Universe, all of space and time and their contents, including planets, stars galaxies, and all ofther forms of matter and energy.

Ruled by God the omnipotent, all-powerful, all-knowing present everywhere at at all times. The Creator of the divine Universe. Underneath the glorius star Arcturus, the planet Sirius and the ancient civilization from the planet Pleades lies the consetallation Bootes and Virgo and a direct portal to realms above the twelfth dimension to all of the civilizations in other galaxies.

A literal "space conference room" where the highest powers protected by anjelic hosts and Archangel Metatron (Enoch after he ascended into the celestial realm and his heavenly metamorphosis near the Throne of Glory) who governs over the entire vast Universe with the Merkabah of sound.

The coordinates would be "Latitute 37" the UFO and paranormal highway where extraterrestrial craft enter and exit the Earth's atmosphere. A parallel dimension in time which runs from California, through Nevada, Colorado, Kansas, Missouri, Illinois, Kentucky and across Virginia and up through Greece and in between the waters of North and South Korea. Protected by the infinate beauty of the choir of the spirits of light and sound of the Universe, a spiritual zone undefined as a nucleus of reality, not just divine conciousness but 'the I that is We'.

While listening to Guns and Roses singing out loud to 'Knockin on Heavens Door' watching dozens of fleets of spaceships descend from the sky at warp speed above the river in his backyard, Ryan-a young man stumbles into a sacred one hundred foot tall divine crystalline portal made of Universal plasma which appears like the inside of a kaliadascope appearing other wordly with gold and diamond shaped Merkahbah's of sound that allows you to see and travel into other dimensions of time including the future. Receive messages from the Divine Creator, Ascended Masters and the Divine Avatars who are an incarnation or representation of God.

Ryan has been given a supernatural key from the Spirit to time travel. Sit in front of the Throne with the lumanaries. Form friendships with civilizations from other galaxies who cruise along Latitude 37 and park their fleets of spaceships above the 'Veil' at Eagle Point and go for rides in their spaceships, give Martians and the Viking Seals from Mars tours of the Plantation and show them the animals on Earth, dechiper dark energy, discuss quantum physics and talk about future events of the human race and life on Earth years before it happens.

Ryan keeps prophesing that the year is 2039 is when the

extraterriestials will come to Earth and save the planet and cohabitate in peace with the few humans that will still exist on planet Earth after saving the Universe from a 'space espionage war'.

A literal Mt. Sinai itself in a tiny little remote town on Earth on the Chesapeake Bay in Virginia lies Eagle Point Plantation. 'An electrifying supernatural celestial realm' overseen by the magnificent power and glory of Archangel Saint Michael, a spiritual warrior in the battle of good versus evil, the leader of all angels and the army of God.

In faster than a split second you can travel back in time to the ancient Lost City of Atlantis-one of the oldest and greatest mysteries of the world discovered by Plato more than 2,300 years ago and as he says the utopian island existed 9,000 years before his time and mysteriously dissapeared one day. The Garden of Eden 'the Terrestrial Paradise' the bibilical paradise described in Genesis 2-3 in the BC Era or fast forward in an instant breaking the sound barrier faster than the speed of light through the atmosphere through the Milky Way and Orion's Belt to a distant galaxy ten million light years away floating through extensive spans of nothingness kown as 'the intergalactic medium' where the moons above represents cosmic events, divine epiphanies and the ephemeral nature of human life and history and civilizations from other solar systems and perhaps the 'Neverending Story' of Eagle Point and the state of humanity may actually end in the year 2039.

Are Nostradameus prophacies coming true? WWIII between Russia and Ukraine and North and South Korea, let alone Iran and Israel? Global warming to be the demise of humanity before a nuclear war? Political unrest, violence, hate crimes are the new norm in society. Drought, pestilence, disease, famine, locust invasions and pollution. Solar flares from the Central Sun. Uncontrollable wild fires, earthquakes, volcanoes disrupting and destructive natural disasters are a daily occurance all over the planet.

And AI Chatbox computer programs that people prefer to socialize with as 'their new best friend to manipulate mass data banks for fraudulous ponzi schemes' who will wipe out millions of jobs and control the stock market and breach national security among other things. Instead of having animals as pets humans will have 'pet' robots who will take over the planet. What will happen to the animal kingdom and the marine life whose eco system has been irripairably disturbed with bactaria and global warming which has provided humans sustainability on planet Earth?

Gods starseeds 'Indigo children" connecting with far superior intellectualy, scientifically and electronicaly advanced civilizations in the Universe to whom a quantum equation is as simple as 1+1. In divine collective consciousness, galactic races who are far intelligently superior and in higher realms than earthlings?

'The Arcturians'

And the mystery continues. Kristin, Ryan's mother is watching out of her kitchen glass storm door as the spaceships take formation around the property recognizing the massive size and glowing red 'disco' lights of the Pleadians ships, with their multidimensional pure light frequency who activate sacred timing. Their titanium sleek ships are propelled by electromagnetic fields made out of oxygen from the atmosphere and their high tech form with floor to ceiling windows shaped like a polygonal prism and operate at the speed of 'quantum entanglement'. And the Arcturian ships spinning faster than the speed of light shaped identically as the Pleadians ships, with their cobalt blue flashing lights, the same color as Archangel Saint Michael 'the Messenger' as they are keepers of the Veil.

Kristin notices some new types of spacecraft she hasn't seen before which appeared in bronze color in the shape of an Octagon with what appeared to be laser beams on each side and some type of glass 'teleport' on the bottom. Grabbing her camera she takes pictures of the ships in awe glimpsing at the occupants in the bronze ships which have a gargantian size and tendrals of long hair wearing high tech armor appearing as protective suits on, guessing they must be from some far out Galaxy.

She waves at the Pleadians and Arcturians and says welcome peace to you laughing at all of light codes and signs from the Holy Trinity that she had chalked on the solid oak cross doors of the Plantation enjoying the whishing sound of the spacecrafts feeling a vibration lifting her to another worldy realm.

Wondering what was up in 'the divine world' Kristin asks Ryan "What are our visitors up to and did you speak with them? Is there another space war going on or are the Arcturians and Pleadians waiting here for the Sirians to change the history of the future? I am sure that they didn't fly all the way here just to hang out with the Martians or visit just you. Well maybe they would. You hang out and channel with them everyday along with the Martians and everything else in the Universe and all paranormal activity. All of scientists on earth says the planet and humanity are in demise".

Ryan replied blushing in an erethal state of mind smiling replies "It was the Spirit and he was telling me all the works of heaven, earth and sea, and all the elements, their passages and going and changes of the stars, the seasons, years and days and hours, the rising of the wind, the numbers of the angels and the formation of their songs, and all human things, the toungue of every human song and life, the commandments, instructions and sweet-voiced singings and all things fit to learn and he annointed me with a sweet smelling oil" looking at his mother as if she was one of the lowest life forms on the planet and then felt sorry for her with the present state of things at their home and with Stewart and with all of the divine intervention taking place and his own personal manifestation demands which are so fucking irritating to her.

Smiling to herself she asks "Are you going on a spaceship ride tonight? Take some pictures for me. Is there a space war in the entire galaxy or just one evil race, or is it the crystalline grid of the Earth? Lightcodes or the imbalance of the electromagnetic field of the North and South Pole? You lucky kid have fun you are probably the only human being on Earth that gets to experience this you know. I am so proud to be your mother" thinking why don't you just write a fucking book and take videos you would make millions or be taken into custody by NASA and interrogated for your knowledge.

Ryan replies "Thanks mom. See you later" and walks out to the backyard and dissapears through the portal. Kristin thinking to herself 'Close Encounters of the Third Kind' in the 23rd century and hears a group of Arcturians surrounding her in the kitchen speaking in light language looking at her with curiousity at her humanly inepthitude so far inferior to their sophistication and intelligence

Even after the Pleadians took her one night into their spaceship and placed her in a 'med bed pod' her chakras are still out of balance most likely from partying too much in Beverly Hills and Hollywood in her 20's when she worked at Universal Pictures in Feature Business Affairs and had her own golf cart and used to lunch on 'Jaws' lake and had full access to their wardrobe department; deep seeded trauma from her parents and her own divorce and being stuck raising and supporting two kids by herself. Most likely Ryan is so psychicly advanced and doesn't share his secretive relationships with his friends from other galaxies with anyone and being on 'the spectrum' is a consorted state of being in itself.

Kristin has been keeping track of the cycles from visits from the extraterrestials in a special journal, which normaly occur on a full moon cycle and during cosmic solar flares from the Central Sun. Laughing out loud reminding herself she could probably sell a video of a Martian spaceship next to her house that crash landed right next to the master bedroom in the east wing in 2019, which appeared a glowing neon green. A radioactive propelled ship in the shape of a cylindar. A small craft that was used transport small groups to explore the planet with the capability of cloaking itself with a Martian appearing outside the craft looking like a radioactive C3PO from Star Wars for a billion dollars to Elon Musk but the money would not satisfy her undying thirst for knowledge or the guilt for NASA destroying them.

And a deep dense fog always appear after they arrive and let themselves be known and their underground 'Martian space camp' beneath the river is very well hidden and appears like a planet in itself with an orange and gray glowing and craters underneath the neon green glowing 'Latitude 37 beacon'. A small slice of the Universe and a whole other world in itself. And Ryan communicates with them constantly.

Kristin says out loud "Welcome friends, peace to you and glory to God". Arcturians have an almost turqoise blue skin with an erethal glow, are about 10 feet tall and seem to be non binary not noticing any differential from feminine or masculine. They have extremely advanced medicinal technology based on the fungiculture from their planet Arcturus 'the divine keeper of the Veil' and inter-abide with the divine and have great compassion and love. Their eyes are triple the size of humans and they have an oval shape and when you stare into them they are almost like a computer system but they feel your pain and demise of the sins of humanity and have great appreciation for planet Earth and love of animals.

They wear some type of oval shaped crystal embedded in the middle of their forehead which is some type of divine connection and they have telekinisis powers and transport to there spaceships like shapeshifting, wear no clothes or shoes and use mental telepathy to communicate with you and they have always been curious about Kristin ever since she moved to Eagle Point and lived through the 'house haunting' which actually was just a distraction to bring her back to Christ and after she discovered that she had 'a Martian Colony' next to her house and learned about Latitude 37 and to her seeing a spaceship is as common as a constellation. Most likely the Arcturians are fascinated about the inferiority of the human mind.

In linear space and time there is no fear, illusion or separation. Ryan adores Arcturians and he tells me they always offer him some type of elixer water from their planet that tastes like Mr. Pibb and a type of glow in the dark wine and that they have banquets of fresh fruit, crudite and platters of desserts on their ships that magically multiply on their own and silver platters overflowing with fish and some type of chicken nugget just like the banquet hall at Hogwarts in Harry Potter, along with vaults filled with thousands of gold bars and crystals mined from planets in far out galaxies to trade goods with other planets occupants and have laboratories of special minerals and rocks collected from their journey through the cosmos and each one of their ships has a med bed pod which is the biggest trend in New Zealand at the moment with people paying thousands of dollars to physic mediums to channel them to the Arcturian spaceships that instantly diagnosis and cures any ailment.

Ryan says the main control room is filled with white captain chairs and a computerized map of every interstellar galaxy. They love music and have instruments made from everywhere in the Universe and that every extraterrestial race has an intergalactic treaty displayed on the outside of their spaceship. And that there are space stations just like 7 Eleven's or 'convening' places where they park and teleport into rooms for 'the meeting of the galactic minds' and trade and buy goods from other galaxies.

Kristin notices her horses with their heads staring up at the sky from the stalls in the barn snorting out of curiousity at the spacecrafts. They are used to them after living here for seven years and horses have sonic hearing. Kristin went and changed into her Dehner english black leather show boots and a pair of tan colored Tailored Sportsman britches and texted her next door neighbor Susan to invite her to go on a trail ride. She hops in her ATV and drives to the barn to saddle up Coconut.

A nasty severe thunderstorm was on its way which always means 'divine symphony of the Merkabah of sound and light codes'. The tidal flooding this year has caused sink holes, ponds and wetlands popping up all over the farm as well as increased tornadoes which means trail riding time is a very short window due to the weather and insects from the humidity and global warming.

Excited about the thunderstorm, Kristin loves to watch the 'light language codes' with all the spacecrafts participating and her desire to connect with the bizarre Octogan shaped ships from a far away distant galaxy and learn why they ended up at planet Earth. Was their planet swallowed by a black hole? Another hostile race blow up their planet or is it just another "Intergalactic Council of Light' meeting. Just like everyone else 'the great unknown' is the hook, line and sinker for any over active spiritual mind with an undying thirst for knowledge of the Universe and the future.

Reflecting on a verse from the Gospel of Judas that reads when he asked Jesus "When shall the Great Festival of Light dawn for all imprisoned humanity?" Jesus left and returned the next day and Judas asked "Where did you go after you left us?" and Jesus said "I visited a noble, sacred people beyond your world". Judas amazed and enquired of him, "What beings are there higher and holier than us, and not of this world?". Jesus laughed "Why are you thinking about them? I tell you nobody on this Earth will ever know them, nor human children ever belong to them. Nor will any angelic force of luminaries reign over them. They don't come from this aeon. Humanity comes from a lower region. They come from another power, not from that force which governs you".

Kristin has always wondered if Jesus is refering to the Sirians. Ryan says that Sirius is the most Holy planet in the Universe and no one is ever allowed to even visit their planet and Kristin is positive that they have cracked the jigsaw pieces of Ryan's autism as he shares pieces of imformation about them unknown to humanity.

In freemasonry, it is taught that the Blazing Star Sirius which is 8.611

light years away from planet Earth and is a symbol of omnipresence (the Creator is present everywhere) and of omniscience (the Creator sees and knows all). Sirius therefore is the 'sacred place', a source of divine powers and the destination of divine individuals.

Kristin smiling to herself can't even imagine the brilliance and sophistication of their minds and technology hypothesizing that humans are brainwashed from their parents from the day they were born and thrown into a world full of demons, greed, jealousy, hate and hypocrosy, corrupt politics and caltholic churches and treason is about the new norm let alone 'unidentifiable sexual gender', open marraiges and multiple wives, physical and mental disabilities and diseases.

'Friendship In The Making'

Susan is a retired litigation attorney who was raised a devout catholic. She and Kristin hit it off immediately after Susan bought the house next door around the cove from Kristin and Stewart stopped coming to Eagle Point as often due to his heart aneurism and low blood platelet count-he can't take Viagra anymore. And of the fifty rental houses he owns thirty of them are empty after the end of the governments Covid rent relief program. He like most landlords doubled their rental prices monopolizing the rental market which Kristin new would eventually bite him in the ass.

He foolishly just bought an empty Suntrust Bank building on the Gloucester Courthouse for $650,000 which brings in no income and is full of lead paint and asbestos and has seven walk in vaults (hey turn it into apartments so people can lock their drugs and hide dead bodies in the vaults, or better yet an adult bondage club) which is normal for Stewart who is a buyer and not a seller and loves empty old historical buildings, he just doesn't want to spend the money to rehab them, instead of paying off the $800,000 balloon payment due in the summer on Eagle Point and is being played by a group of billionaires who love historical architecture who Kristin had given a tour of Eagle Point to recently, who instantly befriended her.

Susan is also single and inherited a million dollars from her parents and a pension from her ex husband and bought a brand new house on the cove that has a dock with a boat and a swimming pool. She rescued a Palomino mare and she does nothing but garden, read books and watch movies all day. She loves to lecture Kristin about the corrupt churches in the world and the ladies get in heated debates about Christianity, take turns cooking each other dinner and go out to lunch and shopping together and swap fresh veggies from our vegetable gardens. Susan brings Kristin fresh chicken eggs from her hen house and she pays Ryan to help her with manual labor and yard work.

Miraculously the County hired Ryan who is 23 in the year 2023 as a housekeeper with assisted employment through the NAMI

Connection, a non profit group that assists adults with autism and depression at Walter Reed Hospital part time. He rides the Bayside Transit who picks him up right in front of the kitchen door back and forth to work two days a week. His confidence has skyrocketed getting direct deposit and he volunteers one day a week at the Helping the Homeless Thrift Store owned by Pastor Wendy. "Fucking talk about gratitiude Jesus" Kristin says out loud. I finally have some much needed time to myself and to do adult things on my own with other women and start dating other men and write books and screenplays and Ryan needs a break from me too.

Teaching Ryan how to manage money is going to be the hardest. Everytime we go to a convenience store there are kids wasting thirty to fifty dollars on high priced name brand junk food. He is hopelessly addicted to scratchers and buying himself new clothes and yes he does think of himself as invincible, most likely from being a cancer survivor and his 'out of this world' channeling skills and his knowledge about the future that no human being on Earth is privy to.

Smiling, Kristin puts on a pair of spurs and grabs her bridle, Nelson Passoa jumping saddle, saddle pad and girth from the tack room. She grooms and saddles Coconut in the cross ties feeding him and Zeus peppermints and molassas biscuits. Adding a few sprays of Avon Skin so Soft on him which repels mosquitoes, she puts on a fancy gold crochet bug net with rhinestones on it over his ears. Loving the comfort smell of hay and pine shavings trying to get an up close look at the Octogan shaped spaceships hovering above her horses pasture and what do you know the clouds started rolling in.

Susan texted she was almost at the mailbox which is a mile down the driveway. Kristin replies 'I will meet you halfway". She mounts Coconut after kissing his muzzle and grabs a crop out of the brush box taking some selfies of herself and heads off down the driveway watching the hundreds of Canadian Geese and dozens of White and Blue Herons swimming in the pond by the barn with the Mallard ducks.

Kristin sees Susan, who could be Nicole Kidman's twin sister, on her palomino quarter horse mare with her long flaming red hair and size 40D boobs bouncing as her horse is jigging, wearing jeans, cowboy boots and a Western hat. Giggling to herself, like most other women neither of us wear bras anymore after the Covid pandemic. You actually get better service in public, guys love to look at nipples. Kristin smiling says "Hi Susan, Goldilocks looks happy to have some company. How did your date with John go last night? I know you were excited. Did you have sex with him? Does he have any good looking single friends?".

Susan replies laughing "Hi sweetie thanks for asking me to come over. I have been dying to go on a trail ride with you. I screwed things up. Well actually he did not me. He mistakingly thought my invitation was to spend the entire weekend which I told him was not the case. He is a nice man but not intellectually stimulating enough for me. I just kind of got the idea that he is playing the field and I have more money than he does. I made us crab cakes, cole slaw and cornbread muffins for dinner and he drank way too much wine. We went skinny dipping in the pool and he grabbed me from behind. I slapped him and told him that 'I was a nice Catholic woman'. I took his car keys away and made him sleep in the guesthouse. After he woke up the next morning with a hangover we talked over coffee and a bagel and agreed that we should just be friends".

Kristin cracking up says "Susan you are a complete prude. I am proud of you by the way. Why did you 'lead him into temptation' skinny dipping with those huge tits of yours. I wouldn't sleep with anyone drunk either. Especially in a pool. Maybe he just really is attracted to you. Don't feel bad dating is absolutely horrifying in your fifties".

And Kristin giggling goes on telling Susan "I went on one last week with Brad who should be renamed 'Ken'. He is an investment banker, tall and good looking. After listening to the sales pitch about himself that he is the 'biggest catch in the world' for over an hour at Outback Steakhouse, I ordered a gin and tonic. Drank it in two seconds and then faked an emergency that I had to go home. I kissed him on the cheek goodbye and blocked his cellphone number. He was obviously looking for a 'Barbie'.

And the one before that was a man named Gary who I met at the Yorktown Beach. He is really good looking and a NASA scientist. He took me out to lunch at Chantillys on the beach. That very same night he texted me a picture of a fifty thousand dollar Tiffany diamond ring with the price tag on it in a Tiffany's box and a picture of his ten inch dick with a hard on. He said in a text 'I want to take you to Bermuda this weekend on my private lear jet. I have a captains license and own a vacation bungelow on the water and the Tiffany diamond is yours'.

I texted him back a picture of me posing in front of the bride's dressing mirror in the foyer wearing nothing but a pink lace thong, pink thigh high stockings and pink open toed high heels with a feather boa around my neck and replied 'share this with your wife. No thank you'. Secretly thinking he was going to do a 'mile high club' thing and then throw my body into shark infested waters. Or even worse make a it a routine weekend thing.

Some women do have affairs like that. But fucking is it worth it? And do any of them have a guilty consciouness just for sex? And why didn't they just marry a women that just wants to spoil their man in bed even if they have kids or careers. Like Stewart says 'Be a sharp professional business women and a whore in the bedroom'. And everytime some creep on social media wants some long distance love affair, meaning phone sex and nude videos. I just respond 'send me a gift card and some flowers and I will think about it' and I never hear from them again, it works everytime" laughing out loud.

Susan laughing hysterically said "I am so glad we became friends. You are right. No relationship is better than a bad or toxic one, that is one thing we both have in common and it takes quite some time to really get to know someone. I think people's social skills in general are lacking due to the Covid thing and working remotely. You know social media is taking over the world, let alone the recession and all of the banks closing. Coconut looks so good you must spoil him rotten. Do you hear that wooshing sound coming from the sky it sounds like dozens of airplanes flying above".

Kristin smiling says "it must just be aliens from outer space visiting the Martians above the cove. I hope they don't abduct us and perform experiments on us, just kidding. Wow look at those lightenting bolts across the river you better go back before it pours, the thunder is starting to roll in. I was making spinach and ricotta manicotti and a spinach salad for dinner do you want to come over?".

Susan replies "Hell yeah. I love your cooking. I will bring a bottle of red wine and we can sit on your back porch and watch the storm. I just have to feed my chickens real quick. 6 o'clock okay?". Kristin blows her a kiss and waves goodbye and turns Coconut back to the barn to switch horses and takes Zeus on a quick spin in the indoor arena before the rain. She fills up their feeders with Timothy hay and gives them a scoop of sweet feed looking forward to girl talk, good food and the light codes tonight.

After feeding the horses dinner Kristin drives the ATV back to the house and sees Ryan walking out of the portal breaking the sound barrier with a huge smile on his face surrounded by angels thinking 'beam me up Scotty'. "Hi Ryan how was your journey, did you go to the Bermuda Triangle or see an intergalactic convention? Did you take me some pictures of the inside of the spaceships and bring me a present back from the Universe? What galaxy were the Octagon spacecraft from? They looked really mean did they blow up a planet or something?".

Ryan replies "Shut up mom. You ask too many questions. I already told you the year is 2039 when they are all coming to Earth. I am going up to my room". Kristin says "Susan is coming over for dinner and to watch the storm. Love you too" and watches Ryan run up to his room and hears him slam the door and hears the voices of RA and Kyron (who are divine light beings who facilitate communication/channeling with the Holy Trinity) along with several other angels channeling to the Arcturians and Pleadians as the windows in the house started rattling from the cosmic vibration of the collective synergy and the grounds start shaking. Wishing she could understand what they were saying as she glances at the sky watching the spaceships spinning flashIng codes of light at each other a 'literal divine symphony orchestra' awestruck by their beauty feeling content like 'a chosen one' to see something so special.

Kristin hears Archangel Saint Michael 'The Messenger' of the Heavens in his magnificent voice channel a message to her "Kristin they are here to save humanity and the planet Earth. There is an alien war going on between the Reptilians and the Draconis in the Andromedae galaxy. The Gargonians are the race with the Octagon spacraft and they are hostile and from far distant galaxy called 'Cosmos Redshift 7".

Blushing Kristin says "Adonai" to the Archangel Saint Michael and curtsies. Dresses the manicotti with some organic marinara sauce and throws it in the oven. She takes off her boots and britches and changes into a yellow polka dot cotton dress admiring her fit body in the mirror and goes and sets the table for Susan who is pulling into the driveway and notices Stewart has sent her 16 text messages in a row. Ugh she tells herself enjoy dinner and the light show and deal with it tomorrow. You never know if or when Stewart is having a narcissist attack.

Susan and Kristin ate like birds and talked about their past over dinner and Susan shyly blurts out "Kristin how did you ever talk Stewart into buying this place when he lives so far away?". Kristin laughing out loud replies "I screwed my way into it. My first come on line to Stewart was 'I have been groomed and molded to please a man'. Sad but true". Susan laughs at Kristin.

Loving to entertain Susan, Kristin goes on "Just kidding. One of his rentals burned down and the insurance company gave him $400,000 and he took me on vacation down here to look at some timber land he inherited. I was looking at estates for sale on the drive and found Eagle Point. We both fell in love with the place and the listing broker Kyle Haus and I became best friends. I told him everything about Stewart and the other 'butler' who lives in his house. The previous owners estate financed Eagle Point with 0% interest and the rental income here pays the mortgage and the crop land income pays the property taxes. Plus he needs a tax shelter" laughing at all the narcissitic bullshit that the man put her through.

"He was going to retire and move here or so he has been saying for seven years and instead of selling any of his rentals he purchased nine more rental houses on a drug infested culdesac near Rustburg from his dad's estate for pennies on the dollar. Actually I was a mail order bride. The person that financed the house I bought in Gladys, an older man named Joe who is now dead, when I first moved to Virginia introduced me to Stewart. A 'Match made in Heaven' or so I thought. I should have listed to Joe when he told me "That man should have his balls cut off. The only thing he cares about is sex and food".

Getting up for more food all of a sudden hungry and not wanting to think about the past Kristin asks Susan "Do you want some more spinach salad? I picked it from my garden. You can take some home with you. Strawberry cheescake for dessert. I am so looking forward to great things to come. Thanks for coming over. Maybe one day we will meet our knight's in shining armour" both ladies laughing out loud.

Both Susan and Kristin had seconds and finished off the entire dish of manicotti, the salad and ate dessert enjoying each others company. Then the loudest thunder rocked the Plantation with the windows rattling and a severe lightening storm knocked out the electricity. Kristin grabbed some candles and Susan said "Thanks for today and dinner. You really cheered me up. I better go home and start the back up generator. I will be in touch. Love you". Kristin gave her a hug goodbye and retreated to her suite which was originally a 'men's cigar smoking room' her intuition telling her 'divine syncronicity' the light codes were about to come.

Sitting on her back porch smoking a ciggarette with a glass of wine Kristin hears Ryan channeling in his room as she watches the spacecrafts stationed at different portals around the property emit 'erethal surreal divine lightening bolts of sound', each with a different rainbow color, sound and frequency with massive crystalline codes coming from 'Beyond the Veil' from the Trinity creating a high frequency vibration, a 'divine orchestra'.

The Arcturians, Pleadians and Sirians were squashing dark matter from the Universe while healing the crystalline grid of the Earth in unison with the Holy Trinity. And then the Octagon spaceships descended out of the galaxy at warp speed through the Milky Way faster than the speed of light running for their life; secretely making plans to come back to Earth and and blow up the Central Sun, she overhears from the voice of RA channeling a message to her.

Kristin, in complete inspiration, awe and fascination of the Universe and the Veil above her house. Thinking no live feature film could ever get any better than this or any other type of Earthly connection with the Christ. Kristin's spirit guides say out loud 'go take a hot shower with lavendar and go to sleep this instant. You will receive a transmisson from the Messenger in your slept. Rest up for the divine convergance and solar flares from the Central Sun tomorrow'.

So she does and after she climbs in bed wearing a white silk nightgown she turns on an Archangel Raphael meditation song from the Well Being Academy from Youtube noticing that the sixteen texts from Stewart are his demanding request to advertise and rent all of his empty rental houses. Well ok, thats easy for me you fucking jerk. Thanks for betraying me and giving up on all our hopes and dreams together. She turns on the music enjoying the frequency.

'The Messenger' Archangel Saint Michael puts Kristin into a deep trance and guides her to a divine primordal jungle completely serene and surreal at the same time, somewhere in Asia, filled with hundreds of Boa Constrictors and Anaconda's wrapped around tree limbs with their forked tounges slithering out of their mouths. Dozens of Otters and pink river dolphins swimming and fishing in a pristine river. Toucans and other colorful birds nesting in trees with hundreds of monkeys as a herd of jaguars walk along the riverbank with the divine sounds of the rainforest with millions of green rainforest frogs croaking. And then Archangel Saint Michael showed her a vision of a herd of wild horses asking her to feed their starving foals which must be a vision of the future of how global warming is going to effect crop lands and wild animals and falls into a deep creative healing much needed sleep.

'New Beginings'

Waking up especially refreshed from a divine nights sleep, smiling as the Transit bus is going down the driveway taking Ryan to work enjoying the peace and quite. Kristin puts on a silver bling sweatsuit and looks at the spaceships from the kitchen window while making a cup of coffee and notices that the full moon is still glowing in broad daylight and laughs out loud.

Grabing a blueberry muffin hoping one day to 'crack the code' herself she texts Stewart "Sure Stewart. I will be happy to do your advertising." thinking you fucking asshole. On a whim needing some socialization Kristin texts her friend Alice, a phsycology professor from Williamsburg "Lunch 1pm Olivia's on the Gloucester Courthouse?" who replies instantly "Absolutely see you later" .

Kristin walks off to the barn enjoying the nature of the farm and watching the neighbors crab potting and jet skiing on the river. After taking care of the horses and getting all dressed up in an Indigo blue colored fancy linen sundress with a beach motif and high heeled sandles, she climbs into her new silver Audi sedan that she paid cash for. She turns on the radio blasting the band Trains 'Drops of Jupiter' singing out loud as she speeds down the driveway glad to get off the farm for a few hours after her 'soul vacation' this morning, enjoying the beautiful scenery of Virginia with the Dogwood trees blooming, wild Lilac bushes and purple wisteria vines after living in Hollywood in the rat race most of her life being a single parent.

Kristin drives down Main Street through the quaint Gloucester Courthouse lined with antique lamp posts with hanging baskets full of red Geraniums and fresh flowers. She pulls up in front of Olivia's Restaurant, an upscale place with an outdoor patio that she frequents and notices her friend John from the Archeaological Foundation who wants to have a 100 seat fundraiser on her front yard at Eagle Point in October with tents and a caterer, outdoor port a potties at a price of $100.00 per ticket and give tours of a few rooms in the Plantation, dining with a group of other prestigious business men.

She pulls up right in front of restaurant with a smile and get's out of her car and walks up to John and gives him a hug and says "How nice to see you John! I am so excited for your event at my house. I have been thinking about the public relations aspect. May I please call ABC 7 news to interview us in advance and of course the local newspapers. Let's do lunch soon I have some other ideas for public events at your historical Plantation's in the area, especially Timberneck and the Roswell Ruins that you might be interested in. A 'Gloucester Street Fair" with old fashioned art boothes, homemade food street vendors with a puppet show and live bands is my favorite. I want to narrate a podcast for you and have you consult on a documentary on 'Archealogical digs at historical Virginia Plantations".

John smiling replies "Yes of course. I can tell public relations is right up your ally. You are a sight for sore eyes. You can do whatever you want with our real estate portfolio and the Architectural Board of Virginia wants to come and tour Eagle Point. I am slyly pressuring Stewart with very little luck, call it reverse phsycology to invest some money in your house. I know you are burnt out on being 'super woman' with that 12,000 square foot place with no help. I give that place ten years until it crumbles into ruins. I will text you this weekend and we all can do lunch and then you can do a tour or vice versa. We all love your storytelling descriptions of the rooms in the house hearing about the 'poltergeists' and spirits and ghosts in the house. It is part of your charm".

Kristin noticing Alice walking down the sidewalk smiles and replies "Fabulous. See you soon darling. Tell your wife to come over and go horseback riding with me anytime. Enjoy your lunch. I am having a 'girl's day' while Ryan is gratefully at work. Nice to meet you gentlemen. Take care" and introduces Alice to the group. Kristin gives her a hug wanting to go in the air conditioning in a private booth and have private talk with her friend.

Alice, a native New Yorker from a family of money, by nature is a modern mind reader and has very good insight into relationships and people in general. Her famous Redskins Superbowl star husband is pushing 78 years of age and has turned to drinking from the pain of his football injuries; which Kristin relates to after falling off of horses more than several dozen times in her show jumping career.

Alice is a complete introvert who can't stand to socialize for more than one hour except for the wild holiday parties she throws at her mansion in the King's Landing million dollar subdivision in Williamsburg where the drama is the equivelant to the 'Desparate Housewives' TV series which must be a living hell. Alice was Kristin's first friend and ally in Gloucester since she moved to Eagle Point.

Kristin has always preferred to live in the middle of no where, most likely from her dad and her first step mother who bought a 5,000 acre ranch in Northern California and built a custom 20,000 square foot 'Gone With the Wind' style mansion with two sweeping spiral staircases handmade from cherry wood, full of handmade custom stained class windows. They had four full time garderners who tended a ten acre fruit and vegetable orchard with the Russian River down a revene where she used to ride his horses through when she was a teenager visiting him for the summer, flirting with all the high school boys.

And ironically he also bred India Blue peacocks and had a deer sanctuary for orphaned fawns whose mothers were killed by hunters. Her first step mother 'Dottie', a Yugoslavian and self made millionaire who bought her first apartment building on the strand in Manhattan Beach, California when she was 18 years old, used to make her iron all of their linens and clothes for $5.00 dollars an hour, probably the only discipline she ever had in her life. Poor Dottie, she should have known after her and my dad bought a vacation home in Oahu that you can't take a surfer away from the wave, just like you keep a horse lover out of the saddle. My dad ended up divorcing her and marrying his secretary and they moved to their vacation home on the beach in Hawaii permanently and he still surfs or paddle boards everyday.

Alice in her nice black linen school teacher business suit wearing a white ruffled blouse with her blonde hair up in a bun and black pointy toed high heels says "Kristin you look so much better, your skin and hair and you finally gained some weight. I was so worried about you the last time I saw you with all that bullshit Stewart put you through. Actually I am suprised that he lasted through the seven year stretch. That is normal for men. You are so kind hearted, I am sure that must of really hurt. Men just turn into assholes when they age and have no testosterone left unless they have tons of money and the time to do nothing. How is Ryan and do you ever talk to your dad?".

Kristin replies "Thanks sweetie. That whole experience with Stewart was absolutely brutal. I could never even imagine or wish such a cruel experience and heartache on anyone. I actually was so weak that I couldn't even drive the car for months. I had to have Ashley deliver horse feed to me and used Door Dash to deliver my groceries. Chalk it up to 'poisonous fucked up choices', American Hustle is one of my favorite movies. That fucking asshole has absolutely zero conscious, remorse or guilt. I actually am so relieved that I already went through that so I can move on to bigger and better things. I have finally gotten my strength back and see all things in a different light. Ryan is driving me fucking nuts with his caffeine addiction and trying to control me with his 'manifestation' skills to take him shopping and out to eat at fast food restaurants which are growing more powerful as he ages. I spend most of my time birdwatching, stargazing, riding the horses and reading and writing".

Kristin smiling at Alice adds "And then I reflect. Ryan never even complained once during his cancer treatment and surgeries after 9 months of chemotherapy, 30 days of radiation and 3 blood transfusions. My dad is swamped with work, Mark Zuckerburg is one of his biggest clients who owns almost the entire island of Kuaia. All of the billionaires in Hawaii are pooring money into their real estate while the rest of the world is starving to death from global warming and food shortages. My veterinarian laughed and said if worse comes to worse you can eat the 40 India Blue peacocks you have and live off oysters and crabs if there is any water left in the river. I brought you a bag of cherry tomatoes, lemon cucumbers and organic yellow zucchini from my garden for you to take home. How are your grand kids and your hubby?".

Alice says "Shit Walter is a grumpy old man and has more money than he knows what to do with. My college students are absolute morons. My side business 'Not Time for Therapy' is taking off. I find working with my clients more rewarding than teaching. I just plan vacations to Iowa to see my son and to Arizona to see my grandkids. Do you want to split a jack cheese and artichoke heart sandwich with the sweet potatoe fries? I have to go soon I am going to be late for class and I want to come and visit you and the horses and Ryan this weekend and bring you some designer clothes that don't fit me anymore. Anne Taylor style casual wear and some sequin evening gowns and a few other summer things. You are so lithe you can wear anything. I hope you find someone to give you companionship and financial security and walk away from that man and put Ryan in a boy's home so you can have your own life. Just join the 'Millionaire's Club' in Newport News and you will get invited to private parties with single men looking for a life partner".

Kristin laughing replies "It is all in the master plan Alice. Sounds great. I am going to stop at the feed store and stock up on horse feed on the way home. I will be home most of the weekend. Let me know if you want me to make you lunch. And actually the honest truth is that I just pray to Jesus everyday for his Mercy. All of that swimming you have been doing agrees with you and Walter's arthritis must be agonizing. Do you guys still have sex"?.

Alice after she orders lunch and ice water with lemon for both laughing and says "No, we sleep in separate rooms. He just rings a bell and I stand next to his bed with a bottle of lube and jack him off". Both ladies laughing hysterically enjoyed their lunch and Kristin autographs a copy of her recently released book and the girls hugged goodbye.

Kristin sped home and unloaded the horse feed, fed her horses and cleaned the stalls. On a whim decided she had to buy a 12 string acoustic guitar. An Ebenezer like the one that she played in high school. And then she found a Steinway baby grand piano for free from an estate sale that just needed to be tuned to place in the vestuble at the main entrance of the Plantation. Joking to herself the ghosts and spirits will play with it in the middle of the night.

'Space Odessey'

Kristin obsessively started researching the 'Cosmos Redshift 7,' wanting to learn more about the Gargonians and their titanium spacecrafts and technology and what gases and minerals their planet emits and why their technology would create Octogon shaped ships with teleports and the only spaceships she has ever seen that have visible lasers. Thinking to herself why don't the Martians just blow them up with their radioactive missles? Intergallactic space treaty must be a trip and why Earth is a target is a motive for them and wondering if there are nearby galaxies that are working as spies for them almost a 'space espionage'. Maybe they threatened the planet Sirius and have a superior super powered engineered nuclear laser.

Quickly she places all of Stewart's rental ads on Craigslist and Facebook and on his website and shoots him a text with a picture of her at Olivia's with Alice with her piercing blue eyes in her beach blue sundress and high heels knowing that he won't respond until she rents all of his houses and probably not after that either.

After researching the Cosmos Redshift 7 which is a high-redshift Lyman alpha emitter galaxy observed 800 million years after the creation of the Universe with a time travel of 12.9 billion light years away from Earth and is one of the oldest most distant galaxies known. Their planets are extremely poor metalicly which inhibits evolution of the luminosity functions in the re-ionisation era which may be why they are surfing the galaxy looking for a hostile takeover, although they have the earliest first stars that produced chemical elements needed for the later formation of planets and life as it is known today.

So the Gargonians do not have the basic minerals on there planets to have a balanced diet or any type of eco system on their planet. Nor do they have any allies. Or gold and diamonds to mine; raise animals or horticulture. And most likely they have a deep seeded hatred towards mankind. And the Fleadians and Arcturians whose planets are rich in minerals and plant and marine life. They will most likely fight until the bitter end or the demise of humanity.

And NASA just discovered coincidentally that Earth has a liquid outer core and a solid inner core but the Martians core seems to be entirely from liquid. 'The uniquiness of Earth's core allows it to generate a magnetic field that protects us from solar winds, allowing us to keep water on the Earth's surface'. Mar's surface lacks a magnetic field and so the planet's surface conditions are hostile to life.

The traces led scientists to believe that Mars once supported a potentially habitable environment but evolved over time to become an inhospitable frozen desert and they just won't give up trying to glorify the plant Mars trying to prove that there was recent traces of water. Kristin thinks out loud and shit what was their food source? And have you even investigated their underground colonies NASA, I mean just use your imagaination for Christ's sake. If they only knew what life was really like there with an asteriod for a moon. Keep it to yourself Kristin is thinking.

Wondering why the Gargonian's think blowing up the Central Sun would accomplish their goals, Kristin watches the Transit bus bringing Ryan home from his job feeling she just didn't have enough time to herself. She walks out onto the kitchen porch staring at the spacecrafts in wonder and asks Ryan as he walks in "What would you like for dinner and what is the deal with the hostile Octagon people? Did you have a nice day?".

Ryan replies "Fried shrimp, french fries, corn on the cob and garlic bread. Just shut up mom. They are an evil miscalculated race that was created by mistake. I am going upstairs. Let me know when my dinner is ready. We have other important visitors here I must go as he grabs two cans of Dr Pepper out of the refrigerator".

Well you brat laughing to herself. Everytime he starts irritating me or drinks too much Diet Coke I will just start asking him questions about the spaceships and he will dissapear up to his wing above the kitchen which was originally a school house in the 1600's and was converted to a suite with a bedroom, a living room and two full bathrooms which have been completely remodeled with Chesapeake Bay blue paint and white crown molding and has two dormers on each wall in every room where he can see every location on the property.

Kristin replies "You are so sweet to your mother" puts on her apron and turns on a cd of Aerosmith's greatist hits, puts his dinner in the oven and returns all of Stewart's emails and text messages to his prospective tenants singing out loud to the song Sweet Emotion waiting for the grand piano to be delivered and walks down to the east wing and notices that the furniture in the library room which was originally the 'ladies sitting room' had been rearranged and there were coffee table books taken from the book shelves sitting on the antique drawing board titled 'the Splendors of Christianity' and the other 'Nature's Blueprint'.

Smiling to herself, the last time she went to take a video of the basement for a podcast on historical architecture there was a children's table and chair set decorated with an antique china tea pot, cups and saucers that was set for a tea party with dolls sitting in the chairs that she had never seen before.

And absolutely nothing would phase me at this Plantation 'In the midst of uncharted waters'. We actually are not to far from the Bermuda Triangle. I am going to pick Ryan's brain about that one over dinner just to piss him off, she says to herself as she sees the Uhaul van driving down the mile long driveway lined with hundreds of ancient magnolia, ash and pecan trees.

Kristin walks out on the front porch of the main entrance which has four Georgian columns which soar up three stories high to the attic and waves at the two guys in the truck both who have the physique of a body builder smiling to herself.

The guys backed up to the front door entrance which has a flight of stairs five feet high off the ground to the main entrance. The guys get of of the truck eyeing Kristin and her smile and the driver says "Hi. I am Tom and this is Doug. This place is absolutely beautiful. Wow. How old is this place? Is it haunted?".

Kristin replies smiling "Thank you so much for bringing the piano. I want to put it in the foyer across from the brides mirror. My name is Kristin. The house was built in 1680 and then was remodeled in 1905. And yes we had a house haunting in 2019. The place was full of ghosts all over the farm. I wrote a book about it called Behind the Veil. You can buy it on Amazon, and no it's not haunted anymore just full of spirits".

The guys look at each other in complete shock obviously wondering why she lives in this place by herself and notices that there is no one else even present on the farm. Tom says "That is so cool. I have never met an author before. I will have to buy your book and read it tonight. I lived in a haunted house in Connecticut when I was a kid and never got over it. Both of my parents mysteriously died in that house. I love haunted house stories and old Plantations too. You have good taste. Let's get this baby grand in the house. We have more deliveries to make. Nice to meet you".

Tom and Doug with their huge arm muscles bulging some how managed to carry the piano up the flight of stairs to the foyer and placed the grand piano where Kristin requested. Looking up and down the hallway Doug said "This place is so incredible. Your hallway reminds me of the Shining".

Smiling Kristin replies "We had a poltergeist in the dining room during Christmas, it is all in my book. I am trying to get Stanley Kubrick to film a movie here. The ariel view at the beginning of the movie zooming down on Eagle Point Plantation with some eerie suspenseful music would be as famous as the beginning of the Shining. The basement is five feet undergound and has a labrynth of catacombs where the servants from Africa lived and has a walk in civil war safe that is filled with bat guam from a bat infestation. Ironically bats only nest in an area over 100 degrees. My website is Eagle Point Plantation. I am having a wine and cheese open house next month if you want a tour. Tickets are fifty dollars a peice. I have to run. I have dinner in the oven for my kid, he is on the spectrum. Thank you so much again" and waves goodbye and walks back into the house after locking the door.

Admiring the Steinway grand piano Kristin walk's back to the kitchen to serve Ryan dinner giggling out load as she hears the piano starts playing Beethovens Symphony by itself and says out loud "I love you angels. Hallelujah. Let us get a harp too" making a mental note to herself. She takes Ryan's shrimp and chips and corn on the cob out of the oven and puts it on a plate with some cocktail sauce and garlic bread and yells "Ryan your dinner is ready" who is already running down the three flights of stairs from his wing and says "Thanks mom.

I am going to eat in the dining room".

Kristin follows him to the dining room wanting to pick his mind for more details about the aliens and what is going on in the divine world and asks sweetly "Were you channeling to the Arcturians and Pleadians? You know the year 2039 many people have predicted is going to be Armagedon. The end of the world and the Second Coming of Jesus Christ, who in all actuality is already here people are just so disuaded by the demon's walking the planet they just don't even notice".

Ryan giving her a dirty look replies "I just like the future and to time travel. And yes it is the year 2039". Kristin smiles knowing he is not going to devulge any further and she laughs to herself and says "They are coming out with a flying car this year. I emailed you a picture of their website. They cost $155,000 each. You should become a flying car salesman just like on the Jetsons and make a fortune and eventually open your own 'mini spaceship' dealership, hire staff so you can buy more gold bars at the 'Intergallactic 7-11 in outer space', spend hundreds of dollars everyday on scratcher tickets, PS4 games, fast food, Dr Pepper and clothes. And hire a maid to clean your room and serve you dinner. I will just stick to walking on dirt on planet Earth. You can just fly everywhere and buy a robot dog and name him or her Pluto. There are chocolate mint Klondike bars in the freezer for dessert." laughing to herself and takes off on a walk to visit with her horses.

Enjoying the sound of hearing Zeus and Coconut whinnying in unison Kristin then suddenly sees a vision and hears a soft nicker of Zackery nudging her on her shoulder that brought tears to her eyes. Zackary, who is a dapple gray ex-race horse from Texas and Ryan's riding horse was euthanized a few months ago due to cancer and thanks to divine syncronicity the farmer Greg who crop shares here happened to have his excavator parked in a field and buried him in a field of wild periwinkles. Sadly she thinks Ryan must really miss Zackary, and the family rides with his sister. At least Zackary had a great life for the ten years that we had after I rescued him from starvation. Jesus held him together for six years longer than he should have lived and he is pain free running in the pristine green fields in the Heavens with all the other horses I have owned in my life that were rescued from slaughter. His spirit comes to visit the horses, me and Ryan quite frequently. Divine timing plays into this one with the recession, inflation and food shortages.

On a whim Kristin texts her daughter Ashley "Early dinner tomorrow at Fliorias, a new fancy Italian restaurant on the Courthouse?. Bring Danny your roomate and his boyfriend Ian. My treat. Love you".

She gives her horses a huge bucket of apples, carrots, peppermints and a scoop of sweet feed. She kisses their muzzles and says "I love you boys. I will be back after the peacocks go to sleep and take you on a ride".

Ashley texted back "Heck yeah. Danny and I both have the day off- 3pm we will pick you up. I can't wait to see you. Let's catch up tomorrow before we take off on our month long cross country road trip. Love you too".

Kristin walks back home watching the eagles kite above the river and noticed a flock of ospreys fishing behind the house, admiring the colorful sailboats cruising down the river in the breeze. She stops at her vegetable garden and picks a basket full of zuchinni, yelow sqaush, green onions, a red bell pepper and a few rainbow carrots, plucks a few leaves of cilantro to make a stir fry with some brown rice and fresh lemon juice and a teaspoon of honey and a few grates of fresh ginger and do some research on the premonition of the year 2039 as the sun sets shining beautiful golden rays through her kitchen windows.

Kristin shops for a used harp on Craigslist thinking to herself that Stewart is going to flip that she is turning the living room into a music room which is actually very appropriate for this Plantation - music, light and sound are humans most creative gifts from the Universe. And he really won't even notice or care. She pulls out her cutting board, knife and a wok to make herself dinner in peace noticing the microwave was flashing 11:11 when it was actually approximately 5:55pm.

Chopping fresh veggies and throwing a few vegetarian egg rolls in the oven all of a sudden starving Kristin hears Ryan walking into the kitchen and he ambushes her over the year 2039 not making any sense after his Dr Pepper binge and his channeling and he keeps saying over and over again "It is all about the future".

Kristin says "Let me eat my dinner. Your sister and her roomates are taking us out to dinner tomorrow. Go pack your lunch and have some chocolate cake for dessert Don't forget to brush your teeth. Love you". Ryan replies "Thanks mom. I am going on a space ride. See you tomorrow" and runs out the door and dissapears through the portal to the 'divine world of the Universe'. Kristin says "Have fun bring me back an asteroid or a crystal from Neptune and send me some pictures".

Kristin is just about to start eating her dinner while watching the moon rise with two angelic hosts governing the moon and stares at the spaceships spinning at warp speed with their bright 'disco lights' eminating from their crafts as they ascend at warp speed above the Central Sun faster than a split second. She turns to reading the Revelations from the King James version of the Bible while listening to Hildegard Von Bingen's 'Voices of Angels' thwarting off any negative energy from every entity that she feels is invading her aura field from this Plantation. Most likely from the spirits that still remain inside the mansion and the ghosts that follow Ryan home from his outings.

'The Bait And Switch'

And two minutes later Kristin looks at the kitchen door as Stewart walks inside looking frazzled amd exhausted thinking 'oh fuck'. She smiles and gets up and gives him a hug, wondering about 'of the other three women you have in your life, no make that two he dumped the married lesbian with the kids after she stole her Covid rent relief check that back paid an entire years lease along with thousands of dollars of antiques from his farm, why do you look so exhausted?'.

She says smiling "Hello Stewart. What are you gracing me with your presence for? Do you need your dick sucked? Are you hungry? Do you want a vegetarian chinese dinner?" She gives him a hug and shoves her dinner plates to his seat and grabs some cheese and crackers and a container of roasted pine nut hummus for herself wondering what his problems were.

Stewart replies "Yes. I just needed to see you and get out of the 'Twighlight Zone'. I am having serious problems at home with Rhonda and Michelle and just want to mow the lawn here. Then I have to meet with my attorney in Richmond tomorrow and go back to work. I just wanted to know that you are okay. I am having serious health problems from my heart aneurism, can you do your Jesus thing?".

Kristin instinctively knowing he is having financial problems with the balloon payment due on Eagle Point. Did he really think that someone was going to pay him nine million for the place? The gossip in Gloucester over his non performance of rehabing the Suntrust Bank Buiding on the Courthouse and Eagle Point are all over the place. And the power bitch struggles going on at his farm Green Hill in Gladys where Rhonda and Michelle live, thinks to herself well thank you for such a sweet loving night to dump your bullshit on me you mother fucking jerk. She just smiles at him and his short comings and why does he really think that I can save his day like I am a 'divine good luck charm'. He has already walked away from that.

Kristin, being 'raised up' feeling Archangel Saint Michael's presence strongly around her with his shield just smiles and makes small talk about the neighbors and his tenants thinking about karmic illnesses that she had a deep conversation about with Ashley over Stewart's health conditions. She will never divulge her business relationships with the people in the town of Gloucester or his own personal and business relationships. Never wanting to be a false representation of Jesus's healing which is like walking with the Devil, offers Stewart some homemade chocolate brownies and a scoop of vanilla ice cream for dessert does the dishes.

Kristin says "Let me tuck the horses in. I will be right back and you can take a hot shower and get some rest" still hungry and knowing better. Stewart replies "That was delicious. Thank you sweetie. I live on Hamburger Helper and hot dogs at home. I really regret all of my choices. You look fantastic and beautiful by the way. Hurry back. I am just going to mow the front yard with the zero turn until it gets dark" in deep seeded fear over losing Eagle Point.

Kristin smiling does a long walk to the barn. She spoils her horses with a quick spin in the indoor arena, feeds them dinner while stargazing at the constellations and the amazing spaceships. She walks back home to wait on Stewart until he leaves tomorrow not falling for his antics walking with Jesus in her heart and soul silently listening to the angels playing the flute in triumph echoing in glory at the spiritual magnificence of the 'Great Festival of Light' in the history of the Universe.

Ryan keeps texting her 2039 over and over again. She has never seen him so obsessed or excited about anything before in his life. The year 2039 is only sixteen years away. Silently wondering to herself if humanity will survive global warming that long let alone all of the wars, the food crisis and the risk of Artificial Intelligence taking over the world. She walks back into the house to get Stewart off to bed wondering if he ever noticed the grand piano in the foyer.

Kristin hands Stewart a fresh bath towel and his robe and slippers and asks him "Did you take your pills?" to remind him. She finishes cleaning up the kitchen while he is showering. Kristin heads down the hallway to take a quick bath in the east wing. She returns to her bedroom and Stewart is in bed snoring fast asleep. She climbs in bed thinking about time traveling, the Universe, spacecrafts and the Plantation full of spirits.

The next morning Stewart says "That was the best night sleep I have had in a long time. I really love it here and your hot body. Now get your crazy ass out of bed and make me some coffee and breakfast" as he grabs her love handles. Kristin, thinking how much he has changed since he can't have sex anymore and is addicted to text messaging multiple women and his tenants, slips on a purple floral strapless sun dress smiling and walks to the kitchen. She turns on the coffee pot and asks "Spinach and swiss cheese omelete, bacon and an english muffin?" as she grabs the ingredients out of the refrigerator.

Stewart nods his head staring at his cellphone reading his texts messages and says "I want you to set up a meeting with Poindexter the billionare that owns Cumberland Plantation that you gave a tour of Eagle Point to and see if you can negotiate a deal for $10 million". Kristin thinking to herself you just fucking amaze me asks "Do I get a commission? Why do you think I can get you $10 million when the current assessment is $2.7 million? And what happened to your grandiose buyer who was offering you $9 million dollars for Eagle Point?" smiling to herself.

Stewart says "The broker never gave me the offer and no I am not giving you a penny. But I have to do a 1031 exchange and you can pick out another Plantation you lucky girl". Kristin knowing that was absolute bullshit smiles sweetly and replies "I will see what I can do for you Stewart. Here is your breakfast. Let me heat up your coffee. I know you are in a hurry".

Stewart finishes his food gets up and said "Wow. You are a great cook. Sorry to eat and run. I have to go to my meeting. Don't forget about Poindexter. Love you. Stay out of trouble". He kisses her on the cheek and throws a wad of cash at her and walks out the door.

 Kristin says out loud after he is gone giggling as she watches him drive down the driveway "You know you just have to laugh. Like I already have made enough fucking money for you Stewart which zero of it did you share with me, out of blatent acts of kindness. You are going to have to up the anti on that one you kind loving soul", planning on teasing the shit out of him with that one.

She goes about her day enjoying the wildlife on the farm looking forward to having dinner with her daughter and her friends, the GenZer's she calls them have such a different mindset they just flat out think differently and they get a kick out of the ghosts stories and pictures of the spacecrafts I take and talking about the future. Both Ashley and her roomate Danny bartend at a high dollar private flapper bar in the fan district in downtown Richmond while they are finishing their college degrees

Danny is getting a BA in Engineering and Ashley an MBA; she eventually wants to go to law school and get a JD in Criminal Justice, having been obsessed with criminal minds and serial killers her entire life. Danny's boyfriend Ian who already has a degree in Accounting does film payroll for Marvel Entertainment and gets to travel all over the world. Ian plans on eventually starting his own film payroll company which is very lucrative business. His family lives in Alaska of all places.

Kristin leases a few of Stewarts houses without even a thank you from him. He is just probably dealing with too much personal and business shit with his own life. Thinking to herself as she feeds and waters the horses after turning them out to eat grass for a few hours. Kristin washes her hair and changes into a sexy plum colored sundress after returning all of Stewart's emails and text messages from prospective tenants and watches Ashley driving down the driveway fashionably two hours late as usual and calls upstairs "Ryan are you ready to go"?.

The kids enter the kitchen and Ashley gives her mom a hug and says "You look great. I have missed you. Do you like my new tattoo? It is a black widow. And my new haircut? They call it 'the baby bitch bang' look. I got a new nose peircing too and Danny got a matching one. Shit you are in good shape mom. Hi Ryan".

Kristin smugly thinking to herself how happy and vivacious the trio is- like their vibe is total 'peace' and the challenges of growing up in your twenties in Richmond, Virginia Kristin hugs all three of them and says "I love it. You look so healthy. I am glad you cut down on the pot smoking. Thanks for coming over. I just wanted to get out of the house and see you guys before you take off on your crazy road trip across country. I hope you stay at campgrounds and bought some bear spray" laughing she says "I am starving. Lets go eat then I will give Ian a 'ghost tour' of the Plantation after dinner".

The kids replies in unison "Heck yeah. Lets go". They climb into Ashley's car who says "I bought a Premium AAA membership, maps of every state and spare tires. Danny and I went to Camping World and bought a tent, camping stove, portable air conditioner and a first aid kit", laughing out loud. Kristin reminisces with the kids about their five day long journey through Arizona, Oklahoma, Texas, New Mexico, Arkansas and Tennesse driving across country when they first moved to Virginia in 2010. Ashley says "Mom that was the smartest move you ever made for us" speeding down the back roads to the restaurant.

As they arrive at the restaurant Kristin notices a new outdoor patio with mood lighting and candles. The inside of the restaurant was packed and says "Do you guys want to sit outside? I like the ambience and it is perfect weather. It is too crowded inside" and they took seats at a big round table under an umbrella reading the menus on the table. A short brunette wearing a black uniform stops by and introduces herself. "Hi. My name is Peggy and I will be your server tonight".

Danny says "Hi Peggy. We would like two bottles of the California Merlot please". Kristin asks Ashley "Do you want to split the eggplant parmesan? It comes with a dinner salad and garlic bread. The portions here look huge. I made you guys a homemade carrot cake for dessert when we get back to the house and bought a gallon of Turkey Hill Vanilla Bean ice cream. Ryan you should order the lasagna and ask for extra bread instead of a salad and no more Dr Pepper. Order a Sprite instead".

Ashley replies "Yes. That is fine mom. Do you guys know what you want?". Danny said "We are both going to have the shrimp pasta primavera, a Long Island Iced Tea and the ceaser salad with chicken" and places everyones order to Peggy who returned with their wine. The kids clicked their wine glasses saying 'Cheers'. Kristin says "Peace to people of good will and here is to a triumphant exploration of America on your road trip. May Archangel Saint Michael be with you for divine protection and Jesus too". The group in unison cracking up says Amen.

Ashley asks her mom "Have you adjusted to grandma's death yet? I really miss her a lot. That whole thing was so morose and drawn out with her in hospice and my grandpa is so far away in Hawaii. Atleast I keep in touch with uncle Erich. He wants us to stay with him and Nicolas in the Hollywood Hills for a few days. We are going through Arizona on the way back to visit Danny's uncle who wants us to come and visit him on our road trip. We are going through the Great Lakes in Ohio, Yosemite National Forest Campgrounds, Idaho to the Snake River and Seattle, Washington and then down through Oregon to California. We plan on staying at public campgrounds that have park rangers and hopefully meet some other cool hippie nature lovers. We have a master plan".

Kristin says "I hope you bought extra water in case you get stranded and a case of canned food and peanut butter and jelly. I am sure you will have a 'spiritual' blast. Yes. My mom has been connecting with me in with my dreams constantly along with my dad's mom, your Grandma Irene. She wants me to finish writing the book 'Three Days to Heaven' the story about Palero that she started writing".

Kristin takes a deep breath and says "It is just going to open up so many emotions about that experience when the Animal Control Police took Palero's (Kristin's first Belgian Draft Horse she rescued from slaughter in Canada at 5 months old and raised as a baby who came down with a deadly case of laminitis at two years old and had three surgeries and lived a year in an equine hosptial while she was going through her divorce) lead rope out of her hand and euthanized him right in front of her children who were 4 and 5 years old at the time at the Los Angeles Equestrian Center from a complaint that a boarder turned the horse in for irremediatley suffering".

Kristin continues "And to this day I will never know if it was her your dad or the veterinarian from the equine hospital that turned me in. I had a complete nervous breakdown and turned to the mortgage industry selling pay option arms. I made my first $22,000 paycheck out of vengeance from the unjust terror on the horses eyes being betrayed and having his legs chopped off for an autopsy by the State of California Veterinarian Board. I had his body cremated. The day we left California I put his ashes from the urn in the garden in front of our house in Lake View Terrace which magically made a crystal vortex like shinning diamonds and his soul was released to the Heavens".

Kristin looks at her daughter and says "I am okay. I have my plate full with your brother and a whole new life ahead of me. I just talk to Jesus Christ constantly, all the time. I am just so happy that you guys have your life in order and enjoy each other's company. You better keep in touch with me on your trip so I know where you are. Ian how did you end up in Atlanta after living in Alaska? My account executive from World Savings that approved all of my pay option arm loan submissions quit his job in San Diego and moved to Atlanta to be a liquor salesman. He said liquor makes everyone happy instead of a negative equity loan. Danny I love your haircut. And your Banana Republic shirt you look great. You and Ian make a great couple. My brother's boyfriend is deaf, six and a half feet tall, is a personal fitness trainer and weighs 275 pounds. He is a narcissist and their relationship is so toxic. I don't know how they can stand it. Maybe the bondage appeals to them" laughing her head off knowing the guy went after her brother for his money and to live 'the kept man' lifestyle. She has already been there and done that.

Ian with an emotional smile on his face replies "Both my mom and dad work for the Government of Alaska. They started fighting all the time. I just couldn't stand to listen to them yell and scream at each other anymore. They agreed to let me go to college in Atlanta and live with my aunt Tonya. I was always fascinated with the entertainment industry since I was a little kid after living in the complete isolation and harshness of the bitter coldness in Alaska. I am glad I came to the States. I really love Danny and your daughter and thank you for welcoming me into your home. This food is absolutely incredible. Garlic and cilantro is my favorite combination" smiling at Danny. The party enjoying their dinner and wine in quite contemplation of what is to come in the future. Ashley pays the check and Kristin the tip and tax and they all share a cigarette before the drive home.

Kristin has the kids stop at barn to pet the horses and feed them dinner. Ashley drives to the kitchen entrance and Kristin brews them a pot of double strength espresso and serves them each a slice of carrot cake and a scoop of ice cream. She packs the kids four grocery bags full of tomatoes, cucumbers, zucchini, yellow squash and potatoes from her garden. She grabs four cartons of fresh chicken eggs that Susan gave her from the fridge and some baggies of fresh rosemary, cilantro and Italian parsley to take home with them. Listening to classic Sting instrumental music smiling as she watchs the red tail hawks kiting as the sun is going down.

Ryan and Ashley give Ian a tour of the Plantation exploring the massive house. All three of them have to get up early to go to work tomorrow. Kristin is going to work on another novel all night and sleep in. The kids arrive back at the kitchen laughing. Kristin giving each of them a hug says "I love you guys. Please be in touch with me on your road trip. I hope to see you soon when after you make it back to Virginia. Look up at the sky under the planet Arcturus. Do you see the spaceships flashing their lights spinning faster than the speed of light? There are dozens of them".

The kids look up in complete astonishment taking out there cameras. Danny and Ian in unison say "Holy fucking no way They are so cool. Wow. I have never seen a spaceship before" and Ian says "I know they travel faster than the speed of light through galaxies from far away; connecting with extraterrestrials is the hottest new thing since Bitcoin. You are so lucky to live here That was the most amazing thing I have ever seen in my life. I can only imagine" and Ashley laughing says "My bro talks to the Pleadians and Arcturians. My mom and I saw them ascend through the atmosphere at warp speed one night from the back porch last year in broad daylight. They connect with you in your dreams too. It happened to me all the time when I lived here".

Kristin says "There are portals to other realms of the Universe all over the property. Ryan time travels too. It is all in my sequel to Beyond the Veil. Did the piano start playing by itself like usual? I am going to buy a used harp too so the spirits and I can start our own orchestra (laughing). Just kidding. It is the angels here. They love music and it suits this old Plantation. Drive safe you guys and don't forget the grocery bags full of fresh veggies and eggs. Love you and don't let the ghosts follow you home" laughing out loud and gives everyone a hug goodbye.

Kristin retreats to the Library room in the East Wing which was originally the 'ladies sitting room'. She picks up her guitar and starts strumming along with Sting's 'Nothing Like the Sun' singing out loud. Thinking to herself she is proud of her kids progress from growing up in a dysfunctional family. They have adjusted well from being uprooted from their family in California-which in all actuallity makes them more adaptable as young adults. And then she plays 'strumming my pain with his fingers, singing my life with his soul, killing me softly with his song'.

Kristin laughs out loud as the grand piano starts playing along with the music echoeing through the house. After doing a Google she finds a used harp from an estate sale in Gloucester for next to nothing and then arranges a purchase with the estate's owners manager. Pleased with her find, the harp is going to be delivered tomorrow from the same delivery service. Grateful that Ryan is out exploring a distant nebula in the atmosphere enjoying the peace and quite in the house and thrilled that he going to work all day tomorrow, needing a break from being a mom for a few hours to rejuvinate.

'A Cosmic Universe'

Waking up to a breathtaking sunrise Kristin watches the Transit bus take Ryan down the driveway to work and goes upstairs to investigate his room on a whim. She finds a glass jar in his window sill labeled 'Jupiter' gleaming a surreal looking neon multi colored aqua, blue and green gas vibrating some type of language glowing in the dark almost like a glass full of the unexplipicable gasses that surround their planet and another one labeled 'moon dust' with a metallic gray substance and tiny moon rocks and another labeled 'Saturn' with a bizarre rainbow substance that resembled silly putty in the shape of a circle.

Laughing she eyes several jars of crystals suspended in mid air glowing with some type of magical dust almost like a jar of 'glow in the dark crystals' or the inside of a crystal ball and a dog that is alive that appears like a 'Gremlin' sneering at her sitting on his bed with several angels shining, one on either side of her as she investigates his 'secret Univerise laboratory'.

Kristin looks at the mirror above the fireplace mantle and sees an image of Ryan staring at her with his glasses on with his head bulging like 'the Incredible Hulk'. Ryan says "What are you doing in my room? You are not supposed to be there you witch. Don't touch the jar of red Martian dust it is radioactive-it will kill you. Stay away from my gold bars or I will hypnotize you into a walking zombie forever. Now get out of my room".

Kristin laughing out loud says "Of course Ryan. Have a nice day", takes some pictures of his collection and waves goodbye as his image dissapears from the mirror. Kristin hearing something else tapping on the door in one of his closets thinks 'will curiosity kill the cat'? Thinking better of it it might be a talking manequin or an evil ghost he has locked in there, she heads back down stairs needing a much needed break from everything.

Shit at least she doesn't have to worry about Ryan financially with those

24 karat solid gold bars the size of bricks thinking out loud "I wonder how many he has and where they came from. The gold texture seemed to have a shining gold field around them like they are electrified or something. They probably came from somewhere way out in the Milky Way" laughing to herself.

Satisfied with her NASA investigation and that Ryan is starting to feel comfortable sharing with her about his Universal experiences. She walks back downstairs to the kichen and puts on a sunhat and glasses not even being able to imagine what Ryan does in outer space. She walks to the barn to see her horses planning on doing absolutely nothing today but plant flowers in the antique urns on the kitchen porch pillars, the back porch behind her bedroom and work in her garden harvesting wild blackberries, rasberries and figs from her yard waiting for the harp to be delivered. She grabs a granola bar out of the fridge in the barn and one for each horse.

Listening to the songbirds on her nature walk she looks at the ground in front of the main entrance to the barn and sees the words "The Messenger" spelled out in pebbles that were what I call 'Archangel Saint Michael' indigo blue color and a picture made of tiny white pebbles of a Sirian spaceship. Kristin is overwhelmed by a complete wave of 'cosmic energy' that shocks through her system. She looks up at the sky as a rainbow is shining straight down on her from Beyond the Veil enveloping her in rainbow colors bouncing off her skin with a flock of hundreds of doves circling above her which dissapeared into thin air after a few minutes.

Completely invigorated with boundless energy Kristin says out load "Amen Jesus. Halleleujah" knowing the divine intervention she has somehow helps her cope with Ryan's other wordly channeling powers. She kisses Zeus and Coconut on the muzzle feeding them carrots. She puts Zeus halter on to lead him into his grass pasture and notices there are seven freshly made crop circles in the field each one with a different 'algabraic' symbol and pattern.

She changes her mind and locks both horses in the indoor arena and turns on the piped in radio to a classical music channel for them. She goes into the field to take some pictures of each symbol texting Ryan the photos hoping he will tell her what message is in the light language.

Then she hears a voice, Archangel Saint Michael's voice 'The Messenger' who says out load "the Seven Seals of Soloman Kristin. Divine love and peace to you".

Blushing at her humanly ineptitute she smiles and says thank you to 'the Messenger'. She heads back to work in her garden after cleaning the horses stalls and putting the boys back inside and collecting all of the 'Indigo Blue' and 'Sirian White Crystals' from in front of the barn, placing them separately into two plastic pitchers she grabbed from the feed room.

After pulling all of the weeds, Kristin picks fresh tomatoes, cucumbers and okra, wondering how many times she has read the Revelations. She makes a mental note to plant seedless watermelon, mini-pumpkins, japanese eggplant, snow peas and bok choy. Crock pot homemade chinese soup made with vegetable broth is a really filling meal and is incredibly easy to make. Then she cuts a basket full of blue hydrangeas and purple iris for the kitchen table.

Almost everyone in town are turning their mini farms into self contained eco preserves, growing their own vegetables and raising chickens for eggs preparing for climate change and food shortages as she watches a flock of five bald eagles kite above her house. Thinking out load "I should buy a bread maker and several hundred pounds of flour and start canning vegetables to stock up the pantry and make fresh preserves from the raspberries and figs and apple butter from the apple trees in front of the barn".

In good spirits Kristin notices Tom and Doug pulling up to the front foyer in a Uhaul truck. She smiles at them and waves and goes through the servants entrance pulling off her gardening gloves and clogs and heads to unlock the front door excited to see the harp.

After unlocking and opening the massive front door with a beveled glass window made out of solid oak and stepping outside admiring the beautiful gold harp in the back of the delivery truck Kristin says "Hi Tom and Doug. Thank you so much for a quick delivery. I just had to have her. Isn't she beautiful? I got a great deal on her".

Tom and Doug smile at each admiring Kristin's body in her skin tight flare legged lycra gold sweat suit. Tom says "Your so welcome. We both read your book. I can't beleive you live in this house after what happened here. Where do you want us to put this baby? You will never be able to move it yourself. She weighs a ton".

Kristin laughing points to a corner of the vestuble diagonally across from the piano thinking shit I have to have an antique organ too. A huge pipe organ like they have in churches. Doug and Tom place the harp where she requested. Doug says "That looks awesome" as the piano starts playing "Stairway to Heaven" by itself.

Kristin laughing at the spine tingling look on the guy's faces staring at the piano with their mouths wide open hears Tom say "Is that I ghost? I can't see anyone". Kristin replies "It does that all the time. Maybe someone cast a spell on it. Just kidding. It is an angel. That is why I have a cross symbol on the front door. Thanks again take care" and watches the guys run out the door as fast as they can.

She locks the front door and starts strumming the harp playing 'Amazing Grace' singing as loud as she can with the music echoing through out the entire house as if she had been playing it her entire life. She glances out the front door and sees the Transit bus bringing Ryan home wondering why he loves to listen to music and dance but doesn't have any interest in learning to play an instrument. She even tried an electric keyboard and a drum set which she ended up giving donating to the thrift store since he never even attempted to play either of them; at least Ashley played to flute in her high school band- anything musical is excellent therapy for PTSD which all three of us suffer from for many reasons.

Ryan walks through the kitchen door with a case of Dr Pepper, his own personal drug of choice along with a bag of Hostess chocolate donuts and walks down the long hallway watching Kristin play the harp singing along smiling at her.

Kristin stopped playing and asks "Do you like it? Jesus gave it to me as a gift to drown out the fucking noise of your cartoons and PS4 games. What is that thing you have locked in your closet. I hope you didn't abduct someone and have them chained to a wall. Or is it an alien from the Cosmos Redshift 7 galaxy? I only went to your room to make sure it was clean and your 'Gremlin' thing was making growling noises. What does it eat and where did it come from. Did you like my pictures of the crop circles?".

Ryan giving his mom a dirty look replies "It is a dog from Mars that I named Star. She only eats bones and some type of fish that the Martians give to me from Mars. She guards my room and the 'it' in my closet is a man from the Ancient Lost City of Atlantis that accidentally followed me home when I was time traveling. I just haven't had time to take him back. If you want to know what the crop circles secret code is figure it out your fucking self. I am hungry from working all day. Can you make me a steak and fries for dinner? I am going upstairs to my room".

Kristin smugly smiling at Ryan's irritation says "Of course. And Archangel Saint Michael already told me about the crop circles. I will pick some green beans out of my garden to go with your steak. And don't forget that Jesus says 'Love one another". Don't drink too much soda. It makes you crazy. Stewart is coming over tomorrow. Aren't you excited? Maybe he will take us out to dinner". Ryan gives his mom a dirty look muttering "That man is evil" and runs upstairs drinking two Dr Peppers through a straw before he even gets to the second staircase landing to his wing.

Kristin noticing the clock on the microwave was flashing 5:55pm and the grand father clock in the living room started chiming puts Ryan's Porterhouse steak and thick cut fries in the oven after dashing them with sea salt and black peppercorns with a dash of Worchestire sauce on the steak. She snaps the ends of the green beans off while snacking on a few throwing them in a pot of boiling water while rocking out to Journey's 'Don't Stop Believin' singing along and dancing planning her outfit for tomorrow.

Thinking the scarlet red lace knee length form fitting dress and opened toed high heeled red sandels deciding which restaurant she was going to have Stewart take her and Ryan to tomorrow night. She takes Ryan's dinner out of the oven wanting to go on a trail ride and puts his steak and fries on a platter with the green beans and texts him 'your dinner is ready' and what do you know he is already standing behind her.

Kristin tells Ryan "There is a chocolate silk pie in the fridge. Put your dishes in the dishwasher. I am going riding. What galaxy are you going to and who with?". Ryan replies "Thanks mom. I am going to the year

2039 and it is none of your fucking business. I have important things to do. Have fun with the horses. See you tomorrow".

Kristin changes into her boots and britches and drives her ATV to the barn wondering what Ryan's night will bring him. She sends a text to Stewart "I made reservations at the Gloucester Marina Yacht Club 6pm tomorrow. You need to wear a button up shirt. Drive safe. All of the tenants have cash for you. See you tomorrow. Going riding" and shuts off her cellphone.

Ambushed by the flock of peacocks fanning in front of the barn entrance she grabs from the feed room a grocery bag and throws them three loaves of bread. In biblical times it was said that 'Christians adopted the symbol of the peacock to represent immortality like the dove represents the Holy Ghost'. To Kristin the peacocks remind her of the terradacytal's from the dinosaur era.

Kristin walks down the barn aisle looking forward to riding, planning on selling all of the pea hen's eggs this summer so the flock can't multiply since Stewart refuses to buy them any food anymore. She decides to do a short ride in the arena and then ride around the loop in front of the Plantation on each horse. And then do a beauty treatment back at the house and sleep in saving her energy to thwart off Stewart's pressuring desparation antics to set up a meeting with Poindexter to make him millions of dollars. Thinking to herself that fucking bastard.

She grooms and hugs her horses with a smile. She rides Zeus first and then Coconut enjoying the warmth of their vibration and bodies between her legs as she watches the sun go down like a big bald head in the peace and quite. She notices that all of the spaceships are gone and sees the constellation of Virgo above the Plantation directly underneath the glorious star Arcturus. After riding and bathing Kristin falls into a deep slumber enjoying the peace and quiet listening to the harp and the piano playing 'Heavenly music'.

'Divine Intervention'

And of course Ryan is up before the crack of dawn after drinking two Dr Peppers and is blasting cartoons on his cell phone from the kitchen. 'You fucking jerk' Kristin thinks to herself. She brushes her teeth and gets dressed in a long sleeved NASA t-shirt and a pair of grey yoga pants. Walks into the kitchen in a bad mood glaring at Ryan. She makes herself a cup of coffee, grabs an oatmeal protein bar and walks off to the barn to feed her horses breakfast. She throws her flock of peacocks a bucket of corn watching the flock devour the corn kernals, in quiet contemplation over life on Earth.

Avoiding Ryan like a hawk, Kristin spends the day brushing her horses, composing music and working outside in her garden. And reading ancient gospels about Christ from a book she found in her library in the Plantation that she never bought titled 'the King', written by a man named Francis Ridley Havergal published be the Rodgers Co. based out of Philadelphia which must be hundreds of years old.

Kristin takes a nap and gets all dressed up for Stewart needing a break from the cosmic energy at Eagle Point and everyday life. Admiring herself in the bride's dressing mirror in her red lace dress she hears Stewart walking down the hallway with the sound of his familiar footsteps.

He grabs her in his arms in a bear hug and says "You are drop dead georgeous. I love that dress and your hair. You need to gain some weight. Let's go out to dinner. I am starving. I drove the Suburu, you lucky girl". Kristin sways her hips and lets him open the door for her and poors on the charm in gratitude of getting out of the house, holding hands while driving to the Yacht Club not even remotely hungry and ignoring Ryan.

Stewart and Kristin smiling walk into the restaurant arm in arm admiring the wharf full of yachts. All of the waiters treat Kristin like she is a movie star from Hollywood and wait on her hand and foot, pulling out the chair for her and placing a dinner napkin on her lap.

Stewart orders Kristin a bottle of brut champagne, a martini for himself and a Coke for Ryan.

Stewart then devulges to Kristin "Rhonda had a nervous breakdown and is on several anti depressents. She tried to run me over with her car last night and says she wants to kill me. She bought a gun to kill Michelle the poor white trash married women with the kids who left her husband thinking I was going to marry her and lives in your old house on my farm. I thought it was funny. And they both say that they want to kill you and throw your body in the Severn River".

Kristin sipping on her champagne just smiles laughing thinking to herself that those are signs of emotional duress from narcissim and replies "That is not even remotely funny at all. They should both be incarcerated or seek mental health before a serious accident occurs. You could have been killed. I don't want to have anything to do with either them. I just lost my appetite. What is that horrilble rash all over your body? That looks painful. What is wrong with your doctors? I would go to a specialist. Poindexter is taking me to lunch Wednesday and John from the Archealogical Foundation is coming on Wednesday to take a tour of the Plantation with the entire Board of Directors. They are going to lunch with us along with the Board of Architects I guess you won't be here. (And that one is a 'divine intervention) It's okay. I love your shirt by the way" (her guides saying to her 'in one ear and out the other').

Stewart obviously entertaining himself with his stories flags the waiter to place their order. Stewart orders himself the steamed lobster, baked potatoe with steamed asparagus dinner and a ceasar salad, a cheeseburger and fries for Ryan. Kristin orders the butternut squash soup with roasted pinenuts in a sourdough boule and a garden salad with balsamic vinegar.

Stewart replied "I am just on steriod injections. No infectious disease doctor can figure it out. I have already had three blood transfusions. They really want to do the open heart surgery soon. I am so sorry for all the bullshit I put you through. Let's eat I am just exhausted. Lets go to bed early. I have to leave tomorrow after breakfast to go to Richmond and pick up rents".

Kristin smiling her ass off says "Okay. Thanks for dinner. I will make you your favorite homemade Belgian waffles and bacon and scrambled eggs for breakfast" watching the waiters and most of the other patrons in the restaurant staring at her. Mostly from her sleek physique and shining white aura field that has been glistened by Jesus and her bubbly, happy kind genuine hearted type of soul. And all of the ballet classes and show jumping she did in her youth which really helps with your posture and composure.

Trying not to show her sadness at Stewart's oblivion over his heart condition and the long road to recovery and her irritation at him leaving her high and dry to fend for herself and take care of the farm and that huge house by herself. But hey. chalk it up to 'divine will' and just go with the flow. Make more allies in town and business connections. And it turns out that John and Poindexter are close friends which is a good thing. Stewart's $30 million in real estate assets are pennies on the dollar compared to their net worth looking forward to what she can learn business wise from them.

Stewart picks up the check saying "Wow that was expensive but it was worth it. The ambiance and company were wonderul" smiling at Kristin probably courting her to do the deal at Eagle Point and Kristin replies smiling back at him "Only the best for you Stewart. Are ready to go home?" and the 'family that once was' walks out to the wharf.

Kristin says to Ryan "Here is my cellphone. Can you take some pictures of me and Stewart in front of the yachts?" She puts her arm around Stewart and her other hand on her hip as Ryan snaps some pictures. Kristin says "Thank you Ryan" and takes a few pictures of her and Ryan. Then they walked off to Stewart's Subaru.

Kristin asks Ryan "How many sodas did you have four or five? Are you time traveling tonight or cruising through the Milky Way. Or are you just going to hang out with Jesus. Where did all the spaceships go? Are they coming back soon? It is kind of boring without them at the farm" and Ryan says "Shut up mom. You had too much champagne. Thanks for dinner Stewart. that was yummy". Kristin turns on the radio to classical music enjoying the silence sitting in the passenger seat, glad that the dinner went as planned. Wondering what God has in store for her next.

Stewart and Kristin both shower in different bathrooms and climb in bed together and fell asleep instantly in silence and didn't wake up until 9:00am the next morning. Stewart kisses her on the head and says "Make me breakfast you whore. I slept so good now I am going to be late. After they fix my heart you are going to have to be my sex slave again. I don't know what is wrong with me to have anything to do with your crazy ass. No other man would want you or your fucked up kid. I hate to leave".

Kristin giggling to herself puts on a floor length pink gauze sundress with ruffled lace short sleeves and says "Your wish is my command". She walks off to the kitchen feeling well rested and hungry. She turns on the coffee pot and heats of the waffle iron and throws the bacon in a frying pan while listening to Stewart bitch incessantly about all of the tenants he is evicting and how they have no respect for him and the sub standard work from his employees that he doesn't pay and just gives them free rent and how his extreme dislike at Rhonda's fucked up emotonal problems that is ruining his home life and all of Michelle's drug addict boyfriends that drive by his house.

Kristin thinking to herself that his female friends personality disorders are a byproduct of the phsycological and emotional torture from his narcsissim. She is so glad that she is not there anymore. She might have to hear about it but doesn't have to see it in person.

Well you know can you ever get away from that life you created for yourself Stewart, Kristin thinks to herself. You created it all. That is what the demons inside you do. And living in hell with your riches is the new norm for you that actually will never bring you any inner peace or true happiness.

I am so glad you bought Eagle Point to get away from that. She finishes breakfast and serves Stewart two waffles, bacon, scrambled eggs and Ryan three waffles and a plate eggs and a slice of wheat toast for herself. She says to Stewart "I am glad you enjoyed your night. I know you need a break from everything. Try to think happy positive thoughts. Laughter is contagious you know".

Ryan says "Thanks mom" on a sugar high from the maple syrup and Dr Pepper and runs out the kitchen door and dissapears through the portal to escape Stewart's insults and negative energy. Kristin gives Stewart a hug goodbye as he runs out the door to go to work completely oblivious to the portal or anything else spiritual here.

He says "Call me later. Love you sweetie" with a look of complete regret and remorse on his face. If he only knew the financial and physical challenges he was going to face in the future. Being humbled and humiliated can be an ever life changing event after his $9 million dollar sale of Eagle Point that never existed falls through. Maybe he will have some gratitude after all.

Taking a deep breath Kristin changes into jeans and a ruffled floral long sleeved t-shirt She takes a long nature walk to the barn to take care of her 'love pig' horses who are her own personal therapy. 'The compelling connection between the horse and humans stimulates a higher vibration leading to a higher consciousness for both humans and horses, a divine awareness of their own collective wisdom' listening to the Whipporwhils and Canadian Geese with their gosselings following them closely planning on rejuvinating, playing her guitar and working on a screenplay all day.

She notices that the Octagon spaceships have returned. She hears thundering and lightening bolts coming from Beyond the Veil talking out loud "How could the Gargonians return here so fast? They must have cloaked themselves. Where are the other spaceships?". Wondering if they are communicating with the Martians or are attempting to transcend out of the darkness.

Well, shit it doen't matter there must be other forces above that she can't see and maybe they are facing their own 'Judgement Day' over their plans to blow up the Central Sun which would destroy planet Earth and humanity in it's entirety. She instincively feels Archangel Saint Michael's shield around her as the future is about to be rewritten. Then she telepathicaly hears Ryan ask her 'Are you okay mom?' and Kristin thinks out loud 'Yes of course I am. I am with Archangel Saint Michael - the Divine Messenger - He that is Unto like God' . The hidden mysteries of the Universe are a never ending story.

Zeus and Coconut were snorting and wildy running around their stalls staring up at the bizarre bronze Octagon spaceships laser beams and the lightening flying out from above cove in front of the Plantation. The forty or so flock of peacocks were screaming and flying looking for safety from some type of dark force. Kristin stares up at the ships noticing a dark cloud enveloping each one. The laser beams were blinking and some type of siren from their spaceships was going off.

Deciding to just lock the horses in the indoor arena so she didn't have to worry about them while she cleans their stalls. She leads one horse at a time and closes and latches the door. She cleans their stalls and puts two bags of pine shavings in each one. She fills their feeders up with hay and grain in their buckets with some vitamens. Then she refills the water buckets.

Gratefully Kristin sees her neighbor Susan drive up to the barn. Susan climbs out of her farm truck with her long red hair looking frantic. She says "Kristin I have been calling you all morning. We just received a mandatory hurricane evacuation notice. They say it is a catagory 3. Do you want to go to town with me real quick and stock up on horse feed and water? I think it is too late for us to make arrangements to evacuate. I need to put Goldilocks in one of your stalls until the storm passes, if that is okay with you".

Kristin says laughing "What is new. Do you see those Octagon spaceships above my horses field? They are planning on blowing up the Central Sun. Let's run for our lives. Just kidding. Take me back to the house to grab my purse. Where do you want to go? Southern States, Tractor Supply or both. And Aldi's please for water I detest Walmart."

Susan giggling "Yeah. I see something bizarre up there. The thunder and lighting coming from above your house earlier was definately a 'supernatural thing'. I am going to take stall number one next to Zeus and stash some extra food in your feed room if you can just feed and water her for me until the storm passes".

Kristin hands Susan a halter and asks "Absolutely. Call it 'horse socialization'. Can you lead Coconut while I lead Zeus to put them back in their stalls? I don't think I should leave them in the arena in case we get stuck. Here take a carrot with you". The ladies walk down the barn aisle, halter the horses and lead them back to their stalls.

Kristin as she climbs in Sue's farm truck "Let's go before the rain. Ryan will probably be home from work early. The whole town always closes the stores during a hurricane. I hope we fucking don't lose power in this heat" not wanting to freak Susan out by telling that Ryan is surfing the galaxy with extraterrestrials in a high tech spaceship.

The girls speed to town and buy everything in sight as the shelves at horse feed stores are almost empty. Then Susan speeds to Aldi's and the ladies buy dozens of cases of water since they are both on wells. Cases of bread and jars of peanut butter and jam. Chit chatting on the way home Kristin tells Susan about her dinner with Stewart last night, watching the sky turn black.

Susan drives back to Eagle Point and they almost didn't make it through Warner Hall Plantation's graveyard, who their nearest neighbor which was already flooded with four feet of water from tidal flooding. Susan stops at the barn. Ryan who was home early quickly unloaded everything in the feed room, lifting the heavy feed bags, bales of hay, bags of shavings the cases of water that Kristin bought.

Kristin says to Susan "Go put Goldilocks in your horse trailer while I get her stall ready. The wind is really kicking up. Do you see all those crazy lights in the sky? I wonder what they are up too. It is almost like a 'divine symphony interstellar conversation'. Thanks for taking me shopping. You should rename your farm 'Yellow Brick Road" for your horse's sake ".

Susan laughing grabs Ryan to unload her truck and help her hitch up the horse trailer and speeds off to get her horse. She returns five minutes later and unloads her horse Goldilocks who gratefully walks into the stall flirting with Zeus and Coconut. Then a severe lightening and thunder 'Veils' the spacecrafts and Susan frantically says "We just got a tornado warning too. I am going home. Will see you as soon as the storm passes. I have to lock my chickens in their coop and start the back up generator. Love you".

Kristin gives her a hug goodbye. Ryan helps her lock all of the dutch doors and close the sliders at the entrance. She throws the peacocks some whole corn. Kristin and Ryan climb into the ATV and make it back to the house a split second before the bands of hurricane rain started pounding the farm with wind just over 100 miles per hour galing off of the cove in front the Plantation. Severe lightning bolts were cracking out of the sky.

Kristin could barely open the storm door in the kitchen from the force of the wind as a lightening bolt crashed behind the house with smoke blowing narrowly missing the back porch. Wowed by the force of mother nature, Kristin looks up at the sky hoping to see a sign from the Heavens.

And the second Kristin and Ryan walk through the kitchen door a lightening bolt cracked by the silo on the other side of the property where the main electrical transformer is located and the power was knocked out. Kristin lights the candles in the kitchen, laughing at the cats looking wild eyed from the sound of the thunder, terrified as they scurry down the hallway in the dark to hide under her bed.

She calls Dominion Power to report the outage and tells Ryan "You don't need candles in your room. You already have all of those glow in the dark jars from the Universe in your secret space laboratory. You will probably just go time travel all night anyways. I will make you a few peanut butter and jelly sandwichs for dinner and eat all the ice cream in the freezer for dessert before it melts. Don't use the power in your cell phone in case of emergency".

Kristin makes some sandwiches on 12 grain bread with raspberry preserves and organic creamy peanut butter and opens a bottle of hard apple cider to calm her nerves from the noise of the storm listening to the wind whip through the house with the windows rattling. Eying the Gargonian's Octagon shaped ships and all of a sudden she just could not stop laughing out loud. The piano and harp started playing 'Jesus Christ Superstar'. Thinking 'Amen Jesus. And gratitude for blessing us with your angels and their characteristic supernatural light and protection'.

'Ask And Receive'

Waking up especially well rested after listening to Gun's and Roses live concert in Japan all night. Grateful that the hurricane drifted up through Maine and New Hampshire instead of anihilatting the East Coast thanks to global warming. Kristin happily responds to Poindexter's and John from the Archealogical Foundation texts agreeing to lunch and a tour. A duo is killing two aces with one stone.

The 12,000 square foot plantation takes hours to walk through. And the meetings of the minds about the future of Eagle Point and Kristin and Ryan's safety in an unfunctional house that requires the most creative solutions is of utmost importance. The both will end up being the biggest divine inspiration to achieve her original dream to do a complete restoration of the Plantation

Her first project is to rehabilitate the horse structures and grounds into a commercial horse boarding facility. Create a therapeutic riding center for special needs kids and women suffering from PTSD and underprivileged children whose families could never afford an extracurricular activity let alone a horse back riding lesson. All of the lesson horses will be rescued from the slaughter house and be housed in the seven stall barn by the silo. Along with a 'Community Wellness Center' in the 10,000 square foot barn by the silo with yoga, candle making, meditation, music, dance and art classes. A petting zoo at the four stall and a summer camp for special needs kids run by volunteers.

Adding a ten acre community garden in her business plan to co-op fresh vegetables and fruit for the homeless. A waterfront restaurant on the cove with a 'Malibu' ambience like the famous Gladstone's Restaurant on the Beach in California, along with a souvenir shop. A medium sized yacht on the dock to do waterfront tours with fine dining through the Mobjack Bay, maybe with a glass bottom like the boat tours from Long Beach, California to Catalina Island (the famous Wrigly gum family island) to view schools of dolphins and sharks which are all of Kristin's hopes and dreams for Eagle Point that

Stewart had been promising her for over seven years that never came into fruition.

Do houses and land have feelings? Absolutely, the Plantation loves her determination and love for the place after all she has put her heart and soul into the farm almost like they are married to each other and that is where Christ comes into play call it 'divine will' and her soul has been saved as she has been time to live in the realm of supernatural existence in the current pitiful state of humanity.

I will 'just ask' and receive and have Susan draft a legally binding letter to Poindexter asking for a $100,000 finders fee and a permanent salaried Estate Manager position at Eagle Point including housing before she sets 'the kill' meeting with Stewart.

And he most likely will sign the contract in a heartbeat to walk away from the overhead and deterioration of the place and move on to dilusioning and trapping his next naive victim forever suffering from his short comings and infidelity and false promises and Kristin will be permanently relieved from the broken chains of bondage.

The clocks are still flashing 11:11, 3:33 and 5:55 constantly everyday in 'Divine Peace' while the angels play Hildegard Van Bingen classical Holy music on the grand piano and harp in the foyer constantly as Kristin shops for a used pipe organ from an abandoned church on the internet enjoying the music.

Ryan who is bouncing off the walls from his Dr Pepper and the divine energies flowing through the house announces "I am going back to the Lost City of Atlantis to take the man back that is living in my closet. Then I am going fast forward to 2039 and travel through galaxies with the Arcturians and Pleadians and fly by the planet Sirius and visit Intergallactic Trading Posts. See you tomorrow or the next day. Get some rest mom. You look really tired and you are going to need it".

Kristin thinking shit, I wonder what the Universe have in store for me now, says "Peace to you Ryan. Glory to God and have fun. Love you. Susan is coming over to pick up her horse, I want to discuss my business outline for Eagle Point and have her draft a legal letter for a high powered business meeting I am having here next week with Poindexter that will greatly affect our future. Say Hi to Jesus for me. I will just hang out with Archangel Saint Michael tonight" as she watches Ryan run out the kitchen door through the portal with hundreds of Angels breaking the sound barrier and defying any quantum physics that is known on planet Earth.

Suffering from a horrilble case of hypertension and stress from Stewart's bullshit way of handling the mortgage which is very unlike him, and stress from existing on Earth and life here itself. The Earth's magnetic field is spinning faster than normal raising the vibration of the human body from all of the solar flares from the Central Sun. Most spiritual people call it 'the Great Quickening' or 'Divine Convergence" which will last until year 2039 should we survive global warming, corrupt politics, food shortages and draught, let alone WWIII and the AI Chatboxs which will attempt to destroy humanity by detinating every nuclear war head on the planet after a mass suicide and mass killing sprees.

Kristin asks Ryan telepathically after reading the Gnostic Gospels of Mary Magdelene quotation 'All of nature, its forms and creatures are interrelated; all will be returned to their original source' to go back in time to the CE era to connect with Mary Magdelene. At that time era women had no privilages and were treated like slaves cooking and for sex and even King Soloman had multiple wives and whores and was not loyal to any of them them, it was just an evil fixation. Kristin connects with sacred Mary watching the celestial stars from the Universe waiting for Jesus to return to Earth feeling divine connections from kindred spirits.

Kristin takes a walk to the stables as Susan drives down the driveway with her horse trailer, pulling up in front of the barn Susan with a sigh of relief says "That storm was wild. We got so lucky. I felt so much better you let Goldilocks stay here. I brought my laptop. We can draft the letter in your stable office, it won't take very long. You look happy and well rested".

Kristin replies "Thank you darling. I listened to music all night and slept like a rock. Just let me feed Zeus, Coconut and Goldilocks breakfast". She opens the feed room and fills a bucket up for each of them with a scoop of alfalfa cubes, a scoop of sweet feed, some vitamens and carrots glad that the foundation of the barn didn't flood from the rain like it normally does.

Susan follows Kristin down the barn aisle laughing at the twenty or so India Blue peacocks roosting on all of the dutch door windows, to the stable office, sits down on one of the leather couches as Kristin sits down in front of her antique roll top desk. Susan turns on her laptop and says "I love this flagstone floor and walnut panneling in your office and the way you have it decorated. I can't believe how much horse equipment you have. I love all of the show ribbons and pictures of you jumping on those georgous warmbloods in California".

Kristin smiling says to Susan "Thank you sweetie. Call it the good old days". Susan is smiling logging into her computer and says "Now from what I remember, your goal is to have Poindexter sign an contract agreeing to give you a $100,000 finders fee should he sucessfully negotiate a purchase deal with Stewart for Eagle Point and a clause offering you permanent employment as either the estate or office manager at Eagle Point with a W2 salary of $120,000 per year including medical benefits, stock options and board for Zeus and Coconut at no charge and housing for you and Ryan and a privacy clause that you do not want Stewart to be privy to this agreement. Am I correct? It will only take me a few minutes and if he needs the language edited just give him my email address".

Kristin replies "Sounds perfect to me. His company is called Criss Cross Properties LLC and here is his business address based out of Texas. I am going to have too much fun orchestrating this one. He is a very kind Christian man. His childhood home was called 'Christ's Cross Plantation' and he loved my business plan. Poindexter and the Architectural Foundation are coming over for a tour Wednesday and then we are going out to lunch at Lulu Bird's on the Courthouse. You are more than welcome to join us. Maybe they will invite us to their private parties so one of us can meet the man of our dreams for companionship and security. Did you know that horses are the symbol of God's creative power, an example of the beauty and strength of his divine creativity?" giggling as Susan is typing away.

Susan replies "You amaze me Kristin. I will keep you in my prayers that this works 'like a divine plan' and yeah I am coming Wednesday we need more allies in town. Isn't Lulu Bird's coat and tie? I heard the food is great and very expensive" as she prints out several copies of the agreement for Kristin and emails her a copy of the document.

Kristin smiling says "Yes it is very upscale. I love getting dressed up and to be waited on. I will text you a picture of the dress I am going to wear, a white and gold silk chiffon floor length with an open back and high heeled gold lame' open toed sandles and I think I will wear my hair up. Be here at 11:00 no make that 11:11am they are coming at 11:30 with a whole bunch of other people. Thanks again for helping me with the contract."

Susan gives her a hug and says "No problem. I am excited. Not much happens in Gloucester accept the supernatural events above your house" laughing, and puts her laptop in her truck. She puts the halter on Goldilocks and loads her in the trailer "See you Wednesday. Let me know if you need more chicken eggs".

Kristin waves goodbye and turns her horses out in a small field in front the barn while she does her barn chores wondering what Ryan is up too who must have heard her and texted her a picture of the planet Sirius from the window of a fancy Arcturian spaceship traveling faster than the speed of light whizzing by billions of stars and cosmic nebulas.

Thrilled for an exciting new adventure Kristin puts the horses back in their stalls full of pine shavings and walks back home and decides to clean all day wondering what the ancient old Plantation will look like after it is restored. Eyeing the Gargonians who are flying their ships above the 'Martian' neon green beacon above the Pine Island graveyard on the famous cove where the Powhatan Indians used to trade goods with the Blackbeard pirates, the Celts and the Norse before Virginia was colonized, Kristin just laughs. She walks down to the library room and starts strumming 'Stairway to Heaven' by Led Zepplin listening to the piano and harp join in laughing to herself.

After three hours of sweeping and mopping the first floor and decobwebbing, Ryan finally appears back in the kitchen with a worried look on his face. He says "Hi mom. I am so glad you weren't abducted. The Gargonians are out to get you. I brought you a peice of the Orion's belt in a crystal jar for your room and for protection. Isn't it beautiful? It's like a diorama of the Universe in a jar. Here is a small crystal from Sirius to wear arround your neck that it is supercharged with divine energy. I am starving can you make me some fried chicken and mac and cheese for dinner?. I am going to my room to feed Star. The Martians gave me a sack of food for her".

Kristin says "Thank you Ryan. I love my presents. I will start cooking" as Ryan runs upstairs. Kristin admires his gifts from the Universe holding the crystal in her left hand which repels negative energy admiring the glass jar full of space air and stars 'a looking glass' into the Universe.

She batters some chicken breast, placing the chicken in a Pyrex dish with corn oil. Places the dish in the oven and makes his American cheese mac and cheese, a loaf of garlic bread with some fresh green beans from her garden blasting 'Hotel California' by the Eagles. Kristin serves Ryan his dinner in front of the TV in the 'ballroom dining room' while he is watching Star Wars.

Kristin makes herself a spinach salad and spoons a bowl full of Mac and Cheese with a few slices of garlic bread joining Ryan watching Star Wars. After they finish dinner Kristin makes him a hot fudge sundae for dessert and one for herself. Kristin says "Ryan can you please carry all of the dishes into the kitchen and put them in the dishwasher. Don't forget to pack your lunch for work tomorrow".

Kristin returns all of Stewart's messages from his prospective tenants which she doesn't get paid for, and is a total inconvenience and a pain in the ass talking to all of those desparate people and rents are double what a mortgage payment would be this year with no end in sight. Grateful at the moment she is not one of them. But hey she may be one day soon if Stewart doesn't perform on his balloon payment and if the structural engineer report affects Poindexter's decision.

There are at least two joyst that are about to crumble in the basement due to tidal flooding and the humidity which are holding up the main structure in between the kitchen and the dining room from the original house before the O'Grady family added to front portico with the Georgian columns and the east wing facing the pool and dock.

After editing her grand business plan for Eagle Point looking forward to her meeting with Poindexter and his associates, cleaning the kitchen and putting the laundry away Kristin drives her ATV to the barn, rides her horses and feeds them dinner. Needing some rest, Kristin drives back home watching the 'cosmic conversation' taking place Beyond the Veil between the Martians and Gargonians and the other unbeknownst visitors that are hanging out at 'Latitiude 37' above her house.

Hoping to receive more guidance and a divine channeled message from Archangel Saint Michael-Kristin takes a hot bath with lavender soap and epsom salt. After drying off and putting on a pink cotton nightie, she retreats to her bedroom. She keeps eyeing the looking glass from Sirius and holds the crystals Ryan brought back to her from the Universe in her hand listening to the piano and harp play choir music and falls into a deep sleep for twelve hours straight not having any interest in talking to anyone and gratefully the angels music is drowning out the thundering and lightening bolts and the sirens from the spaceships.

'Inspiration And Hope'

Waking up to silence and solar flares from the Central Sun, Kristin watches the Transit bus take Ryan off to work down the driveway and brews some decaf coffee, pulls out a few oatmeal cookies from a jar and a banana wondering if she even knows herself anymore. The 'old Kristin' has metaphorically been transformed like a snake that sheds it's skin, a 'divine rebirth' which is a great thing.

And then she hears a knocks on her kitchen door and sees Brad standing there with several dozen long stemmed red roses. Kristin is wearing nothing but a see through floral silk camisole and pink lace panties thinking fuck you Brad for showing up at my home unannounced. He must have found my address on the internet, you jerk. I really just wanted to relax. Kristin opens the door and says "Hi Brad. What a nice suprise. Thank you for the flowers. They are beautiful" as he walks in the door and embraces her admiring her body and skin with no make up and bed tousled hair.

Pushing Brad away Kristin says "Would you like a cup of coffee? I am sorry about our date. I just don't need a sales pitch and your insecurities are worse than my own. Sometimes we have to do our own soul searching and the owner of this place shows up unannounced constantly. He is a narcissist so I can't have you over here. Why haven't you invited me to your place you know?". Brad blushing thinking she will grab his arm and drag him to her bedroom replies "I am just not over her. I mean my ex and she still has all of her things at my house. I thought we could just have fun together".

Kristin laughing out loud says "I do not need a fuck buddy Brad. I am in my fifties you know. You should have been up front about that. You cannot have any intimacy without honesty. I am sure you will have no problem finding someone else with your charm. Good luck to you Brad. I have a very important business meeting today. Have a nice day. Can you please leave now? Maybe we can have lunch some day soon and just be friends. I can probably give you some advise on you to 'catch a whore' properly" smiling at him as she shoves him out the door and locks it.

Kristin puts the roses in a vase and fills it up with water. She places the vase in front of her tenants house with a Happy Birthday card on her walk to the stables and goes to play with her horses after getting dressed in a pink velour jumpsuit, snapping some photos of the 'otherwordly advanced spaceships' who were flashing laser beams at each other in a interstellar conversation with scientifically advanced civiliiations from other galaxies on this planet Earth full of nature, minerals, birds, wild animals and the demons that stalk the human race.

And then a 'literal' vortex opened up in the sky. The Octogon ships were pulled into the vortex which appeared to be some sort of 'black worm hole'. The spaceships dissappeared into some other realm as the vortex sealed itself up and a dazzling crystalline divine white Christ like mist instantaneously covered the entire farm. The grass turned emerald green and the sky indigo blue with flocks up hundreds of white doves circling above the mansion. And then earily complete silence came upon the farm almost as if time was standing still.

Kristin smiling says out load "Amen Jesus. Hallelueah" - syncronicity, omnipressence and divine timing. She lets her horses loose who both take off at a dead run to the yard in front of the Plantation happily munching on clovers in peace surrounded by angels. She whizzes through the barn chores and calls to the horses who trot back to their barn with their blonde manes flapping in the breeze against their solid gold coats and Zeus walks in his triple sized stall and Coconut in his double sized box stall with a gleam in their glistening gold eyes.

Kristin thinks to herself all of the money in the world could never buy her the happiness that she experienced this morning, the peace, love and light from Christ. Kristin gives her horses some carrots, satisfied with their well being she jogs back to the Plantation to beautify her self for the high powered business meeting and a few last minute straightening up of things. Looking up at the Heavens in awe and wonder as her spirit guides are telling her 'Go for it Kristin. You are fighting for your and Ryan's life. Just do it and cement the deal. We will help you'.

Kristin smiling to herself says out loud 'fuck yeah' (Help from above throughout all of the realms of Heaven are about to rewrite Kristin's future) and walks up the three flights of stairs to her pink marble bathroom under the attic. She washes her hair enjoying the help and gets dressed with very little makeup in her floor length dress. She puts her hair up with all the confidence in the world. She slips on her open toed gold sandels and hears Susan walking down the hallway.

Kristin turns and looks at Susan and says "You are fucking hot. I love your sexy 'attorney grey business suit with your deep v neck blush colored lace top'. It goes great with your red hair. Where did you get those patent leather sandals? I absolutely love them. You smell delicious".

Susan smiling replies "from Saks Fifth Avenue on the internet. There are absolutely no clothes worth buying in Gloucester. We should open our own clothing store on the Courthouse and ship truck loads of clothes from the garment district in downtown Los Angeles and New York City and make a fortune and call the store 'Divine Grace' or something along that line. Now you have me mind cycling, stop it" as she laughs being a true entrepreneurial spirit just like Kristin.

Kristin smiling at Susan says "Let's take some pictures they should be here any minute". The girls pose in front of the bride's mirror in the vestibule with big smiles on there faces at the excitement of the day snapping selfies and a video while the grand piano is playing 'Jesus Take the Wheel' by Carrie Underwood along with the harp .

Susan says "What the hell was going on at your place this morning?. It was like watching a live Star Wars movie. That vortex 'black worm hole' think that appeared out of nowhere and those bizarre blinking lights and laser flashes coming from the sky above your house were definately not of this world. And the emerald green grass and indigo blue colored sky was absolutely surreal. I was worried about you. And then this white mist covered everything and silence became so breathtaking still".

Kristin looks at Susan laughing and replies "I am writing a book about it titled 'The Messenger'. Call it a 'divine intervention day' or the 'Great Purge' of God's starseed 'Indigo Children'. Actually the Trinity was here re-writing the future of planet Earth and my own future, just kidding. Here they are I am going to walk first and you entertain the rest of the group okay? Let's go!" and the ladies walk off to the kitchen covered by His grace, surrounded by angels.

The ladies stand at the kitchen entrance with the glass storm door open, watching Poindexter pull up in his brand new grey Range Rover and John in his new shiny black Cadillac Esplanade with groups of people loaded in a caravan of new fancy cars. Kristin steps out on the kitchen landing holding out her hand and says "Hello Mr. Poindexter. Thank you so much for coming. I believe that we met briefly at Eagle Point a month ago. You were driving through town and loved the setting of the place. I am pleased to have you here with us today. John I am so thrilled that the Architectural Board of Virginia wants to tour the house. Welcome to Eagle Point Plantation. This is my friend Susan, my next door neighbor who is a retired attorney who will be helping me with the tour and joining us for lunch".

Kristin and Susan smile at each other watching car loads of business men wearing designer suits and ties pulling up in front of the mansion in brand new fancy cars. Kristin feels no humility at her situation here or at the condition of the Plantation and intuitively knows that both John and Mr. Poindexter know everything about her and Stewart as well.

Mr. Poindexter with a twinkle in his blue eyes places his arm on Kristin's shoulder and says 'This place is absolutely beautiful and your business outline is right up my alley. You and I can most likely be an asset to each other and achieve our dreams together. Nice to meet you Susan and thank you for your help" as he kisses her hand admiring her breasts and the 'walls that speak in the mansion'.

After the group of thirty nine convene in the kitchen, Kristin announces "I will nararrate the tour and let me know if you have any questions" as the Architechural Board is awing over the architecture and age of the house. And Kristin is finally recovering from all the emotional and pshycological torture from Stewart's controlling narcisistic ways knowing that someone will actually believe in her and treat her with decency and will she ever grow up? Most likely not.

Kristin flashing her TV smile announces "My name is Kristin, and I will be your tour guide. Welcome to Eagle Point Plantation and thank you for sharing your expertise and time. I will give a short narrative of each room and a description of how the space was used in the 1600's when Jonathan Bryan owned the Plantation during the civil war; and in the 1900's after the O'Grady family added the East Wing and the front portico. And here we go gentlemen".

Taking a deep breath smiling brightly at her audience, Kristin is a natural in front of the camera and can hold a room full people all to her self even in the highest company and counts to five backwards and recites "This is the original kitchen from the main Plantation built in 1680 with the original fireplace that has an osprey nest in it. I named her Olivia. She comes back every year and meticulousy spends weeks rebuilding her nest. You naturally take a liking to bird watching when you live here. The main house is 12,000 square feet and consists of twelve bedrooms, nine bathrooms and fourteen fireplaces. There are several layers of rotted subflooring from Hurricane Katrina. One of the caretakers named Bill that previously lived here told me that the entire farm was covered under ten feet of water. The windows are original from the 1600's and this room was a butler's pantry.

Leading them to the other side of the kitchen, Kristin shows them a stairway that leads to the basement that was used for ventilation and leads them to the 'butler's pantry' off the kitchen that has a swinging door to the 'ballroom dining room' which has two Georgian columns and a fireplace mantle to match that was remodeled in 1905 by the O'Grady family.

She then leads them through the first floor to her bedroom 'the men's cigar smoking room', the front vestuble, living room, library, the yellow children's nursery and the gutted master bedroom in the east wing and then to the upstairs east wing, back downstairs and up to the wings under the attic which were Ashley's rooms, her office and into the attic and then back downstairs to the wing above the kitchen which is Ryan's world 'the old schoolhouse'.

Laughing Kristin says "My son is heavily into scientific experiments. Please don't be shocked" and then leads the group down into the basement and showed them the walk in civil war safe, the pool full of snap turtles and what remained of the dock, the original ice houses and the main pump house, the three rental houses and three horse stables and indoor riding arena and the apartment above the 10,000 square foot storage barn, the peacock aviary and of course she couldn't resist showing off Zeus and Coconut as the group was treated to a flock of bald eagles fishing in the pond in front of the barn.

Intuitively knowing that the group was impressed with the place she announced "Should you want to bring any of your colleagues for a tour and more photographs just let me know. A well known architect professor from North Carolina named Mr. Bradford toured Eagle Point a few months ago and is filming a documentary on the architecture at Monticello and is planning on including Eagle Point in his film".

Mr. Poindexter fondly says to Kristin "I don't know how you do this yourself. It is humanely impossible. Let's go to lunch. I am driving you and Susan. I booked the entire restaurant for our group. We can go over your proposal when I take you back home" looking at her innocence and gumption to turn the farm into a showplace completely intrigued. Kristin looking at Susan in triumph replies "Thank you so much Mr. Poindexter. I am hungry. And we all have to manage when we have no choice. I have help from above and it just builds character".

Kristin sits in the passenger seat as Poindexter holds open the door for her. He places Susan in the back seat and shuts the door after her. The entire caravan heads off to Lulu Birds on the Courthouse. Mr. Poindexter is talking to his secretary April giving her lists of calls and things to do and asks her to order a structural engineer report on Eagle Point and other reports from Gloucester County regarding the zoning and conditional use permits while Kristin is listening in immense satisfaction with a huge smile on her face.

The caravan arrives at the restaurant with red carpet treatment from the owners who introduce themselves as 'Tim and Tina' shaking everyone's hands and they recite "Welcome to Lulu Birds we are so happy to accomodate you. We hope that you enjoy your meal. Let us know should you need anything".

Mr. Poindexter seats Kristin on his left and Susan on his right next to John in the banquet hall with fine linen table cloths, gorgeous flower arrangements, fine china and silver and bottles of fine wine placed on the table that the waitresses were pouring in everyone's glasses. Kristin and everyone in the group are studying the menu.

Kristin says "This fondly this reminds of the fine dining in Beverly Hills. My girlfriends and I used to go to happy hour at the Four Seasons Hotel on Rodeo Drive almost everyday after work. Great choice Mr. Poindexter, thank you very much" who asks "What are you having? I will order for you. I love the food in Los Angeles too. Virginia is definately lacking in culinary skills".

Kristin smiling replies "The Greek salad with Mediteranian feta cheese and Kalamato olives. I am a vegetarian" as the young brunette waitress named 'Linda' places appetizer plates of grilled shrimp skewers, stuffed Bella mushroom caps and fresh crudite with Gouda cheese, avocado slices and flatbread in front of everyone. Linda says "Please let me know when you are ready to order". Surely drooling over the huge tip she is going to make.

Susan says "I am going to try the grilled ahi with asparagus and the lobster bisque soup". John says "Excellent choice. I am going to have the same. Tell me more about your law practice Susan before you retired. Are you still consulting?".

Susan replies "I do wills and trust on occasion and other complex time share documents for the Hyatt Hotel Coporation in the Netherland Antilles. I am enjoying my farmette and spend most of my time gardening, reading books, watching movies and riding my horse with Kristin. Call it a spiritual quest to just enjoy nature after all of those years working 80 hours a week and then going through a divorce".

Mr. Poindexter orders the clam chowder and prime rib and placed Kristin, John's and Susan's order. After Linda completed the rounds Mr. Poindexter clinked his wine glass with a spoon and said "I would like to make a toast. Here is to a bright future for Eagle Point Plantation and our future working endeavors. Building long lasting friendships and successful business relationships in Jesus name. Amen" smiling at Kristin and everyone at the table says Amen and toasts their wine glasses with 'a positively contagious synergy' flowing through the room as the group is talking and laughing together.

Kristin enjoying listening about Mr. Poindexter's empire and business accomplishents says "Mr. Poindexter I am thoroughly impressed with your success. I have to say you are one of the most down to Earth billionaires I have ever met. I grew up on the show jumping circuit and rode for Huey Lewis, Cher and Joan Rivers and other well knowns and catch rode for the biggest horse show judge in the United States, Dale Peterson. I was spoiled riding million dollar grand prix jumpers and hunters. Unfortunately it has become such an elitist sport. My father built the first million dollar custom home in Manhattan Beach and bought me a $7,500 show horse to keep me away from boys, that I ended up winning more than my fair share on, we were not rich. It is a great sport that teachs you self discipline, comradery and the skills to compete and definately helps you with business endeavors as an adult, as well as meeting a lot of fascinating people. I had to groom and braid the rich kids horses to pay my own show fees when I was a teenager" smiling as she nibbles on an appetizer.

Mr Poindexter said "I know. Both of my girls grew up show jumping. I bought a hunter and a jumper for each of my girls, Erica and Melissa. We winter in Florida at Ocala and horse show for eight weeks straight. Actually I bought a $10 million dollar vacation home next to Palm Beach to make things easier. I did it to keep them away from boys. My wife Julia loves the horse show life too. It gives her something to do connecting with the other horse show moms and and gives her well rounded and eccentric people to socialize with who really just want to keep their kids out of trouble and focus on something positive. That is something that we all have in common" drinking his wine and watching the group of professionals at the table in smug satisfaction. He shows Kristin pictures of his girl's on their horses with champion ribbons and coolers covering them at the horse show in Florida.

Mr. Poindexter continues "I will most likely bring my horses to Eagle Point Plantation when they are ready to retire and turn most of the 190 acre crop lands into retirement pastures. They need run in sheds with fly spray systems and automatic watering stations and an area of sand. Both of my girls are going to Harvard and won't have time for them accept on holiday's. I think I will put an outdoor grass hunter derby field along the water so you can have horse shows at Eagle Point and have sponsors pay high dollar prize money for the Hunter Derby classes. The 'horse show dad's' can go boating, fishing and crab potting while their kid's show. They will absolutely love it. A marketing thing really. I will donate a percentage of the profits to 5C1C3's in the area. I am really looking forward to this project Kristin. This is absolutely delishes, how is your salad?" slicing into his prime rib, smiling at her with a twinkle in his eyes.

Kristin says "That smells fantastic. Really good, the best one I think I have ever had. There is a big market subsidized from the Virginia Race Horse Association to retrain and retire ex racehorses and they also pay very well. Probably enough to cover most of the maintenence staff and gardners. Or you can establish a separate 501C3 non profit organization. A multi-facated well rounded continual stream of income" and finished her entire salad.

After the waitresses cleaned the table and recited the dessert menu Kristin is the first one to say "Chocolate mouse please. I can't resist" and Susan orders the same. Mr. Poindexter and John order New York cheesecake and the Linda returns with dessert and coffee. Kristin thinking I could get used to this silenty says 'Thank you Jesus'.

After dessert Mr. Poindexter picks up the tab and all of the gentleman shake hands and say thank you. Poindexter says to John "I will see you at the Board of Director's meeting next month. I am going to take the ladies home and discuss a few details with Kristin and Susan". The parties in good spirits leave the restaurant and Mr. Poindexter opens the door for Kristin and Susan and they drive off back to Eagle Point.

Kristin says to Mr. Poindexter "Just so you know Stewart is unscrupiously greedy and if he thinks you really want to buy the place he will absolutely gouge you since he knows about your wealth. And then he will try to stick you with every piece of real estate he doesn't want in the deal that he paid more than they are worth at triple the market value. Maybe talk to your attorney about setting up a silent entity. You know he is having open heart surgery and will be 73 this year. He will never sell any of his rentals in the poor depressed town of Brookneal. It would take away his identity of the slumlord that owns the entire town 'The big fish in the little pond'. I am sure you have done your due diligence background on him" smiling.

Mr. Poindexter laughing responds "You are smart Kristin. Yes I do know everything about Stewart. Call it 'due diligence'. I and have dealt with many people like him in business. You are doing to the right thing for that Plantation you love, yourself and your family and your own future. You are still young. It is not easy starting over in your 50's, especially with a kid with autism and your horses. You have the rest of your life ahead of you, take pride in your work and have great social skills. And you are honest. Your business outline is more than viable and professional. You can become a consultant on historical home restoration after I am done with the place since you will out live me too. Restoration is a very niche market on the East Coast".

The trio arrive back at Eagle Point as the Transit bus dops off Ryan who dissappears thankfully to his wing after drinking to much Diet Coke. Susan hands Mr. Poindexter a copy of the agreement who reads it thoughtfully while absorbing the energy from the Plantation. He looks at Kristin directly in the eye affectionately and says "Kristin you are brave and underated. I agree to your terms. I am going to have my tax attorney contact you with and discuss your best interest over a cash finders fee or stock options".

Kristin smiling in victory replies "You do realize that I gave up my own successful business saving peoples homes from foreclosure that I pulled in $150k a year working at home being a single parent to manage Stewart's business. I have made him millions buying up short sales and historical homes that were foreclosed on. He has left me high and dry here. Well no he said he left me a three bedroom log cabin on thirty acres in Appomatox in his will which I have never seen. And 'new beginnings' are everything. I would be satisfied with refinishing the loft apartment above the four stall barn while converting the workshop on the first floor to a kitchen and living area for the stable manager. Ryan should have a waiver from Gloucester County to move to a group home by the time the project is finished. The apartment above the seven stall barn can be converted to an office for the horse boarding business. I think the 8x12 solid gold antique bride's dressing mirror needs to stay in the main Plantation and the musical instruments. Thank you so much for everything" smiling gratefully and gives him a hug as he turns to leave.

Mr. Poindexter says "My secretary April will be in touch with you to schedule the structural engineering report and several of my professional contractors that I will be sending over to look at the electrical, drainage and plumbing systems on every structure on the property. Just keep track of your hours and send an invoice to April for your time. Have a blessed weekend ladies" as he admires the view to the river with the colorful sailboats floating out into the Mobjack Bay in the breeze and the multi-million dollar yacht owned by Tom Cruise which is anchored in front of the Plantation with a helicopter parked on top and a pontoon in tow, and the grounds in complete satisfaction of his future conquest of Eagle Point Plantation.

Susan and Kristin embrace screaming "Hallelujah" laughing together. Susan says "Kristin that man is a human angel. I had an absolute blast! Just think of all of the people and connections we are going to meet here at Eagle Point and in Tidewater Virginia. It will help my legal consulting business too. Let's do a celebration barbeque at my place this weekend-Sunday afternoon is good. I will grill Ryan and I sirloin burgers and you can bring the veggies from your garden to grill and maybe we can go for a swim and do a jumping lesson afterwards".

Kristin smiling at Susan replies "Sounds fantastic! I love baked potatoes on the grill too. It's a date. I think I will do asparagus, zuchinni, squash, onions and carrots with herbs, olive oil and lemon juice. Let's do homemade strawberry daiquires. I will bring supplies to make S'mores for dessert. Invite your son Clay. I need him to look at the farm truck and his unfriendly stuck up girlfriend. Let's invite Teresa and Bob-the owners of Warner Hall Plantation. She is a vegetarian too. I will tell her to bring a salad and bread. I can only imagine the relief that everyone in the neighborhood is actually going to have when someone with money actually does a restoration with Eagle Point. We can eat outside on your patio by the pool. I might have to go for a swim too. See you Sunday afternoon, love you. I wonder how many years that the rezoning and artchitect plans will take to put a restoration into fruition that I will still be able live in this house" relishing at their greatest accomplishment of their lifetime...and the whole new world that is opening up to them. And Susan takes off to resume her own life.

'Ultimately'

Kristin takes each horse on a full moonlight trail ride after making Ryan a spaghetti and meatball dinner with garlic knots and returning all of Stewart's prospective tenant's phone calls. In complete inner peace watching the spaceships, singing a song she wrote 'And Heaven and Angels Sing". Walking with Jesus and the extraterrestials that are already living on Earth and are parties of the 'Divine Master Plan". She feeds Zeus and Coconut a scoop of grain and three flakes of hay. Turns off the lights and walks back home under the moon light.

Kristin thinking fuck yeah laughter is the best contagious medicine walks into her 'men's cigar smoking bedroom' after a hot shower. Laughing out loud she is planning on writing a whole new chapter of the future until the year '2039' as the clock is flashing 11:11. Which makes her laugh reminiscing fondly over the house haunting at Eagle Point when the 'house came alive'.

With the poltergeist in the dining room and the Christmas tree ornaments flying around the ceiling and rolling back and forth down the hallway. The evil ghosts in Ryan's bedroom with all of the children ghosts he had stashed in his closet. The previous owners spirits talking to her through the bride's dressing mirror in the foyer. Hundreds of civil war soldier ghosts stalking her all over the farm trying to scare her out of the mansion. Let alone the demons that planned 'the Conjuring' in advance from the very first moment that she set foot in the Plantation.

And the servant ghosts wrecking havoc on the farm. The Powhatan Indian Chief ghost on his white horse that terrorized her horses. Let alone the blackbeard pirate ghost that stalked her and tried to kill her cats with poison. Her own personal 'kindergarden class into the supernatural world' and the years after that it would take her to transcend to the light. She drifts off to into a deep sleep in the midst of unchartered waters 'Beyond the Veil' while channeling with "the Messenger".

Grateful that Ryan is off to work and the house is silent. Kristin peaks out the kitchen door noticing all of the spaceships are gone. Enjoying the complete earily silence. She sees dozens of text messages from April, Stewart and prospective tenants which she doesn't read. She grabs a cup of decaf coffee and a few cranberry oatmeal cookies. She walks off to the barn to see her horses, admiring the sound of the song birds, smiling at the blue and pink hydrangea bushes blooming in front of the two ice houses, wild Rose of Sharon bushes and mounds of honeysuckle vines covering the horse board fencing. And the hundred of wild Jacaranda trees that are growing everywhere, which are native to Africa of all places.

With a dire need to relax and just do nothing but play with her horses, garden and work on her screenplays. Wearing a white cotten sweat suit with the breeze off of the bay rippling through her long blonde hair with no makeup and a big floppy sun hat, a cross necklace looking up at the sky and the sun and the moon who is still shining bright governed by two angelic hosts and all of the cords and symbols that Jesus has left in the house and around the farm to protect her pretty little ass from the demons that are stalking the planet. She smiles to herself thinking peace, 'divine intervention for a day of peace' and creative writing and then explosive supernatural things will take place for days on end with the 'intergalactic counsel of light' after a few days of rest with nature. Amen.

Kristin walks back into the kitchen after taking care of her horses to her satisfaction as the microwave clock is flashing 11:11 and the piano and harp are playing Hildigard Von Bingen. Grounded in nature and invigorated to face the day. She plants nastursium seeds in the planters with cherry tomatoes in the butler's pantry off the kitchen with a smile on her face enjoying the angelic music looking forward to her day. And then Stewart shows up at the front door with a furious look on his face looking for a war.

Kristin just smiles as her lip is quivering not knowing if she has the energy for a battle or to be ripped apart and walked all over. I mean what did I do but just try and survive and take care of this place with no help.

Stewart grabs her in a tight wrestlers hug and says "You crazy fucking bitch. Why did you reduce the price of my rental house in Richmond to $2,000 when I told you that I wanted $2,500? And turn on the fucking air conditioners? Your electric bill was $600.00 last month. Your are a bad naughty girl. I can't trust you with anything. I am going to mow the grass. You better make me a nice fucking dinner to keep in my good graces or I will throw you out on the street with your retarded kid and worthless horses. Let me know when dinner is ready. I need you to update my profit and loss statement. I doubled almost everyone's rent during the Covid pandemic. I have a meeting with Marcus and Millichamp tomorrow morning in Norfolk then I am having lunch with Chuck the attorney in Richmond to go over my dad's estate on my way back Brookneal to show a few empty houses".

Kristin, beside herself, tries to smile and replies "All of the prospective tenants that I sent to your rental in Richmond complained that the house is in absolute deplorable condition full of trash and rats. There is furniture and trash all over the porches and yards from the previous tenants. It has been 105 degrees here everyday thanks to global warming. It is hurricane season. Nate gave me two pounds of fresh crab meat. Crab cakes, steamed brocolli, cole slaw, potatoe salad and hushpuppies? Carrot cake for dessert with cream cheese frosting. I will get started".

Knowing better to even respond or say anything she slips into a pink floral lace sundress and matching sandals with rhinestones. She puts her hair up, turns on the radio singing along to Guns and Roses 'November Rain' and goes to work cooking dinner making the carrot cake from scratch first smelling the cinnamon and nutmeg wafting from the oven.

Ryan slips into the kitchen and says "Goodbye mom. I am out of here until Stewart leaves tomorrow. He is evil. Love you" as he dissapears through the portal to some unknown galaxy while Kristin and her spirit guides are creating a 'love potion' dinner to knock Stewart to sleep until he leaves the next day.

Kristin sets the table in the dining room with antique Canton china and puts a bottle of champagne in the refrigerator to chill. She turns up the radio to drown out the noise from the zero turn lawn mower. Then she brews a cup of peppermint tea after smelling the pollen from the fresh cut grass.

She drives the ATV to the barn to put the horses in their stalls admiring their beautiful shining gold hair coats. She gives each of them a hug and returns back to the Plantation to finish cooking dinner.

Dancing to Boston's 'More than a Feeling' glad that Stewart is done mowing around the house as he heads the zero turn toward the rental houses. Kristin boils a few red new potatoes. Walks outside cuts a few stalks of broccoli from her garden along with a purple cabbage, spinach, yellow plum tomatoes and a few scallions. She chops up the broccoli and then makes a bowl of cole slaw adding sliced radishes and dried cranberries-her famous cole slaw secret recipe. She mixes the crab meat with an egg yolk, a few smashed saltine crackers, the scallions and fresh parsley. She then mixes the hushpuppy batter wondering where Ryan is.

And she wonders what it is like to participate in an 'Intergalactic Convention' and cruise through the Milky Way with civilizations from other galaxies. She shuts the solid oak cross door to his wing on which the previous owners wrote in indelible ink the words 'Quarentine Zone - Do Not Enter' to disuade Stewart from going up to his room snooping through his Universe laboratory and the 'Gremlin' dog Star. Even after she painted ten layers of Kilz paint the words still show through.

Kristin finishes the potatoe salad. Glazes the frying pans for the crab cakes and hushpuppies with extra virgin olive oil. She texts Stewart dinner is ready in ten minutes. Forms four perfect crab cakes squeezing fresh lemon juice on top and turns on the burner to steam the brocolli. Carries the dish of coleslaw tossed with poppy seed dressing and the bottle of champagne to the dining room giggling to herself that Stewart loves homemade food and will leave tomorrow.

Stewart puts the zero turn up in the tractor barn and drives his Suburu back to the kitchen entrance appearing more relaxed and as he walks in the door. He says "That smells delishes. I am starving. Sorry for being mean to you. I just have to keep you in your place and am under a lot of stress with my business and the open heart surgery coming up. Rhonda and Michelle keep getting in bitch fights threatening to call the police and put restraining orders on each other and they are both jealous as hell and hate you I still haven't received the SBA loan check that is supposed to pay off the balloon note on Eagle Point next week" as the clock is flashing 5:55.

Kristin who fucking detests the smell of crab, smiling to herself turns down the music and replies "You poor baby. That sounds horrible. And why would anyone be jealous of me being a single parent with a special needs kid. Maybe it is because I am smart, beautiful, great in bed and a good cook? You do realize that since you bought the Suntrust Bank builing that produces no income and refinanced Green Hill (the Plantation he lives at with Rhonda in Gladys) into a thirty year mortgage your debt to income is too high to qualify for a traditional mortgage. Interest rates for a non-owner occupied mortgage would be around 8.5%. Your payment would be almost $9,000 per month. This place would never appraise with the repairs it needs". In complete shock, thinking you mother fucking bastard. You should have stayed loyal to me. I am a loan officer and my brother is the CEO of the Royal Bank of Scotland".

She flips the crab cakes and hushpuppies and drains the broccoli, melts a pat of real butter and very little salt and pepper. She places two crab cakes and a scoop of potatoe salad and broccoli on Stewart's plate.

Kristin says with a smile "You can take the other two crab cakes home with you". She makes a vegetarian plate for herself and places the hushpuppies on a separate plate and carries the dishes into the dining room, lights a few candles and asks Stewart to open the champagne. Stewart asks Where is Ryan? And I want to take the other pint of crab home so Rhonda can make me crab imperial".

Kristin replies "No problem. He is spending the night with a friend. He will be back tomorrow. She recites grace 'In the name of the Father, Son and Holy Spirit thanks be to God' and clicks her champagne flute with Stewart saying cheers".

Stewart slicing his crab cake says "This is absolutely delishes. I love your cooking baby". Kristin eying him sipping on her champagne eats as slowly as possible with a knife and fork watching Stewart gobble down his food and serves him seconds.

Kristin then asks "Would you like a scoop of vanilla ice cream with your carrot cake for dessert? Here have more champagne. I am glad you enjoyed it". She carries the dishes back to the kitchen and slices herself a tiny peice and Stewart a huge peice of cake and a small scoop of ice cream and retreats back to the dining room, serves him dessert while sipping on her champagne in victory of tweaking his bad mood into a pleasant night enjoying the peace and quite while Ryan is out exploring the Universe.

She sighs thinking how could you risk loosing this place. And no she is not going to tell Poindexter-he is so sophisticated he probably already knows. Thinking to herself Kristin says maybe I should talk to Susan about it tomorrow.

Kristin says "Stewart did you want me to call my brother Erich to see if he can help you get a mortgage to bail you out? Once they start foreclosure proceedings that don't have to accept the payoff and if they do you have to pay attorney fees".

Stewart replies "Yeah. Call him and see what he can do for me, thanks baby". Kristin sends Erich a text 'Call me asap tomorrow. Stewart needs a mortgage on Eagle Point ASAP. He is in pre foreclosure. His SBA loan fell through'.

Stewart well fed and tired from his drive and mowing the lawn follows Kristin to the kitchen and watches the news and reads text messages while Kristin loads the dishwasher making small talk.

When she is finished with the dishes she announces "Greg your farmer planted soy beans the other day and wants to put the blade on your tractor and redo the driveway. I am going to tuck the horses in I will be right back you look tired" and kisses him on the head not really wondering or caring who or which woman he is texting.

Stewart yawning says "I don't know if I want to pay him again to fix the driveway. Hurry up. I am so tired. Love you sweetie" as he is eyeing her body wanting to crawl in bed naked together. Kristin tired as well from the stress of a suprise visit and all the cooking gives him a quick hug.

Kristin walks to the barn to takes care of her horses, brushing them and giving them extra hay and shavings. She shuts the fans off so the barn doesn't burn down in the middle of the night and all of a sudden receives a message from Archangel Saint Michael who says "Kristin it is the 'Great Purge". Go to bed and rest. Ryan is fine and you will receive messages from your great ancestors in your dreams. Divine love be with you. You did good tonight", chuckling as he dissapears in an instant.

And Kristin obeys. Her and Stewart shower separately, climbing into bed together in silence. Kristin, thinking about Archangel Saint Michael lays next to his shoulder listening to him snore in a deep sleep. Then she changes her mind and turns over and sleeps on her stomach holding a pillow next to her head. She sleeps in peace listening to the quiet.

Stewart wakes up at the crack of dawn and grabs Kristin's hand to his crotch and says "Suck it baby". Kristin holds his dick in her hand and grabs a jar of Astroglide. She gets up and stands next to the bed and jacks him off, not wanting any intimacy at all, grateful for the advise from Alice. Thankfully he comes in two minutes and falls back into a deep sleep. Kristin listens to the birds chirping staring at the ceiling. Stewart wakes up as Kristin is staring out the window and says "I needed that baby. Thank you. Now get up and make me breakfast. I am hungry".

Kristin replies "I aim to please. Omelet and hash browns?". She gets up and puts on a red strapless sundress, puts her hair up and waltzes to the kitchen. She turns the coffee pot on glad that he is not angry anymore. Sex definately decreases stress. She goes through the motions of cooking him breakfast and makes a fresh fruit salad of blueberries, cantaloupe and strawberries to go with the cheddar cheese hobo omelet, hash browns and an everything bagel. She sits down to eat while Stewart is texting 'her, we and us' thinking you fucking jerk. How can you live with yourself.

After finishing the breakfast, Kristin follows Stewart up three flights of stairs after loading up the dishwasher to her office overlooking the driveway to edit his profit and loss with his ludicrous rental prices not saying a word as he rubs her back and kisses the back of her neck while she is printing out his paperwork for his approval which he does. And as he runs downstairs. Grabs his suitcase and throws a wad of hundred dollar bills at her saying "Wish me luck. Love you baby". He walks out the kitchen door, climbs in his Suburu and speeds down the driveway.

"Well whatever fucking turns you on Stewart" Kristin says out loud to herself. Kristin using her arms and hands rubbing her torso to shake off negative energy just like sweeping dust off the floor with a broom. She puts both hands on the foor to ground her energy. She changes into her riding outfit in disgust and texts her neighbor Susan to go for a ride.

'Embracing Change'

Krisitn holds her head up high and walks to the barn. Her solice place, feeling used. She feels better after hearing her horses whinny at her her enjoying the fresh air. She glances at the Plantation watching Ryan fly back through the portal with bags of specimen jars, crystals, gold bars and whatever else he brought back from his trip through the Universe last night with a huge smile on his face and a vibration that could break any sound barrier from any galaxy in the Universe.

Kristin feeds her horses a double breakfast for their patience and hugs them unconditionally while she waits for Susan to ride Goldilocks over. Thinking to herself 'You have to do what you have to do. Just forgive yourself. You have done nothing wrong' and feeds Zeus and Coconut carrots, apples and peppermints. Grateful that Jesus brought them back from death numerous times each and blessed the barn with his angels and all of a sudden she laughs out loud in immense peace.

She leads Zeus out of his stall in his new pink bling halter and puts him in the cross ties and brushes him as Susan rides her horse into the barn aisle and puts her horse in stall number one which used to be Zachary's stall. Wearing a cowboy outfit with a distressed look on her face

Susan asks Kristin "What the fuck is going on here. I saw a bank representative snooping around your farm last night while you and Stewart were having dinner. He gave me his business card 'Thomas Breyer from a division of the IRS' and he said it was regarding the estate sale and asked me for my phone number, I think for a date. He was cute too. I didn't want to bother you guys" as she gives Zeus a kiss on his muzzle and grabs some carrots out of the refrigerator.

Kristin replies "That stupid fucking idiot waited until five days after his balloon payment was due on this place to come up with $800k. And that jealous bitch Michelle that lives in my old house at his farm put the wrong company name and bank account information on his SBA loan application which I knew was a complete lie this whole time. The

Small Business Administration doesn't loan money on residential property when an entity has no employees and neither does the County of Gloucester give millions of grant money to real estate investors to rehab properties zoned residential and that are not owner occupied. She has been playing him this whole time and why would he ever say he didn't trust me? He has too much debt to qualify for any traditional mortgage, nor could he afford the payment".

Susan in shock says "Kristin sometimes things happen for a reason. That is horribly irresponsible and poor money management on his part. I am praying for you babe that Poindexter will cement a deal and hire some staff for this place. Just think about how much less stress that you will have".

Kristin smiling at Susan says "I like that. I feel so violated by him. And then he fucking wanted to have sex this morning. I jacked him off standing off next to the bed and he just ran out the door like there is nothing wrong. He said he was trying to get an extension on the balloon payment. The contract with Poindexter won't be valid should Stewart no longer own the place. Poindexter can buy Eagle Point at a silent auction in front of the Glouster Court House. And you know Susan, I am just going to trust my heart on this one that things will play out in my best interest with this situation. It actually would take me at least six months to pack up the 12,000 square foot house let alone the stable and arena".

Kristin grabs her Nelson Pessoa saddle and bridle and tacks of Zeus admiring his gleaming solid gold hair coat and his white tail that reaches the ground. She says to Susan "Well shit. Let's go cruise in the indoor arena with the fans on. I killed a copperhead snake in here last night. Do you want to ride Coconut while I ride Zeus? You can borrow my english boots and chaps?".

Susan replies "Kristin anything with Stewart is depressing, stressful and flat out cruel. Don't ever forget what a narcissist does to you with no remorse. Yes I want to ride Coconut in an english saddle. I am hot too. And just look at it this way-'the best is yet to come' for both of us and Poindexter and John aren't going to let anything happen to this place or you. Love you sweetie".

Kristin saddles and bridles Coconut for Susan and puts a pair of leather jumping boots and him, hands the reins to Susan and leads Zeus into the indoor arena sliding the door closed and turns the fans and lights on and leads him to the six foot tall mounting block and hugs him after pulling the stirrups down from and saddle and vaults on his back and watches Susan do the same appreciating the moral and emotional support from someone that cares about her and this farm.

Kristin says "Do you want me to teach you to jump? There is a thirty acre farm right next door to your property that isn't very expensive. Clear cutting all of the timber should pay for the purchase price. I would have to live in one of those tiny homes with Ryan I can't imagine the torture from that. You look great on Coconut. Isn't he comfortable?'. Susan with a huge smile says "Kristin I have this gut feeling everything will be fine. I love Coconut. He is a blast compared to Goldilocks. I will try a cross rail and follow you and Zeus".

Kristin in 'divine joy' in the saddle picks up the posting trot legging Zeus forward in perfect rythym watching Susan over her shoulder and says "Heels down, look up around the corner and hands in front of you relaxing your elbows". All of a sudden missing her successful horse business and teaching beginner riding lessons she is bound and determined with the 'Fire of the Holy Spirit' to work with Poindexter and bring Eagle Point back to life. Kristin does a diagonal across the arena and uses her outside leg nudging Zeus into a canter laughing as he bucks and lets him hand gallop a few laps.

Kristin brings Zeus back down to a walk petting him and says to Susan "You did great. Beleive it or not I broke both Coconut and Zeus myself when they were two and three years old and had a blast doing it. I hereby elect you to be the horse show co-manager with me after Poindexter rehabs this place. I am going to have WSET TV have a live crew and put the horse shows on the news. I think you would really enjoy it. Horse people are just a breed of their own and it pays very well. And hey, you only live two minutes away" thoroughly enjoying a riding friend.

Susan patting Coconut on the neck while she catches her breath replies "I absolute love that idea. Learning to horse show was always a fantasy of mine that never transpired after law school, marraige and working my ass off. I just don't think Kristin that it was a coincidence that I bought the house next door. God does work in mysterious ways. I love Coconut. You did a great job training him. He is so comfortable and steady. I like English riding much better that Western except for on the trails. I don't know how you would ever get back on if you had to dismount on the trail" giggling to herself.

Kristin smiling says "Time to jump. Just follow me and keep your weight in your heels for balance and say 911 if you think you might fall off. Just kidding". Kristin nudges Zeus into a sitting trot and guides him over a cross rail with ground lines three times in a row and then canters over a small oxer watching Susan to make sure she is hanging on and then she steers Zeus to a post and rail jump with a set of brightly colored yellow flower boxes underneath and then a combination of red brick wall jumps decorated with fake pine Christmas trees and then heads towards a liverpool oxer filled with water that Zeus jumps five feet high over. Kristin laughing at the thrill, enjoying the escapism and the company and Susan is smiling hooked on jumping as well.

The girls walked the horses around the arena who were panting from the heat talking about Poindexter in delight. Susan announces "Kristin this place is going to become famous again with a little help from a friend. This was all just ment to be. I read that they used to have fox hunts her in the 1900's".

Kristin responds "I know they did in the 1950's as well. I met many of the decendents who used to fox hunt here. They carried flasks of whiskey with them and were drunk as a skunk by high noon. The previous owners, the Carrithurs family had four Virginia Equestrian Society sanctioned horse shows here a year. Warner Hall donated all of their flower arrangements from their weddings and they had white linen clothed tables next to the show arena".

Smiling at each other Kristin and Susan walked the horses back to the barn. Susan picks out the stalls and spreads the pine shavings while Kristin hoses them off with warm water, sweat scrapes the water off, brushes out their tales and manes. The ladies put the horses back in their stalls. Kristin feeds them a scoop of sweet feed, hay and a few carrots.

Susan says "I have a dentist appointment in Richmond tomorrow that is going to cost me thousands of dollars. I will be in touch with you when I get home. You are a strong woman Kristin. You will be fine. Thanks for letting me ride Coconut. I am officially in love with him and jumping. There is an Amazon delivery van coming down your driveway" and takes Goldilocks out of the stall and mounts her in front of the barn and waves as she is trotting down the driveway to go home. Kristin blows her a kiss and waves goodbye thrilled with her horses performance.

Kristin in a great mood throws her flock of Peacocks a bucket of scratch grains watching the squirrels and songbirds devour the food with the birds and walks back home dying to see Ryan's treasures from the Universe as 'God is giving her a distraction to cope with the upcoming future events' that she will need warrior and emotional super human strength to make it through a life changing event that she has waited so long for. She enters the kitchen entrance of the Plantation which has been her home for over seven years and her official college course of 'Supernatural 101' continues eternally.

Thankful for the reprieve and internally in deep agony over Stewart's failing business after all the years that she has been devoted to him and always made sure that everything went right as planned. All of those years of work building his empire and net worth and Kristin's networking with succesfull real estate investors and high dollar master planned community construction companies. Pondering should she help him 'save the day' or walk away and decides to just be herself and things will fall into place without a care in the world for the night.

Kristin pours herself a glass of Ocean Spray cranberry juice and lights a ciggarette on the kitchen porch mesmerized over the river view with the Bald Eagles and Blue Herons and the neighbors boats sailing down her back yard pulling crabs out of their pots that they placed in the river.

Kristin in satisfaction enters the kitchen looking at awe over Ryan's overflowing bags of Universal treasures. She sees jars full of peices of astoroids and a magazine called 'The Intergallactic Times" dated May 2039 with a picture of an enormous mile long luxury spaceship with aliens of all different sorts looking out the windows. A bag full of golf ball sized solid white diamonds or are they crystals? And glowing ameythists and what appeared to be emeralds which had a neon glow about them that were completey surreal and obviously mined from some far out galaxy billions of light years away. Then she eyes a crate full of solid gold bars with that same erethal electromagnetic glow about them like the ones in Ryan's room.

(I can only imagine what the FBI would do if Ryan tried to explain where they came from) and eyes something of interest a drawing on a peice of bark painted blue with a picture of Jesus painted in white with his wings on him after he ascended into Heaven which obviously was not crafted in any dimension or planet in the solar system surrounding Earth which is worth more to her than any cargo ship of gold bars. She picks up the painting of God and puts it on the shelf in her room with all of her other heavenly gifts, the angel feathers and coins and crystals from Archangel Saint Michael in satisfaction

She walks back to the kitchen and makes Ryan and herself a banana split. She gives Ryan three scoops of neopolatin ice cream and drizzles chocolate and caramel fudge on top and ads the whipped cream, a chopped banana and diced walnuts. Kristin makes a one scooper for herself and she asks Ryan "How were your celestial travels to the cosmos? What did you order from Amazon?".

Ryan after finishing his ice cream replies "I ordered a new wallet and a Pokeman game. I just love space and the future. I had a spiritual and Universal blast. I am so sorry for you mom. Everything will be okay. Thanks for dessert. I am going to work tomorrow at 8:00am. Get some rest. Love you and peace be with you" and hugs her goodnight as he dissapears upstairs to his 'school house wing'. Kristin just smiles back at him grateful for the break tomorrow.

Kristin, caressing handfulls of the fresh mined diamonds or are they 'divine crystals' through her hands that must be worth millions wondering where in the fuck that they came from, knowing that she can't share this with anyone. And then she laughs out loud thinking that she and Ryan would probably go to Federal prison trying to explain how Ryan mined them.

All of a sudden crying to herself about the house and Stewart's fucked up responsibility that he really just wants people's attention from to worship him as 'a big time real estate investor'. She decides to call her dad in Hawaii since her mom is dead and has no one else to talk to but her spirit guides as she listens to God's angels play the piano and harp in angelic healing music that no human on Earth could ever compose or orchestrate.

Kristin calls her dad who answered the phone "Hi honey. How are you. Is everything okay?" and she replies "Well Ryan is still working and I am in the middle of writing my third book and Stewart banked on getting a bogus loan from the Small Business Administration to pay off the $800,000 balloon payment on Eagle Point which was due on May 5th, five days ago. I am just besides myself. He has too many mortgages to qualify for a traditional bank loan and is just absolutely dillusioned. He is going to have the open heart surgery on June 12th".

Kristin's dad responds "Oh no. I am so sorry honey. I don't know what the hell is wrong with that man and it may work out to your best interest in the long run. After Dottie and I moved to Northern California we were shopping for ocean front property in Carmel and we found a great beach house with a rental on the water and tried to buy it and the couples living in the houses had lived there for a decade rent free as caretakers with no lease and the listing broker told us that both of the couples had rights to the property and monetary wise as they could not be evicted because they were not tenants. And with the deterioration of your house and the grounds it might be in your best interest for someone else to buy the place and pay you to manage it while they do a historical restoration".

Kristin says "Yes, you are right dad. One of my friends who is an attorney and I have been networking with other real estate investors. One in particular named Mr. Poindexter who is a billionaire and has a great tract record on restoring historical homes. He signed a contract with me after I gave him and his group a tour of Eagle Point, to manage the place after he negotiates a purchase deal with Stewart. It is he just dropped the bomb on me. This is my seventh year here and there are absolutely no rentals on the market anywhere in the county. The economy here is horrible and it is only going to get worse. In case something goes wrong with the deal, Mr. Poindexter will probably be happier to buy Eagle Point at auction rather than to deal with Stewart's fucked up greed anyways. It is just very stressful for me".

Kristin's dad replies "I need to talk to your brother. I have things I need to discuss with him regarding my will and other ideas about Eagle Point. Let's touch base in a few days. I am glad you are writing your third book. I heard to more you write the better you get at it. Hang in there. Love you and tell Ryan I said hi. He texts me constantly asking for Amazon gift cards". Kristin "Okay dad. I am glad you are swamped with work. Thanks for listening to me. Love you too".

Feeling better after connecting with her family Kristin walks off to the barn needing therapy from her horses and fresh air and peace and quite and thinking better of it will not let Stewart pressure her to bail him out of his foreclosure. New beginnings can be scary and stressful but anything is better than being used by a narcissist. He already abandoned her years ago. He lives with two other women and has affairs with any women he wants with no remorse. He doesn't support her financially anymore so really what do I have to lose?

'Kindred Spirits'

As she looks at the beautiful old Plantation and the flocks of Bald Eagles kiting above the river. Takes a deep breath and walks to the barn her 'happy frequency place'. Kristin grooms both Zeus and Coconut and lets them loose in a small pasture in front of the house waiting for Mr. Poindexter's structural engineer Mark Smith to come over and due his investigative report in the basement and of the Plantation. She sees his brand new black GMC truck pull down the driveway and walks over smiling and waving to him in front of the house.

Kristin in a flirtatious mood holds her long pink floral sundress to the side carefully avoiding the pot holes and rocks in the dirt driveway with her long blonde hair blowing in the breeze. She eyes Mark getting out of his truck and thinks herself 'Oh baby. Oh yeah. You are gorgeous. Please be single'.

Kristin puts on her TV smile with a twinkle in her eyes and holds out her hand as Mark gently takes her hand. The two look at each other like a spark of energy was flowing between them. Kristin says "Hello Mr. Smith. Welcome to Eagle Point Plantation. It is so nice to meet you! Mr. Poindexter speaks very highly of you" thinking to herself he must be from California. He has that hot surfer build and beach blonde hair.

Mark smiles at her staring into her blue eyes and her sensual composure says "Hello Kristin. I have heard so much about you too. Are these your horses? They are absolutely beautiful. This place is georgous. Look at the river view. I can see why Poindexter has to have the place. Let me guess. You are from Califfornia too? Huntington Beach here" pleased with everything about her.

Kristin laughing says "How did you know Mark? Born and raised in Manhattan Beach. As an adult I migrated through Beverly Hills and Hollywood. My horses are Zeus and Coconut. I bought them from the Shafer Draft Horse Farm in Winfred, South Dakota when they were three and five months old. They are fifteen now and were a by product of the Wyethurst Pharmeceutical Corporation's 'Premarin' drug-the women's estrogen replacement hormone which is made from pregnant mare's urine. The drug company sends all of the foals to slaughter. Sorry I am an animal activist. I bought dozens of them and gave them away. I did an undercover story with Christine Lund on 20/20 and one with Artie Burkcow from Dateline NBC about the horse slaughter industry when I worked at Warner Bros and had access to their press release ticker. I love this place too. Sorry for the unkempt grounds. I just look at the river and bird watch to take my mind of things".

Zeus and Coconut walked over to the fence happy to have company as Mark scratched them both on the neck petting there faces with a smile saying "I love horses too. But took to surfing instead. I miss California do you"? Kristin replies "The food, the clothes, nightlife yes. But my son is on the spectrum so the peace and quite suits me, as well as the cost of living. My dad makes hollow wooden big gun boards that the surfers use at the Pipleline Contest in Waimea Bay. His business is called Haleiwa Surfboard Company. His surfboards sell for $22,000 a peice. Follow me I will show you the basement".

With smug satisfaction of making a new friend from her hometown Kristin leads him to the house and down through the trap doors to the basement saying "The Plantation was originally built in 1680 and the east wing and the portico and the columns were added in 1905. It's freezing down here I always wondered why they only did a 6 foot tall ceiling down here. The basement at Warner Hall Plantation was turned into a walk in wine cellar. Here are the Roman basins, or cisterns that were used to trap water from the tidal flooding" and showed Mark the dozens of catycomb rooms walking through the labryinths feeling an overwhelming creepy feeling from the ghosts that were watching and following them.

Mark astounded with the architecture of the Plantation while staring at Kristin and her femininity says "I have never seen anything like this ever in my career. It would take half a day just to open the spider windows down here for ventilation. I absolutely can't believe that servants lived down her in the damp cold. There are snake skins wrapped around the pipes everywhere. I have to go back to my truck and get my materials. It will probably take me an hour to do some tests and compile the information for my report" while staring at her sexy ass obviously enchanted by the place and with Kristin.

Kristin following him back outside smiles flirtatiously at and Mark replies "I am going to put my horses back in their stalls in the barn. I will be in the kitchen doing paperwork. Come inside let me know when you are done. I would love to give you a tour of the Plantation" as he hands her his business card which Kristin reads as Mark Smith Structural Engineer Incorporated with a Virginia Beach address staring at his hot surfer body. Kristin smiles up at Mark and says "You are in Virginia Beach!. That is not to far away from here. Let me know if you need anything".

Mark smiles fondly at Kristin with his baby blue eyes and replies "I would really like that Kristin. Thank you very much. See you in about an hour". With a smile she walks back to the pasture, looking over her shoulder waving at Mark and opens the gate as the horses follow her back to the barn with no halters on looking forward to their grain. After tucking them in she returns to the house to make herself a salad for lunch.

She picks a picnic basket full of vegetables from her garden, turns on the soaker hose watching the colorful sailboats and someones yacht sailing down the Severn River, watching a flock of bald eagles that were soaring above the river in a gentle breeze. Happy to have a distraction from everything Krisitn flirts with Mark going in and out of the basement and takes a few pictures of the boats with the eagles above them and sends them in a text to Stewart 'Isn't it a beautiful day in paradise' thinking you fucking jerk. Listening to Mark walk around the basement with a smile on her face wanting to get to know him better.

Kristin chops up a bowl of fresh red leaf lettuce, cherry tomatoes, brocolli and green onions. She adds a few spoonfuls of feta cheese, garbanzo beans, dried cranberries and a dash of balsamic vinegirette and olive oil.

She sits and eats lunch while returning her business emails and schedules the appointment with Scott who is one of Poindexter's contractors for the next day. Kristin looks out the kitchen storm door as Ryan suddenly appears through the portal with a look of sureal bliss and victory on his face as he runs to the kitchen. Kristin thinks to herself smiling. I am so glad Mark did not see you do that Ryan.

Ryan says "Hi mom. You look happy. How was your day? I just had too much fun flying through Orion's Belt with the Sirians. We went to a space trading post. I ate all this food from other planets that is so much better than ours. They gave me these gold coins with a secret code embedded in each one. You have to collect all 111 of them to reveal the core to quantum phsyics. Can you make me a lasagna for dinner? I have to work at 9:00am tomorrow" holding the coins in the palm of his hand like winning the lottery. He grabs two Dr Peppers and a straw from the fridge bouncing off the walls and runs upstairs and slams his door talking to his spirit guides Tina, Linda and James and then turns on some tunes on his Iphone to drown out their conversation.

Kristin laughing to herself as the piano and harp start playing 'Equal the Splendor' by Kansas starts singing along and grabs a box of lasagna noodles, a pound of gound sirlion and a container of ricotta cheese from the refrigerator and dances around the kitchen preparing his lasagna. She picks fresh basil, Italian parsely from her garden with a pound of roma tomatoes that she dices and puts into a blender to make the sauce, pouring it into the sauteed meat. She grabs a bag of shredded mozarella and minced garlic and makes four layers of noodles, ricotta, cheese and sauce in a lasagna pan.

Mark walks into her kitchen salivating at the aroma. Staring into Kristin's flirtatious blue eyes wondering why she is here alone and obviously hooked on the smell of Italian food. Mark announces "Well that went better than I thought it would. The basement needs a considerable amount of work. Lasagna is my favorite, a childhood thing. That smells so good and so do you. I will email you a copy of the report when I am done. Poindexter wants to do another meeting with me here at Eagle Point to show him in person my results. After my consulting is done can I take you out to dinner"?.

Kristin smiling with a glint in her eyes grabs Mark's hand and says "Absolutely. I would love to. I am so glad you asked! You really cheered my up today for several reasons Mark. It is a date. Come and let me show you the first floor". Kristin leads him to the butler's pantry and then through the swinging door into the 'ballroom dining room'.

Kristin admiring his body says "I seated 29 people in her for a liturgical mass several months ago. The Pastor held the sermon on the front porch. And if only these walls could speak. And they do". She leads Mark to her bedroom and says "This room was originally 'the men's cigar smoking room' in the 1600's. The previous owner's staged it to be an office".

Kristin eyes her king sized bed with pink floral Laura Ashley linens staring at Mark smiling with desire and walks to the front vestibule. She continues "The civil war safe is directly underneath. Do you like my harp and grand piano? I have learned to play both in my spare time". Mark looks at the 8x12 foot gold bride's dressing mirror in the foyer and says "That mirror is very suiting to you Kristin. This place is massive. Poindexter's contractors are dying to get their hands on this place" as smiles and stares at their reflection together standing in front of the mirror as Kristin stands close to him smiling up at him.

Kristin replies "The French family that owned the place in the 1950's renamed the farm 'Ces't Le Rue' or 'Water Street". They had a staff of twelve, and that was just for the house not including the grounds. They had an airplane runway behind the house and the socialites used to fly here for concerts on the front yard and extravagantly catered banquet dinner parties".

Pouring on the charm Kristin shows Mark the living room and then leads him down to the library and then the yellow room. She says "This room was originally the women's sitting room. I use it as a spring and fall room to have a change of pace. Mark looking at the lingerie and high heeled shoes hanging all over the dresser's with Victoria Secret's bags looks at Kristin seductively.

Kristin giggling says 'Mark I have worked at home for almost eighteen years in the mortgage industry with horses in my backyard. After my divorce, a higher up veterinarian friend advised me to always get dressed every day like I was going to a business meeting. To keep my dignity and self confidence. And it worked and helped me from getting depressed being at home most of the time working and raising my kids"

Mark smiles at her and says "Kristin I admire that about you. Your voice is very soothing. I can imagine that the mortgage industry suited you". Kristin walks through the double oak cross doors the gutted master suite. Laughing Kristin says "Do you like the pool? It is full of snap turtles. The Blue Herons stash their eggs next to the pool vents until the baby birds can fly. Thank you for the compliment Mark. That was definately a challenge for me. It just builds character. I am using this room as my closet. All of that walking keeps you in great shape" laughing. Kristin watches Mark eyeing her wardrobe of sequin evening gowns and sundresses loving the feminine side of her.

Mark says "Is that where the dock used to be? What an incredible view of the Mobjack Bay. The deep water yachts can come and anchor here. I bet that you look incredible in that dress. I am going to have to take you out to a five star dinner Kristin".

Kristin blushing says "Why Mark. Are you courting me? The answer is yes. I really enjoy your company. I spend most of my time here taking care of the Plantation and my son Ryan who is 23 and works for the County as a housekeeper. And my horses. I have a few close friends in the neighborhood and find most of my solice in writing novels and screenplays. I better go check the oven". Mark walks side by side putting his arm around her down the long hallway back to the kitchen secretely wanting to put his arms around her and pull her close. And kiss her.

Kristin pulls the lasagna out of the oven. She looks Mark in the eyes and says "I will give you a tour of the rest of the Plantation when you come back with Mr. Poindexter and his entourage. Thank you very much for everything Mark. You enlightened my day. I hope that you have a great night". And then she adds admiring his physique "I would hug you and invite you for dinner. But we have professional protocal here" smiling brightly at Mark.

Mark says to Kristin "I will take a rain check on a home cooked meal. And the hug. Among other things. I will be thinking fondly of you". Kristin breaking all rules puts her arms around Mark and hugs him, never wanting to let go. And she just stands there, feeling his warmth and kindness. Mark completely relishing Kristin's affection hugs her back enjoying her smell, her body and he kisses her cheek.

Kristin takes a deep breath filled with emotion and hands Mark her business card watching him smile at her. Mark says "Hold that thought Kristin" as he walks out the kitchen door to his truck waving goodbye to her. Kristin blows him a kiss flirtatiously and smiles as she waves at him. Kristin out loud thinks 'Oh God he is georgous. And sexier than hell. I adore him. Poor Mark probably really wants a good home cooked meal. I should have just given him the lasagna. And why is he still single? Probably because he is obssesed with his business and has no time just like things were when I was a loan officer'.

Kristin covers Ryan's lasagna with tin foil enjoying the wafting smell of garlic and marinara sauce herself. She takes a loaf of garlic bread out of the freezer and places it on a baking sheet. Felling so much better. Then returns dozens of emails and text messages from Stewart's prospective tenants, thinking why bother anymore.

She drives the ATV to the barn and feeds Zeus and Coconut dinner, brushing their manes and tails just loving their scent. She throws the peacocks scoop of whole corn and drives back home looking at the sky and the portal thinking to herself 'just when you think you hit rock bottom is when the light shines in' watching the sunset.

Ryan runs down the stairs and says "Well do you like him? You two have a lot in common being from California and not having any family here. He loves your horses and is successful. You deserve to be with someone that loves you mom after that evil man Stewart. Is my dinner done?" on a sugar and caffeine high.

Kristin remembering that Ryan knows, sees and hears all that I say and do and the goings on of this house even when he is ten million light years away smiles and replies "Yes I do. And I think he liked me too. Adults get lonely as well. Let me take your garlic bread out of the oven and then your dinner should be ready. Are the Gargonions stuck in the black worm hole forever? Or can they blow it up with their high powered lasers. Or will other ships from their planet try to rescue them. Just curious. I am glad you had fun today. I think you get paid tomorrow. I will take you to Walmart, my least favorite place in the world this weekend and you can buy yourself something you like".

Ryan obviously irritated says "You deserve to be with someone who is loyal to you. That smells so good I am starving and am going to buy myself some new cool clothes this weekend and eat at the Subway in Walmart. I am not sure. The Gargonians are being punished for their evilness and plans to blow up the Central Sun to planet Earth. There are many more of them still in the Cosmic Redshift 7 galaxy. I will let you know when I hear something. We are going on a field trip to Beaver Dam Park and having a barbeque with hamburgers and hot dogs and corn on the cob tomorrow after work. I will be home late".

Kristin laughing "How exciting for you. Your dinner is ready". She serves him two huge slices of lasagna and half a loaf of garlic bread in the dining room and says "Enjoy your dinner. Have a chocolate drumstick from the freezer for dessert. I have more business meetings and contractors coming over tomorrow. Have fun at your picnic in case I sleep in and don't see you tomorrow. Love you" and walks back to the kitchen to put the left overs in the refrigerator as Ryan is blasting Gremlins 2 on the TV, glad that he is enjoying his dinner and will have a fun outing tomorrow. She heads to the east wing afterwards to her dressing room to pick out some clothes to wear for her meeting with Mr. Poindexter's contractor Scott tomorrow.

Kristin hears Susan calling her from the hallway "Where are you sweetie?". Kristin shouts "I am in the east wing darling". Susan walks into her dressing admiring her clothes and says "I just wanted to know how the inspection went. What did you cook for dinner? That smells intoxicating".

Kristin laughs and gives Susan a hug and smiles at her glam country western sweat suit and says "You look adorable. It is a homemade bolognese lasagna and garlic bread. I just put it in the fridge. Do you want a slice for dinner? I was just picking a different outfit out for one of Poindexter's contractor Scott is coming over to tour the place tomorrow. The engineer Mark the Poindexter sent here today was really handsome. Shit he looks like a GQ model. He has a body to die for. And is educated and sucessful. Not only is he very kind, I flirted with him outrageously. He is from California too. He loves horses and is a surfer. Do you want to come over tomorrow? Scott is coming at 1:00pm. Ryan will be at work".

Susan replies "Yes. I can't resist your cooking. Are you going on a date with Mark? I would love to come over and meet Scott tomorrow.

Wear the plum colored Anne Taylor linen pantsuit with that white lace v neck blouse, it goes great with your blonde hair".

Kristin smiling says "Yes. He asked me on a date. I have the hots for him already. He just has to sign off on his report and go over the details with Poindexter in person here. Let me serve you dinner. Do you want another jumping lesson tonight? Ryan should be asleep soon. I am just so excited to see things happening here and am glad hurricane season is almost over".

She walks back to the kitchen after throwing her outfit on a pink antique chair in her bedroom. She serves Susan dinner and grabs a bowl of fruit and some cheese and crackers for herself and cracks open a Wicked Grove Hard Apple Cider for herself and gives one to Susan as well.

Susan says "This is the best lasagna I have ever eaten. Yes. I love riding Coconut. Thanks for sharing him with me". The ladies say 'cheers' and clink their beer bottles and finish their dinner chit chatting and then drive the ATV off to the barn to saddle up the horses. Kristin saddles up both horses while Susan cleans the stalls. The horses are in the cross ties ready to go for a ride. Kristin fills up their water buckets and hay racks with hay, giving each horse a scoop of grain.

Kristin asks Susan "Do you want to borrow a pair of my chaps so you don't get saddle sores? Please put the snaffle bridle on Coconut so he has more go" She hands Susan her extra chaps and then bridles Zeus and leads him into the indoor arena turning on the lights and fans looking up at the constellations in the sky. She leads Zeus to the mounting block and vaults on him after pulling her stirrups down and watches Susan do the same on Coconut.

Kristin breaks Zeus into a trot posting doing a figure of eight as Susan follows her smiling. Kristin then knudges Zeus into a canter in the two point position which men loves to watch and canters a few laps and then brings Zeus into a walk for a few laps.

She then asks Susan "Are you ready to jump? We are going to trot the cross rail combination gymnastic and then do a turn back wheel to the gate and then the oxer and the red brick wall in and out. Coconut will just follow Zeus. Grab his mane if you need balance and sink your seat into the saddle with your weight in your heels. One, two, three lets go".

Kristin kicks Zeus into a trot through the exercise and a left turn back to the gate and canters him over the oxer and through the in and out and pulls him back to the walk watching Susan giggle having a blast.

The girls walk the horses around the arena cooling them out. Susan says "That was so much fun. I want to learn to horse show and get all dressed up in those fancy show outfits. Maybe you will loan me Coconut and you can be my trainer. I can tell great things are going to happen at this place. I researched it and you can have four Virginia sanctioned horse shows here on the outdoor derby field Poindexter plans on building with permanent outdoor jumps".

Kristin says "Of course. I love to horse show too. And it will be easier in my own backyard with Ryan home almost all of the time. You did great sweetie". Both ladies are laughing and petting the horses sweaty necks as they walk the horses through the covered breezeway back to the barn.

The ladies dismount, untack them and hose them off. Susan brushes off their hair and puts them back in their stalls. The horses are pigging out on their grain and carrots happy for the attention. The girls carry the saddles and bridles back in the tack room. Kristin shuts the lights off and climbs in the ATV to drive back to the Plantation.

Susan says "Kristin thanks again. I will see you tomorrow. I am so excited to meet new people here and I really enjoy your company. Love you". Kristin smiles at her and waves goodbye as Susan opens the door to her Mercedes. Kristin says "You too honey. Goodnight and thanks for helping me the the horses. Have a great night".

Kristin retreats to the foyer and picks up her guitar strumming Joni Mitchell's 'Pave Paridise' singing out loud with the piano and harp strumming along. Pleased that she had positive energy 'tweaking gray matter' in her day. And absolultely thrilled with meeting Mark. She just can't stop thinking about him. And all of the upcoming business meetings filling her with hope. Kristin stands in a steaming hot shower making mental notes on lists of things she has to do enjoying the silence while Ryan is fast asleep.

Kristin climbs into bed wearing a pink cotton camisole drifting off into a deep slumber and all of a sudden feels Stewart climb in bed next to her hugging her with his awful car drive smell and beard stubble. Kristin just layed next to him with his horrible rental house odor, thinking she is going to have to strip all of the sheets and wash the blankets tomorrow, fell asleep not wanting any conversation at all.

Stewart wakes up every hour or two looking at his text messages on his cellphone disturbing Kristin's sleep. He wakes her up at 6:00am and says "Make me some coffee and breakfast you crazy bitch. I have an emergency and have to go back home. Sorry I can't cut the grass" and kisses her on the forehead. Kristin exhausted gets out of bed and puts on a pink silk kimono bathrobe and heads to the kitchen with a headache and turns on the coffee pot not even wanting to know what Stewart's emergency is.

She serves him coffee and makes a cheddar cheese and mushroom omelet with fresh cherry tomatoes and an English muffin with apricot jam. She sits down to breakfast listening to his last minute plans to try to salvage his mortgage on Eagle Point. Kristin just smiles and listens sipping her coffee and picking at her breakfast. She gives him a brief hug as he walks out the door and says "Stewart it was so nice to see you too" as he waves goodbye and speeds down the driveway.

'The Enchantment'

Kristin closes the door and takes her coffee to her back porch and lights a cigarette watching the birds flying above the river trying to console her nerves grateful for the 'divine timing'. She puts on a pair of yoga pants and a red long sleeved cotton t shirt with the words NASA on the front with a picture of a spaceship and walks to the barn to take care of the horses in time for her meeting with 'Scott and Susan' thinking that is a catchy phrase. Maybe they will hit it off. She turns the horses out in the pond field full of trees in front of the barn and arrives back at the house at approximately 11:11 to get ready for her meeting.

After getting dressed in a form fitting cream linen pencil skirt and a silk coral sleeveless ruffled silk blouse. She puts on a pair of heeled black patent slides and curls her long blonde hair putting clips behind her ears with a pair of diamond studs. It was too hot to wear a pantsuit. She returns a few of Stewart's tenants calls and thinks I will never have to do that again. Hallelejuah!

Susan shows up early looking fabulous in a teal sundress with her flaming red hair as she walks in the kitchen door. Susan says "I brought you lunch. I hope you like it. I made roasted red bell peppers and eggplant spread on brushetta with fried sweet potatoes" with a smile on her face. Kristin applying her favorite berry colored lip gloss smiles at her best friend.

Kristin gives her a hug and says "Thank you Susan. That looks delicious. You look beautiful. All of that swimming, horseback riding and gardening really agrees with you. Let me grab some plates. I made a fruit salad this morning. Stewart showed up in the middle of the night and left after breakfast, whats new. Actually that was another divine intervention believe it or not. How is Goldilocks and your son Clay?'.

Susan said "Goldilocks is fine. She just stands there and eats grass. I doubled her feed. She has lost weight from sweating in the heat this summer. And Clay? Well you know. All he ever does is ask me for money. At least he comes over and mows the lawn for me" splitting the food she brought on the two plates.

Kristin laughing takes a bite of the bruschetta and says "This is incredible. Give me your recipe. Being a vegetarian can get boring. And it has finally sunk in that I will have to support Ryan for the rest of his life to. His disability check and the income from his job is not enough to barely survive eating let alone anything else. Maybe he will invent something that will go viral, who knows" as she sees Scott's brand new Black Chevrolet Dually pull up in front of the house. Scott is tall, handsome, no-drop dead georgous with short brown hair, blue eyes and is in really great shape.

Kristin smiling says "Hey Susie Q. Look out the front door. You will be very pleased with what you see. This may be your lucky day darling" giggling out loud. She gets up to open the kitchen storm door for Scott. Kristin holds her hand out to him as he gently takes her hand and walks into the kitchen.

Kristin smiling at him with a gleam in her eyes and says "Hello Scott. Welcome to Eagle Point Plantation. Thank you for scheduling us in so fast. I know your are busy. It seems that Mr. Poindexter is buying up the entire state of Virginia. This is my next door neighbor Susan. Give me two minutes to finish my lunch and then I will take you on a tour" noticing Scott and Susan's instant connection as they are both slightly blushing. It is not very often that you meet someone and develop instant sexual chemistry. Scott holds his hand out to Susan, the left one with no ring on it.

Scott says to Susan staring at her cleavage "Very nice to meet you Susan. My sister has natural red hair too. That food smells so good. This place is beautiful and in dire need of repairs and maintenance. And yes Poindexter is on a buying spree. He is also doing some humanitarian projects to balance things out. Not very many people have the expertise in historical tax credits and the millions it takes just to restore one structure. It is all my pleasure to meet you Kristin" looking at her fondly keeping it a secret that he is best friends with Mark Smith who has been after her for years.

Kristin finishes her lunch laughing and says "Scott, just think of how much money you will make from Eagle Point and how grandeous this will be for your companies reputation. In addition to the priceless friendships that I suspect will transpire between us all." In smug satisfaction watching. Scott and Susan flirting with each other.

Kristin says "Okay ladies and gentlemen. Lets go tour the Plantation. Susan will lead and I will narrarate and then you can do your inspection after you know where everything is" smiling brightly as Susan gets up giving Kristin 'that look'.

Scott follows her into the butlers pantry. Kristin, Scott and Susan wander through the massive house room by room and then the basement and the grounds. Scott obviously impressed at the setting says "This place is incredible. I read your book Behind the Veil and the sequel Beyond the Veil Kristin, by the way. I can only imagine what you went through here. Virginia is notorious for haunted old plantation's and vanity fair publishers are as poisiness as corupt politics. Wow-look at that yacht out there sailing behind the Plantation. I am going to have an absolute blast on this project. Is that your house across the cove Susan?" who replies "Yes. That is my retirement home. I have thirteen acres, a heated swimming pool and a small stable for my horse. Kristin and I ride together all the time" smiling at him watching him try not to stare at her tits.

Arriving back at the main house Scott says "It will probably take me several days with a crew to finish all of the reports I need for this place. The house is huge and I have to do a separate report for each rental house, the pump house and all three of the barns. My secretary will call you later Kristin and schedule it in next week. It was great to meet you ladies. Thank you for your time" shaking both of their hands.

Kristin replied to Scott "You are so welcome. It was my pleasure. I have a lot of pride in Eagle Point and love giving tours. I am so excited to see this place come back to life. It has been my dream for over seven years whichs seems that fate brought Mr. Poindexter here to bring that into fruition. Susan will be here next week as well. We are co-op gardening together. Thank you so much Scott! I very much enjoyed meeting you. Take care". Susan shyly but cunningly replies "I will see you next week Scott. It was a pleasure meeting you" with a demure smile on her face.

Kristin after he left said "Let's get all dressed up in our boots and britches when he comes back. I have an extra pair of show boots you can borrow. I am sure that my khaki colored Tailored Sportsman show britches will fit you. I have dozens of them. Let's trail ride around the Plantation while he is working with his crew on the reports. I could tell he was dying to ask you for your number. I will schedule a picnic lunch for all of us on his last day of work here so you guys can get to know each other. I thought he was very professional and down to earth. I think he has more money than you too. Maybe I will plan a double date for us" laughing.

Susan smiling back at Kristin says "We are just having too much fun with this. I liked him too. There is something special about him, his smile and the instant chemistry. Riding together sounds like a fantastic plan as long as you let me borrow Coconut. I have old friends from New Mexico coming over this afternoon to visit. They are the ones I told you about that bought my house with a hundred acres of land and built a Monestary on it. They have never been to Gloucester. I have to cook them dinner. I will be in touch love you" and heads on her way.

In good spirits Kristin loads the dishwasher as Ryan walks in the kitchen on a Dr Pepper high and says "Hi mom. How was your day while I was gone?. Did your meeting go good? I saw Susan leaving with a big smile on her face when the Transit bus dropped me off". Kristin says "Yes 'divine intervention'. I had a great day thanks for asking. How was your day at work? And what do you want for dinner?".

Ryan replies "I just had a really great day. I worked really hard. We had a great time at Beaverdam Park. Pamela rented motor boats and we sailed around the lake after lunch. I had two cheeseburgers, potatoe chips, grilled Italian sausage, cake and ice cream. I have to think about what I want for dinner. I am going up to my room to play my PS4 game. Love you" and runs upstairs to his Universe laboratory room as fast as he can hiding the bottles of Dr Pepper in his backpack.

Kristin smugly laughing at Ryan's new found roots in Gloucester. Not really sure what she is going to do about his caffiene addiction and the lengths he goes to hide it. Kristin opens a bottle of California red wine and lights a ciggarette on the front porch watching the sunset.

Completely relaxed she blasts a few social media accounts with pictures of angels and spaceships. Then she refreshes Stewart's ads and updates his website and goes to work editing her third manuscript which is a gift from the Spirit who tells her 'you have the ability to weave words together in a way the will affect others profoundly with there magic'.

And so it is listening to the Eagles Greatist Hits singing out loud to 'Hotel Californa' dancing around the kitchen looking forward to the future events at Eagle Point. Kristin grabs a vegetarian pizza from the freezer, dices a green bell pepper, two mushrooms, a red onion and diced pineapple from a can and places it on the pizza and puts it in the oven and returns Stewart's business emails and completes his loan application to return to her brother Erich.

Erich obviously feeling put on the spot thinks his bank can do a 7.99% interest only loan with a balloon due in two years with a payment of $5,000 per month. Stewart will have to carry flood insurance which costs $40,000 per year and pay one point at the cost of $9,000. She emails a copy of the loan application to both Erich and Stewart. She separately advises Stewart that the bank will only have to do a desktop appraisal since he has more than 50% equity. But that could change due to the acreage. She eats three slices of pizza and a spinach salad all of a sudden tired.

'Persuation'

Kristin walks off to the barn to see her horses enjoying the sweet smell of hay and pine shavings which is an instant mood lifter and the fondest of her childhood memories. Stargazing at the constellations wondering what is happening in the Universe. Thinking hey Eagle Point is it's own Universe in itself. Glad that she doing the right thing bailing Stewart's greedy ass out on the mortgage.

Kristin grabs a bag of carrots from the fridge, grooms both Zeus and Coconut and feeds them dinner, shuts of the lights and closes all the doors walking back home to the Plantation under the stars.

Erich emails Kristin back that the bank wants to do a full appraisal at the cost of $4,000 and see the inside of every structure on the farm. Stewart agreed and Kristin has to go to work spending undending hours and money on cleaning supplies to try and 'dress stage the place up' and goes to work cleaning the east wing first with the spirit of Lorna Bryant haunting her as she sweeps, mops and cleans the mirrors thinking 'Cinderella' to herself while listening to the piano and harp playing the Beatles 'Revolution' music to the tune of Archangel Raphael.

Working her way downstairs dusting the corner cuboards in the living room and vestuble and cleaning the bride's mirror while the spirit of Elizabeth O'Grady is staring at her waltzing up and down the hallway in her vintage corset and hat with her dainty lace up boots. Kristin, trying to relax and receive a message from Archangel Saint Michael which may be a statistical unknown thing cries while cleaning the dining room.

Fond memories come to mind from all of the lavish parties that she threw in this room and the grandeous family holiday dinners that she spent hours on end cooking from scratch. Hanging out with angels, irritated at having to listen to Ryan blast Taylor Swift in his room while channeling to the Martians she hears him runs downstairs.

Ryan says "Mom I am going time traveling. Have a good night. See you soon" and Kristin watches Ryan run out the kitchen door and sees him run through the 'divine portal' as his human body dissapears into some far away realm in a distant galaxy.

All of a sudden laughing to herself outload enjoying the quiteness. She finishes the dining room and the kitchen and throws her rubber gloves in the trash can, pours herself a glass of wine and lights a ciggarette sitting on the back porch behind her bedroom trying to unwind, watching the colorful sailboats flow down the river and a huge yacht anchored on the other side of the river. The black clouds start rolling in she notices a beautiful Pleadian spaceship situated directly to the left of the planet Artcturus just hovering there as she stares at the stars and space.

Hearing her cell phone ring Kristin notices it is from Mark Smith smiling to herself. She answers the phone "Hello Mark! I am so happy to hear from you". Mark replies affectionately "Hi Kristin. It is nice to hear your sweet voice. Mr. Poindexter and I will see you on Monday. We are taking you out to lunch after I show him the results from my report. I really can't wait to see you Kristin. I think you are beautiful and I really enjoyed talking to you and seeing your horses. We have a lot in common. I will most likely be consulting at Eagle Point for the next four or five years. Have a great night doll".

Kristin blushing replies "Thank you so much Mark. I can't wait to see you too. I am so thrilled that we crossed paths in life. Thank you for the compliment. I am sure that you were a GQ model with that body of yours. Everytime I think about you I just smile Mark. See you on Monday take care darling".

As soon as she hangs up with Mark the phone rings again. Noticing that the call is from Scott. Kristin laughs guessing that Poindexter is orchastrating 'his master plan' answers the phone and says "Hi Scott. I just got off the phone with Mark Smith. How are you sweetie?". Scott replies "Excited to be a part of this team. I am booking Tuesday through Friday at your farm with my co-workers to complete our reports. Poindexter is moving fast forward on this one. Are you available at that time?".

Kristin says to Scott "Absolutely. Susan will be here with me too. I am home almost all of the time. I am in the middle of my third manuscript and shopping for a talent management agent. We will help you with any way that we can or just stay out of your way. Susan and I thought maybe on Friday we can do a 'wrap up potluck lunch' on my back porch and enjoy the view of the sailboats".

Scott responds "Of course. I like that idea. Sounds like a plan. Let me know if you want me to bring anything. I really like Susan I am sure you could tell". Kristin giggling to herself "I beleive that is a mutually satisfying arrangement. I will make a sign up sheet for Friday's buffet lunch. Sounds like we are going to be one big happy family". Scott fondly replies "See you Tuesday morning around 9:00am. Have a great night darling".

Then Stewart calls Kristin and frantically says "Kristin the appraisers are coming at 3:00pm tomorrow and I am coming too they want me to be there. I will take you shopping at Trader Joe's in Newport News when we are done and I am taking you out to dinner too, you lucky girl. I am an absolute nervous wreck I don't know what is wrong with me. I even forgot to pay my car payment. My credit score went down a hundred points".

Kristin laughing to herself says "That is fantastic. Let me get busy cleaning. You are just under too much stress and you should probably fire your property manager Michelle. Everything is going to work out fabulously. Just have some Faith. See you tomorrow. Drive safe".

Kristin knowing Stewart is probably frantic and in desperation and just isn't showing it says out loud 'too little, too late on that one" and I have errands to run all day and buy and unload horse feed. Why the fuck do you do this to yourself or me. It just throws me off and somehow she will survive the entire ordeal simply because she has no choice.

Kristin, thinking about Mark, heads to the barn and grooms her horses. She rides Zeus and Coconut in the arena going over the jumping course two times on each horse and tucks them into their stalls after giving them a bubble bath and feeds them a bucket of grain and alfalfa cubes.

Picking a few armloads of blue and pink Hydrangeas in front of the ice houses on the way home thinking fresh flowers will spruce the place up a bit. She takes three crystal vases stored under the kitchen sink. Arranges the flowers and puts one vase on the kitchen table, one in the dining room and the last in her bedroom. And then Kristin spends an entire hour sweeping and dusting the living room.

Then she decides to clean the bathrooms again and empty all of the trash cans. Satisfied she washes her hair in a hot steamy shower, puts on a pink cotton spa bathrobe and blows her hair dry. She sends a text to Stewart "The house is clean. See you tomorrow" after playing the guitar for an hour in the library room trying to imitate 'Slash', her guitar hero.

Kristin calls Susan happily and says "Scott and his crew will be here Tuesday through Friday. I scheduled our picnic for Friday on my back porch. He really wants to get to know you. Mark and Poindexter are taking me out to lunch on Monday to Bangkock Thai on the Courthouse at 1:00pm. It is business casual and they have an outdoor patio. Do you want to go with us? Come over Tuesday so we can go on trail ride together on Zeus and Coconut and you can tantalize Scott with your horse show riding outfit and your tits. Honestly no man could resist you Susan. Mark and I are really hitting it off together. He told me that Scott is going to be Poindexter's project manager at Eagle Point for at least four years if not longer. I am so attracted to Mark. Sometimes you just need someone after being raked through the coals in a bad toxic relationship".

Susan replies excitedly "Absolutely. I would love to go to lunch with you on Monday. Tuesday is perfect to go riding, I have to run to Washington DC on Wednesday. I can't wait. I will stop by this weekend to go riding with you and bring you some fresh chicken eggs. We can work in the garden. Love you". As they both need someone to talk to with all of the solar flares from the Central Sun and 'divine convergence' and the energies from the aliens.

Kristin thinking where in the fuck are you Ryan, in the Milky way? Writes her meetings on the calender in the laundry room, needing rest for a busy week. She calls her friend Alice in Williamsburg leaving her a message to call her to catch her up on the drama at Eagle Point. She climbs into bed in a sexy nude colored cotton lace nightie. Tired of sleeping and being alone she turns on the radio listening to angelic choir music hearing the piano and harp join in and passes out from deep exhaustion needing to store up on warrior strength to survive the next week cuddling with her cats Eva and Fruit Loop sleeping next to her feet in the 'self contained terranium world, the divine Universe of Eagle Point Plantation' while Ryan is hanging out with extraterrstials surfing the cosmos.

Waking up to a bright sunny day Kristin walks to the kitchen watching Ryan drinking two Dr Peppers through a straw. Then he eats three Belgian waffles and four sausage links while listening to music from Itunes "Knocking on Heaven's Door" by Guns and Roses.

Kristin looks out the kitchen storm door behind Ryan and watches the Gargonian spaceships breaking through the 'black worm hole' flying at warp speed in a desparate last attempt to escape space espionage in the sky above her back yard with their laser beams shooting nuclear energy at the Central Sun.

Kristin pulls out her camera after turning the coffee pot on and turns on the video recorder watching the thunderbolts flying out from 'Beyond the Veil' and a massive rain storm that instantaneously covers the farm with black clouds as dark as night and red blinking lights from the Pleadians ships in the sky as the moon is shining as bright as day.

Ryan throws his dishes in the sink and says "Cool. This is like a live video game. I am so excited I am going to the Pleadians spaceship and make a video for you and cruise around the Universe afterwards. See you later mom. Love you" and runs outside through the portal in front of the kitchen and dissapears.

A few seconds later a huge ligthening bolt strikes the Gargonian spaceships with a sonic boom and nuclear clouds emit from above and the remnants from the spaceships are disintegrated into thin air so no human will ever find any artifacts.

And then suddenly a double rainbow appears accross the river like crystalline diamonds of color. A rainbow sybolizes the divine connection between Heaven and earthings. The song birds sing in unison with an aroma mixed with sage, rose and lavendar wafting across the farm. In absolute awe and wonder thinking out loud "Space Oddessy" in the 23rd century. Thank you Stanley Kubrick I may have your next blockbuster feature film. And thank you and gratitude to you Jesus Christ.

Sipping coffee while watching her own personal Star Wars movie on her video recorder, Kristin thinks it will be a perfect story beat board to use as a visual aide to film directors when she finishes her book and adapts it into a screenplay. She heads off to the barn after grabbing a blueberry muffin and a to go cup full of decaf coffee, enjoying the peace and quite while Ryan is out surfing the Universe.

Slowly wandering around the grounds she heads to the barn and feeds the horses a scoop of grain for breakfast, an apple and a few carrots. Kristin laughs out loud hysterically, watching dozens of rockets from the Langley Airforce Base in Newport News flying back and forth above the Plantation.

She throws the peacocks some bread and opens the horses stall doors when they are done eating breakfast and lets them run loose to the yard in front of the Plantation at galloping at a dead run, their favorite place to graze.

Kristin cleans the barn and as soon as she is done hears the thundering sound of hoof beats making the ground shake and sees Zeus and Coconut running, bucking and leaping into the air running from a swarm of horse flies that were chasing them.

Kristin laughing to herself another 'divine intervention day'. Thinking I wish the farmers would plant lavendar or sunflowers instead of corn. She locks the horses in their stalls and turns the ceiling fans on and heads home to do some more cleaning and wait for Stewart and the appraisers at approximately 2:22pm.

Kristin changes into an Anne Taylor white knee length linen eyelet sundress and a pair of red low heeled cork slides and curls her long blonde hair while she is returning Stewart's tenants calls at the same time.

She notices Stewart is sitting in front of the kitchen in his Subaru talking on his cell phone in an animated conversation with someone. He was wearing an old ripped up work t shirt and jeans oblivious to everything. Kristin wonders why he didn't atleast put on a polo shirt.

The appraisers pull up behind him in a brand new fancy grey $100,000

Chevrolet dually and park the truck. She unplugs the curling iron placing it back in her vanity as the men walk to the kitchen porch walking by Stewart's car.

Kristin is sure that they are wondering why he is not even acknowledging them. Kristin opens the door, takes a deep breath turning on the charm and says with a bright cheerful smile "Welcome to Eagle Point Plantation. So nice to meet you. My name is Kristin. I live in the Plantation with my son Ryan. We moved in on May 22, 2016," and holds out her hand.

The shorter mean looking bald man grabs her hand and shakes it gently announcing "I am Andy and this is Greg my partner (who is six and a half feet tall with a grey beard and mustache) nice to meet you. We are going to take the measurements from the outside of the house first which should take us about a half an hour then you can give us a tour of the inside and the three rental houses" as Andy turns and eyes the overgrown vines and peeling paint on the rentals he asks "Are any of those structures habitable?' obviously shocked at the lack of yard maintenance at Eagle Point.

Kristin laughing says "The Hobbit House" is the one bedroom with the dome shapped roof beyond the two ice houses and is completely remodeled but the sunroom is leaking, they never installed any flashing on the place and it needs a new roof, drywall repair and mold abatement. I have tenants in the two bedroom two story house next to the 'Hobbit House', Brittany the tenant is home and said she will let you in at 5:00pm after she picks her son up from the school bus at the mailbox, her kid has autism. The house has newer laminate flooring and designer paint but needs a new roof as well. The one on the end is called the 'Sunset House'. Has three bedrooms, two full bathrooms and has not been cleaned since the last tenant moved out. It doesn't have a furnace, Stewart needs to order a dumpster and I will have my son Ryan clear all the furniture and trash so I can clean it and lease it out".

Smiling to herself adding "The original occupants of the 'Sunset House' were decendants from the witches that were burned at the Salem Witch Trials and practiced witchcraft and black magic in that house".

Greg asks Kristin "Who does the yard work here?". Kristin smiles and replies "Stewart. He won't let anyone use his tractor or zero turn mower". Greg looks at Kristin in disgust at the weeds and tall grass everywhere and says "He should be fired."

Andy and Greg looking at each with a curious look on their faces go grab their clipboards and tape measures from their truck, lock the truck and start taking measurements for their report not doing a very good job of keeping quiet about their opinions that the farm is in dire need of repairs.

Kristin smiling calls out and says "I will be sitting in the kitchen doing paperwork. Just come in when you are ready to see the inside of the house and I will be happy to give you a tour. Let me know if you need anything or have any questions".

Kristin watching Stewart sitting in his car still talking of the phone who doesn't even get out to introduce himself to the appraisers, whose report he has to pay $4,000 for whether or not the loan funds just shakes her head and smiles.

Kristin works on editing her screenplay sitting in front of her laptop at the kitchen table and watches Andy and Greg walk through the kitchen door. She gets up and smiles and says "Are you ready for a tour. Let's start in the butler's pantry".

Kristin does her normal tour noticing that Greg was taking hundreds of pictures of every unfinished areas in the house, the plaster that had fallen off of the ceilings over the years, the insides of the closets that were gutted and the hardwood floors, only half of which have been refinished.

After they finished their inspection of the inside of the Plantation Kristin leads them outside to tour the rental houses, all three of the stables, the storage barn, the apartment by the silo at the other side of the property noticing the disgusted look on their faces. She smiles and says "Here is my business card. Should you need anything further just call or come by. Thank you so much for your time".

Kristin waves goodbye and watches the men get into their truck and speed down the driveway. She knocks on the window of Stewart's Subaru and says "Let me change my clothes real quick and we can take off" watching him smile at her.

Kristin changes into a floor length linen aqua blue sundress and high heeled cork slides and grabs a blue chenille cardigan sweater and drinks a glass of wine. She calls to Ryan who is already waiting in the kitchen. Irritated and starving from a food disorder and all of the stranger's energies in the house and grounds. Ryan's routine is to eat dinner at 4:00 or 4:30.

Kristin says "Ready to go? Close the kitchen door all the way" and they both climb into Stewart's car. Kristin smiles and says "What are you in the mood to eat? The appraisal did not go over so well. They were taking pictures of every flaw in the house and said they cannot give you any value for the unfinished rooms with no power or water. Oh well. You should have more than 50% equity with the $2.2 million you already paid for Eagle Point".

Stewart laughing says "Scoots BBQ and then across the river to Trader Joe's you lucky girl. Thanks for doing all of that touring. Fuck them both. If I don't like the appraisal I will just hire someone else. Unless the Carrithur's estate forecloses on me before that. The County of Gloucester is going to grant me millions of dollars that I will never have to pay back to rehab Eagle Point and all of the rental houses and stables" acting like he doesn't have a care in the world about anything. Kristin thinking to herself dementia? And her guides say just enjoy your night and stalk up on food that you like from Trader Joe's.

Stewart orders a double bbq pork platter and Ryan a cheeseburger and fries dinner. Kristin orders a side of cucumber salad, mac and cheese and a sweet potatoe. She fills a glass with ice water with lemon slices and slides into the booth next to Stewart. Stewart blurts out "Rhonda wants me to give her a house free and clear and live by herself. She says I owe it to her. Michelle wants me to make you move from Eagle Point and take over all of my real estate portfolio. Rhonda hates her guts and says she feels sorry for you".

Kristin laughing hysterically explains to Stewart "Rhonda can't start over in her seventies. She owns nothing. You should give her a house. She will never move out of Green Hill. She is to jealous of Michelle. And if you take a good hard look at how your business is operating these days you would be an absolute fool to let Michelle make any decisions with your real estate. I am sure that you already know that".

Kristin just changes the subject and talks about all of their past real estate conquests feeling emotional about Stewart's naiveness. She finishes off her cucumber salad, macaroni and cheese and sweet potatoe and just smiles. After they are done eating Stewart says "Put your GPS on to Joe's'. That was really good food".

And so she does smiling in the best way that she can 'covered by His grace'. They arrive at Trader Joe's and Kristin fills up a shopping cart with her favorite things and heads in line to check out eyeing Stewart's antics just wanting to go home and pet her horses.

Stewart pays the bill and loads the groceries in his Subaru and drives back to the Plantation talking about all of his tenants and Michelle and unloads the groceries into her kitchen and says "I have to run. Rhonda won't let me spend the night with you anymore. I might get a disease from you and your retarded kid. Talk to you later put more ads on Craigslist so Michelle doesn't have to waste her time. Love you" as he grabs her ass and runs out the door. He must be thinking that she will have a temper tantrum and beg him to come back, at the abandonment and gossip about his other 'not so girlfriends'.

And this routine actually will work out better for both of us. Between Stewart's unidentifiable skin disease and he most likely needs some time to himself since Rhonda quit her job and is just an unpleasant person in general. Call her a complete frustrated bitch if you will. And Michelle will eventually get caught with her lies about the bogus loans and fake grants for his Suntrust Bank Building and Eagle Point that he will never receive a check for. Thinking to herself his mind is definately twisted.

'Synergy'

She takes a deep breath and decides to 'chalk it up to divine will'. And think about nothing but Mark Smith. She puts the groceries away and watches Ryan run outside towards the portal who excitedly yells out ' I am going space traveling to another galaxy with the Pleadians. See you tomorrow". Kristin laughs, reminding herself what a narcissist does to you.

To take her mind off of things Kristin goes and rides Zeus and Coconut in the indoor arena after changing into a pair of shorts and a tank top. Kristin leads Zeus bareback to the arena and vaults on his back from the mounting block. Smiling and petting his neck feeling the warmth of her horses hair on her bare legs looking forward to what the future has to bring and especially her new friendship with Mark Smith and Poindexter. Kristin puts Zeus away and rides Coconut on the loop around the Plantation admiring the water view. She puts her horses to bed and feeds them dinner.

Letting it all go because all that Stewart ever did was throw some money and empty promises at her and then let her down like a bomb was dropped on her. At least he admits that he does nothing but use people. Kristin is surrounded by angels and the spacecrafts that were descending from the atmosphere at warp speed above the Plantation as the sun goes down. And the brilliant star Arcturus appears in the sky with a crescent moon above the river and concurrently cosmic sonic booming sounds appear from "Beyond the Veil" like fireworks.

Intuitively knowing a transmission from "the Messenger" will come to her as Kristin stands in the doorway to her 'men's cigar smoking room' listening to a mission bell ring as the voices are calling from far away. And Archangel Saint Michael who will program her in her sleep tonight like calling up the Captian in the middle of the night. That she will never leave Eagle Point until after the 'Greatest Coming of Eternal Light' in the history of the Universe in the year 2039. We are all just prisoners here by our own device.

Kristin listens to the angels in the house play the harp and grand piano to the tune of Hildegard Von Bingen's 'Celestial Heirarchy'. She grabs her Ebenezer guitar from the library room, sits down on the leather couch and turns the amplifier on high and strums along. She then switches to Skid Row's "I Remember You' and then the Black Crowe's 'She Talks to Angels'.

Musically invigorated Kristin pours herself a glass of Merlot and lights a ciggarette on her back porch lounging on her fainting couch covering her legs with a chenille blanket. When she is finally tired, she hops in a hot shower rubbing jasmine scented body wash all over herself and climbs into bed and falls into an instant deep sleep.

Watching the Bayside Transit gratefully take Ryan to work enjoying the silence, Kristin makes an appointment at the hair stylist and for a pedicure. She texts Susan a message if she wants to join in. Excited about Mark and Poindexter's visit and all things to come she drinks a cup of decaf Rasberry tea, eats a blueberry muffin and dresses in a simple jogging suit colored in red and heads off to the barn her 'instant happy frequency place' and feeds each horse a scoop of sweet feed and vitamins.

She lets Zeus and Coconut loose in front of the Plantation and gets their stalls ready. Susan texts her back "Just pick me up. Yes". Kristin feeds the peacocks, checks the weather and fills up the horses feeders with Timothy hay. Watching the blue herons and mallard ducks swimming in the pond she calling out to the horses. Zeus and Coconut lift their heads up and take off into a trot back to their stalls leaping and bucking in the air with their golden eyes shinning bright grateful for their freedom. The boys walk into their stalls. Kristin watches the spacecrafts in wonder, curious about their Universal occupants and closes the stall doors as Zeus and Coconut are pigging out on their lunch.

Kristin jogs back home to get dressed for her girls day with Susan excited to see Mark and Poindexter tommorow. She changes into a cotton beige v neck floor length sundress wth lace inserts after putting her hair up. Satisfied with her appeance she grabs a lemon cream yogurt from Trader Joe's out of the fridge and sits at the kitchen table spooning mouthfuls of the delicious yogurt in her mouth salivating.

She texts Susan when she is done "I will be at your house in five minutes. Let's grab a bite for lunch in town".

Grabing her purse she climbs in the driver's seat, turns on the radio listening to Bon Jovi's 'I'll Be There for You' singing along and speeds to Susan's house. Turning down into Susan's private driveway admiring her gardens and the lagoons that wash under her front porch, the planters full of red geraniums and purple petunias on her pool patio. And her vegatable garden looks like a jungle over loaded with things to pick. 'Realistic living' Kristin thinks to herself instead of trying to take care of a 12,000 square foot house and 400 acres by herself.

Susan runs out the door and says "This is so exciting. Thanks for picking me up. I go stir crazy here by myself too. You look happy and your skin is glowing. I take it you are excited about your future with Mark and Poindexter and moving on from that fucking asshole Stewart. I think that I will just get layers and a trim at the hair dressers and maybe a few blonde highlights and ruby red nail polish at the nail place. You should go almost platinum blonde I think. And why do you always do gold glitter nail polish? At least do a sparkling berry color to make it stand out" laughing her head off.

The positive contagious synergy in Kristin's car makes her say "You are absolutely right. I will go Platinum blonde, maybe just highlights. Gold and pink are my favorite colors. The bullshit from Stewart's greed and Ryan's demands are just way to much for me anymore. At least Ryan has an excuse. I am his lifeline to the world. I have to hold my head up high, budget money like crazy and live on my pay from the State as Ryan's caregiver until Poindexter officially hires me and gives me a paycheck. I don't want Mark to think that I am a rescue case even though that is what men want. 'Equal the Splendor' you know. He probably spends 60 hours a week working and wants someone at his disposal like all men do. But at least he loves horses and surfing and will appreciate homemade cooking. And a blow job and sex" giggling out loud.

Susan replies "Kristin-Ryan has roots here and your family is so far away. I am impressed by your courage with that one Things are going to get so much better for both of us. Just wait until Poindexter owns Eagle Point and puts all of your dreams into fruition. You will have staff and really good income. In addition to a new love affair with an honest man that likes you for who you are" laughing out loud.

Kristin smiles back at Susan and says "You are right. And what the fuck. Scott is going to be here all day everyday for at least four or five years. That is better than any super lotto jackpot you could win-that is going to be so convenient for the two of you. Mark lives in Virginia Beach and owns a waterfront beach house-it is atleast a three hour round trip drive to Gloucester. I am so sick and tired of being lonely here without any help around the place. I am one of those 'cuddle bunnies' that loves to snugle up all night-the same old song and dance. So hey where do you want to go on our first double date to dinner? And no skinny dipping before" smiling at Susan with fond affection.

Kristin adds "I read all of those books that you loaned me about Chistian Martrydom. That was the most evil horrifying event that I ever read about in my life. Thanks to God that he blessed me with Archangel Saint Michael as my guardian angel to surf the great unchartered waters of 'Eagle Point' after being with a narcissist after all of this time. And you better not abandon me after you fall in love with Scott".

Susan hugs Kristin and says "I have always suffered deep seeded abandonment issues myself too Kristin. I believe in destiny as well. And our predetermined paths in life. 'Gratitude to the most High' for that one. On to bigger and better ones. I have a feeling that Mark will sweep you off of your feet and devote himself to you. Your lives will soon be completely interwined. Stewart will remorsely be out of the picture permantly. I have been fantising about Scott and I. Maybe we will have a double wedding in front of your Plantation after it is restored. Anything is possible when you have Faith".

The girls pull up in front of the hair dressers appropriately named 'Split Endz". The two go all out on hairdoes and hair color and then stop at the 'Nail Expo' and do manicures, pedicures and eyebrow waxing in good spirits. Aferwards they stop at Macy's and buy several alluring summer outfits each to share with each other. Susan picks out a formal in blush silk with rhinestones and a sapphire blue below the knee sexy sleeveless sundress. Kristin in a naughty mood picks a gold sequin backless dress with a cowl neck and a form fitting black lace formal dress with a sequin bodice with a matching bolero jacket.

Kristin asks Susan 'Do you want me to stop at the Wareneck Deli on the way home? I am all of a sudden starving. They have really good sandwiches. We just spent a fortune". Susan says "Yes please. My treat. I am hungry too". Kristin pulls up in front of the deli and the girls sit at the counter studying the menu.

Susan asks Kristin "Are you going to do just a veggie melt with jack cheese?". Kristin orders two ice waters and says "Perfect. No mustard please. That was too much fun shopping. We are almost the same size and can share our dresses". Susan places their order and said "I have tons of jewelry and accessories. I was obsessed with my apperance when my fucked up ex husband started cheating on me. And then he dropped dead of a heart attack and I never really had any closure to our marraige".

The waiter serves the ladies sandwiches with a dill pickle and a side of cole slaw. Kristin bites into her sandwich and says to Susan "Call it karmic illness. And it was his loss. He will have to roll over in his grave out of guilt. At least you can live with your self and Scott adores you. This is absolutely delishes" and finishes everything.

Susan responds laughing "Yes I know. And fuck that bastard. I was a great loyal wife to the jerk. His girlfriend was forty years younger than him and was just using him for drug money. What an idiot. I love the food here too" as she cleans off her plate and pays the bill. The girls walk back to Kristin's car and turn on the radio listening to country music.

Kristin asks Susan "Do you want to go jumping for a while on the horses before I take you home?. Ryan is just way out there somewhere in the vast Universe. Who knows what he is doing". Susan replies "Head on. Let's go. I can't wait".

Kristin drives down the mile long driveway at Eagle Point and parks in front of the show stable. She switches the flood lights on along with the radio which has speakers in the indoor arena, and sets it to a classical music channel. Zeus and Coconut whinny in unison in excitement.

The girls change into boots and britches in her tack room. Susan feeds

Zeus and Coconut carrots and apples while Kristin tacks the horses up with their saddles and bridles. The girls lead the horses to the indoor arena and mount. Kristin starts trotting around the arena and then puts Zeus into a canter.

Susan and Coconut follow Kristin and Zeus. Kristin pulls Zeus back to a halt. Kristin says "Here is my jumping course for tonight. Susan let's start with trotting the yellow daffodil flower box, canter the oxer filled with the cedar trees, the line with the two red brick walls and then the combination with the topiary trees next to the jump standards with hay bales set underneath and finish with the neon green triple bar oxer with the words 'Martians Rule' written on the planks. Ryan painted that one for me" laughing hysterically.

Susan smiling with glee says "That is great that Ryan likes to paint and helps you with the horses. He needs other things to do besides video games. They hadn't invented the cellphone yet when you and I were growing up. And you really need that Kristin. This place is nothing but all work. Artsy things are very therapeutic for people on the spectrum. Let's go. I absolutely love riding Coconut. Thanks so much sweetie".

Kristin smiling picks up the sitting trot and steers Zeus over the flower box, canters around the corner and jumps the oxer across the diagonal, the outside line with the brick walls in five strides and then the 'Martian' triple bar oxer which Zeus jumps five feet high over in her inner 'special place' which is in the saddle ever since she was a little girl.

Susan catching her breath and laughing says "This is too much fun. I am addicted to jumping. It is like an adrenalin rush" smiling in good vibes. Kristin laughing says "I know. My secret desire that I never shared with anyone was to compete in the Grand Prixs over the five and six foot high jumps at timed speed. A Grand Prix horse is syndicated for at least ten million dollars these days. Actually retraining a young thoroughbred from the race track that has no use but to head to the slaughterhouse is much more rewarding. The State of Virginia subsidizes a special horse show circuit just for ex racehorses with huge prize money".

After walking around the arena several times cooling the horses off the girls dismount and lead to horses back to the cross ties. Kristin removes their tack placing the saddles and bridles back in the tack room. Susan sponges off the horses with Vetrolin astringent in hot water and put the horses away in their stalls. Kristin walks to the feed room and places three flakes of hay for each horse, two buckets full of grain and turns on the ceiling fans on in the stalls.

After turning off the lights Kristin drives Susan back home and gives her a hug saying "The power of His grace. Love you sweetie. Thanks again. See you at noonish tomorrow. I can't wait to see Mark and his sexy ass. And I adore Poindexter too. He is just so sophisticated, intelligent and down to Earth. I love that he does everything 'in Jesus's name". Susan smiling replies "Love you too Kristin. Get some rest. At least we give each other Hope no matter what. That was a blast. Thanks for the jumping lesson. See you soon" and dissapears into her chicken coop.

'The Universe'

Kristin drives back home remembering what it is like to 'Live and Let Live'. She reflects on the Beatles song 'giving inspiration and hope in this ever changing world that we live in'. And then she watches in fascination as the Pleadian and Arcturian spacecrafts flash their divine disco lights like morse code spinning faster than the speed of light descending from the atmosphere under the Central Sun above her home. The stars were lighting up the sky like crystalline diamonds while the constellations Bootes and Virgo above the Plantaion ascend on the farm as the sun goes down into the black night and is replaced by a waning moon sitting above the famous 'Cove' next to the Plantation.

Ryan appears through the portal in a split second breaking the sound barrier as soon as Kristin arrives back at the house with a look of elation on his face. He is carrying two silver latex looking bags, one in each hand, with a picture of a spaceship on the front of the bags and the words 'Intergallactic Trading Post' on it, filled with treasures from his cosmic trip through the Universe. He is wearing a backpack made out of the same material with pictures of distant galaxies and nebulas and the words 'Greetings from the Universe' written on the backpack.

Ryan follows Kristin into the kitchen he says "Hi Mom. I had a blast surfing the Universe and visiting 'cosmic space outposts'. We dined at 'Intergallactic Restaurants' floating in the air. Their food is so much better than ours. They have a space flavored Dr Pepper served in a star shaped glass cup and some type of ice cream that I have never tasted before that I fucking love. I will give you your presents tomorrow. I am tired. Have a good nights sleep with the angels. That was definitaly a divine vacation for me. I can't wait to go again".

He leaves a neon green cup made out of titanium with a picture of a Martian on the front of the cup and the words 'Martian's Rule' on the kitchen counter and then Ryan runs up stairs to his 'school house wing'. Kristin cannot only imagine what is in the 'Intergallactic Trading Post' bags. Smiling to herself thinking 'the Jetsons meet Space

Oddessy' in the twenty third century.

She walks up the three flights of stairs under the 'previously haunted attic' that has been turned into a 'tabernacle' to Ashley's pink marble bathroom. Kristin takes a hot bath with sage and primrose oil and then crawls into bed wearing a silk kimino with pictures of India blue peacocks on it. She falls fast asleep in a deep slumber wondering what the next day will bring her in good spirits.

Well rested and in a great mood Kristin dresses in a pair of leggings and a pink lycra Eagle Point Plantaion t shirt and goes to the kitchen to make some coffee. Ryan is sitting at the kitchen table listening to cartoons on his cellphone oblivious to anything. Kristin taps him on shoulder and says "Turn these fucking cartoons off. Do you want me to make you an everthing bagel for breakfast?" noticing two empty Dr Pepper soda can's sitting in front of him. Ryan jumps and says "You scared me. Yes please. Do you want to see what I brought you from my space vacation?".

Kristin smiles and says "Ofcourse". Ryan pulls out of his silver 'Greetings from the Universe' bag a coffee table book titled 'Welcome to the Future' with the numbers 2039 centered underneath and a picture of a galaxy with billions of stars super imposed on the cover which were radiating like glow in the dark crystals and places it on the table. Ryan smiling says "It is like a bible of the futuristic times. Sorry it is written in Sirian language. You won't be able to read it. But you can look at the pictures".

He then hands her a heavy solid crystal bowl with a solid crystal pestel with a huge smile on his face and says "You rub the outer edge of the diameter of the bowl like this with the crystal pestel. It creates divine energy and then you ding it like this with the pestel and it creates a ball of rainbow colors and energy that you can use to heal and manifest. You can use your hands or mind to elevate the balls of energy to do anything you want. You can enlarge the ball of energy around your body or make dozens of small ones. I thought that one was so cool. I bought one for myself too. We went to a place called 'The Orion's Belt Space Emporium'. They have tons of cool stuff there".

Ryan reaches into his bag of space treasures and continues "And here is a peice of an asteriod embedded into a looking glass from the Milky

Way. This cool glass jar has a peice of a shooting star inside that exploded in the Andromedea Galaxy. She is still energized and glows in the dark. I bought myself this cool space helmet that has virtual space games and alien wars that you play with all of the other galaxies without the internet and you can drive a spaceship faster than the speed of light trillions of light years away and blow up other spaceships. The Martian's gave me the titanium cup for you that I left on the counter. They gave me one too. This mini Universal computerized tablet which is voice activated has diagrams in it on 'how to build you own spacecraft and manipulate electromagnetic fields for a self propelled luxury craft'. It is so cool and has all of these options you can add nuclear laser beams and robots to fly it for you".

Kristin laughing and thinking shit am I really a human being on planet Earth, looking in fascination at his 'out of this world' treasures. She hugs Ryan and says "That was very thoughtful of you. I absolutely love them. Thank you very much darling. Are you going to volunteer at Helping the Homeless Thrift Store today? The Bayside Transit left me a message they were picking you up at 9:30am. I am so glad you had a cosmic blast. That sounds so very exciting since there is not much else to do here at Eagle Point".

She puts his bagel in the toaster and grabs a $20.00 bill out of her wallet and hands it to him and then ads "Are you and your friends going to McDonalds today for lunch? I think that is great that you guys have your own routine. You can invite them over to Eagle Point if you want to hang out with them here and play video games if you ever are not surfing the Universe".

She butters his bagel and spreads Strawberry preserves on top and serves it on a plate in front of him. Ryan replies "Yes I am. We just love McDonalds and order vanilla ice cream cones for dessert. Thanks mom. Have fun at the Thai place with your friends and new boyfriend. See you later". He places the $20 bill in his wallet, grabs his bagel and another Dr Pepper from the fridge and runs out the door to the bus who is an hour early.

Ofcourse Kristin never told Ryan about her lunch date with Poindexter, Mark Smith and Susan as she opens the 'Welcome to the Future' book that he gave her...history that is written before the future...in complete awe and wonder of God's omnipresence and the Holy Trinity's omniscience, Jesus Christ and the 'Greatest Coming of Eternal Light' in the Universe.

Leafing through the book fascinated by the pictures of other worlds in far away galaxies, distant astral realms and the photos of extraterrestrials. Kristin hears 'The Messenger' chuckling at her who says out loud "Kristin go look in your library and you will find a book titled 'Translating Sirian Light Language for Earthlings, circa 2039' . Divine love and peace to you".

Overwhelmed by that warm fuzzy feeling and divine love that no human being could ever imitate Kristin says out loud "Glory to God, Halleleujah. Amen". She runs down to the library room excited and sees a book with a Sirian Blue color cover with an 'unwordly vibration' sitting on the coffee table titled 'Sirian Light Language' with the numbers 2039 centered underneath. She grabs the book to her chest and kisses it and puts both books inside her nighstand in her bedroom and drives the ATV to the barn in a hurry.

'Covered By His Grace'

Zeus and Coconut whinny at the top of their lungs glad to see their mom. Kristin smiling at her prized possessions who have hearts of gold, feeds them sweet feed, hay cubes, apples, carrots and peppermints and turns them out in the pond field watching a flock of five bald eagles kite above the pond filled with blue and white herons and mallard ducks as the peacocks perch on the dock next to the pond. Laughing to herself 'bird world' on Earth admiring her horses gleaming good health eating grass under the ancient ash trees.

 She whizzes through her chores. Returns a few of Stewart's business calls and text messages and opens the pasture gate. The horses walk back to their stalls full from eating grass and they both lay down for a nap in their stalls filled with pine shavings and hay. Kristin says "I love you boys, see you later" thinking to herself thanks be to God. Kristin gets into the ATV to drive back home to beautify herself for the lunch meeting noticing a floral delivery truck pulling up in front of her kitchen.

She drives the ATV back home as the delivery man brings a crystal vase filled with three dozen pink and white roses out of his truck. He smiles at Kristin and says "Is this 4100 Eagle Point Plantation Road? I have an anonymous delivery at this address. But there is a card attached". Kristin grabs the vase of roses and card and says "Thank you so much. They must be from a secret admirer. Or an an alien. Have a great day" and waves goodbye intuitively knowing that the flowers are from Mark.

She walks into the kitchen with a big smile on her face breathing in the intoxicating aroma of the heirloom roses. She puts the vase down and opens the card which reads 'Kristin I haven't stopped thinking about you since the second I met you. Get used to it beautiful. Affectionately yours, Mark'. Kristin places the vase of flowers in her bedroom on an antique ivory marble side table. She takes a quick selfie next to the flowers and texts it to Susan, smelling the aroma from the roses wafting through the hallway.

With a smile she runs upstairs to her pink marble bathroom after selecting a below the knee length form fitting blush colored linen Anne Taylor skirt with a matching blazer and a Laura Ashley style ultra-feminine pink floral silk camisole, a pair of beige opened toed sandles with rhinestones on them from her dressing room.

Kristin showers and gets dressed deciding on a natural makeup look. She curls her long blonde hair. She puts on her jewelry admiring the pink diamond tear drop earrings, matching necklace and bracelet that were a gift from her father for her fourty ninth birthday. Kristin puts a pair of rhinestone boby clips behind her ears showing off her cheek bones.

Satisfied with her appearance, Kristin puts on a berry colored lip glaze and notices Mark's truck coming down the driveway pulling in front the kitchen entrance. Kristin glowing with excitement walks slowly back to the kitchen. She walks out on the kitchen landing with a smile waving at him. Mark climbs out of his truck wearing khaki pants and a Ralph Lauren long sleeved pin striped blue and white business shirt and a blue designer tie looking like a million bucks as he smiles back at Kristin - you know a 'fate accompliss'.

Kristin holds the kitchen storm door open for him and says "Thank you for the beautiful roses Mark. Are you trying to court me like a gentleman? You look like you should be on the cover of a GQ magazine. Are you for real?' as she gives him a big hug not wanting to let go. He is in great shape and smells incredible embracing her and running his hands up and down her back and hips. Kristin feels his you no what getting hard and whispers in his ear "Let's try to behave ourselves over lunch. Susan just pulled up and Poindexter is behind her".

Mark kisses her on the head with a triumphant smile on his face admiring her natural beauty and honesty and puts on his 'business persona' and says to Kristin "Let me court you Kristin. You deserve it. I have all the respect in the world for you. I just feel this passion about you that I have never experienced before. You just 'shoot for the stars' with Poindexter plus I love your horses. Sunday night dinner? I have a job in Maryland on Friday and Saturday and want to go surfing on Sunday afternoon. You pick the place and I will pick you up" and squeezes her hand staring into her eyes. Kristin with a twinkle in her eyes replies "Oh Mark! Of course. I would love that. It's a date! I will pick some place elegant with ambiance so we can talk" squeezing his hand back smiling at his bright blue eyes.

Kristin watches Susan let herself in the kitchen smiling at Kristin and Mark hugging. Susan pulls out her phone and says "Say cheese" and snaps a few photos as they pulled out of their embrace. Susan says "You might appreciate those pictures someday as a fond memory. You too make a great couple. I love your outfit Kristin. And Mark you are in really great shape like a sophisticated athelete".

Kristin laughing says "Hi Susan. You caught us. Aren't the roses Mark sent me beautiful? I absolutely love your dress. Emerald green is your color and those matching emerald earrings are gorgeous. That really sets your outfit off. And no man would ever be able to resist you with that cleavage".

Kristin smiles and opens the door for Mr. Poindexter, establishing direct eye contact with him like they were seeing through each other's souls admiring his tailored khaki pants and Yves Saint Lauren aqua business shirt and tie with his gold Ray Ban glasses sitting on top of his head as she looks at his sleek brand new Range Rover. He just reminds her of George Clooney.

Kristin gives him a hug and says "Welcome to the greatest aquisition in your real estate career Sir. In the midst of unchartered waters" smiling affectionately at him. Poindexter laughing says "I absoluteley love this place. There is just this feeling of peace here. Like I am coming home. And the water view is outstanding. I have never seen anything like it. Kristin let me handle everything and we will move fast forward" as he shakes Mark's hand not hiding his smile knowing what is going to transpire between Mark and Kristin in the future.

Poindexter looks at Susan smiling and says while he is holding her hand "You should be on the cover of Vogue Magazine. Emerald green is my favorite color. I hear that Scott is starting his construction reports with his crew tomorrow" affectionaly raising his eyebrows at her.

Susan blushing says "Thank you so much for the compliment. Thank you for having me for lunch. I would be happy to work with the

County of Gloucester on the rezoning applications since I live right here should you need the help Mr. Poindexter" smiling at him while he is staring at her cleavage. Poindexter smiles and says to Susan "You are officially hired. Welcome aboard".

The group heads out the kitchen. Poindexter leads the way and seats Susan next to Mark in the back seat of his Range Rover and holds the door open for Kristin while gently holding her hand and places her in the passenger seat. He shuts the door and announces "My wife Julia loves Asian food. We fly to Thailand, Japan and China constantly just for the cuisines" as his secretary April dials his bluetooth on the speaker phone interrupting his conversation talking about business endeavors. Kristin pulls down the front window visor looking through the mirror and winks at Mark and Susan just 'enjoying the ride of her life'.

The foursome arrive at Bangkock Thai on the Courthouse with a valet opening Poindexter's car door and chaufering them into the restaurant down a red carpet and seats them at the nicest booth in the restaurant next to a floor to ceiling aquarium filled with lion fish, starfish, blue crabs and lobsters. Poindexter politely touches Susan's elbow guiding her to to sit next to him staring at her tits. Kristin knows this is a harmless thing. Most men can't resist looking at beautiful breasts and I'm sure he could tell that Mark and I wanted to sit next to each other.

Mark slides Kristin in first on the other side of the booth smiling at her and puts his leg next to hers admiring her body as she smiles back at him. Kristin was going to behave herself and not slide her hand under the linen napkin sitting on his lap, thinking about their hot date on Sunday night.

The waitress says "My name is Erica and I will be your server today. If their is anything not on the menu that you would just ask and the chef and we will be happy to accomodate you". Erica smiles and pours a French Pinot Grigio into all of their wine glasses and hands each of them a menu while reciting the daily specials. She leaves the table to let them study the menus.

The owner's of the restaurant then stopped by their booth introduce themselves as Mr. and Mrs. Nguyen. Mr. Nguyen says "Thank you so much Mr. Poindexter for choosing Bangkock Thai. I hope you enjoy your meal" bowing and smiling at his enterauge. Mr Poindexter replies "Thank you for your hospitality Mr. Nguyen".

Mr. Poindexter picks up his wine glass smiling at his group to make a toast and the group follows his lead. "Here is to friendship, family and a rewarding business venture at Eagle Point Plantation. Comradery and the finest things in life yet to come. In Jesus name. Amen".

The party says Amen and clinks their wine glasses. Kristin and Susan are eyeing each other soaking up their new found good fortune. Susan says "I think we are just going to be one big happy conquering business family. I think I am going to have to try the Peking Duck special. Duck is the one thing I could never master cooking at home".

Poindexter says "Excellent choice Susan. I will have the same. My wife Julia loves duck as well. Julia never mastered cooking duck either. Duck is one of those dishes that is more enjoyable at a five star establishment. We probably only have it once a year. Susan, I hear Scott is working at Eagle Point for the next four days" smiling fondly at her as she blushes.

Poindexter asks "And you Mark and Kristin?". Mark nudges Kristin who says "The vegan red pad Thai noodles with steamed brown rice and the papaya salad please". Mark responds "Thai Chicken Curry with the papaya salad. Thank you Sir". Erica brings a huge appetizer sampler tray and Poindexter places their order.

Kristin smiling says to Mr. Poindexter "I absolutely love Thai and Japanese food. When I worked at Warner Bros in my twenties, my friends and I used to frequent a place called Yamashiro's Restaurant in the Hollywood Hills next to the Magic Castle and the Playboy Mansion after we took pole dancing lessons as aerobics after work. Yamashiro's has a floor to ceiling glass bar overlooking Japanese gardens and outdoor seating with firepits. Airplaning is completely claustraphic to me. Glory to, Julia. She is braver than I am".

Smiling at her new best friend and business partner just wanting to take Mark home to her bedroom and climb into her bed with him. Having a kid on the spectrum absolutely makes your sex drive skyrocket. And the need for company from someone else who cares and accepts you for who you are. We all have needs for love, companionship and sex.

Kristin serves one of everything from the appetizer platter to Mark and Mr. Poindexter on a salad plate and places a spring roll and a potsicker for herself. Kristin expertly picks up a pair of chopsticks, fondly remember her childhood Sunday night chinese dinners at 'The Hibachi Grill' in downtown Manhattan Beach, where her dad taught her how to use chopsticks before her parents were divorced. Susan picks the sushi for herself using chopsticks as well.

Mark grabs her knee laughing and says "Kristin you amaze me. One of clients that I did a project for before I moved to Virginia worked for Amblin Entertainment. He took me on the Warner Bros lot tour. We had lunch at the commisary with Steven Speilberg. Movie people are a bit eccentric. They all think they are 'Gods' in some sort of way".

Kristin laughs and Poindexter says "Try having dinner at the White House with Donald and Melenia Trump. Julia and I were invited there twice. It takes several hours just to pass the Secret Service to get inside. Trump is actually very funny and has a great sense of humor. The 'political lingo' makes you just not want to say anything at all. They have cameras and tape record everything. The food is great but the ambiance is the equivalent of being in a court room with 007".

Susan says "My most exciting or worst business trip was when the Board of Directors for the Hyatt Hotel Corporation hired me to litigate their parent corporation and flew me to their offshore timeshare in the Netherland Antilles. They gave me the presidential suite overlooking the water to try and impress me. Little did I know I had to work eighteen hour days the entire week I stayed there. I ordered Dom Perigion every night to make up for it at their high powered business dinners where I had to bring my laptop to. And needless to say when I heard someone knocking on my door in the middle of the night I didn't answer it. I ended up billing them for overtime for my entire stay." laughing to herself as Mark and Poindexter laugh out loud.

Mr. Poindexter says "Mark I am so impressed with your work on the Birmingham Palace in London. That was an absolute brilliant and creative idea to save that place. You are probably the only structural engineer that could have desinged that solution. Not to mention the project that you did for Oak Glenn Plantation Estate in South Carolina. That project turned out absolutely breathtaking. I am glad that you are still making the time to consult for me after all of your accomplishments. I am sure that your fees have tripled and that you have a waiting list" smiling at Kristin who just is too innocent about the people that she is connecting with.

Mark replies with a smile "Thank you sir. I thoroughly enjoyed salvaging that Palace. And actually I am only getting better with tenure. Criss Cross Properties will always be my top priority. Cumberland was my favorite project out of my entire career for personal reasons as well. And Eagle Point Plantation is going to give Cumberland a run for her money" sliding his hand up Kristin's thigh.

Poindexter says "As soon as I have time I am going to take you, Kristin, Susan and Scott on a road trip to Cumberland with Julia. We are throwing a grand Christmas celebration for my entire staff and consultants this year the week before Christmas. I think April said the event planner was having a catered dinner by a famous restaurant in New York after a short Mass by a local pastor. And a live band with ballroom dancing. A raffle and other fun events and gift bags. We will stay there overnight and charter a yacht the next day with a champagne brunch".

Kristin smiling at Poindexter says "I would absolutely love that. I haven't had a night of off Eagle Point in almost eight years. Could I possibly have an email copy of the construction files from your project at the Cumberland Estate to familiarize myself further with the terminology on historical restorations? I would be fascinated to read them. The appetizers here are delicious" picking up a spring roll dipping it in plum sauce with her chopstick taking a bite as Mark is watching her tease him licking the sauce off of her lips.

Poindexter replies smugly "Just send April my secretary an email. You will learn very fast from Scott and his crew too, as well as Mark-he is an expert. Don't forget to send her an invoice for your time giving tours of the Plantation. Susan I have heard many stories of corrupt things about those boys at the Hyatt Group. I am glad you stood up for yourself. Kristin you have a whole new world open to you. I treat my employee's like royalty for life. We all have something to contribute and give each other an enormous amount of moral support in every way shape and form for life".

Erica the waitress serves everyone there lunch and asks "Is there anything else I can bring you?" as she refills their wine glasses. The party seeming content said no. Erica says "Enjoy your lunch. I will come by and check on you soon" smiling at the group, clearing the empty appetizer platters.

Kristin says to Mark "That smells absolutely wonderful. You can try my Pad Thai if you want and picks up a peice and places her chopsticks in his mouth" smiling at him and brushing his leg with hers. She says "I actually never tried duck although it smells delishes. I love curry too and Indian food". She raises her wine glass and says "Here is to mentorship and priceless friendships".

The group impressed with the quality of their food finishes off their entire plates as Poindexter is telling anicdotes over his life as a Billionaire. Erica returns to clear the plates and serves coffee. She returns and announces "I hope that you enjoyed your meal. Green tea sorbet glazed with dark chocolate, strawberries and sticky rice for dessert" with a smile.

Susan says "That was fabulous. Thank you Mr. Poindexter. Kristin and I usually just eat vegetables out of our gardens. My Aunt Judith stayed at the Cumberland Plantatioin last year and said it was the most beautiful place she has ever been to in America. Aunt Judith told me that the staff was very professional. She stayed for a over a week and will books the same vacation every year from now on. I can't wait to go there myself. I took ballroom dance lessons for years while I was going to law school'.

Kristin smiling says "Susan, we can practice together. Ballet was my thing when I was younger. I was in the Nutcracker recital at the famous outdoor 'Greek Theatre' in the Hollywood Hills. As soon as I graduated to toe shoes 'the horse show fever' hit me hard". Poindexter laughing says "Kristn, my girls did ballet, tap shoes and jazz dancing until Julia and I introduced them to show horses. They fell for it hard as well".

Mark joins in and says "I can only imagine how beautiful both of you ladies will be in formal ballroom dance outfits. I am going to give Kristin surfing lessons and she is going to teach me how to jump. That is if you Mr. Poindexter every slows down on acquiring every historical

Plantation on the East Coast" chuckling out load.

Erica returns to serve Poindexter the bill and clears the table and says "Please come again". Mr. Poindexter pays the bill and tips her $100.00 in good spirits. Poindexter says "Thank you for joining me for lunch. I have great plans for all of you and have another business meeting in Richmond. I very much enjoyed your company and we will have another lunch with Scott present very soon" smiling at Susan.

Susan blushing replies "I would very much enjoy that. Your intelligence and accomplishments are very comforting to me for many reasons and thank you for welcoming me to your group. I think Kristin and Mark thoroughly enjoyed themselves too" as she eyes Mr. Poindexter admiring her cleavage.

The foursome waltzs down the red carpet to wait for the valet who shows up instantaneously and opens all four car doors. Mark holds Kristin's arms and seats her next to him in the back seat as Poindexter holds Susan's hand and seats her in the front. Poindexter climbs in the driver's seat and speeds off to Eagle Point listening to dozens of messages on his Bluetooth speaker phone from April.

Kristin whispers in Mark's ear "I can't wait to see you on Sunday. I will be thinking about you every second. I love your touch and will never get enough of you" as Mark is rubbing her leg smiling at her and whispers back to her "I need you too Kristin. Let's go slow and let me handle everything and just trust Poindexter" watching Susan smile at them through the rear view mirror. Kristin puts her head on his shoulder for a minute and then resumes her composure and replies "Okay Captain" smiling at him and enjoying the warmth of his body during the drive.

As they arrive back at Eagle Point Plantation, Mr. Poindexter pulls Mark aside and says "Ladies we are going in the basement for a few minutes to look at Mark's conclusive reports then we will meet you back in the kitchen. Kristin and Susan walk into the kitchen, bear hugging in excitement for the future.

Kristin says "That was incredible. I think I am going to fall in love with Mark. He is the man of my dreams. And Mr. Poindexter is an absolute godsend and so completely genuine. It seems that he just wants to share being in peace with everyone that surrounds him. Thank you for the pictures Susan. Shhh here they come".

Mr. Poindexter walks into the kitchen door admiring his soon to be aquisition with Mark following him and says "Ladies until next time. Can I have a word with you alone Kristin?". Kristin smiling at Mark follows Mr. Poindexter to his car as he says "Kristin you are just too innocent. I am going to meet Stewart in Lynchburg with my attorney on Friday and cement the deal on Eagle Point Plantation, including all of the possessions in the house and implements on the property. The meeting would be too stressful and humiliating on Stewart's behalf for you. I don't want you to have to worry about him coming back here to fuck with your life. I am going to buy that bank building on the Courthouse in the deal too to keep him out of Gloucester. Go out with Mark and enjoy your love affair. That man absolutely adores you. Let me know if you need anything. As soon as I close escrow I am sending a landscaping crew and a maid over here so you can take care of yourself. See you soon cutie" and he gives her a hug.

Kristin smiles and kisses his cheek and says "Thank you for everything Mr. Poindexter, you have no idea how much gratitude I have for you. And for Mark". Mr. Poindexter smiles at Kristin and walks over to his Range Rover with Mark. She overhears Mr. Poindexter, no he wanted her to hear in solice tell Mark "Wine and dine her Mark. Spoil her rotten. Give her anything and everything that she wants. Take good care of her. She deserves it and so do you Mark after all of these years being alone. I think she is absolutely beautiful, smart and a great catch".

Mark looks up admiring Kristin's beauty and sexuality, who is smiling at the gentlemen as she stands on the kitchen landing. With a smile of satisfaction on his face, his renewed open heart, inner lust and a wave of passion not wanting to leave Kristin Mark mouths "See you Sunday Beautiful". Kristin waves goodbye blowing them a kiss as both of the men get in their vehicles and speed down the driveway.

Kristin looks at Susan and says "Okay. I have to let this all sink in. I don't ever remember being this happy in my entire life. Not happy, elated. Grateful. Thank you Jesus. Mark is just fucking incredible. I absolutely love everything about him. You better get some rest. Be here at 11:11am tomorrow to hang out with Scott all day. Thanks for being my friend Susan. Love you".

Susan smiling gives Kristin a hug, thrilled for her and says "It's a date. Mark truely is genuine Kristin. I can just tell, He absolutely adores you. 'May the love and light from God be with you'. I am going to go home and take care of my chickens and Goldilocks sweetie. See you tomorrow. I can't wait to see Scott too" laughing as she walks out the door.

And in a split second after they all leave the Transit bus drops Ryan off who says "Mom I love your outfit. Did you have a great day? You look happy. I worked so hard and we ordered Dominoe's pizza for lunch and watched Return of the Jedi. I love my friends. Are the horses okay? Are you going to marry him? Think of how much money you will have working again. I am starving can you make me dinner?".

Kristin says "Sure. Steak and a baked potatoe? The horses are fine and I love Mark already. We will have to see what happens. I am glad you enjoyed your day. I have another meeting tomorrow and yes we all like money so we don't starve to death. Let me make you some cornbread and pick you fresh green beans out of my garden. You need to rest after working so hard. I will let you know when dinner is ready".

Kristin hangs up her clothes in her dressing room and changes into a comfy pink velour sweatsuit, gathers the ingredients for Ryan's dinner and puts the steak and two potatoes on a broiler pan in the oven. She mixes the cornbread batter and pours it into a baking pan and walks out to her garden smoking a ciggaratte and picks a bowl of fresh green beans in incredibly great spirits.

She turns on the radio singing along to Free's 'All Right Now' dancing around the kitchen and throws the green beans into a pot of boiling water and takes the cornbread out of the oven. She calls to Ryan "Dinner is ready" who runs downstairs. He says "That smells yummy. I am starving. Thanks mom". Kristin puts his top sirloin steak and a potatoe on a plate. Grabs a stick of butter, slices and dresses the potatoe with salt and pepper, spoons the green beans on the plate and slices him three large peices of cornbread.

Kristin says "You are welcome Ryan. Love you too. Enjoy and oh there is a Peppridge Farm Coconut Cake in the freezer. Save some for me" watching him grab his plate with a bottle of Dr Pepper in hand. She puts the other potatoe on a plate with the rest of the green beans to eat later in the microwave.

She heads down to her dressing room to pick out some clothes for tomorrow listening to the harp and piano play "Glory to God". Smiling to herself she sings as loud as she can drowning out the noise from Ryan watching Star Trek in the dining room. Grabbing her favorite beige show britches and a matching pair for Susan she then picks a Land's End bubble gum pink and white striped long sleeved lycra top and a black leather belt with rhinestones on it to wear later this week.

Stopping at her office under the attic on the way back she prints out a 'Potluck Lunch' sign up sheet with the words 'Eagle Point Social' centered at the top for her and Susan's party on Friday. She writes on the first line 'spinach tortellini salad with feta cheese and sun dried tomatoes' with her name next to it and on the second line 'Ghirradeli dark chocolate covered strawberries' and also her name.

She texts Susan 'Reminder for Friday. I need your help setting up the buffet tables on the back porch and let's do plastic plates. I will leave a pair of beige show britches in the stable for you with my spare black leather show boots'.

Kristin places her clothes in her bedroom and heads back to the kitchen. Still full from a huge lunch she pulls her plate out of the microwave and eats her potatoe plain with a few green beans and a small slice of cornbread. Ryan waltzes in and says "That was delicious. I am going on a walk to get the mail and then stop at the guest house to take a shower. I am tired".

Kristin says "I am glad you liked it. I will pack your lunch for you tomorrow. I have a business meeting tomorrow here and Susan is coming over to go riding with me. We are having a buffet lunch on Friday afternoon on the back porch". Ryan says "Cool. See you tomorrow".

Kristin waves goodbye and finishes her dinner and loads up the dishwasher. She looks at the picture that Susan sent her of her and Mark over lunch in smug satisfaction. She picks up her cell and forwards a copy to Mark with a note 'Mark-Thinking fondly about you darling'.

Kristin grabs a pair of gloves and drives the ATV to the outdoor jumping field on the old airplane runway behind her house. She walks around lowering the jump sizes for Susan admiring the colorful sailboat jump standards with rainbow colored jump rails that Ryan painted for her, the built in faux stone wall with live cedar trees on each side and the glittering silver gate between two silver jump standards with UFOs on them. The liverpool jump is her favorite with stars and planets painted on the neon inidigo blue jump standards. She lowers the oxers in the triple combination painted neon pink and yellow to cross rails and moves the flower boxes full of fake colorful flowers in between two rainbow colored jump standards as a warm up fence.

Satisfied with her derby field jumping course she drives to the barn and spends an hour clipping the horses muzzles and bridle paths, grooming them with a curry comb afterwards. She plugs in her horse vacuum and sucks all of the dirt and pollen out of their hair coats kissing them both on the nose telling them sweet nothings of the great things to come at this place. Admiring their solid gold hair coats shining she brushes out their manes and tails and adds a handful of leave in conditioner rubbing it in the bottom of their tails.

Fuck Kristin thinks to herself. Zeus and Coconut are going to be so happy to have other horses here for companionship. Let alone having the foundation and roof of the barn repaired along with the electricity and plumbing. Kristin fills up two buckets with wheat bran and sweet feed. Throws a handful of peppermints in each and a drizzle of molassass, fills the buckets up with warm water and places them in the stalls. Watching the horses salivate at their treat she pulls the halters off in the cross ties. The horses walk into ther stalls eating their dinner with a grateful look in their gleaming gold eyes. Kristin throws a few extra flakes of hay in each stall, fills up their water buckets, shuts off the lights and heads home.

Kristin retreats to the library. She picks up her Ebenezer twelve string acoustic guitar singing out loud while she plays Journey's 'Don't Stop Beleivin' and then 'Faithfully' reflecting on her teenage years when she and her high school friends used to drive a hundred miles an hour twelve hours straight to San Francisco to go to Annie Lennox concerts and stay in seedy hotels in Chinatown, then drive back home and go to school the next day.

Kristin up early happily watching the Transit bus going down the driveway to take Ryan to his volunteer job at the Helping the Homeless Thrift store and his McDonalds date lunch walks to the kitchen and turns on the coffee pot. She scrambles two eggs, adds parsely and cream and puts two slices of whole wheat in the toaster looking forward to her day. Kristin turns on the radio as Kansas's 'Wayward Son' is playing, singing along and dancing around the kitchen.

Reading her messages while eating she reads one from Scott "Running late 11:00am. Change of plans. Tuesday: Architects Wednesday: Plumbers Thursday: Electricians Friday: Contractors" and another from Mark "I can't get you off my mind baby doll. And Sunday. Have fun with the crew today". Kristin texts Mark back "Mark, thinking very naughty things about you darling. I can't wait to be with you. And to have your arms around me".

She heads to the barn and turns out Zeus and Coconut in their field attached to the indoor arena after feeding them a scoop of grain and a bucket full of treats. Kristin cleans their stalls as fast as she can, loading them up with cedar shavings and hay and returns home to change into her semi formal casual business dress.

Kristin takes a hot shower and puts three layers of Dr. Teals lavender scented lotion and a layer of SPF 100 all over her body. She choose an Anne Taylor pale yellow knee length linen sheath dress, a colorful yellow floral silk scarf and a pair of white patent leather sandals with a low heel. After getting dressed, spraying lavendar scented perfume and Este Lauder SPF 70 day cream, she applies very light makeup and does her hair in a updo with rhinestone clips, a pair of diamond studs and a matching necklace. Kristin hears Susan walking down the hallway calling her "Kristin, where are you sweetie".

Kristin says "I am coming downstairs Susan". Kristin meets her in the foyer and says "I absolutely love that dress. The bronze silk and gold hem goes awesome with your red hair. And that v neck with your cleavage. I love your updo too. Aren't you excited to see Scott? I love those gold lame sandals. You look like a professional sex kitten" giggling out loud.

Susan smiles "Thank you sweetie. That pale yellow dress makes you look so innocent until someone looks into those flirtatious blue eyes of yours. I love that scarf around your neck. Very demure and sexy at the same time. Fuck I have to buy a new well pump. They want ten thousand dollars plus installation".

Kristin laughs and says "Susan, maybe Scott will have one of his workers fix it for you. Use your feminine charm and act desparate. Just shove your tits in his face and he will probably do anything for you. They are headed down the driveway let's go".

Kristin eyes a fleet of brand new shiny black Suburbans following Scott's new dually truck down the driveway. She and Susan look at each other and Kristin says "Yellowstone series? Wow. I absolutely love this".

Scott opens the kitchen door eying Susan in complete desire. He smiles at her and Kristin, wearing navy blue dress pants and a white polo shirt with his brown chest hairs poking through below his neck. Kristin notices his expensive brown leather belt and matching boots and the same ying and yang tattoo on his right shoulder that Mark has.

Scott says "Hello ladies, sorry for the change of plans. Poindexter does that quite often" chuckling with affection. Susan says "Hello Scott. You look incredibly handsome. Nice to see you darling" flirting with him. Kristin smiling replies "Absolutely no problem Scott. Can you take the sign up sheet for our Friday potluck lunch to your secretary to distribute?. It's a 'getting to know you thing'. Wow you are in great shape Scott. Were you a Chippendale dancer in college?" smiling at him noticing that the clock was flashing 11:11.

Kristin counts a group of eight architects enter the kitchen shaking Scott's hand eyeing Susan's cleavage and Kristin's legs. Kristin smiles and projects her voice in the calmest manner and says "Hello gentlemen. My name is Kristin and this is my associate Susan. We will be your tour guides today. Welcome to Eagle Point Plantation. Thank you for taking the time to visit us today".

Gleeming at the enterauge Kristin notices the entire group are wearing Rolex watches and designer clothes staring at the architecure of the house in awe while shaking Scott's hand one after the other. Scott smiling says "Kristin lives here with her son and is a permanent fixture here. She will be working for Mr. Poindexter and Susan is a legal counsel consultant for Criss Cross Properties. Thank you for coming on such short notice" with a twinkle in his eyes glancing at Kristin and Susan.

Kristin leads the men through her usual narrative, used to it after giving thousands of tours of Eagle Point Plantation. The men are taking measurements, pictures and videos of every room smiling at Kristin's ass in deep conversation over their architectural finds. Susan is flanking them and Scott is following last watching the show.

When they are done with the house Kristin tours them the three guest houses. And then the three stables and apartment above the 10,000 square foot barn. She leads the men laughing back to the barn and introduces them to Zeus and Coconut. She fondly announces "These boys are the official mascots of Eagle Point Plantation" as the flock of peacocks run down the barn aisle. She hands Scott and Susan a bag of carrots to feed the horses and leads them back to the Plantation as the group watches a flock of Bald Eagles kite above the river as the colorful sailboats float by.

One of the architects by the name of Jeff says "Thank you so much for your time. This place is absolutely incredible. I feel like I have been on vacation to another world. I am very impressed with you Kristin. You are a fabulous tour guide. I can't wait to see Poindexter restore this place back to it's original condition" as he shakes her and Susan's hands. Kristin flashing her TV smile says "Thank you kindly Jeff. I aim to please". The men take a few photos of the birds and boats.

Scott says Kristin "I will see you tomorrow around lunch time. Thank you again sweetie" as he mouthes silently to Susan 'You are beautiful. Call you later' winking at her and they wave goodbye. Kristin and Susan watch the fleet leaving down the driveway laughing and hugging.

Susan says "I could really get used to this instead of being in front of a sterile judge in the courtroom. I want him. No, I have to have him. He is so handsome and charming. Love you sweetie. I have to get ready for my trip to DC tomorrow. See you Friday". Susan kisses her on the cheek and runs out the door.

Kristin elated with the day and her new found friendships thinking very highly of Scott and any business professional that works under Poindexter. Ryan runs off of the bus with an Achievement Award from the thrift store for superior volunteering work. Kristin says "Ryan that is so fabulous. I am very proud of you. Did you have a great time at McDonalds with your friends?".

Ryan bouncing off the walls on a Dr Pepper high says "Yes I did. I had a Big Mac and brought home a twenty pack of McChicken nuggets for dinner. I like your dress. See you later" and runs up to his room channeling to everything in the Universe with his spirit guides. Kristin turns on the CD player blasting Eric Clapton to drown out the noise and puts a comfy pair of yoga pants and a tank top relishing the day.

'Salvation'

After working on her manuscript for several hours Kristin makes a quesedilla with fresh spinach, yellow squash, red onions and handfuls of queso cheese. Pouring pineapple salsa from Trader Joe's and a spoonful of sour cream Kristin starving after all of that walking devours her food. Her phone rings at 5:55pm with a call from Mark.

Kristin answers and says "Is this my knight in shining armor? I was just thinking about you Mark. And your hot sexy body. Thanks for calling darling". Mark laughing says "Kristin I heard great accolades from Scott about your pure professionalism today. All of the architects loved you and Susan. They gave you a glowing review to Poindexter. You are handling everything well sweetie. And Scott says that you look like a virgin sex toy. Lucky me".

Kristin says "Mark I am just being myself and I am the lucky one. You have no idea how much that means to me. I am so looking forward to seeing you on Sunday. I have given thousands of tours of this place and am so grateful that everything is falling into place. And you are the one that is going to be my sex toy" seductively laughing.

Mark glad that she is being honest says "Kristin just lean on me. I will never let you down. I think about you every second like you are a gift from God. Enjoy the ride doll. There is a swell up and I am going to ride a few waves. I have grueling business meetings for the next few days and need to de-stress. Let me take care of you. I will be in touch. Love you and your sexy ass'.

Kristin laughs says "I did a refinance for my dad in Hawaii. The worst client I ever had in my life, by the way. The title company closes their office every time 'the surfs up'. And I need you for everthing. And more. I am grateful to have you in my life. Watch out for sharks and have fun Mark. And thanks for being you. Love you too handsome". She hangs up the phone, finishes her dinner and does the dishes in quite contemplation listening to the harp and piano playing angelic choir music to soothe her soul.

Kristin grooms her babies and sponges them off with lavendar epsom salts in hot water feeding them a double scoop of grain and hay, kissing them admiring their beauty and loyalty. Walking back into the kitchen, she throws her wet clothes into the washing machine Kristin grabs an oatmeal cookie and retreats to her pink marble bathroom to take a hot bubble bath fantisizing about Mark. Lathering her body using a loopha about to doze off. Kristin dries off, slathers Dr. Teals lotion with Melatonin all over her body. Throws on a white cotton bathrobe and walks downstairs and climbs into bed listening to Archangel Johpiel on YouTube.

Dead asleep in two seconds Kristin wakes up every several hours at 2:22am, 3:33am and then again at 5:55am receiving transmissions from 'the Messenger'. He gives her visions of the Plantation in all of it's glory completely restored with fine furnishings and velvet wallpaper. Beautiful crystal chandeliers and hand painted al freco artwork of angels on the ceilings. And life and visitors. With beautiful boxwood gardens and rose trees. The pastures full of show horses and retired ex race horses. And visions of Kristin with Mark wearing wedding rings. And Ryan living in a 'tiny high tech home' behind the storage barn next to dozens of other tiny homes filled with workers. 'The Messenger' transmits to Kristin "Divine love, peace and glory to you Kristin".

Kristin wakes up especially refreshed until she hears Ryan's fucking cartoons. She makes a cup of coffee and runs out the door to the barn. She turns the horses loose watching them run all over the farm sipping on her coffee eating a PBJ granola bar that she stashed in the barn. She does her barn chores and steps out into the lane in front of the barn admiring her beautiful horses and the water view. She calls Zeus and Coconut who trot back into their stalls. She fly sprays them and feeds them pepperments and goes home to take a shower.

Dressing in a caramel colored linen pant suit with a gold lace v neck tank top, leaving her long blonde hair down with curls. She slips on a pair of low healed velvet open toed sandals. Chocolate diamond earrings. And gold bangle bracelets with rhinestones. Very little makeup and berry lip gloss. She walks back into the kitchen at 12:12pm as Scott is sitting in front of the kitchen entrance with eight brand new white Mercedes plumbers trucks behind him with 'Criss Cross Properties LLC' emblazoned on the doors.

Kristin opens the kitchen door, smiles and says "Hello Scott. Welcome home. Hello gentlemen. Welcome to Eagle Point Plantation. Sorry the plumbing here is worse than a bad algabriac equaticn. Albert Einstein will connect with you from his grave if you can figure this one out".

Scott chuckling says "Kristin you are too entertaining and should be a talk show host. And a model. Or both. These guys are experts and can figure out anything or Poindexter would have fired them years ago. You look beautiful by the way".

Kristin smiles at the group and says "My name is Kristin. Are you ready for the worst plumbing journey you have ever had in your life? Please give me some hope" and flashes her blue eyes at them and says "Come follow me". She gives them a tour of the house and then takes the group into the basement where they spend hours mapping out their plans.

When they are done Kristin says "You think that one was complex just wait until you see the rental houses, pump house and the three barns. Thank you for your bravery. You guys are absolutely brilliant". She walks next to Scott giving the group a tour the rest of the property.

After they arrive back at the house the men say "We love a challange and are installing a new Artisan well in the pump house. You and horses will be able to drink the water and it won't stain your laundry. Thank you for your time Miss. We will see you soon" and they wave and walk to their trucks.

Scott says to Kristin "Excellent job entertaining Kristin. That went better than I thought. Keep their minds inventing new things to make their egos happy. See you around the same time tomorrow? Mark is head over heals for you baby. Treat him the same way Kristin" walking away with a twinkle in his eyes. Kristin replies laughing "Scott, let's just Knock on Heaven's Door together. Susan is hot after you. And Mark. Mark. I already love him Scott. See you tomorrow 'partner in crime?'. Have a blessed night."

Kristin thinking fuck yes. She throws some fried shrimp and fries for Ryan in the oven and turns on the laundry. After serving Ryan dinner she walks to her dressing room and picks out a teal long cotton ruffled sundress with tap sleeves and then changes her mind and puts it back.

She stops at the library and picks up her Ebenezer guitar and strums along with Slash to "Sweet Child O' Mine' by Guns and Roses. Invigorated with new life she drives the ATV to the stables and takes care of the horses. She drives back home tired and takes a hot shower and climbs into bed needing some rest after all the extra walking.

Ryan is off to work and Kristin is looking forward to her day and the quiteness not having to listen to his obnoxious video games. Grabbing a peach ice tea she walks up to Ryan's Universe laboratory wing to make sure every thing is in order. She says to Star "Behave yourself. We have visitors again'. Peering at Ryan's collection of treasures from his space travels completely organized and in order. Kristin laughs out loud "Seems Ryan has come down with a case of OCD. I love it" and walks back down stairs. After eating a poached egg and avocado toast she heads off to the barn.

The horses whinny looking forward to their breakfast. She let's them loose in the pond field watching them itch their necks on the hundred year old ash trees and drinking water out of the pond with dozens of Mallard ducks and Blue Herons swimming around.

She takes a picture and emails it to April with a note "Two or three commercial sized pond aerators and night lighting would make this picturesque don't you think? Have a blessed day". That was one of the first thing she wanted to do at Eagle Point after she moved here.

Kristin cleans the barn to her satisfaction and puts Zeus and Coconut back in their stalls admiring their gleaming gold hair coats. Heading back home Kristin notices an Amazon delivery truck driving up to her house. Hoping Ryan didn't steal her fucking credit card again. The driver hands her five small packages which appear to be a video game size and says "for Ryan Osborne. Have a nice day" and gets in his truck and leaves. Krisitin leaves the packages on Ryan's seat at the kitchen table and heads down to her dressing room.

Admiring the beautiful clothes that Alice gave her, Kristin eyes an aqua blue linen pencil skirt and a matching sleeveless cowl necked blouse made out of rayon embroided with sapphire blue starfishes. She grabs a pair of white flat sandals with rhinestones walks up the three flights of stairs under the attic, bathes and changes her clothes. She puts her hair into an updo with pearl clips. Adding a pair of pearl earrings and a pearl necklace that her dad sent her from Oahu and red lip gloss.

She heads back downstairs and takes a few pictures in front of the bride's dressing mirror in perfect natural light. Pleased with the photos she sends them to Mark in a text "I hope this makes your day my darling. You are always on my mind Mark. I can't wait to see you" as she hears Scott pull up in front of the kitchen.

Kristin waves to Scott through the storm door and walks out on to the kitchen landing counting seven brand new white Mercedes work vans and vinyl signs on the side which read "Criss Cross Properties LLC".

Scott smiles at Kristin and gets out of his truck and leads the group of men, all fourteen of them who are each wearing jeans and a black t-shirt with the logo 'Criss Cross Properties LLC on the front with a super imposed picture of the Cumberland Estate and black work boots.

Every single one of them were in excellent shape and good looking. Wearing tons of tatoos and facial piercings. Kristin was happy to see several African Americans and Asian men in the group. Each wore a flat top haircut and had brown work belts filled with tools. The men were waiting for Scott for instructions eyeing the massive Plantation. Scott leads the men up to the kitchen mouthing the words "You look like Cinderella" smiling at her.

Kristin assuming her natural in front of the camera persona smiles as she eyes the group and says 'Hello Scott. So nice to see you again. We must have mental telepathy. Great color on you! I love your shirt (he is wearing an aqua blue Ralph Lauren polo shirt)". Scott laughs and says "Kristin you have an excellent grasp of the color wheel, and historical Plantations. You look beautiful".

Kristin eyes the group taking a deep breath and says "Hello my name is Kristin. Thank you for coming to Eagle Point Plantation. I hope that you will enjoy the tour. Please don't be shocked by the condition of the electrical and non-existent electrical systems. The original house was built pre circa 1680". Scott laughing says "That was priceless. All right gentlemen. Kristin has lived here for seven years and knows more than anyone about this place. Let's head on".

Kristin in her normal narrative trying not to be silly gives the group a tour of the house and makes a special speculation at the ancient round breaker boxes in the vestibule. The head electrician with a name tag 'Leon' says "Is there a reason why this house hasn't burned down yet?. This is the most sub standard installation I have ever seen". Kristin laughing says "I turn off all of the power at night in the house and the barn. I thought about buying those antique oil lanterns but changed my mind".

Scott says "Ready to see the main breaker panels in the basement"? and leads the group holding Kristin's elbow heading out the kitchen door. Entering the basement another worker Moe says "Did people actually live down here? There are live wires everywhere. Whoever did this should have their license taken away".

Kristin can't help herself and says "Moe. There is speculation that the basement was once used as a torture chamber". Scott takes them to the main breaker boxes underneath the kitchen which are full of corroded lug nuts from the moisture. The crew eyes the romex wires which are not in conduit zig zagging over heater ducts and joists through out the entire basement.

Kristin noticing the shocked look on the crews faces announces "Just think of how much experience you will gain ripping the entire electrical system out and replacing it with a new one up to code".

Smiling she says "I will show you the main panel behind the house. Dominion Power just replaced the breakers but they failed to label any of them" and walks outside with Scott behind her and points to the panel which is filled with wasp nests. Kristin walks back in front of the house laughing. She says "I know where the main breaker is in the thirty one stall show stable but am not sure of the other structures. Follow me".

Scott walks next to her to the main barn as Zeus and Cococut whinny. A worker name Greg with a horrified look on his face says "Who did this?. Your horses are beautiful. Why do you have extension cords every where?. Don't leave those portable fans on at night. Is that a peacock? My wife loves those things".

Kristin eyeing Scott says "Yes it is a an India Blue peacock. They free range here. I would be happy to give your wife some peacock eggs to incubate". She grabs a few apples for the horses and walks down to her office and shows the group the breaker panel.

Moe says "Oh my God. Jesus be with you. I have never seen such bad work. Your horses are beautiful". Kristin says "Wait until you see the 10,000 square foot storage barn and the rental houses".

She leads them into the indoor arena and then through the back rear doors as a short cut to the storage barn. Laughing to herself as the guys brains are on overload. Scott says "Are you ready to see the main pump house and rental houses?" smiling at Kristin. Greg says "Yes. Of course sir".

The group makes their way back to the Plantation watching a deep water yacht fishing boat cruise the river behind the house followed by the Gloucester High rowing team. Scott announces "Thank you Greg and everyone in the crew. I need your reports in by the end of next week with a list of materials. Should you need to return and do further measurements please let me know".

The group is awing over the water view and the potential of the place. Greg responds "Thank you sir. We will get right on it. This is a beautiful place to work. Thank you Miss Kristin. Take care".

Kristin smiles and waves to everyone as they climb into their Mercedes work vans and looks at Scott laughing. Scott says "They have seen worse believe me. I am looking forward to our potluck tomorrow and seeing Susan. Call it 'a hook line and sinker'. It's almost like a high school infatuation. She is just drop dead georgous. And highly intelligent. You did good with the group of sparkies. You are just going to love my group. We are like family. I hand picked them over the years. See you tomorrow doll. Are you going to call Mark later and sweet talk him?".

Kristin giggles and says "Susan is elated with you too. And that is an excellent idea and I will. I absolutely adore him Scott. He just makes me feel so beautiful and sexy. And he accepts me for who I am. With a special kid and a toxic past. I trust him with all of my soul". Singing out loud and swaying her hips to the song 'Pour some Sugar on me' she laughs and says 'Mark this one is for you'. Thanks for everything Scott. Here is to TGIF. And our whirlwind weekend". He waves and gets into his truck smiling at her.

'Compassion'

Kristin notices the Transit bus coming down the driveway and goes to hang up her nice outfit in her dressing room and changes into a pink cotton romper, taking off her jewelry. Ryan is on a fucking Dr Pepper caffeine high and says "Did you have a good day.? Can you make me a tuna sub I forgot my lunch today".

Kristin looking at him irritated says "Of course. Yes I had a wonderful day". She chops up celery and onion and takes a foot long french bread loaf out of the pantry and two cans of solid white albacore and makes his dinner serving him on a paper plate with a bag of Sun Chips in the dining room.

Glancing at the clock in the kitchen which is flashing 5:55pm her phone rings with Mark's number. Kristin answers the call in her seductive voice "Hello my darling Mark. I am so glad to hear from you sweetie. How did your day go?". Mark says "I loved your pictures doll. You are exquisite. And mouth watering. Not all clients are pleasant to work with. My maid from Guatamala just left and her cooking is horrible. I couldn't focus on my meeting because I was thinking about you. And us. And everything about you. That is happy and peaceful. And taking you to bed".

Kristin laughing says "Mark-you are an extremely succesful business man. Just like me you have not had someone by your side for a long time. Plus we have chemistry. Scott and I were talking about you today. I told him that I was going to 'pour the sugar on you' and sweet talk you. You are all I ever think about too. I need you Mark. You just struck a chord in my heart hot stuff".

Mark replies "Kristin I have spent years building a muti million dollar self generating business with unending referrals. And now all I want is you. Scott said you were great with the sparkies today and looked like a supermodel. I guess I just miss you. And it is only a few days until Poindexter closes on Eagle Point and you will be mine. I am going to make arrangements soon to take you on a weekend vacation and slow down".

Kristin says "Mark I would absolutely love that. And I support your business in every way shape and form. Take the clients with your outstanding reputation. I miss you too sweetie. It's only a few days until Sunday. We are having a TGIF potluck here tomorrow with Scott's crew".

Mark replies "Your voice is dripping like honey. Your smile is everlasting. I love your body and your innocense. Kristin I just want to be with you and take care of you. You are one in an inner circle of support from Poindexter's group. I guess I just never expected to fall in love again".

Kristin says "Mark love is priceless, endless and pure joy. I trust you. And I can't wait to do very naughty things to you. I get lonely too. I am going riding later to distract myself from driving to Virginia Beach and knocking on your bedroom door".

Mark laughing says "Kristin it is an honor to know you. And of all the great things to come in the future. And you might fuck me but I will make love to you. Maybe after several hundred times. Enjoy the potluck tomorrow. Scott is hot after Susan. I hear that there is a private celebration party coming up soon. I am going to make arrangements to take you home with me afterwards. I might not let you ever leave".

Kristin giggles and says "Oh Mark, I would love that darling. Your voice is intoxicating. I adore you Mark. And will never get enough of your body. Or you". Mark says "Kristin. My love. I am going to continue courting you. Be prepared and enjoy it. I will call you tomorrow. I am going jogging on the beach and think about you. Send me some pictures tomorrow. Love you baby doll". Kristin says "I will. Sweet dreams sugar. Love you more".

Kristin eats a few slices of cheese and crackers and a peach. Thinking of nothing but Mark. And how things will play out. Imaging him jogging on the beach in sexual frustration and playing his cards right with his billionaire clients. She drives the ATV to the barn and rides her horses in quite contemplation.

Realizing that the entire farm and house are going to be gutted. Watching Ryan run out through the kitchen door as he breaks the sound barrier dissapearing through the portal, eying the divine spaceships in the sky puts her horses to bed and drives back home to fall into a deep 'coveted sleep' covered 'by His grace".

'The Pure In Heart'

Susan arrives early to set up for their 'TGIF Potluck Lunch' looking like a million bucks with her long red hair and alabaster skin. Wearing a sapphire blue strapless sundress and rhinestone sandals with a huge smile on her face. She says "Can you call Ryan to carry the food from my Mercedes? I made grilled teriyaki chicken skewers and stuffed Bella mushroom caps. I brought a ten pound bag of ice and several cases of Wicked Grove Hard Apple Cider".

Kristin says "You are fucking georgous. I love your dress" as she hears Ryan running down the stairs from his wing. Susan says "Ryan can you please carry the food and boxes of ice and beer from the trunk of my car?". Ryan, drinking a Dr Pepper through a straw says "Sure. I am excited about the party". Ryan carries everything from Susan's car in three trips and puts the food in the fridge and the ice in the freezer.

Kristin wearing a white floral floor length spaghetti strap sundress with pink roses on it and a pair of pink suede cork sandals with her hair up says "Here is Scott and his enterauge. Looks like there are a dozen fancy cars and trucks following him". Kristin walks out on the kitchen landing and waves hi to Scott with a smile on her face. Scott waves back and directs the vehicles to park on the front yard wearing the sexiest of Ralph Lauren jeans and a royal blue polo shirt with a dark brown leather belt.

His crew who all look like they are Chippendale dancers, and one feisty looking girl with purple hair and tons of tattoo's follow Scott into the kitchen all carrying trays of food and cases of beer. The are all wearing black Criss Cross Properties LLC black t shirts with matching ball caps with the same logo. Kristin counted eleven of them plus Scott and introduces herself and Susan.

Kristin smiling says "Welcome to Eagle Point Plantation friends. The next best happy frequency in your life for the next four or five years. Make your self at home". Laughing she gives Scott a quick hug and says "Just leave your potluck's on the kitchen counter and Susan and I will take care of everything.

Scott staring at Susan's cleavage and her ass walks up to her, kisses her on the cheek and whispers into her ear "You are the most beautiful woman I have ever seen in my life. I am picking you up at 5:30 tomorrow". Susan blushing admiring his buldging arms and crotch says "So nice to see you again Scott. I am very much looking forward to it. Kristin and I are going to set up the tables on the back porch and then take the horses for a ride while you are doing your reports" licking her lips while eyeing the magnificent physique of his crew.

The crew recites their names one after the other and they shake Kristin and Susans hands and say "Hi Ryan. You are too cool"and leave enough food on the kitchen counter to feed an army. Kristin says "Please use the restroom in the one bedroom guest cottage. That house has central air conditioning. Lunch is at 1:00pm. Let me know if you need anything. Pleasure to meet you all and welcome to your new home away from home. Scott and Mr. Poindexter speak very highly of you and your accomplishments". Not only being able to imagine what it will be like to have help here.

Scott replies to her affectionately "Thank you Kristin for your hospitality. I hear that Mark Smith is taking you out to dinner on Sunday. He is extremely fond of you Kristin. He is a best buddy of mine. Be good to him" with a smile on his face. Scott says "Word spreads fast". Giving her that look 'just go for it' as he and the crew are looking at all of the work that needs to be done on the place with gusto.

Kristin thrilled with everything says "Yes he is. Mark is my new best friend. We have something special going on. I just adore him. For many reasons and everything. Susan and I are planning a double date with the two of you all. Maybe a celebration dinner in ten days?". Winking at him Kristin starts loading up the fridge with Susan's and Ryan's help.

Scott and his crew of eleven who Kristin decides to call 'the dirty dozen' head down the hallway to work on their complex investigation deciphering the work the house needs to be restored laughing and in good spirits ripping apart the construction of the Plantantion.

Kristin and Susan drive the ATV to the barn as the crew is ripping apart the mansion and tack up the horses after changing into their boots and britches. Susan wears a long sleeved skin tight white lycra shirt with the beige Tailored Sportsman show britches and thankfully she puts a sports bra on. Kristin hangs up their dresses on the coat rack and pulls on her boots and britches and her pink and white striped lycra shirt.

The ladies mount the horses in the indoor arena and walk the horses on the loop in front of the Plantation watching Scott's crew staring at them from the windows taking pictures. Kristin leads Susan through a small fence gate to the outdoor jumping field behind her house. She walks around letting Zeus get used to the surroundings and all of the visitors. She picks up the posting trot for a few laps glancing behind her to make sure Coconut is behaving himself. She canters a few laps and brings Zeus back to the walk.

Kristin glances at her back porch noticing that Scott is standing there with his crew watching them taking pictures. Kristin waves and smiles and nudges Zeus into a trot and heads him towards the flower boxes. Lands cantering and steers him towards the sailboat jump, the stone wall, the silver glitter UFO jump and then jumps through the neon pink and yellow triple combination expertly. Zeus lands bucking and she steers him towards the lattice gate in and out, and then the 'Universe' liverpool jump as the sailboats breeze down the river, performing perfectly with Coconut following their lead with his perfect training. Susan walks Coconut up beside Kristin on Zeus as Scott and his group start clapping and a few of them have their video cameras on. Greg one of the crew men yells "I want a riding lesson. You girls are fantastic. I love it here".

Kristin and Susan giggling wave to the crew, pet the horses necks and walk back to the barn. Kristin and Susan untack the horses, put the saddles and bridles and put the boys back in their stalls after a hot bath. Kristin feeds Zeus and Coconut a scoop of sweet feed, impressed with their stellar performance. Kristin and Susan change back into their dresses in her office, fixing their hair in 'divine elation' impressed with Scott and his crew.

Susan tells Kristin "That was an absolute blast. I have never had so much fun in my life. I can't wait to horse show. I can't only imagine our future here together Kristin. Scott is so incredibly handsome. I just want him. Bad". The ladies grab hands smiling at each other driving back to the house to get lunch ready.

Kristin, Susan and Ryan go all out placing the dozens of platters of home cooked food on the buffet tables in the dining room, copper buckets full of ice, water bottles, hard cider and beer. Pink champenge on ice. And trays of desserts. Arranging the seating for the group.

Kristin helps everyone fill up their plates and sits next to Leyla, the only other girl there besides Susan with the purple hair. Kristin asks "How did you end up in construction sweetie"? Is it a family trait?". Watching Susan and Scott sitting close next to each other in deep conversation.

Leyla said "My dad is a general contractor. I grew up with a hammer and a saw instead of a Barbie doll and got hooked. College was just not my thing. Plus, I love to be outside. I am kind of crass and love hanging out with construction workers. I have a foul mouth And carpentry is an art form in itself. I worked for my dad for ten years after high school and ran into Scott at a trade fair. He knew of my dad's high quality work and offered me a job. I said yes on the spot and have been with him for almost ten years now. I am a lesbian, by the way".

Kristin smiling says "How fascinating. My dad built the first million dollar custom home in Manhattan Beach, California where I grew up. His crew used to smoke pot and play the conga drums after work everyday at my house when I was in elementary school. Contractors definetely have pride in their creations. I moved to Virginia from Los Angeles in 2010 and fell in love with historical architecture. Nice to meet you! I am going to get seconds".

Kristin makes the rounds chit chatting with the guys serving them plates of food and Greg says "How do you ever manage taking care of this huge house by yourself. It must take you forever to clean this place with three separate wings". Kristin laughing says "I have help from above. Plus the staircases keep you in great shape. I am just used to it I guess. Plus I have no choice. The French family that owned the place in the 1950's as a summer home had a staff of twelve. And that was just for the house. Not including the gardners or maintenence people".

Greg and the guys say "Let's do a potluck every Friday when we start working here. And we want to learn to jump too". Kristin laughing "Sounds like an excellent plan. And of course. I will teach you in the indoor arena. Once the rehab project is done we are going to do guided waterfront trail rides around the farm with a string of ranch horses. Would you like another beer?".

Kristin gets up and serves everyone another beer and makes a plate of chocolate covered strawberries noticing the Scott and Susan are deep in conversation oblivious to everyone. She walks over to their loveseat and says "Hi love birds. Smile" and takes half a dozen pictures of them and hands them the plate of strawberries. "Can I get you two anything else?".

Scott and Susan smile at each other and Scott says "Please. Another plate of everything. This is a real treat for me and my crew. Susan your teriyaki chicken skewers are delicious". Kristin says "Coming right up. Greg and I already decided to make this a weekly Friday event once you guys are here full time. Susan can I get you seconds?". Susan says "I am good. I will work on the strawberries" smiling at Kristin. She fills up another plate and hands it to Scott with a hard cider for each of them.

Kristin heads back to chat with Leyla and the guys with a slice of key lime pie. After tasting it she says "Whoever made this pie it is absolutely delicious. And where did you find real key lime juice in Virginia? Can I have the recipe please". Leyla laughs and says "It is my Grandmother's recipe. Whole Foods in Richmond has real key lime juice. I will email you the recipe. My girlfriend Sasha loves it too. We are both natural bakers. Thank you for the compliment".

Greg says "That girl can bake anything. Leyla you should write and publish a cookbook and do a podcast in your spare time" smiling at her. Leyla laughing says "You are so fucking right Greg. I think I will". Kristin notices that Ryan is on his third plate of food with his head phones on watching Return of the Jedi.

After almost all of the food is gone Scott gets up to make an announcement. He says "All right team. Excellent work this week. I think we have accomplished everything we needed to do here for the mean time. I need your individual reports emailed to me by next

Wednedsay and we may plan another walk thru after I study the reports and turn them into Poindexter for review. Next Monday and Tuesday we are working at the Cumberland Estate on the wine cellar remodel. Coordinate with my secretary Ruth, she has a caravan sign up sheet. Thank you very much Kristin and Susan. We can call our potlocks 'TGIF lunch'. There are trash cans in the kitchen to throw your paper plates in. Greg will take them with him" laughing and smiling at the contagious synergy of his group.

In great spirits everyone shakes hands and throws their plates in the trash and grab their almost empty serving platters. Greg says "Thank you ladies that was great. I can tell our crew really enjyed this and are going to love working here. See you soon" and heads off to their vehicles.

Scott gives Susan a hug and a kiss. Scott playfully raising his eyebrows says "Be good to him Kristin. He is a great catch". Kristin giggling says "Your wish is my command. I will worship the ground he walks on. And the air that he breathes." and Scott hugs her goodbye. He says to Susan "See you tomorrow darling" and kisses her again and walks off to his truck.

Kristin and Susan estatically hug. Susan says "That was so much fun. I love his co-workers. They are just so fucking cool. I adore him Kristin. You are so natural with people. I can't wait until they rip this place apart. And give you some dignity living here. I still can't beleive that Scott and Mark are still single. They must be workaholics". Kristin texts Susan the pictures that she took with a note 'Couple of the Year'.

She laughs and says "Susan they can't beleive that we are still single too. And I suspect that it has something to do with being intertwined in Poindexter's elite inner circle. Call it 'Divine syncronicity'. Like breaking the sound barrier. Thank you so very much for your help orchestrating today. I am going to change into a jumpsuit and do some cleaning. I will let you know as soon as I hear something. Love you".

Susan looks at the pictures and says "He is smoking hot. We do make a good looking couple. Thanks for the pictures. Talk to you soon. Love you too" and heads out to her Mercedes with Ryan carrying her platters loading up the car.

'Victory In The Light'

Late afternoon Kristin receives a phone call from Stewart who sounded overflowing with guilt and greed at the same time. He says "Hi Kristin. I am coming down to Eagle Point to mow the lawn tomorrow. I need to talk to you about something important in person. I will take you out to dinner so we can talk".

Kristin smiling to herself replies "Of course I will be home. Is everything okay? My brother said you didn't show up at the title office to sign your loan documents". Stewart says "Yes. I just made a life changing event that you need to know about. It is going to affect you too".

Kristin says "Wow. I can't wait to hear all about it. Drive safe, see you tomorrow" knowing exactly what he is going to say to her and she is going to hold to her guns until two days after the new Deed of Trust is transferred to Criss Cross Properties LLC, as sings along to the Steve Miller Band's 'the Joker' playing on the radio.

Several minutes later she receives a call from April. Smiling Kristin picks up the phone and says "Good afternoon. Thank you for calling Eagle Point Plantation. This is Kristin speaking. May I help you?" in her business voice. April says giggling "Hi Kristin I like that. Happy Friday to you. Mr. Poindexter is on an airplane to Texas right now. He wanted me to call you and tell you 'Victory in the Light' and to have a great weekend".

Kristin replies elated "Thank you so very much Miss April. That is fantastic news. I am looking forward to meeting you at the Christmas party at Cumberland in December. Peace to you doll, thanks again". April replies "I will be in touch. Don't forget to email your invoices. Take care".

Kristin texts Susan "If you are not busy come over for a ride. I have great news". Kristin changes into a pair of jean leggings and a white cotton ruffled blouse and opens a bottle of hard apple cider letting everything sink in. Susan shows up five minutes later dressed the same way as Kristin. She walks in the kitchen in anticipation with a smile and says "Can I have one of those. You look incredibly happy. What happened?".

Kristin opens another bottle of cidar and hands it to Susan and says "April, Poindexter's secretary called me this afternoon with a message 'Victory in the Light'. Stewart signed the contract. Can you fucking beleive it? And Stewart called me this afternoon and says he is coming down to mow the lawn and tell me about 'his life changing event' over dinner completely full of guilt and that suffocating greed thing".

Susan says "Cheers Kristin. We won! I am so happy for you. I mean us. We. Scott is taking me to the Severn River Yacht Club for dinner tomorrow night. I am going crazy deciding what to wear". Kristin says "I am so excited for you. Wear a cocktail dress with a plunging v neck and high heeled sandles with rhinestones. You are sophisticated. He probably is just as nervous as you. Thanks for telling me where you are going. I will have Stewart take me and Ryan way on the other end of town. Do you want to go jumping again?". Susan gleaming says "Let's go-partner in crime" giving her a hug.

The girls hop in the ATV laughing and head to the barn. The boys whinny as loud as they can over the excitement of being ridden together again, enjoying the attention. Susan takes some carrots from the refrigerator and feeds them to both horses and halters and places them in the cross ties next to each other. Kristin grabs the saddles and bridles from the tack room and places them on the saddle racks. They give the horses a quick brushing and saddle them up.

Kristin grabs on extra pair of black leather schooling chaps and hands them to Sue along with a crop. Kristin zips up her maroon colored chaps with fawn colored fringe on the zippers with her name embroidered on the back belt that she had custom made from a booth at the Del Mar National Horse Show.

Kristin says "Susan you look sexy in those chaps. Let me take a picture of you. Smile. I did a semi nude photoshoot for the cover of Easy Rider Magazine sitting on a Harley Davidson motorcycle wearing nothing but a pair of black leather chaps and stiletto patent leather black high heels when I was in my twenties". Kristin snaps some photos of herself, bridles Zeus and leads him into the arena. Susan does the same and the ladies mount the horses walking side by side giggling in excitement of things to come.

Susan says "I am so excited to go out with Scott. I really hope things work out between us. And Mark is taking you out on Sunday night. I am so happy for you Kristin. You need adult life away from Ryan. Scott talks about Mark like he is his hero. Let me tell Stewart off for you that fucking asshole that coped you out. I knew Poindexter would come through. We are going to have the whole world at our fingertips right here at Eagle Point" giddy with excitement.

Kristin laughing says "That one will soon be permantly in the past. I am going to have him take us to Olivia's and order a bottle of Crystal champagne. I will think about you the whole time while he drops the bomb on me".

Kristin nudges Zeus into a trot as Coconut picks up the same. She does a figure of eight several times around the arena and brings Zeus back to a walk. She picks up the canter in the two point position for several laps around the arena smiling at Susan's improved riding skills happily watching Coconut canter around the arena.

Kristin halts Zeus and says "We are going to trot the crossrail and come back to the trot through the gymnastic. And then pick up the canter and figure eight the gates and end up with a gallop over the liverpool oxer. Ready? One, two, three let's go".

Kristin guides Zeus through the jumping course with Coconut following enjoying the rythum and her advanced riding skills. After they were done jumping the liverpool Kristin brings Zeus down to a walk after changing leads in the corner. Susan pets Coconuts neck and says "I absolutely love this. Thank you so much Kristin. This is like a life's dream to me. I cannot wait to see Poindexter put some money into this place after all of those years that you waited. Be tough tomorrow night and don't take that man's bullshit".

The ladies walk the horses around the arena to cool them off and dismount in the barn aisle and put the equipment away in the tack room. Susan sprays of the horses with hot water in the cross ties while Kristin fills up their feeders with hay and a scoop of grain in their buckets. She adds an apple and a few carrots out of goodwill. Susan puts the horses back in their stalls filled with cedar shavings and closes the dutch doors. Kristin turns off the lights and says to Susan "Thanks sweetie for your help. Let's make a memory book together. And just be yourself with Scott. Everyone loves you".

They climb in the ATV and drive back to the Plantation in the dark. Susan says "Are those spaceships above your house? They definatley are not aircraft or stars. Wish me luck with Scott. We will be going on a double date soon with you and Mark. Thanks for the jumping lesson. I have to lock up my chickens and feed Goldilocks dinner. Be in touch. Love you sweetie". The girls hug and Susan takes off home. Kristin goes to take a hot bath and sleeps like a rock facing the drama Stewart is going to put her through tomorrow.

The next morning Kristin notices Ryan is not in the house thinking he is out surfing the Universe. Looking up at the Central Sun and the golden rays shinning on the Plantation. Kristin spends the entire day relaxing with her horses and bird watching. Mark texted her a picture from his job in Maryland in front of a multi million high tech house with floor to ceiling glass windows hanging off the side of a cliff on the Atlantic Ocean. And one of her and Susan jumping yesterday that Scott must have sent to him with a note 'You and me. Sunday. Beautiful. And forever". Kristin texts him back "You take my breath away Mark. An put a sparkle in my eyes" with a picture of her and Susan in their dresses yesterday, and one of her in her sexy riding chaps.

Kristin especially refreshed to hear from Mark makes a cappucino turns her horses loose who take off at a dead run to the yard in front of the Plantation after giving Ryan a carrot cake muffin. Kristin says "Stewart is taking us to dinner at Olivia's at 6:00pm tonight. Behave yourself" and she eats one herself.

She feeds the peacocks a bucket of corn and returns April's and Scott's emails. Filling up her horses feeders with hay and their stalls with shavings, grain in their feed buckets. She watches the Blue Herons fishing for oysters and calls to the horses "Come on boys. Lunch is ready". The horses jog back to the barn and run to their feed buckets. Kristin walks back home in dread over Stewarts visit and takes a nap until 3:33pm.

Her guides wake her up as Stewart is mowing the front yard who doesn't even say hello to her. Kristin walks off to the barn and waves at Stewart and cleans the stalls and gives her horses an early dinner. She walks back home and washes her hair and picks out a form fitting black lace formal dress for dinner and a pair of black patent leather heels. After putting on very light makeup, curling her hair wearing diamond tear drop earrings and a matching necklace. Kristin texts Stewart "Our reservation at Olivia's on the Gloucester Courthouse are at 6:00pm. We need to take off". Kristin puts a cherry bomb red colored lip gloss on waiting in the kitchen.

Stewart parks the zero back in the tractor barn and picks Kristin and Ryan up in his Subaru at the Plantation. Stewart says "You look georgous" full of guilt and drives her to the restaurant in silence. Kristin makes small talk and says "Alice is coming over tomorrow. She gained some weight and is bringing me an entire closet full of expensive designer clothes. I am so excited".

Pulling up in front of the restaurant Stewart eyes the Courthouse in shame but full of greed. They walk into the restaurant and the owner seats them in his 'personal booth' and serves Kristin a glass of red wine and Ryan a Diet Coke and gives them dinner menus and says "It is so nice to see you again. Enjoy your dinner".

Stewart orders the crab cake special and Ryan a beer battered fried cod fish and chips plate. Kristin orders a dinner salad and a baked sweet potatoe. Stewart looks at Kristin and says "I know you are going to be upset but I sold Eagle Point and the Suntrust Bank yesterday to another real estate investor for more money than I paid for them. I just can't do this anymore with my health problems, Rhonda and Michelle. You are going to have ten days to vacate Eagle Point and move your horses after we close. I included all of the furniture in the house in the deal too. I don't have the time or anywhere to move it. You can move to a two bedroom apartment in my office building in Brookneal if you are desparate. And you will have to work under Michelle cleaning my rental houses to pay off your rent".

Kristin smiling at Stewart "I have ten days to pack up my life possessions? And you gave away all of the furniture I shipped from California? You are absolutely incredible. Thank you so much Stewart.

After all of that work my brother and I did to help you with the refinance at Eagle Point". In complete disgust at the way Stewart is saying goodbye just she thinks about Mark and new beginnings. Stewart replies "I know. The buyers are paying all cash and wanted to close immediately. If I have a heart attack and die tomorrow my kids would just auction the place off anyways".

Kristin smiles at Stewart and says "It is amazing how someone's life time dream can change so quickly. I am sure you are burnt out on the overhead a flack you are getting from your cave women. I have to say I am completely shocked Stewart. But I do understand. You have to do what is best for your empire. I thought you said you were going to do a 1031 Exchange and buy another Plantation down here?" thinking you fucking scumbag. Poindexter saw right through you from the beginning.

Ana our usual waitress serves our dinner and refills Ryan's soda and pours Kristin another glass of wine. Ana says to Ryan "It is so nice to see you again. How is your job going? Do you like getting your own paycheck sweetie?". Ryan smiling while biting into his fish filet says "I love it. I am going to make lots of money and work really hard. I am saving money to buy a moped. Thank you". Ana smiles "Let me know if you need anything. Enjoy your dinner".

Stewart said "I am just going to save it all for my retirement. I am content with everything in Brookneal and I will never leave Green Hill. And Kristin I have been stringing you along for years. You are still young. Go find yourself another sugar daddy". The group finishes off their meal and Stewart pays the check acting like there is absolutely nothing wrong.

Kristin gets up and grabs Ryans' hand and says "Stewart thank you for the advance notice and driving all the way down here to tell me in person instead of your usual text messages. I appreciate that. I will have to think about your offer overnight. I will have someone else give us a ride home. You look very tired. Thank you for dinner and congratulations on your riches. Goodnight".

Kristin flags a car down on the Courthouse to ask the man for a ride home. Kristin says "Can you possibly give us a ride home? My dinner partner had a temper tantrum and left us stranded". The driver said

"No problem. My name is David. I think I met you years ago when we were searching for a boat with a mayday call at your place that we never found" smiling at her. "I know the way to Eagle Point. I saw you on the front page of the Gloucester Gazzete a few months ago about a book that you recently had published".

Kristin smiling says "That was Beyond the Veil, the first sequel to Behind the Veil. My publisher is adapting the book into a screenplay for me to sell. I remember that day. After you and the Marine Police left we had a lightening storm and power outage. I made one of my tenants search the Plantation with me and the basement for hours with flashlights to make sure there was no one hiding there".

David speeds down the back roads and drops her and Ryan off in front off the house at the kitchen entrance and gives her his business card from the Search and Rescue Squad of Gloucester and says "Call me if you need anything and lock your doors". Kristin says "Thank you very much David. Have a great night". She waves goodbye and walks into the kitchen with Ryan and locks the kitchen door.

Ironically Mark just sent her a text message that read "Ten days to Heaven Kristin. I can't wait to see your beautiful face tomorrow. Take care baby doll". Kristin texts Mark back "I need you too darling. You make my heart sing. I can't wait to see you. Hugs and kisses". Kristin appeased at what she knew would transpire. Mark must have heard the good news about Poindexter's speedy closing. Kristin says out loud "Thank you Jesus Christ".

Changing into a sweat suit and hanging up her evening dress she heads off to the barn and grooms Zeus and Coconut, kissing their noses and feeding them treats. She fills up their feeders with Timothy hay and refills their water buckets and gives them each a scoop of grain. Puts the boys back in their stalls, shuts off the lights and walks home staring up at the beautiful stars and Arcturus aligned directly above her house under a waning moon. After taking an Advil she climbs into bed and falls into a deep slumber out of sheer exhaustion and the stress of the day wanting to look well rested for her date with Mark tomorrow.

Soul Mates

Feeling refreshed and excited to see Mark tonight Kristin hears Alice calling her from the kitchen "I brought you Starbuck's coffee and an egg and cheese biscuit doll". Kristin puts on a pair of jeans and a blouse and says "I am coming. That was so sweet of you" and meets Alice in the kitchen and gives her a hug. Kristin says "You look fantastic. What is your secret to never aging at all"?.

Alice laughing hands Krisin her coffee and breakfast and another bag on the table for Ryan says "Expensive face cream and makeup. I have an entire car load of clothes for you. I left them on hangers. Tell me about your date tonight. I only have a few minutes Walter and I are going to the Florida Keys for the weekend".

Kristin sipping her coffee says "I am jealous. You guys vacation all of the time. How exciting take some pictures for me. Mark Smith is the structural engineer who I gave a tour of Eagle Point to for Mr. Poindexter who is my new boss and the new owner of Eagle Point. He is paying Stewart all cash and closes in eight days. Stewart doesn't know that Poindexter hired me and I am not going to tell him until after they close and record. Mark is georgous, highly intelligent, very sucessfully self employed, a surfer and is from Huntington Beach, California. We hit it off immediately and he has been single for years just like me. He said he will be 'courting me'. He loves horses too. We are going to the Marina in Matthews for dinner. He lives in Virginia Beach. Aren't you excited for me?" biting into her biscuit.

Alice looks at Kristin and says "I am so happy for you Kristin. You need to get married again before you get any older. Surfers are in really great shape. Sounds like a match made in Heaven for you. I have heard about Mr. Poindexter. He the richest billionaire in Virginia and is buying up all of the real estate in the state. I heard he is a great family man and his wife Julia is absolutely stunning. He also donates big money to some very good causes. Well this is going to work out just perfect. The house looks like it needs some work and you will get to stay here and get paid for it".

Ryan runs down the stairs and says "Hi Alice. That smells good. Thanks for visiting my mom. I got a job and get paid every week. I have my own bank account and take the bus to work". Alice hugs Ryan and says "I am so proud of you that is great. Can you please go out to my car and carry all of the clothes from the trunk for your mom? I brought you two chicken biscuits and hash browns from McDonald's for breakfast".

Ryan smiles "Sure. thank you. McDonalds is my favorite" and runs out the door and makes several trips to Alice's Lexus placing the clothes on the dining room table and then grabs his McDonalds bag and says "I am going to eat in my room. Bye Alice" as he runs up his staircase.

Alice follows Kristin to the dining room and says "Wear this cherry bomb red long formal sundress with ruffles. You look great in v necks and it has a delicate floral pattern that is so sexy and feminine at the same time. It has a matching chocker and a scarf you can wear around your shoulders. Actually I have never worn it" and holds the dress up to Kristin and adds "perfect color with your blonde hair".

Kristin says "Thank you so much Alice. I absolutely adore it. These clothes are stunning. You have such great taste. I really appreciate it. I can't afford to buy designer clothes right now with my food bill for Ryan and the horses. You really cheered me up" gives her a hug noticing that almost all of the clothes still have price tags on them.

Alice replies "You are very welcome Kristin. It must be really hard for you not having any family here and being responsible for Ryan all of the time is a huge burden. Let me help you carry the clothes down to your dressing room. I think about you quite often and am glad that things have taken a turn to the best. You have to remember to nurture yourself too". The girls grab armfuls of clothes and make three trips down the long hallway to the East Wing.

Kristin says "John the Chairman of the Fairfield Foundation is having a hundred seat fundraiser with tents on the front lawn catered by Olivia's in October. It is a hundred dollars a ticket. Do you and Walter want to come? I have a feeling Poindexter and his wife will make an appearance and you can meet Mark. I absolutely love this gold sequin cocktail dress. And these Anne Taylor pant suits are beautiful. I love this one too. And the white formal gown with the gold trim is to die for".

Alice thrilled with her exquisite taste in clothes hangs up dress after dress and says "Defintely. Send me the link to buy tickets, I am sure they will sell out fast, This white halter dress will look fantastic on you with your figure. So will this pink linen mini dress with those long legs of yours. Well it is starting to look like a department store in here. Sorry my shoes won't fit you. I have an entire room full of accessories and purses that I will go through when we get back from the Florida Keys" pleased with her act of kindness.

Kristin laughing says "I feel like I am at Macy's Alice. I will arrange for you and Walter to sit next to Poindexter at the fundraiser. Thank you so much again" gives her a hug and the ladies head back down to the kitchen. Alice says "Enjoy your date with Mark tonight. You deserve it. Love you". Kristin walks her to her car and says "I love you too Alice. Have a geat time in Florida. Call me when you get back and I will give you an update".

Alice heads down the driveway and Kristin walks to the barn, feeds the horses breakfast and turns them out in their pasture. Almost teary eyed at the nice gifts from Alice. Her and Walter have millions of dollars and have always been kind to Kristin and her kids. Ryan walks into the barn and grabs a Dr Pepper and an ice cream bar from the fridge and says "Hi mom. I love your new clothes. Are you excited to go out to dinner tonight?".

Kristin says "Yes I am. I will order a Dominoe's pizza to be delivered at 6:00pm for you. The tenants will be here if you need anything. Don't forget to pack your lunch for work tomorrow night in case I sleep in". Ryan on a sugar high from the sugar and caffeine says "Thanks mom. Extra large double pepperoni please. I am going to eat pizza and watch Star Wars movies tonight. I am going on a walk".

Kristin smiles and thinks good for you Ryan. She cleans up the barn and calls to the horses who run to the open gate and walk back into their stalls. Kristin feeds them a few apples and carrots admiring their gleaming good health from all of her caregiving and the exercise they have been getting jumping with Susan, and walks back to the Plantation.

Kristin sees Susan wearing a cowboy hat riding Goldilocks down the driveway in a western saddle and sits on the kitchen porch to wait for her. Susan has that look of being struck by 'cupid's arrow' on her face grinning from ear to ear. She says "Kristin I think I am falling in love already. I had such a great time last night. Scott is such a gentlemen and very intelligent. We sat and talked for hours. He brought me two dozen red roses when he picked me up and ordered Crystal champagne at the restaurant. His family is absolutely fascinating. His father is Chief of Construction for Markel Eagle in Short Pump. They have built dozens of master planned comunities all over the United States".

Kristin laughing replies "Markel Eagle builds 'self contained communities'. I am friends with one of their executives, Nate Van Epp. I am so thrilled for you Susan. Scott must be courting you too. Mark keeps sending me the sweetest messages and calls me every night. I am glad after all that heartache we experienced turning us into damaged goods that we are both at the point to open our hearts to someone new. Do you want to come over tomorrow and see the new wardrobe my friend Alice brought over this morning? Most of the cocktail dresses should fit you too. They all still have price tags on them. Then we can go for a ride if you want. Ryan will be at work. I will fill you in on my date with Mark tonight and we can share details. Did you kiss him?" giggling.

Susan smiling "Yes we did. He is a great kisser too. We made out like teenagers. He felt so good. Tomorrow sounds perfect. I can't wait to hear everything. I will share all of the details about our date then. That was priceless of Alice. I will see you around 11:00. Now try and behave yourself tonight and don't do anything I wouldn't do. I have to show you the videos Scott's crew made of us jumping. You will love it. The pictures came out great too. Goldilocks is been eaten by swamp flies. Have fun at the Marina. Love you" and Kristin waves goodbye as she trots down the driveway.

Picking a huge ripe heirloom tomatoe from her garden and a lemon cucumber Kristin makes herself a tomatoe cucumber sandwich on sourdough bread with mayo and a slice of Gouda cheese. Eats lunch standing up reflecting on her great fortune to go out with Mark and to have a few close friends.

On a whim she whips up a double batch of chocolate chunk and walnut homemade cookie dough, using an ice cream scooper placing the batter on cookie sheets in her double oven. She grabs two oversized cookie tins from the pantry and cuts off a few sheets of parchment paper. Turns on the radio listening to Jim Croce's 'I've Got a Name', singing out loud enjoying the smell of fresh baked cookies filling up the kitchen. She orders Ryan's pizza online and leaves a double tip.

After the four dozen cookies were done she puts two dozen in each container. Sets aside one for Mark and the other she gives to Ryan. Driving the ATV to the barn to give the horses an early dinner suspecting that it is going to be a late night. Kristin opens the feed room listening to her horses whinny and fills two buckets full of grain, hay cubes, apples and carrots. She puts both horses in the cross ties, fills their stalls up with shavings, hay and their dinner buckets glancing at her watch. Divine timing she calls it. I have exactly one hour to beautify myself for Mark. She puts the horses away says "I love you boys. I will be back late tonight". Turns on a classical music channel on the radio for them, throws the peacocks a bucket of corn and drives back home.

Kristin showers and puts on her favorite lavendar scented body lotion. She does her makeup in a natural way and then curls her hair. After putting on her new dress she picks a pair of sparkling ruby earrings and necklace to match her dress. Sliding on her favorite nude colored open toed heels in excitement. She takes a picture in front of the bride's dressing mirror in the foyer surrounded by a shimmering light. She puts her wallet and lip gloss in a small gold hand purse with her cellphone-shutting off the ringer watching a brand new black AMG Mercedes sports car pulling up in front of her kitchen. Thinking to herself, shit Mark. You are too good to be true.

Kristin watches Mark walk in through the storm door absolutely drooling over his fit body and designer khaki pants and custom fit white linen dress shirt. Which was unbuttoned down to his cleavage showing off his blonde chest hair. Wearing a very cool gold rope chain necklace and a white muscle tank top underneath Kristin smiles at the small 'ying and yang' tattoo below his shirtline on his right shoulder.

And his tailor made brown loafers probably cost $500.00 themselves. Not including the pricy Rolex watch.

Kristin with a twinkle in her eyes gives her flashy TV smile to Mark and says demurely "Nice car darling. Are you trying to sweep me off my feet Mark?". He walks up to her and gives her a bear hug. Kissing her neck and rubbing her ass, holding her tight and carressing her. He whispers in her ear "You are absolutely tantalizing. In an innocent way Kristin. I love your dress and everything about you" as he strokes her thighs. He lifts her chin up with his fingers and French kisses her listening to her moan.

Kristin blushing kisses Mark caressing his hot fit body and says "Well thank you kindly sir. I aim to please. Being an arm peice comes naturally to me. I have been groomed and molded to please. I just baked some homemade chocolate walnut cookies for you. You can think about me every time you sink your mouth into one savoring the delishes chocolate". She licks her lips teasing him and rubs his ass thinking fuck Mark you are hot.

Mark smiles fondly at Kristin loving a seductive woman. He pulls a jewelry box out of his pants pocket and places it in her hand. Kristin looks into his eyes with raw emotion and opens the box revealing a diamond tennis bracelet. "Oh Mark! It is absolutely beautiful. I love it. Are you seducing me I hope?". She holds out her left hand and Mark puts the bracelet on her arm.

He says "No I am courting you. You are seducing me. The diamonds suit you well. I am going to have to buy you more. Let's go to dinner". Kristin hugs him again wondering if this is all real and kisses him on the lips and grabs her purse as he takes her by the hand and leads her to his Mercedes and opens the door for her admiring her legs.

Kristin says "I love your car. I made reservations at the Marina in Matthews. It is on a yacht club with a sandy beach. I will GPS the directions. Sorry you have to drive so far. And Mark I am so glad I met you. Call it one of those syncronicity things. You have no idea how attracted I am to you not to mention how impressed I am with your accomplishments".

Mark looks at Kristin and says "You need a man in your life. I need a mate. Call it fate. I drive all over the US for business. Kind of relaxing to me listening to music looking at the scenery. I really can't wait to make love to you Kristin. You are so sensual. I have never had that before" as he holds her hand.

Kristin smiling replies "To be honest with you Mark I am just content to sit in the passenger seat. And go on Sunday drives. I love to make gourmet meals and entertain. Plant flowers and vegetables in my gardens. And I love music and dancing. Secretely I would love to horse show again. And sensuality-I am just behaving myself Mark. I am a very submissive woman".

Mark laughs and says "Kristin my sister Cecilia has a daughter on the spectrum. She is married and her husband owns half of Merrill Lynch and is filthy rich. She has a maid and a nanny. And a chauffeur. I know exactly what you have been through. Ceclilia does nothing but shop, go to spas and lunch with friends. She is a complete sex fiend from the stress of a special kid. Her husband loves it. I give you a gold medal for that one raising Ryan by yourself" as they pull in front of the Marina.

A valet opens the door for Kristin and Mark who walk arm in arm into the restaurant in complete lust over each other. The hostess seats them at an intimate table with a waterfront view and says "Your server Hannah will be here shortly. Are you two newlyweds?" pushing up her sleeves revealing tatoos of marine life on her arms". Mark smiles at her and says "How did you know. We are on our honeymoon shopping for a waterfront estate. We would like two ice waters with lemon and a bottle of dry brut Dom please".

Kristin giggling says "Mark I adore you". Mark is massaging Kristin's thigh with his hand with his arm around her holding her tight studying the menu as Hannah opens the champagne and pours it into their flutes. Hannah says "The specials are Swordfish grilled with garlic butter and a 20 ounce Porterhouse steak each with two sides" and leaves a loaf of brown bread and butter on the table obviously jealous.

Mark picks up his champagne glass and so does Kristin and he toasts her and says "Here is to us my darling sex kitten". Kristin smiling flirtatiously says "You are the man of my dreams Mark" and kisses him on the lips while rubbing his thigh.

Mark says " I am going for the steak. What would you like darling?" sliding his hand up to her crotch under her dinner napkin. Kristin about to have an orgasim replies "You. The spinach dip appetizer-we can share. A baked sweet potatoe and a dinner salad with poppy seed dressing please".

Hannah returns to take their order watching the lovers enviously. Mark says "the Portherhouse special well done, loaded baked potatoe and steamed asparagus. The spinach dip appetizer to start. My lovely lady here wants a dinner salad with poppy seed dressing and a baked sweet potatoe. And a side of steamed asparagus for her too. Thank you Hannah".

Kristin just smiles as Mark hugs her and touches her face with his fingers. He kisses her and says "Just enjoy it Kristin. Things will only get better. You have been through a lot. And you handled yourself magnificently with Poindexter". And then he kisses her neck as she is rubbing her thigh. "Poindexter and I have been co-working together for a decade. He won't make you work very hard. You will have a ton of staff to boss around". He whispers in her ear 'I can't wait to taste you".

Hannah serves the two dinner with a shitty fake smile and opens another bottle of Dom pouring it into their glasses. Kristin says to Hannah "Thank you for your kind service and sips her champagne as Mark is rubbing his fingers through her panties under the dinner napkin and feels her come in two seconds. Kristin lays her head on Mark's shoulder in relief and whispers "Thank you sweetheart. You are so good to me darling. I adore you".

She picks up her composure relaxes and says "How is your steak master?. You are too much fun, which besides riding with Susan I have had a complete lack of until Poindexter brought you into my life." while kissing his neck. Mark says "Fantastic but not as good as you that I am going to lick off of my fingers. Have some more champagne doll. Eat all of your food I want you to be happy. All of the time".

Kristin and Mark finished their dinner and Hannah brings them a dessert menu. She says "I highly recommend the apple tart". Mark says "We will share the triple layer chocolate fudge cake please". Hannah returns with their cake and Mark feeds her with his fork watching her demurely licking the chocolate off of her lips. Kristin says "This is delicious. Excellent choice darling". Hannah brings the bill and takes the dessert plate away. Mark paid giving her a generous tip.

He puts his arm around Kristin holding her close and opens the car door for her one upping the valet and leans into the car French kissing her, brushing against her breasts as he fastens her seatbelt. He grabs her hand while he is driving and says "Kristin. I want to spoil you rotten in every way I am going to give it to you at least two times a day when I am here. I travel a lot and you have hobbies and kids. We have seven more days to go. And then you will be all mine".

Kristin lays her head on Mark's chest while he is driving and says "Of course darling. Anything and everything that you want. Susan told me that you and Scott were doing an inspection at the Suntrust Bank building on the Gloucester Courthouse this Wednesday. I wanted to do a condo project there called 'Bird Walk Commons' with a mixed use commercial tea room and natural hemp product store in the original bank front and botanical gardens with bird baths and fountains. Susan and I want to cook you guys a special lunch and meet at Susan's house. Game on?".

Mark smuggly says "Indefinately of course. I would love a home cooked meal" as he pulls up in front of her kitchen. He opens the car door for her and holds her hand walking into her kitchen. He puts his arms around her and hugs and kisses her rubbing her ass. Mark says "Kristin only a few more days. I think I already love you. I will see you on Wednesday at Susan's house beautiful".

Kristin burries her head in his chest and kisses his neck rubbing his buttocks and whispers to him "A few days goes by fast. Thank you very much for the bracelet. I absolutely love it. 'A circle is a neverending sign of God's undying love' and the symbol of the Universe. I will miss you. I can't wait until Wednesday sweetheart. Don't forget your cookies. I love you too Mark. Drive safe and thanks again for dinner. Oh and Susan has a heated outdoor salt water pool. And a pool vollyball set. Bring a bathing suit. I am bringing a coral colored string bikini with me. I grew up playing beach vollyball on the Strand in Manhattan Beach. Sand castle contests and everything".

Mark laughs and says "Kristin everything about you is a fairytale. It is part of your charm. I was on my high school's vollyball team called 'the Sharks'. We won the state championship. I haven't played in a while". Kristin kisses him and says "You definately have an athletes body. You are so incredibly sexy. Don't ever leave me. I did indoor water polo in high school. And drama. And choir practice. The good old days. While I was away at a horse show in Santa Barbara as a teen where I was circuit champion by the way, my mother sold our childhood home after my parents divorce and leased a waterfront condo in Redondo Beach. I had to switch high schools for the last semester". Mark rubbing hips and kissing her neck says "My poor little darling how traumitizing. Kristin I want to know everything about you and more".

Kristin says "Actually I am very down to earth and old fashioned Mark. Working in Beverly Hills and in the entertainment industry just makes you more adaptable. And the wealthy horse show patrons. My personal motto is 'the only thing money can buy you is time to do the things you love'. And of course the freedom to have someone special in your life. And of course schedule your meetings around adult time. In the bedroom. At lunch time" smiling up to him.

Kristin kisses him again. Mark hugged her forever not wanting to leave or end their embrace. Mark kisses her on her forehead stroking her cheek and then on the lips and she kisses him back. He says "I better go home before you seduce me into your bedroom. I have an 8:00am business meeting tomorrow. I jog three to five miles on the beach every morning". Like a true gentlemen he walks back to his Mercedes blowing her a kiss in quiet satisfaction pleased with his new conquest. Kristin waves goodbye and blows him a kiss elated. She looks up to the sky and says 'Thank you Jesus. I love him. Hallelujah'.

Ryan is off to work and Kristin wearing a comfy yoga outfit makes a cup of decaf while scrambling an egg. In absolute satisfaction over what is to come she makes an avocado toast on wheat bread and places the egg on top and eats breakfast. Walks off to the barn to feed Zeus and Coconut taking an inventory of the feed room.

She lets the horses out in the pond field smiling at them. She starts to clean up the barn as a Gloucester Floral delivery van pulls up in front of the breezeway. The driver carrying three dozen red long stemmed roses in a crystal vase asks "Are you Kristin at 4100 Eagle Point

Plantation Road?". Kristin chocking up says "Yes. Thank you sir" and grabs the vase with a sealed card attached. The driver says "You have an admirer. Have a blessed day. Your horses are so beautiful. This place is so cool". He gets into his van and heads down the driveway.

Kristin sits on the bench in front of Zeus stall and opens the card that reads "My princess. I loved last night. Thinking about you baby doll". Kristin almost started crying wondering if this whole thing was real after all of the phsycological and emotional torture that she went through with Stewart.

She picks up the phone and calls Mark and receives his voice mail and leaves a message "Mark. You are kind, loving and the sexiest man I have ever laid eyes on. You made my day. And my night. And you are my prince. Going to visit with Susan today and shop for our lunch on Wednesday. I still beleive in fairytales baby. Love you sugar".

After cleaning the barn Kristin puts the horses back inside all of a sudden emotionally exhausted. Not ever remembering being treated so well by a man as Mark treats her. Maybe it is his 'divine masculine side'. And although she may not be quite the intellectual match for Mark, he seems to be ok with it since all he ever does is work. And surf. And jog on the beach. She sees Susan pull her farm truck in front of the kitchen and walks back home carrying the vase of flowers.

She says "Hi Susan look at the beautiful flowers Mark sent me. I just want to cry. He is my fucking soul mate. I love him with all of my heart. We have so much chemistry together. I absolutely loved our date. He has a great sense of humor too. And is so protective. Thank you Jesus" and gives Susan a hug who is giving her a huge smile.

Susan says "Kristin I feel the same way about Scott. I am in absolute euphoria and will die if he ever leaves me. Do you want to go to Kroger to plan our lunch to take our mind off of things? After stalking up on horse feed from Tractor Supply. I need more mealy worms for my chickens". Kristin not ever remembering being so happy in a very long time says "Absolutely. Let grab my purse and cell phone out of the butler's pantry".

The girls take off and buy half of the horse feed left on the shelves at Tractor Supply and Kristin purchases ten bags of pine shavings. Susan buys $300.00 worth of mealy worms for her chickens and the girls request a stocker to load up the supplies at the checkout. Susan is playing country music in her farm truck without any air conditioning listenting to Reba MacIntire. The ladies are chatting about their new boyfreinds and new found independence as they pull up to Kroger and Susan grabs a shopping cart.

Kristin says "Lets just make surf and turf. That is so easy and simple and appropriate for the river view. I will do a stuffed bell pepper dish for the side and a fruit salad. You pick the dessert. We will probably be in your pool the entire time anyways". Susan says "I agree. I will just fire up the grill for a few minutes and then we can play volleyball".

Susan pushes the cart through the fresh fruit and veggie section as Kristin picks a bag of four yellow bell peppers, a cantaloupe, fresh kiwis, blueberries, raspberries, strawberries, cilantro and a can of whipped cream. Susan picks out two pounds of fresh jumbo tiger shrimp deveined and two pounds of round steak, a jar of Houisen sauce and a package of fresh Naan bread. Kristin grabs a crudite tray, French Onion dip and a tray of pre sliced Boar's Head gourmet cheese. She adds a bag of shareable Peanut M&M's and heads to the checkout.

Loading up the groceries Susan and Kristin smile at each other making girl talk. Kristin asks Susan "Do you want to go and get a manicure and pedicure with me Tuesday afternoon? Ryan will be at work". Susan pulls up in front of her kitchen handing her the bags of fruit and vegetables and says "Absolutely. Just text me when you want to pick me up. I am going home to call Scott. This place is so beautiful. Love you sweetie".

Kristin waves goodbye and puts the veggies and fruit in the fridge. She heats up a sausage and pepperoni pizza in the oven for Ryan and serves him dinner. Ryan says "Thank you mom. I am going to eat the whole thing. I am starving". Kristin says "You are welcome Ryan. There is a Pepperidge Farm Chocolate Cake in the refrigerator for dessert. Don't eat the entire thing and brush your teeth before you go to bed please".

Kristin's cellphone rings at approximately 5:55pm from Mark. Kristin overwhelmed with love and desire answers the phone and says "Hello darling. I was just thinking about you. And your hot sexy body. Did you have a good day? I absolutely love the roses. Thank you so much

Mark. Susan and I are making you surf and turf on Wednesday on the grill. I am going to get a manicure and pedicure tomorrow".

Mark excitedly says "Kristin, my baby doll. Poindexter is closing early on Eagle Point and is chartering the famous 'Blackbeard Pirate Ship' in Yorktown on Saturday night to do a cruise along the Severn River to see the back side of Eagle Point. It is a formal tuxedo, evening gown dress celebration dinner with most of his staff and a catered five star dinner. There are going to be newscasters and newspaper reporters. Most likely magazines too, seeing us off on the boat. I have to work at a job in Nags Head that day. I have arranged for Scott to pick you and Susan up Saturday late afternoon. I want to take you home with me to Virginia Beach after dinner to my house and have you spend the weekend with me. I will take you back to Eagle Point Sunday night. I am sending my maid Guadelupe over on Saturday afternoon to stay with Ryan and help him take care of the horses while you are gone".

Kristin excitingly replies "Mark that sounds like the best idea I have ever heard in my life. I am absolutely thrilled. You are making me wet. You just made my day. That is absolutely great news about Poindexter. You are a master planner Mark. That is perfect. I can't wait to see your house and spend the night with you. You probably won't get any sleep. I may just seduce you all night long. And then fall asleep in your arms. I think about you every second Mark. And wonder what did I do to deserve you in my life" almost in tears.

Mark says "Kristin. Just follow my lead and 'I will take you to that special place'. You are my lady in waiting. I am going to take care of you. And everything else. Forever. Just smile during Poindexter's high powered executive speech. We are sure to be on prime time news. You will do fine. They all will probably offer you riches to take you away from me".

Kristin laughing says "Mark I only want you. And us. And I need you. Just show me the way baby". Mark says "I am taking you the way. And I heard that girls that love to ride horses love to be on top". Kristin giggling says "Mark you are the Captain. I am the wench. I aim to please and I adore your sexy hot body. One more day and we get to frolic in the pool. And five more days until you have me".

Mark sighs and says "Kristin you are too good to be true. I am going to have to buy you more diamonds. And hire a body guard to protect you. Get some rest baby doll. Behave yourself on Wednesday if you can. I have tons of paperwork to do and I can't concentrate after listening to your sexy voice". Kristin says "Your wish is my command Master. Will be thinking about you all night darling. Love you Mark". Kristin hangs up the phone signing 'Glory to God' fuck yeah.

Susan texts Kristin "I heard the fantastic news from Scott. Halleleujah". Kristin messages back "Amen love. See you tomorrow". She heads down to the library and picks up her guitar playing classical music in deep thought unwinding from the excitement. Afterwards she goes through her evening gowns in her dressing room wondering if they are sophisticated enough for the celebration dinner thinking she will have to ask Susan and walks back to the kitchen and makes a bowl of angel hair pasta and grabs a slice of French bread. Twirling the pasta with a spoon savoring the taste watching the sunset from the kitchen storm door. The words 'divine manifestation' pop in her mind out of nowhere.

Giggling she pours a glass of Merlot and texts Ashley "I need you and Danny to come over early Sunday morning and help take care of Zeus and Coconut with Ryan. I am spending the weekend with Mark my new boyfriend at his house in Virginia Beach. Watch the news Saturday night. Love you". Ashley messages back "Good for you mom. We will clean the stalls and feed them. Why are you going to be on TV?".

Kristin responds "Poindexter, the famous Virginia billionaire closed escrow on Eagle Point today. He offered me a great paying management job to stay at the farm. Poindexter chartered the Blackbeard Pirate ship in Yorktown for a celebration dinner. It is a black tie event. The TV stations and news reporters are going to do an interview, as well as several magazines. Tape record it for me if you can. Mark's maid Guadalupe is staying at Eagle Point overnight with Ryan". Ashley messages "Sounds like you hit the big time. Of course. I am so happy for you. That is incredible. Love you".

Kristin drives the ATV to the barn to tuck the horses in and feeds them a bucket of sweet feed, carrots and apples. She fills up their water buckets and gives them a few extra flakes of hay after brushing them off. Kristin says "I love you boys. Sleep tight", her muscles needed a break. The horses seemed content to stay inside after all of the jumping her and Susan have been doing. She turns off the lights and closes the breezeway doors and drives back home under the stars observing that all seems to be quite in the 'Divine world'.

Kristin says to Ryan who is eating a half gallon of Breyer's chocolate ice cream with a spoon "Don't forget to brush your teeth. I am going to get my nails done with Susan tomorrow. Have a nice day at work. See you when you get home tomorrow". Ryan responds "I will. Have fun tomorrow. I am glad you have a new boyfriend" He puts the empty ice cream container back in the freezer and says "Goodnight mom" bouncing off the walls on a sugar high. Kristin sighing to herself says "Goodnight Ryan. I am going to watch a movie. Love you".

Kristin goes to her bedroom and puts on a soft cotton pink bathrobe. Washes her face and brushes her teeth, applying Este Lauder face cream and body lotion. She turns on the air conditioner to drown out the noise of the ruckus going on up in Ryans room. She climbs into bed resting a pink floral bolster under her knees and streams Netflix on the TV watching Yellowstone reruns and drifts off to sleep thinking about Mark with a smile.

Waking up with a smile Kristin laughs as the Transit bus is driving away from the Plantation. She puts on a periwinkle blue capri jumpsuit and grabs a peach ice tea and a slice of pumpkin bread after eating a blueberry greek yogurt and goes on a walk needing a break from Ryan.

 Noticing the farmer's soybean crops are sprouting looking at the massive amount of yard work the place needs. Thrilled that Eagle Point will have live in gardeners and a full time maintenence crew, she grabs a bag of carrots out of the refrigerator in the barn for the horses. Kristin feeds the horses breakfast and turns them out in a grass field in front of the barn with the pond.

Sitting down on a bench sipping her tea and eating the pumpkin bread enjoying the silence watching the horses eat grass and the Mallard ducks swimming in the pond in immense satisfaction. Kristin laughs out loud and says "After I get my nails done today is officially 'watch grass grow' day" in incredible great spirits of things yet to come.

Kristin cleans the barn putting extra pine shavings and hay in the horses stalls with their lunch. She opens the pasture gate and watches the horses trot back to the barn with their golden eyes gleaming. She fly sprays them and turns on the ceiling fans fondly watching them munch on their sweet feed. She heads home to grab her purse and change her clothes and texts Susan "Half an hour okay?".

Susan responds "Perfect". Kristin feeds her cats a can of tuna fish and makes a PBJ for herself. Changing into a white cotton sweatsuit and a coral colored blouse. Kristin hops in her Audi and speeds off down the driveway to pick Susan up listening to U2's 'In the Name of Love'.

Susan is waiting on her front porch throwing her chickens a loaf of bread. She waves at Kristin as she parks in the driveway. Kristin says "You look stylish as usual. I love your jumpsuit. Royal blue is a great color on you. It makes you look so expensive. And authoratative. Your chickens have gotten huge".

Susan smiling gets in the car and says "I am collecting a dozen eggs a day. I have been donating most of them to the food pantry. I never thought I would like raising chickens as much as I do. Each one has a different personality. They come to me when I call them." laughing at herself's fond affection for her birds.

Kristin says "I have heard the same thing about chickens from other people. They get really attached them. Susan you have no idea how happy I am Poindexter closed early. I feel like a black cloud has been lifted from the farm. And me too. We are going to have a blast tomorrow. Mark asked me to spend the weekend with him in Virginia Beach. He is taking me to his house after the celebration cruise" laughing and says "In addition to that he is sending his maid to Eagle Point to stay with Ryan while I am gone. I am falling really hard for him Susan".

Susan giggling said "I know Scott told me. I am thrilled for you sweetie you deserve it. I invited Scott to stay overnight at my house. He said 'I thought you would never ask'. We will go check on the horses Sunday morning for you. I have absolutely no idea what I am going to wear. I assume most of the other women are going to wear designer evening gowns. I can't wait to see Scott in a tuxedo".

Kristin smiles at Susan "I bet Mark looks better than James Bond in a tux. You can come over and look at my dresses and see if you like one. I don't know what I am going to wear either. Emerald green really sets you off. I can't wait to be on the news. I love that stuff. Call it Los Angeles nostalgia. Are you going to be bad sleeping with Scott? I am going to seduce Mark. It won't take very much effort" and pulls up to the nail spa.

Susan says "Kristin you are naughty. I am sure it won't take more than a smile from you with Mark. Scott says he is dying to sleep with you". The girls walk in as the nail artists wave and direct them to the pedicure chairs. They stop and the nail color turnstyle and Susan picks a ruby red and Kristin chooses a sheer garnet color. The ladies sit down next to each other and kick off their sandals and turn on the massagers with a remote control and put their feet in the hot water with epsoms salt.

Kristin says "I could do this everyday. Ohh yeah that feels so good". Susan is giggling and says "That tickles" as the nail tech is loofaing the bottom of her feet. After their toes are done they head to the manicure stations while the nail techs do their fingernails.

Kristin says "I love that nail polish color on you. I am bringing a bikini tomorrow. Text me if you need anything else. Mark played volleyball on his high school team. He told his team 'The Sharks' won the league championships. He is so athletic. You are so lucky to have a pool. Swimming is so soothing. It doesn't matter how many therapeutic things I do, Ryan just stresses me out in general. Hopefully Mark's and I soon to be outrageously satisfying sex life will help with that. And getting off the farm for the weekend".

Susan replies "Okay. I am picking out a one peice. You are in better shape than I am. Your nails look great too. I paid all cash for my house. I was lucky that there was already a brand new pool installed. I rented an auger for my tractor and Clay installed the pasture board fencing for me. I still can't get him to paint it for me. I can't stand that snobby bitch girlfriend of his."

Kristin laughs and says "Atleast the boyfriend Ashley is with now owns his house and works full time. He drives a Suburban. They waste so much money going out to eat and at bars. Well, she is twenty four now and her boyfriend is twenty nine. How old is Scott? Mark is sixty. Five years older than me". Susan smiles and says "You are a baby. Scott is sixty two and I am fifty eight". The nail techs hands the girls an invoice and places their hands in the polish dryer.

The girls pay their bills waving goodbye to the salon techs and climb in Kristin's Audi. Kristin turns on the AC and says "Do you need anything while we are in town?" Susan says "I am okay. I am going to turn on the pool sweeper and clean the restroom in the pool house and spruce things up for tomorrow. Come over around 12:30-I think Scott said that they will be over at 1:00pm".

Kristin turns down Susan's driveway and says "It is a date. I think it's really neat that Scott and Mark are so close. I love that. I am sure they feel the same way about our friendship. That is a whole new world to me. Let me know if you need anything. Love you". Susan waves goodbye and heads off to her pool house. Kristin drives home an stops at the barn to check on the horses.

Loving their whinnies Kristin feeds them dinner, peppermints and molassas biscuits. She drives back home and sees the Transit bus coming down the driveway. She heats up a bolognese lasagna out of the freezer that she made from scratch in the oven and a loaf of garlic bread. Kristin walks out to her garden and picks a basket of green beans as Ryan gets of the bus waving at his bus driver and says "Hi Ryan. How was your day?. Your dinner will be ready in fifteen minutes".

Ryan follows Kristin into the kitchen hiding a backpack full of Dr Pepper bottles and replies "It was great. Thanks mom. Let me know when dinner is ready" and goes to the dining room blasting a Transformers DVD. Kristin sighs and turns on the radio listening to REO Speedwagon's 'Keep on Loving You' singing along to the melody. She serves Ryan dinner and heads down to her dressing room.

'Shameless'

Her cellphone rings at approximately 5:55pm with Mark's caller ID. Kristin answers the phone "Hello Mark. I was just thinking about you darling. How was your day handsome? I can't wait to see you tomorrow". Mark says "Kristin I can't stop thinking about you. I even dream about you every night. Even Poindexter said 'Mark you caught the love bug'. You make me feel invincible baby doll' laughing out loud.

Kristin replies "That is a great thing Mark. And I feel the same way. Dreams are a divine way of healing and expressing your inner most desires. My own personal desire is you. And I have been having crazy sexual dreams about you too. And I wake up and say to myself 'where is Mark. Does he really exist?".

Mark says "Kristin your voice is so intoxicating. It is like a drug to me. I just want to take care of you and protect you. Forever". Kristin giggling says "I will just have to whisper sweet nothings in your ear. All of the time. As I rub you all over. Everywhere. And send you audio messages. I am the luckiest girl in the world Mark. And that one is from the heart. You have given me hope at one if the darkest points in my life. I never thought I would have to function in 'survival mode'. Maybe we just inspire each other baby to live our dreams together".

Mark replies "Kristin. You have a huge heart. And the innocense about you is more sensual than anything. You make my heart beat. It has been a whirlwind since I meet you. You are just so naive in the sweetest way. I just want to spoil you rotten".

Kristin says "Where have you been all of my life Mark. And I will spoil you back in everyway that I can handsome". Mark says "Kristin you are turning me on. I have tons of paperwork to do. Behave yourself and I will see you at Susan's house with Scott tomorrow. Until them my damsel in distress. Sweet dreams sugar".

Kristin giggling says "Please rescue me darling. I need you too. And thank you for everything. You are always on my mind too Mark. And

I am going to 'strum all of my pain with your fingers'. Among other things. Along with your hot sexy body. Love you too sugar. Goodnight".

With a huge smile on her face Kristin retreats to her dressing room to pick out some clothes. She tries on the coral bikini with bows on the side with a strapless bikini top that ties in the back to make sure it still fits. Admiring her fit body she grabs a beach bag and puts a sarape that ties around your waist that her dad sent from Hawaii to cover up her ass. Adds a pair of rhinestone flip flops and a tube of Hawaian Tropics SPF 100 sunscreen

She picks up a white floppy wide brimmed sun hat and a pair of gold Rayban sunglasses and a beach towel. Going through her dresses she picks an ultra feminine floor length pale pink rayon sundress with capped sleeves with a v neck and ruffles on the trim. And ads a pink floral scarf to the bag to cover up her shoulders. Even SPF 100 doesn't protect her sensitive skin enough from the sun after global warming and the toxic ozone layer of planet earth.

Kristin puts the dress in her bedroom and places the beach bag in the butler's pantry. She grabs a pita bread, feta cheese, spinach that she picked from her garden, and a jar of sundried tomatoes and makes herself a quick sandwich. Polishing the pita off she has a chocolate mint Klondike bar for dessert.

Deciding to make the stuffed peppers in advance she makes a pot of yellow saffron rice. Dices a red onion, snips of the ends from a bunch of purple asparagus and chops a bunch of cilantro leaves with a pair of scissors. She mixes the veggies in the pot of rice and cuts off the tops of the bell peppers and scoops out the seeds. Spooning the rice mixture back in the bell peppers adding two cups of shredded Wisconson cheddar cheese and places the tops back on the peppers. Grabing a heavy duty metal baking dish puts the peppers in and covers it with tin foil putting it in the fridge.

Satisfied, she decides to do the fruit salad in the morning. Kristin drives the ATV to the barn to take care of the horses. She goes on a bareback walk around the indoor arena on each horse to let the them stretch their legs. Singing out loud to Bruce Springsteen's 'Glory Days' absolutely enamoured with Mark. Then retrospectively thinks about all of the recent visits from the Arcturians, Pleadians and Sirians and the divine power they have to change the future.

Laughing out loud, knowing that surely it was the Holy Trinity and the otherwordly Universal beings that wrote the current coming of events with Poindexter conducting a smooth sailing purchase of Eagle Point and bringing Mark into her life. Satisfied with her discovery Kristin puts the horses back inside. She feeds them grain, hay and some treats kissing their muzzles goodnight. After throwing the peacocks whole corn she drives back home under the moonlight needing some much needed rest.

Kristin takes a long steamy hot shower with lavender soap. Dries off and slathers lotion all over her skin. Brushes her teeth and applies Este Lauder night cream all over her face and neck and then eye serum. Exhausted she puts on a red silk nightie and climbs into bed after turning in the AC. Listening to angelic music from Archangel Saint Michael who will be channeling a message to her 'in her deep divine sleep' that will guide her through the weekend and fill her up with unending energy and light.

At approximately 3:33am Kristin wakes up and goes outside on her porch to smoke looking up at the unidentifiable objects in the sky that are flying with high tech lights spinning at warp speed. Giggling Kristin waves peace to you friends. Recognizing the Pleadian and Arcturians spaceships.

She goes back to sleep, falls into a deep trance is guided by Archangel Saint Michael, through a vortex to Mont St. Michel in France. He guides her through the magical island in Normandy topped b a gravity-defying abbey. Then she is shown a ley line that runs through a parallel universe through an electromagnetic field connected to the center of the Earth from the island. 'The Messenger' then shows Kristin a vision of her and Mark staring into each others eyes in a deeply connected in pure divine love and inner peace and Archangel Saint Michael's voice says "You and Mark are soul mates. The divine will of the Universe. Love and light to you Kristin".

Kristin wakes up invigorated vividly remembering her 'divine vacation' at Mont St. Michel in France, remembering 'The Messenger's' words. She says out loud ecstatically "That is it. Mark and I are soul mates.

That is where the instant connection came from. I absolutely love it. Thank you Jesus Christ".

The legend of Mont St. Michael goes that 'One night in the year 708 the Archangel Saint Michael, leader of God's armies against Satan, appeared to St. Aubert, the bishop of Avranches, in a dream and ordered the bishop to build a sanctuary in his name at the top of the island, which St. Aubert ignored saying it was just a dream'. Mont St. Michael is known today as a sacred Christian holy place.

Slipping into a pink jogging outfit she hears Ryan in the kitchen making himself breakfast. She notices two empty Dr Pepper bottles, three empty pop tart wrappers and two banana peels. She says "Wow Ryan! That was a healthy breakfast! Waffles and saugage links from the freezer would have been a better choice and turns on the coffee pot".

Ryan giving her that 'fuck you mom' look on a sugar and caffiene high says "We are going on a field trip to Colonial Williamsburg with my co-workers today. Can I have some lunch money? The bus will be here any second. We are going to eat lunch at one of the restaurants there".

Kristin grabs him two $20's and a $10 out of her wallet smiles and says "Have a great day Ryan. That sounds like a blast. I am going to an adult lunch at Susan's house. See you when you get home. Love you" and hands him an aerosol bottle of SPF 70 sunscreen and a red baseball cap as the bus pulls in front of the kitchen door as he waves goodbye.

Looking up at the Heavens in gratitude, Kristin says Amen Jesus. Pours creamer and three sugar cubes in her coffee. She eats a raspberry protein yogurt and a banana and grabs a handful of oatmeal cookies and a to go cup and walks to the stable absolutely ecstatic about seeing Mark today and spending the weekend with him after their celebration event Saturday night.

Ambushed by her thirty six peacocks she throws them a bucket of corn down the driveway and says "Hi lovies. Did you miss me?" to Zeus and Coconut. She grabs their breakfast buckets from the feed room and hangs one in each stall. Sitting on a bench in front of the barn she sips her coffee and eats a few cookies. Hearing Zeus bang on his stall door with his hoof she walks in the barn aisle, gives each horse a cookie and slides their stall doors open watching them walk down the road towards the Plantation eating grass and munching on vines on the fence line. "Priceless" Kristin says out loud.

Kristin turns on the radio to classic rock and cleans up the barn doing a horse food inventory. Making a mental note to ask Susan to take her farm truck to town and stock up before the weekend. She cleans the water buckets and fills the feeders up with Timothy hay and puts another scoop of sweet feed and a few apples in their buckets.

After using the electric blower to clean out the barn aisle she sees Zeus and Coconut standing in front of their stalls swishing their tails from the swamp flies. Kristin smiles "poor babies" and puts them back in their stalls. She pours a bottle of Avon Skin so Soft on a towel and rubs it all over both of their bodies. After putting a mesh fly mask on both horses she turns the ceiling fans on and heads back to the house.

After washing her hands she takes all of the fresh fruit from the fridge and a cutting board from under the sink. Pulling out a butcher knife and a large antique Canton serving bowl with a lid she cuts the cantelope open first cleaning out the seeds. Using a small ice cream scooper she places balls of cantaloupe on the bottom of the bowl. Does the same to a fresh papaya loving the color texture. She peels and then slices the box of kiwis with a mandolin arranging the slices on top. She does a pint of strawberries next and then adds the containers of blueberries and raspberries. Pleased with her creation she covers the bowl with saran wrap, places the lid on top and puts it back in the fridge noticing the clock was flashing 11:11.

Loving divine timing Kristin heads upstairs and takes a hot shower with wild orchid scented body lotion and washes her face. She drys off and puts two layers of SPF 100 suscreen over her entire body. After the lotion dries she ads another layer of orchid scented body lotion and lathers Este Lauder SPF 70 all over her face.

Putting on a very light layer of nude colored foundation and powder she plays with some eyeshadow and brow liner, curling her eyelashes and adding waterproof mascara. She brushes her long blonde hair and uses a set of jumbo sized hot steam rollers and sprays coconut scented hair spray on the curlers.

Putting on a pair of nude colored lace hipster panties and her pink sundress she decides on a simple pair of real diamond stud earrings that her brother gave her for Christmas a few years ago and adds a gold chain bracelet and anklet. After sliding on her rhinestone sandals she takes out the curlers, fluffs out her hair and slides a rhinestone bobby pin behind each ear. And takes a big rhinestone clip with her to put her hair up while they are swimming.

Kristin heads down the three flights of stairs to the foyer takes a few pictures of her posing in front of the bride's dressing mirror-planning on making a photo album for Mark as a gift with pictures from the first day that they met. She grabs the fruit salad and stuffed bell peppers out of the fridge and carries them out to the back seat of her car.

She returns to the kitchen to grabs her beach bag, purse and cell phone as the clock is flashing 12:12pm. She says out loud "Glory to God. Thank you angels" and locks the front door heading to her car. Turning on the AC she cruises down the driveway to Susan's house listening to 'Maybe I'm Amazed' by Paul McCartney singing along admiring the greenery of Virginia.

Pulling up to Susan's house she parks under a shade tree next to the barn. Takes the platters of food from her back seat and says "Hi darling. I love your dress. The aqua blue beach motif is so fitting. You look beautiful and in love". Susan opens the kitchen door and clears a place on the counter for her dishes.

Susan replies "Kristin I am in love. And so are you. You are so fucking feminine, innocent and sexy at the same time. I was so excited about today I stayed up all night watching movies. Scott was playing raquetball. This is the most exciting weekend I have ever looked forward to in my entire life".

Kristin giggling says "I slept like a rock at the Mont St. Michael abbey in Normandy, France. And I had a divine inspiration dream from Archangel Saint Michael. Scott and Mark are our soul mates. Plain and simple. It is a 'divine will' match made in Heaven. I have to grab my beach bag and purse from the car. Be right back". Susan says "I believe you on that one Kristin. I never though I would have a soul mate in this lifetime until I met Scott".

Kristin grabs her things out of the car admiring the simplicity of

Susan's life with a two bedroom house on nine acres staring at the massive size of Eagle Point Plantation across the cove. She places her beach bag on a lounge chair next to the pool noticing that the table under the umbrella is all set with plates and silverware and serving utensils and carries her purse into Susan's kitchen.

Kristin says "I love your place Susan. Just you know, 'simplicity'. Eagle Point is just such a beast to take care of. Do you want me to help you with anything? The bell peppers are in a grill pan they only take 10 minutes. Here put on my peach scented lip gloss-the smell is irresistable".

Susan applies the lip gloss and says "I love that. Scott is pulling up in front of the house and Mark is in the passenger seat" with an excited look on her face. Kristin glances out the window looking at Mark with a huge smile on her face as her heart is swelling with pure desire.

Kristin walks out to Scott's dually noticing both men are wearing Ralph Lauren designer jeans and matching black Ralph Lauren Polo shirts with the 'Criss Cross Properties LLC' emblem. And gold Ray Ban cop sunglasses like they both just came from a GQ Cover shoot.

Kristin smiles with her flirtateous baby blue eyes and says "Thank you for Gracing us with your presence gentlemen" and walks up to Mark and puts her arms around him hugging him tight and caresess his tight ass and whispers in his ear "I am going to pour my sugar all over you sweetie" and kisses his neck. Mark rubbing her breasts against his chest gently pulls her face close to him, french kisses her and sqeezes her ass rubbing her thighs.

He pulls up his Ray Bans and says "This is what I want to come home to. Everyday. Forever. Baby doll" staring into her eyes with lust. Scott affectionately laughs "Get a room kids" and walks up to Susan embracing her kissing her neck.

Mark says "My special darling I have a package from Julia, Poindexter's wife for you" and pulls an oversized Saks Fifth Avenue gift bag from Scott's truck. Mark pulls out an Yves Saint Lauren desinger backless evening gown made of pale gold layers of silk with a crystal gold embroidered neck and hemline and cap sleeves and gold sequin bodice with a matching scarf. Mark holds up the dress and whispers in her ear

"Wear your hair up darling. And I am going to lick all of that sugar off you. You are officially part of the family. I have never in all of my tenure with Poindexter seen Julia give a gift like this. And you deserve it Kristin. Poindexter has other public relations people from the press coming to the celebration dinner. He is absolutely thrilled with Eagle Point Plantation. Just smile and let me hold your arm. Until I take you home with me. Then you can moan as loud as you want. You look beautiful by the way. I love your dress". Kristin about to cry says "Anything and everything you want darling".

Mark puts his arm around her and the couple walks towards Susan's house eying her and Scott making out. Susan embarrased as Kristin and Mark are laughing. Susan says "Hi Mark so nice to see you. Can you guys fire up the grill and Kristin and I will carry the food out". Scott kisses Susan on the cheeck and says "Of course honey". He and Mark head to the grill admiring the water view and their women.

Kristin carries the peppers and fruit salad and Susan the grilled flank steak skewers and shrimp on bamboo sticks. Susan returns inside and grabs the crudite, cheese and crackers and French Onion dip in a serving bowl. Kristin looking at several cases of hard cider on ice in a copper bucket decides to open a bottled water.

Scott says "Bring me the steak and shrimp woman" smiling at Susan. Mark sits down at the table admiring Kristin and she sits in his lap and kisses him as he puts his arms around her caressing her back. Kristin is stroking the back of his neck and whispers in his ear "It came to me last night in a dream I had about you darling. You and I are divine soul mates. That is where our instant connection and chemistry comes from. I can't wait to see you in a Tuxedo. 007 doesn't hold a candle to you. If you only knew the naughty dreams I had about you and I in bed together last night".

Mark replies "You are pure innocence Kristin. I am going to spoil you rotton in every way. You are absolutely beautiful" staring into her eyes kissing her. Kristin picks up a a piece of brocolli from the crudite tray and covers it with french onion dip and puts it in her mouth licking off the dip with her toungue. And then puts one into Mark's mouth who is obviously thrilled with Kristin's sensuality staring at her flirtatious eyes. Kristin giggles and kisses him.

Susan says "Okay love birds lunch is ready" as her and Scott place the platters of food on a picnic table next to the grill. Kristin says to Mark "Let me serve you darling" and picks up a plate and fills it up with the steak and shrimp skewers and a stuffed bell pepper with two slices of Naan and puts the plate in front of Mark brushing her tits on his chest.

She grabs a bell pepper and bread for herself and sits down next to Mark and puts a few slices of cheese and crackers on their plates. Susan serves Scott the same and a plate for herself and a hard cider in front of all. Scott picks up his beer and says "Here is to many more happy times. And to our celebration cruise this Saturday." and the group clinks their beer bottles saying "Cheers" and digs into to the intoxicating smell of the food.

Kristin daintily slices a small peice of the pepper placing it on a peice of Naan and slides it into her mouth savoring the flavors of her homemade dish. She pulls out her camera and takes a dozen pictures of the group smiling behind Mark. She gets up and serves everyone a small plate of fruit salad and sits back down devouring her lunch.

Scott says "Susan this is delishes. Are you trying to seduce me with your cooking? I love this fruit salad" sipping on his beer. Mark laughs and says "Buddy you better get used to it. I love the bell pepper and the steak. And the fruit reminds me of Kristin and her sweet taste. Ladies you did a great job. This is a real treat for us". Susan smiling at Scott says "Anytime. I love to cook sweetie". The fabulous foursome finish off there meal sipping the rest of their hard cider.

Mark eyes Kristin playfully and says "Ready for a volleyball game beautiful? I think I am going to have to make Susan my team mate since Scott hasn't played as much volleyball as we have. I will go easy on the two of you".

Kristin, spending most of her life with under advantaged people and competing at horse shows with wealthy people replies sticking her nose in the air "That sounds like a fantastic idea Mark. Scott and I just might surprise you darling. I am up for a challenge" winking at him.

Kristin says "Let's go change in the pool house sugar". She grabs her beach bag and waits for Mark to grab his swimming suit from Scott's truck. Scott goes to change in Susan's house. The duo dissapear into the pool house and Kristin runs into his arms as he hugs her and kisses the top of her head. Mark sticks his fingers through her panties rubbing her moist clit and feels her climax moaning out loud clinging to him in all of two minutes. He pulls up her chin and kisses her and says "Good girl. Let's change before I get carried away with you. You are mine all weekend baby doll".

Kristin eying his crotch says "Of course master. I can't wait to see your chambers". She let's her dress slide off of her body onto the floor and pulls down her panties as Mark is watching her drooling. She steps into her bikini bottoms and pulls out her bikini top and says "May I ask that you tie a bow behind my back?". Mark caressing her skin with his fingertips kissing her shoulders ties the knot and turns her around admiring his new lover. Kristin kisses him on the lips and says your turn. I will shut my eyes.

Mark not shy at all from being a surfer undressess and lays his clothes on a bench pulling out his bathing suit slowy from his duffle bag. Kristin staring at his crotch watching his dick get hard licks her lips in desire. Kristin says "Mark you are in incredible shape. You are so hot. I love your tattoos too. They really turn me on" smiling into his twinkling baby blue eyes.

Mark staring at her says "Behave your self darling. Only a few more days. You bad naughty girl". He pulls on his trunks and picks Kristin up in his arms and opens the door to the pool house and runs to the pool watching Scott with Susan in her periwinkle blue one peice bathing suit in his arms on the other side of the pool and the guys say in unison "Come Sail Away" and the guys throw the girls into the deep water of the pool and dive in after them.

Kristin absolutely thrilled with the guys playfulness not wanting to have to be perfect with perfect hair all of the time eyes Mark and says "Game on doll". She gives the volleyball to Scott and asks "Can you serve?". Scott picks up the volleyball and slams it over the net directly at Susan while staring at her tits. Susan bumps up the ball laughing as Mark spikes it over at Scott laughing. Scott manages to bump up the ball falling back into the pool and Kristin spikes the ball hard back at Mark. She says "Ouch that hurt" looking at her hand watching Mark fall into the pool after trying to catch the ball.

After an hour of laughing and playing volleyball the couples are tired and climb out of the pool toweling themselves off, grabbing handfuls of peanut M&M's out of the sharable bag downing bottles of water. Kristin puts on her sarape and sits on Mark's lap smiling at him kissing his neck.

Scott says "That was a blast. Wait until I take you three to the basketball court at my house in Virginia Beach. We had better take off Mark before the traffic through the Virginia Beach tunnel. We both have reports to do".

Mark grabs Kristin's hand and takes her into the pool house. He pulls off her bikini bottoms and kisses her navel. Licks her thighs and then unties her top and kisses both of her nipples. He turns her around and rubs his cock in between her legs. Kisses the back of her neck and helps her into her sundress. Kristin says "Mark I am in Heaven. Your touch is so sensual. I love you darling".

Mark says "Kristin. I insist that you do nothing but rest the entire time until I see you on Saturday. Just read books, watch movies and eat. Ice cream. Lots ot it. And think about me." He kisses her neck and lips hugging her.

Kristin says "I am going to miss you darling" as she watches him pull his bathing suit off and she just can't resist to suck his dick for a minute while cupping his balls. Mark moaning says "Kristin. You are mine forever. You are so fucking hot. And sweet. Let me get dressed doll. Scott is waiting for me".

Kristin regains her composure as Mark gets dressed, fucking thrilled with his sexy body. Mark hold's Kristin's hand and walks out to Scott's truck and hands Kristin her gift bag from Julia. He whispers in her ear "Wear your hair up. Darling. With the rhinestone clips she gave you behind your ears. And the diamond tennis bracelet that I gave you" kissing her neck.

Scott says "Kristin I will swing by Eagle Point at 4:30 on Saturday to pick you up. We are going to drive Susan's Mercedes. The boat leaves at 5:00pm from the Yorktown dock and we have to do an interview with the news stations, magazines and newspapers before we go on board the ship. Susan has my home phone number if you need anything Kristin while Mark is in Nag's Head. Until then our partners in crime" smiling at Kristin and kissing Susan goodbye from his window.

Mark embraces Kristin and whisphers in her ear "Hold that thought my darling. See you in three days. And I will cherish you Kristin. Forever. I will call you tomorrow baby doll". Mark hugs Kristin, caressing her ass and kissing her on the lips staring into her eyes until Scott starts honking the horn. Mark climbs into Scott's truck staring at Kristin with a fondness that only soul mates can relate too. Kristin blows him a kiss and looks at Susan giggling.

The ladies absolutely overwhelmed with joy from their afternoon look at each other smiling. Kristin giggles and says "Is he your soul mate? Your true love? A gift from God?. That was so down to earth and special. Both Mark and Scott are workaholics. I loved playing volleyball. And Mark's body-fuck he is sizzling hot. Thanks for everything Susan. Let me grab my dishes do you want me to help you clean?".

Susan gives Kristin a hug and says "The evening gown that Julia gave you is stunning. We are going to light up the town. It was my pleasure. I just want to relish the energy here and Scott's scent. It won't take me very long at all. Here take the left overs home to Ryan so you don't have to cook him dinner. Love you too sweetie. Let's go riding on Friday and stock up on horse feed. Let's bring Ryan with us to unload everything for you in the barn. Have a blessed nights sleep love". Kristin hugs her goodbye and carries her platters to the car. Kristin speeds back to Eagle Point and stops at the barn.

Not remembering the last time she ever felt so happy inside, almost wanting to cry. She looks at her beautiful horses with a smile and feeds them some apples and carrots. She puts Zeus in the cross ties and curry combs him. Brushes his mane and tail admiring his gentleness. She wipes him down with a towel, picks out his stall and gives him three flakes of hay and an extra bag of pine shavings. After doing with same with Coconut she grabs their dinner buckets and hangs them in their stalls. Watching the boys happily much on their grain she throws the peacocks a scoop of cracked corn and heads home.

Kristin unloads the car and hangs up the evening gown in her dressing room admiring the rhinestone hair clips that Julia gave her. After almost coming close to being homeless Kristin is so grateful for Poindexter taking her under his wing. And for Mark. And Scott too. And in deep gratitude that Archangel Saint Michael and her angels guided her to stick to her guns to see 'the Grand Play' through.

She walks back to the kitchen and stops at the piano, sits down and starts to play a classical melody with the sound of the music echoing through the house. She sees Ryan walk down the hallway. He says "Hi mom. I like the piano. I love Williamsburg. We toured the Governer's Mansion and had lunch at Cracker Barrel. How was your party?". Kristin smiles and says "Like Heaven. We went swimming and grilled steak and shrimp. Susan sent you a plate home to you for dinner. I am glad you had fun on your field trip".

Kristin follows Ryan to the kitchen and heats up his dinner in the microwave and shucks an ear of corn for him. Ryan says "Thanks mom" and takes his plates to the dining room and turns on the movie Alien 3. Kristin says well fuck you kid hating noise stress. She grabs her laptop and heads to her bedroom turning on the AC to drown out the noise from the TV and starts working on a manuscript that she is almost finished with. After a few hours of 'creative writing' thrilled with her work she eats two scoops of Strawberry ice crem and goes to tuck the horses in for the night.

After washing the salt water out of her hair from the pool and applying a leave in conditioner mask in her hair, Kristin puts on a yellow frilly cotton bathrobe and sits on her bed admiring the pictures she took at the pool party. The foursome has a synergy like no other. We all look hopelessly in love with our eyes twinkling. She picks the best ones and sends them in a text message to Mark with a note "Sweet Emotion. Mark-you are my cream come true. Thinking about you and your georgous body. Love you sugar". She texts Susan a copy of each picture. Shuts the ringer off her phone and turns on a Divine Meditation music channel and falls into a deep slumber.

Thursdays are one of Kristin's favorite days of the week. Ryan leaves to go to work at 7:00am and she usually sleeps in until nine or ten o'clock. Pulling on a pair of grey yoga pants and a tie dyed long sleeved blouse slipping on a pair of tennis shoes with no agenda on her day makes a cappucino pouring it into a to go cup grabbing a banana nut muffin.

Sitting on her front porch eating and sipping her drink Kristin watches the eagles and herons kite above the river in the gentle breeze. She looks at her text message from last night to Mark who responded 'You are priceless baby doll. You are all mine'. Susan responded 'You and Mark are the couple of the century. See you Friday around noon. Thanks for the pictures. Love you'.

Kristin walks to the barn finally having someone to look forward to spending the rest of her life with. And a group of supportive allies-her new family. And a whole new world open to her. The horses whinny as loud as they can looking forward to their breakfast. Kristin feeds the boys hugging them and rubbing their necks. She turns them out in the pasture with the pond and closes the gate and just stands there watching the horses eat grass and drink water out of the pond filled with Mallard ducks swimming and quacking listening to the song birds.

Enjoying no demands from Ryan for the moment and so looking forward to spending the weekend with Mark. She calls her dentist and asks "Do you happen to have an opening today for a cleaning?". Maria the front office clerk replies "Yes we had a cancellation Ms. Osborne. 1:00pm". Kristin says "Perfect see you then thank you Maria" realizing that she has almost completely quit smoking.

Kristin cleans the barn watching the horses and birds thinking about what to pack to take to Mark's house. Not ashamed at all about her sexuality, Mark and I are both consenting adults. And Mark is so sophisticated and has a great sense of humor at the same time. And the divine timing thing. I am glad that he is open and honest and doesn't expect anything from me but to be myself. Kristin laughs remembering a card her brother sent her a few years ago with a picture of an owl on the front with a saying 'I love who you are'.

Kristin picks up the phone and calls her brother Erich, gets his voicemail and leaves a message "Call me next week for an update. Poindexter closed on Eagle Point and bought the Suntrust Bank building on the Gloucester Courthouse too. We are going on a chartered yacht in Yorktown Saturday night for a celebration dinner with high powered businessmen. Watch the news then. Several TV crews are going to be there for an interview. I have a new boyfriend and am hopelessly in love. He is originally from Huntington Beach. I am spending the weekend at his beach house on the strand in Virginia Beach for the first time this weekend. He is a surfer too and highly succesful. Love you Erich" and hangs up the phone.

Kristin opens the pasture gate and calls to Zeus and Coconut who raise their heads from the grass looking at their mom and trot off to the barn with their blonde manes flowing in the breeze. Kristin closes their stall doors and applies fly spray to each of them putting a fly mask on both. She turns on the ceiling fans admiring her horses beauty. And how much solace that they have given her in hard times. And how many times that she cried on their shoulders from the anguish of a toxic relationship. And the challenges of raising Ryan. Kristin walks back home picking Magnolia blooms from the trees. She places them in a bowl of water on the dining room table.

She heads down to her dressing room to look through her wardrobe and pack a bag to take to Mark's house this weekend with a smile on her face. Immediately drawn to a raspberry colored off the shoulder floor length sundress made out of a rayon fabric with ruffles that won't wrinkle. She grabs the hanger from her dressing rack, thinking she can wear the dress at breakfast with Mark.

And then eyes a skin tight indigo blue ankle length floral pencil skirt with a matching sleeveless v neck blouse with a feminine white and purple floral pattern. She puts two pairs of pink lace panties and a cosmetic bag full of face cream, an extra electric toothbrush, cosmetics, sunscreen and hair accessories. And ads a pair of nude colored rhinestone medium heeled cork sandals that go with anything. She lays everything on her dressing table and pulls out a pair of nude colored sheer thigh high stockings, a gold lace garter belt a pair of matching panties to wear under the evening gown on Saturday night.

Her phone rings at 5:55pm. Kristin admiring Marks's photo on his caller ID answers and says "Hello my darling. I was just thinking about you. I never stop thinking about you. How was your day honey?". Mark chuckling softly replies "Kristin. You are pure honey. And I can't stop thinking about you for even one second. Not only are you priceless, you are just my everything. I can't remember life without you baby doll".

Kristin giggling says "Do you want some sweet talk baby? I don't know what I did in life to deserve you Mark. You have no idea how attached I am to you. Hymm, charisma, charm, a to die for body. Intelligence, successful and a heart of gold who knows how to treat a lady. Is that a good start not to mention ummm 'your package" seductively giggling.

Mark laughing says "Kristin you are the woman of my dreams. I have so much admiration for you for so many reasons. Not just for your beauty and sensuality. There is a pure gentleness about you. You have perservered at that place for a long time with no help. And you have class. Sophistication and are wide open and honest. I have great plans for our future baby doll. Just lean on me. All of the time. I will give you everything. Including all of my heart. And I loved the soul mate thing that you told me about yesterday. And the time that you and Susan spent to have me and Scott over for lunch and play games. And yes. I love your beautiful body and your needs for sexual attention. You just make me feel like a man. Be prepared my sweet darling. I am going to take you on the ride of your life. Just relax and enjoy being spoiled Kristin".

Kristin says "Mark, that means so much to me. You have no idea how much I adore you. And need you". Mark replies "Kristin. I need you more than you need me. The boat tour press thing is very important to Poindexter. We will most likely be on the cover of Forbes Magazine and People Magazine. You can hold your own Kristin. Just smile and let Poindexter do all of the talking. I will be by your side holding your arm protecting you. And then I am taking you home with me. That is the victory for me darling. I may not ever let you leave".

Kristin laughs saying "Mark I love you too. I can't wait to see you on Saturday and I eat up all of the press and TV stuff. It is a sentimental thing for me from living in Hollywood. Do you care for thigh high stockings darling?". Mark says "Kristin you are giving me a hard on sweetie. Your voice is driving me crazy. I have to turn in reports tomorrow. I will meet you and Scott in the parking lot at the Yorktown beach. I want to see you before we depart for the tour and walk you to the boat in front of the papparizzi. I love you baby doll. I will call you again tomorrow night. Sweet dreams darling". Kristin seductively giggling says "You are my knight in shining armor. I will be dreaming about you all night too Mark. I can't wait to see you Saturday. Goodnight handsome" and hangs up the phone.

Kristin wakes up at 9:00am after dreaming about Mark all night. She walks in the kitchen in her bathrobe grateful that Ryan is in the guest cottage doing what ever in the fuck he does. Turning on the coffee pot and eating an oatmeal cranberry cookie relishing seeing Mark tomorrow. She squirts some heavy whipping cream in her coffee to go cup in great spirits. Eats another cookie and puts on a silver velour sweat suit and a pair of tennis shoes after massaging her face cream in her skin. Heading to the barn in the ATV sipping her coffee she feeds her horses breakfast thinking to herself she hasn't had a day off from this farm or Ryan in over seven years.

She turns Zeus and Coconut loose in front of the Plantation watching them explore the gardens and the swimming pool. Taking an inventory of the feed room and the fridge-fucking Ryan already drank four Dr Peppers before she woke up. She cleans out the barn and places buckets of feed in the horses stalls. Adds flakes of hay and pine shavings and fills up their water buckets.

The horses see Ryan walking down the driveway from the guest house and follow him to the barn. Ryan takes another bottle of soda from the fridge in the stable as Kristin puts the horses in their stalls. He says "Hi mom. Did you sleep good? I can't wait to see Ashley on Sunday. I love my sister. Are you going to get married to Mark?".

Kristin seeing clearly that he is on a caffeine high like a drug addict replies "Yes I slept good. I love your sister too. I am leaving you a chore chart to take care of the horses for me while I am gone. You will have to ask Jesus if Mark and I are going to get married. I hope that we do. Susan and I are going to the feed store and will take you to McDonald's for lunch. Then I need to get some rest. Guadalupe who is Mark's maid is going to stay with you Saturday night until I come home. She can sleep in Ashley's wing. Do you want a ride back home I have to go change my clothes". Ryan says "Cool" and climbs in the back seat.

Kristin drives home, feeds the cats and dissapears uptairs to change clothes and wash her face until Susan arrives, avoiding Ryan like a hawk. Brushing her hair looking in the mirror Kristin wonders what Mark really sees. She puts on a baby blue sundress and tons of face cream. Grabs a beach blue scarf to cover up her shoulders and puts on a pair of comfortable sandals as Susan pulls her farm truck in front of the kitchen entrance. Ryan runs down stairs as Kristin grabs her purse and sunglasses. Kristin says "Are you ready to go Ryan? Close the kitchen door all of the way" and walks out to Susan's truck.

Kristin kisses Susan on the cheek and says "I just can't wait until tomorrow. Thanks for taking us shopping sweetie". Susan says "I am so nervous about the newscasters and Scott spending the weekend. You are a natural at sex. I hope I can please him".

Kristin laughs and says "Susan he will just stare at your tits. And suck them. He will probably get off in two minutes. He really loves you. Just let him do his thing and lay there in bed and enjoy the pleasure. The man is crazy for you. And as far as the TV people, just put on a professional business face and stare at the cameras and stick your nose in the air and think 'fuck you' next to Poindexter with Scott's arm around you. You won't have to say a thing. And the magazines heavily edit all of the photos. You are going to have to get used to it. Poindexter loves the media. I can't wait to meet his wife Julia".

The ladies drive to Southern States and buy as much hay, sweet feed and shavings that they can fit in her truck. Susan stops at Tractor Supply and spends two hundred dollars on mealy worms for her chickens and takes Ryan to Mc Donalds and buys him a double quarter pounder meal and an ice cream cone for her and Kristin. Kristin takes her cell phone and snaps a selfie of her licking the ice cream with her toungue and sends it to Mark with a note "Wishing this was you" laughing at the excitement of the weekend. Susan says "I saw that" giggling and does the same thing to Scott.

The trio drive home and Ryan unloads all of the horse supplies in Kristin's barn and Susan takes Ryan to her house to unload all of her horse supplies and drives him back to the barn at Eagle Point as Kristin is grooming the horses. Susan says "Can we go jump for a while to take our minds of off things?".

Kristin says "Go get your saddle cowgirl". Susan and Kristin change into their boots and britches and carry the saddles and bridles to the cross ties. The horses loving the attention nuzzle the girls while they are tacking them up. Kristin bridles Zeus and hands Susan a crop and they walk down the barn aisle into the arena.

The ladies mount the horses and Kristin says "Mark said there are going to be journalists from Forbes and People magazine at the dock. With professional photographers. I hope that we make the cover" laughing out loud. Susan smiling replies "Wow. This is just so exciting. I know you love it. I am so happy for both of us Kristin. I never thought I would meet anyone again. Let alone fall in love". Kristin says "I know Susan. I call it 'God's Master Plan'. I have lived at Eagle Point for over seven years in complete isolation. Time just goes by so fast".

Kristin picks up the posting trot with Susan following behind her on Coconut. Kristin trots around several laps and then does a figure of eight trotting over some ground poles and switches directions trotting around the arena. The ladies pull the horses back to the walk.

Kristin says "Your riding has really improved. You should be proud of your self. I can't wait to meet Julia Poindexter. I read that she collects angel figurines. I bought her a nice thank you card and a Swarovski crystal angel letter opener. What do you give people with billions of dollars that have everything. Poindexter is so effervescent and kind. I am sure she is an angel herself".

Susan says "Kristin you are just so used having no help and being used by a narcissist. Plus you have no family here. Julia is a mom too. I am sure that she relates to you being a single parent with a kid on the spectrum. A good analogy would be you have survived and forged ahead 'Against All Odds'. I have a lot of respect for you girl. And now that you finally have found your own dignity to start a new relationship with someone who will treat you like a goddess. And you are just the sweetest person. That is my favorite thing about you. I love your sense of humor too. You are just wide open". Kristin says "That is one of the biggest compliments I could ever ask for doll. Thank you Susan. Are you ready to canter?".

Kristin picks up the sitting trot and nudges Zeus into the canter sinking into the saddle enjoy his perfect rythum. She canters three laps and then crosses the center line and does a flying lead change and switches directions and canters three more laps. She says "whoa" and laughs as both horses halt immediately from her voice training. Kristin looks at the smile on Susan's face and clucks and both horses walk off.

Kristin says "We are going to trot the double x oxer with the ground rails back and forth four times. After that let's canter the 'Universe' colored lattice gate, then the line of neon pink post and rails with the flower boxes underneath in a count of five strides and then the silver triple bar oxer UFO jump off the left diagonal and finish over the outside line of stone walls in four strides".

Kristin picks up the trot and heads towards the gymnastic exercise feeling Zeus jump three feet higher than the jump. Susan follows Kristin. They halt at the end of the ring and trot of the excercise three more times. Kristin walks a lap to let the horses and Susan catch their breath and then picks up the canter and heads Zeus towards the lattice gate and through the rest of the course.

Susan pets Coconut on the neck and rump and says "Good boy Coco. That was so much fun. You did a great job training both of them Kristin". Kristin giggling says "The horse is my power animal. 'They give you warrior strength to overcome any obstacle. And divine feminine sexual energy'. Most horse lovers even the rich ones are just down to earth. And the inner beauty and devotion of the horse is just priceless".

The ladies walk the horses around the arena to cool them out and Susan says "I one hundred percent agree with you on that one Kristin. I can't wait to enter Coconut in a horse show some day. I am getting much more comfortable jumping after all the training sessions we have done lately". Kristin says "That can be arranged darling. You will have to pick out a show name for him. I still remember how to braid manes and tails. And no you can't name him "Tin Man', or anything to do with Dorothy or Toto, hey 'Wizard of Oz' might be a catchy show name for him", laughing out loud.

Kristin steers Zeus back to the cross ties and dismounts kissing his muzzle thinking about Mark. Susan puts Coconut in the cross ties and the girls untack the horses and put the saddles and bridles away. Susan grabs a bag of carrots out of the fridge feeding the horses while Kristin is sponging them down with a bucket of hot water mixed with Absorbine Linament. Susan picks out their stalls and gives them each of scoop of grain and a few molassas flavored horse cookies. They put the horses in their stalls and go into her office to change clothes.

Kristin feeling silly says "Is your heart fluttering over sleeping with Scott? Just think of posting the trot and say to yourself 'up down, up down' while he grabs your hips, licking your nipples" cracking up. And then she ads "Or just whisper in his ear 'You can come in my mouth. I swallow'. You will have an engagement ring on your finger in no time at all" trying to help sooth Susan's nerves about having sex with Scott. And then adds "Or you can just be a bitch and say 'I am a devout Catholic. I am not putting out until we are married'".

Susan laughing hysterically says "Kristin you are so funny. But that one is true. The first time might be akward but hey, practice makes perfect. I am wearing the emerald green gown with the green beaded sequin bodice that covers up my cleavage for the photo shoot. And a pair of really fancy beaded high heels. Maybe a diamond pendant and matching earrings. I think I will wear my hair in a bun at the nape of my neck with all of those sophisticated executives. Don't forget to bring a fancy jacket in case we go on deck. The wind off the ocean can be really chilly".

Kristin says "Sounds dazzling. I am sure you will steal the show. I just can't wait. I am so excited! Think of it as 'the glory of the anticipation of the first time'. I sneaked a peak at Mark's 'package' while we were in your pool house. He is the perfect size for me and has huge balls. And just practice kegel exersices. I better go check and see what Ryan is up to. Thanks for your company today" and gives her a hug. Susan kisses her on the cheek and replies "You are so welcome sweetie. That really helped me lighten up. I feel like we have both graduated from lonliness to Cinderella's. Riding Coconut has helped my confidence too. See you tomorrow. Love you".

Kristin waves goodbye. She walks back home as Susan drives down the driveway in excellent spirits. Kristin walks into the kitchen and hears Ryan talking to his sister Ashley with the speaker phone turned on. Kristin says "Hi boo. How is your day? Thanks for coming over Sunday. You know how obsessive I am about the horses. I will leave some cash in my bedroom if you can stop and bring Ryan Subway or Burger King or whatever. Lock the horses in the indoor arena while you clean their stalls and give them hay and grain and fill up the water buckets. Clean the stalls again at 2:00 and 5:00pm. There are tons of carrots and apples in the fridge and extra bags of shavings".

Ashley says "I am so excited for you mom. You really deserve this. I hope that fucker Stewart watches the news and sees you with your new boyfriend" chuckling out loud. Kristin replies "You are silly. I never think about him at all anymore. Wait until you see how fucking handsome Mark is. He looks like a GQ model. And he is an absolute sweetheart. I will text you some pictures later. I will be home sometime Sunday, probably after dinner. Love you".

Ashley says "Believe in miracles mom. Sounds like a plan. Don't worry about a thing just have a blast. Love you too, see you Sunday". Kristin texts Ashley some photos of her and Mark. Ashley sends back a message "Couple of the year. He is drop dead georgeous".

Kristin asks Ryan "Tacos for dinner and corn on the cob?". He replies "Sure mom thanks. I am going to watch a movie" and goes into the dining room blasting 'Predator 2'. Kristin turns the stove fan on high to drown out the noise and puts a pound of ground sirlion with a chopped red onion in a frying pan. She takes a bowl of spinach, diced zuchinni, onions, queso cheese and fat free refried beans and spreads the mixture onto two flour tortillas. Browning Ryan's taco meat she fills a plate with corn taco shells for Ryan.

After adding taco seasoning and letting the meat simmer for five minutes she scoops it into taco shells and brings Ryan his dinner. She throws her bowl of veggies in a separate frying pan with avocado oil. Places the mixture onto the flour tortillas and fries them folding them over. Adding sour cream and pineapple salsa Kristin devours her food.

Ryan leaves his plate in the sink and says "I am going to surf the Universe". Kristin replies "Have a celestial blast for me" and watches him dissapear through the portal in front of the kitchen door. Kristin says "Thank you God". She finishes almost all of her meal and throws the rest in the front yard for the wild critters.

And again her cell phone rings at appromately 5:55pm. Kristin answers the phone taking a deep breath "Mark how did you know I was just thinking about you honey. You remind me of a childhood memory where everything is a bright blue sky. Limitations and love without conditions. How was your day sugar. I know you work so hard and have demanding clients".

Mark responds "Kristin. Kristin. I think about you every second and look at the pictures you send me. Call it inspiration. I just want to be with you and hold you in my arms. All of the time. Everyday. I really worry about you alone at that house. It is really hot here in Nags Head".

Kristin giggling says "I feel the same way about you darling. Even more so. Susan took me and Ryan to town in her farm truck and she bought Ryan McDonalds for lunch and had him unload all of the horse feed. We went jumping in the arena. I tried to cheer her up. She is an absolute nervous wreck over having sex with Scott".

Mark laughs and says "I wonder why. He is fucking crazy over her. That is too funny. Maybe after he pleasures her she will change her mind. She must have had a bad experience or something. She must be nervous about the paparrazi tomorrow. She also has you and your sexy ass for an example. It must be the huge boobs of hers that have given her a complex with men staring at her chest all of the time".

Kristin laughing says "Mark you are too good to be true. Sexual love is an affection without any limitations. Or love without conditions. And I want it all sweetie. Mark I want your heart, soul, the sex and friendship. Sorry that sounds so demanding. Love me unconditionally Mark. Even when times aren't perfect. It builds character and a rock solid relationship. You and I just click. Just thinking about you puts a smile on my face and a twinkle in my eyes".

Mark says "Kristin. I am going to spend the rest of my life with you. Love, honor and cherish you unconditionally. Forever. And make love or fuck you every chance I get. You are my dream come true Kristin. Get some rest darling I have to finish my report. Your sexy voice is distracting me. And tomorrow you and I will be together. All weekend. I may not ever let you leave".

Kristin says "Don't get me too excicted. This is a real treat staying off of this place for a night. I can't wait to see your house Mark. You have no idea how much I appreciate you. I haven't been to Virginia Beach in five years. My overnight bag is packed master. I absolutely adore you

Mark with every move you make and every word that you say with every breath that I take. And thank you for inviting me into your home and your life. I will be dreaming about you all night my. Get some rest sugar. I love you".

Mark replies "My darling. Kristin. You will be in my arms before you know it. Kristin. And I am going to hold you tight in my arms all night long after making love to you and cherish you after you set the paparazzi on fire with Poindexter. Sweet dreams my baby doll. I will see you and your sexy ass tomorrow". Kristin hangs up the phone absolutely elated.

Kristin finishes the dishes and writes a list for Guadalupe of emergency numbers and instructions for Ryan to feed and water the horses dinner and seals it in an envelope with the key to the ATV. Fondly reflecting on her childhood. Her mother hired a live in maid named Lupita who got caught stealing her mother's jewelry. And then her mom switched to Japanese foreign exchange students that my brother and I used to terrorize. Every single one of them quit.

She sits down at her laptop working an her third manuscript in front of the air conditioning letting her imagination run wild creating intensely emotional flawed dynamic characters and non-stop dramatic tension. After two hours of writing and editing Kristin calls it quits for the night wanting to look well rested for the dinner cruise tomorrow. And for Mark especially.

In synchronicity Kristin drives her ATV to the barn and feeds the birds and grooms both horses for a while kissing them and giving them treats. She fills up their dinner buckets and adds a small scoop of Phenylbutazone (anti inflammatory) after all the jumping they did today. She opens an extra bag of pine shavings for each stall and fills up their hay racks and water buckets.

Kristin raised Zues and Coconut since they were three and five months old smiling at their gleaming good health after all the bizarre accidents they suffered during the house haunting at Eagle Point in 2019. Kristin has lost count how many times Jesus has saved Zeus's life since she has lived at Eagle Point. And Coconut's life four times at least. She tucks the horses in and drives back home.

Kristin grabs a towel and a bathrobe and decides to stop at the library room. She picks up her Ebenezer guitar and sits down on the leather couch strumming 'Knockin on Heavens Door' singing as loud as she can. And then she plays 'Hotel California' singing along. And then 'Stairway to Heaven'. Thinking music is so relaxing and singing is excellent exercise for your lungs.

Completely relaxed she climbs up the three flights of stairs to her bathroom and soaks in a hot tub wearing a mineral fascial mask on her face. About to fall asleep she washes her face and applies tons of face cream and body lotion, brushes her teeth. Puts on her bathrobe and walks back down stairs and turns the crystal chandelier in foyer off. She climbs into bed and falls asleep instantly.

'The Fabulous Five'

Waking up refreshed and invigorated about her night and weekend Kristin throws on a yellow cotton sweat suit and heads to the kitchen deciding to make Ryan pancakes for breakfast. She turns on the coffee pot and heats up the griddle. She puts four breakfast sausage links on the griddle. Whips up the pancake batter and makes four double sized pancakes. Cracking two eggs on the side she flips the pancakes and serves Ryan three flapjacks and the eggs and one pancake for herself. Adding creamer and sugar to her coffee she slices a pat of butter and pours pure maple syrup on top.

Ryan sits down at the kitchen table and says "Thanks mom. That smells delicious" and digs into his food. Kristin says "You are welcome. Susan and Scott are picking me up at 4:30pm today. Guadalupe is staying with you until Ashley comes over tomorrow. She can sleep in Ashley's room. Don't forget to feed Zeus and Coconut at 5:00pm and again at 8:00pm and clean out their stalls and fill up their water buckets. Brittany and James the tenants will be home tonight too if you need anything. Make sure that you do not let the horses escape and turn off the lights in the barn. Don't forget to turn on the news tonight. I am going to be on TV". She finishes her breakfast and Ryan replies "Okay mom. I am going to play my PS4. Have fun with the horses. Kristin loads the dishwasher and heads off the the barn.

Kristin feeds the horses breakfast and turns them out in the field in front of the house to eat grass. She stands there watching them graze listening to the birds sing just absolutely thrilled to spend the weekend with Mark. She cleans the barn contently and throws the peacocks a scoop of corn watching them fan their beautiful tail feathers. She brings the horses back inside and grooms them in their stalls while they are munching on hay. Fly sprays them and turns on the ceiling fans in complete peace. Kristin drives back home with no agenda but to rest.

Kristin asks Ryan who is sitting at the kitchen table bouncing off the walls on a Dr Pepper high "Would you like a tuna sandwich and potatoe chips for lunch?". He replies "Sounds good to me. I am playing my Nintendo Switch online with Christina my friend from work". Kristin whips up a sandwich and hands him a bag of Sun Chips and goes down to the library room at the other end of the house and takes a book titled 'the Gnostic Gospels of Judas, Thomas and Mary Magdelene' out of the book case and sits down and starts reading. She finishes the entire book and lays down on the couch and dozes off. Kristin wakes up at 2:22pm and makes herself a PBJ and goes to feed the horses lunch well rested.

She heads upstairs and washes her hair and shaves her legs. Sitting at her vanity in a red cotton bathrobe she dries her hair and spends half an hour curling it, and then setting it with Argan oil hairspray. She does her makeup in a photo appealing way. Puts on her lingerie and the gold evening gown and the tennis bracelet that Mark gave her with a pair of diamond studs. She plays with her hair and an updo placing the rhinestone clips that Julia gave her behind her ears as Mark requested. Pleased with her appearance she heads downstairs and puts her essentials in a gold clutch purse with the card that she bought for Julia. She stops at the brides mirror in the foyer and takes a few pictures.

Kristin walks into the kitchen loving the diving syncronicity day. She sees Guadalupe pulling up in front of the kitchen in a new cherry red RAV 4. She walks up to the kitchen door and Kristin lets her in saying "Hola Guadalupe. Muchos gracias senorita. Here is a letter with instructions and emergency numbers. This is my son Ryan. He will give you a tour of the house and show you the guest wing. And the horses. Ryan loves Dr Pepper and food. Thank you again. I am so excited to stay with Mark this weekend".

Guadalupe replies "You are so welcome Kristin. Mark loves you. I grew up with horses and have five grown up children. Have fun tonight". Scott pulls up in Susan's Mercedes. Kristin grabs her bags and waves goodbye and walks out the door to the car.

Scott looking dashing in his tuxedo gets out of the Mercedes and opens the door for Kristin kissing her check. He says "Kristin you are absolutely beautiful. And look hopelessly in love. You are glowing". Kristin with her radiant smile says "Why thank you Scott. You are dazzling yourself in that Tux yourself. It suits you". He helps her in the car smiling at her innocence and beauty; thrilled for his best friend

Mark and Kristin's future together. He closes the car door and the trio speed down the driveway.

Kristin says "Susan you look radiant. Your dress is gorgeous. I love your hair up too. You have a sensual neck. Don't you think so Scott? It's almost like it wants to be kissed and caressed" laughing to herself. Susan replies "Thank you for the compliment. You look breath taking. I can't wait to see you and Mark together. You need to do this more often sweetie. And take a break from Ryan and your horses. I feel like a princess" as she is staring at Scott in his tux holding hands with him".

Scott driving 80 MPH says "Ladies. I am very impressed with the both of you. And your friendship. I have never in my life had a couple friend. I really like that the two of you are supportive of each other. I bet men stalk you and follow you two all over town. And Susan I agree with Kristin. Your neck is begging to be kissed. And touched" as he laughs out loud.

Scott pulls into the parking lot at the boat launch and parks a few rows in front of the entrance. For a reason. He parks the car staring at the dozens of television crew's vans recognizing Poindexter's Rolls Royce limosine.

Mark pulls beside them in his black Mercedes like a bat out of hell screeching to a halt. He opens the door eyeing Kristin with a huge dazzling smile on his face. Kristin looks at him in his tuxedo with his blonde hair and dazzling blue eyes in complete admiration of everything about him. He opens her car door and gently takes her hand and helps her out of Susan's Mercedes. Eyeing her body ravenously with her naive elegance he hugs her and kisses her neck.

He whispers in her ear "My darling princess. You look absolutely ravishing. And delicious" and puts a Tiffany's box into her hands. Kristin swelling with emotion opens the box and lifts out a diamond chocker necklace studded with thousands of dollars of diamonds. She looks straight into Mark's eyes and says "Are you courting me sweetheart? It is absolutely beautiful. And you are just the man of dreams sugar. You mean everything to me. Thank you so much darling" about to cry.

Mark turns her around and puts the necklace on her breathing in her ear discretely rubbing her ass. He turns her around and kisses her as Scott and Susan get out of the car. Mark says invigorated with divine energy "Poindexter's chauffer is opening his door. Let's go get them and make history".

The foursome looks at each other and then at the news crews and walk in stride overflowing with positive energy and synergy side by side full of confidence looking like they could conquer the world. They stop at Poindexter's limo as he and Julia steps out.

Julia eyes Kristin with a smile staring at her and Mark in admiration. She says "Kristin you look exquisite. My name is Julia. You have made my husband very happy. It is a pleasure to meet you darling" and kisses her on the cheek. Kristin pulls her thank you card out of her purse and places it in her hands. Admiring Julia's chiseled cheek bones and shining brunette hair, solid gold sequin embroidered gown and the chocolate diamonds around her neck. And shit a million dollar diamond wedding ring.

Thinking pure sophistication, elegance, a mother and horse lover too replies "Julia. I absolutely love your dress. You are so elegant and beautiful. And thank you for your blatent act of kindess picking out my dress. You are a very special lady". Julia replies "You are so welcome. You and Mark make a fabulous couple" smiling at them. A security guard and an escort takes Julia onto the boat keeping her away from the newscasters.

Poindexter shakes Mark's and Scott's hands fondly admiring Susan and Kristin. Thrilled with his press conference he announces "Mark and Scott walk on either side of me with the ladies on either side of you 'a five lineup'. I am thoroughly impressed with all of you. Let's go". Poindexter's contagious energy flows through the group as they walk in stride with all of the confidence in the world in front of the dock.

The group turns around staring at the press who takes dozens of pictures with their cameras flashing while the camera men are filming and the reporters are holding their microphones in front of Mr. Poindexter while the press continues to photograph the group. Kristin holds her head up and gives the cameras 'a look that could kill' with her bright smile. After hundreds of photos with the tight nit group 'playing the game' Mr. Poindexter holds his hands up and says "I would like to make a speech".

Poindexter continues "Thank you for joining us tonight to see us off on our celebration cruise. It is in my greatest pleasure to announce that Criss Cross Properties LLC has officially acquired the famous Eagle Point Plantation in Gloucester, Virginia. My beloved team here will be instrumental in orchastrating a full restoration of the pre circa 1680 Plantation and all of the structures on the grounds. My business plan will create hundredes of jobs and provide services for the under privileged. And create a convening place for the community to strengthen relationships within. Including wellness activities for all of the surrounding cities. My group has a great fondess for this project and thanks you for your support. Thank you for your interest and joining us here tonight. In Jesus name. Amen".

The press goes crazy taking pictures of the group. Kristin eating it up just smiles changing poses. Linda, Poindexter's press secretary holds up her hand for questions as the group walks up the dock and enters the famous Blackbeard Pirate Ship. Several security guards close and lock the door.

The hostess at the front door leads the party to a large oval table in the center of the dining room. Mark seats Kristin next to Julia pulling out her chair for her with Scott on Poindexter's other side with Susan next to him. Kristin and Julia smile affectionately at each other and Mark puts his arm around Kristin and his other hand on her thigh. Kristin looking at Scott and Susan is feeling euphoric. And then she sees a group of journalists sitting at the bar watching them with name tags from Forbes, Esquire, Town and Country and People Magazine. And the dozens of men in Tuxedos seated next to their wives staring at the oval table.

The waitresses serve caviar and escargot and plates of brown french bread with butter. The waiters fill up their glasse with Crystal champagne. Poindexter raises his champagne glass to make a toast. Standing up he clears his throat and recites "Here is to the glory and prestige of Eagle Point Plantation and her future. And to my new associates Kristin and Susan." He points to an architects rendering simulating the finished exterior of the Plantation and the grounds which is streaming on a large screen TV. "The estimated completion will be done in the year 2027. Thank you for joining me on another succesful journey gentlemen. Enjoy the cruise. In Jesus name. Amen". The entire group stands up giving Mr. Poindexter a standing ovation clapping, clinks their glasses and says Amen in unison.

Kristin staring into Mark's eyes feels Julia grab her hand who gets up and says "We are going to the powder room". Mark gets up and pulls out Kristin's and Julia's chair thrilled that Julia is going to take her under her wing. Mark and Kristin stare into each other's eyes with lust as she and Julia walk off to the ladies room.

After closing the door Julia smiling looks at Kristin and says "My husband William thinks of Mark as his son. He is part of my family as is Scott. We are a very tight nit group. I have deep admiration for you Kristin. Being single with a special child surviving at Eagle Point by yourself for all of those years. I want to help you. Mark is hopelessly in love with you. He needs a wife. And a lover. William and I love our employees. I have dozens of rooms of brand new designer clothes that I have never worn that are going to be delivered to you. We are the same size Kristin. Make him happy in everyway. Let him give you everthing and spoil you Kristin. I am going to have William bring me and my girls down to Eagle Point soon for a tour. He is so proud of that place. Enjoy your love affair with Mark. He is worth his weight in gold. And I think you are too. Enjoy your weekend Kristin".

She grabs Kristin's hand and leads her through the dining room walking with Grace with her nose up in the air. And the Forbes and People Magazine journalists in a craze are flashing dozens of photographs. The ladies embrace and Mark and William pull out their chairs and seat the ladies for dinner.

Julia and Kristin clink their champagne glasses together smiling fondly at each other with their new found friendship. Mark grabs her thigh rubbing her leg in immense satisfaction admiring her composure with Julia and the press. Scott and Susan smile at her as the waiters serve them dinner salads, more bread and champagne.

The waiters remove the salad plates and bring trays on dinner plates on silver platers and the group is served prime rib and suffed lobster tails, roasted new potatoes and grilled vegetables. The waiter serves Kristin a huge vegetarian plate smiling at her.

Kristin says to Mark "That smells delicious. The garlic butter on the lobster tail is intoxicating" rubbing her leg against him and picks up her fork and knife cutting small bites of the roasted potatoes, sauted asparagus and slices of Jarlsburg cheese eating like a lady from all of the fine dining she did in Beverly Hills.

Mark replies "This is wonderful. Scott and I will introduce you to the rest of the group when we go up on deck as we near Eagle Point. And you smell delicious Kristin". Poindexter and Julia are in a heated conversation discussing which interior designer to hire for Eagle Point.

The party finishes their dinner and are served an apple flambe with Grand Marnier and vanilla ice cream for dessert. The waiters bring coffee in sterling silver carafes while the guests are eating dessert. Kristin says "This is outrageous. Simply delectible" rubbing her foot against Mark's ankle.

She and Mark finished off their entire desert as the Captain says over the speaker phone "We are sailing down the Severn River and should arrive at our destination in just a few minutes". Poindexters security guards come to the oval table and lead the group first to the viewing area on deck. Mark holding Kristin's elbow brushes against her body smiling down at her fondly.

Just as the sun is starting to set Poindexter says "Look at my baby. What an incredible view. Now that is a Plantation" as the colorful sailboats are drifting out to the Mobjack Bay. Noticing every single light is on in the mansion Kristin smiles at Mark and says "I guess Ryan and Guadalupe have been busy. Thank you darling. I didn't think of that one". Mark strokes her check with affection staring into her eyes. He replies with a twinkle in his eyes "You are so welcome doll. Anything for you. And everything for you. And us". Kristin mouths the words "I love you".

The Captain turns the ship around and heads back to the Yorktown dock. Scott and Susan walk over to Kristin and Mark. Scott says "What an incredible view. This is the first time I have been on a dinner cruise. We will have to do it again sometime. Let's go back to the cabin. Poindexter wants to do a closing speech" and they follow Mr. Poindexter down to the galley.

Everyone resumes their seating and Mr. Poindexter stands up reciting "Thank you ladies and gentlemen for accompanying us tonight. I want Eagle Point Plantation to be of the highest priority on your project list's. My assisant April is scheduling a meeting at our headquarters in two weeks. Please turn all of your reports to her by that time. You will be receiving an agenda shortly. Here is to 'Victory in the Light'. Amen". The guests stand up and clap in admiration.

Several dozen guest service members hand out gift bags to the guests with an artist's redendering of Eagle Point Plantation on the front. Kristin opens her gift bag and pulls out a royal blue colored windbreaker jacket, a Ralph Lauren polo shirt and a baseball hat all embroidered with Eagle Point Plantation in large print and Criss Cross Properties LLC underneath. She smiles at Mark, feeling so at home with people that have class.

Kristin says "Thank you Mr. Poindexter for a beautiful evening" who replies "Get used to it Kristin" winking at her and smiling at Mark. The Captain annouces "We are pulling up to the dock. The security guards will lead you out to the parking lot. We hope that you enjoyed your time on the Blackbeard Pirate's dinner cruise".

The guests follow the security guards down the boat ramp in great spirits. Poindexter's body guards open the door to his limosine as William and Julia wave to Mark, Kristin, Scott and Susan. The foursome carying their gift bags head to their Mercedes. Susan says "I had an incredible time. You looked like had fun with Julia in front of the reporters. I wonder if we are going to on the cover of all of those magazines".

Kristin smiling with Mark's arms around her says "I am sure that we will. Poindexter is a hot news item. I loved the redendering of the restored Plantation. You two are an amazing couple. Can you tape record the news broadcast? Mark and I are going to be busy".

Scott laughs smiling at Kristin "Of course we will. I am sure Poindexter's PR department will too". The couples arrive at their cars and Mark gives Kristin a hug, holding her tight rubbing her ass, kissing her neck. He says to Scott and Susan "Have a great night you two. We are off to Virginia Beach". Opens the car door for Kristin, French kisses her on the mouth as he fastens her seat belt. Shuts the door and gets in the driver's seat as Scott and Susan giggling wave goodbye.

Mark starts the car and drives eighty miles an hour through the Virginia Beach Tunnel, exits on the Ocean Drive off ramp and heads towards Ocean Drive. Holding Kristin's thigh he says "You handled yourself magnificently baby doll. You are a real head turner. The press adored you and so did Julia. According to Poindexter they both have had their eyes on Eagle Point and you for years".

Kristin giggling replies "Julia speaks very highly of you Mark. And Scott too. It's a mom thing, she said she couldn't imagine being a single parent living at Eagle Point for all of these years by myself. She is sending me a wardrobe of designer clothes. Poor darling, you are going to have to take out and wine and dine me".

Mark says "That will be my pleasure Kristin. I know all of the best restaurants in Virginia Beach and will kidnap you and take you home with me" as he pulls his Mercedes into his driveway on the strand. Kristin says "Mark your house is georgous, I love the contemporary architecture. I haven't been to the beach in so long. The ocean is absolutely intoxicating". Mark kisses her and gets out of the car and opens her door holding her hand like a true gentlemen.

He picks her up in his arms and carries her through the front door using a remote key. He places her on her feet hugging her tightly kissing her. He puts both hands on her face and says "Welcome home baby doll". A large brown German Shepard dog runs up to them barking and licking Kristin's feet wagging his tail".

Kristin says "I didn't know that you had a dog, petting his head". Mark says "His name is Rex. I raised him from a puppy. He obviously loves you too". Mark takes her hand and leads her to the kitchen and gives Rex a bone out of a jar. Kristin says "Mark I just love this. The floor to ceiling windows are incredible. Everything here is masculine and perfectly clean. I love you too Rex" watching him eat his bone.

Mark picks Kristin up again and carries her to his bedroom. With a king sized platform bed and marine life wallpaper and a sea blue duvet set covering his bed. He has a sliding glass door that leads to a deck with a lounge chair set, colorful bougainvilla and hibiscus tree plants in pots and a telescope on a tripod.

Kristin says "Mark I am moving in with you. Forget historical Plantations". Mark French kisses her while massaging her back and thighs sliding his hand between her legs. Holding her close he rubs his crotch against her with desire. He turns her around and unzips her dress and lays it on a blue chair covered with a whale motif. He takes off his Tuxedo jacket as Kristin unbuttons his dress shirt, unties his bow tie and unzips his tuxedo pants. Mark lays his clothes on top of Kristin's dress and kicks off his shoes pulling down his socks and underwear. He gently lays Kristin in the middle of the bed and pulls down her garter belt, panties and thigh high stockings and throws them on the floor next to the bed.

Mark admiring her body buries his head in between her legs rubbing her navel kissing her inner thighs. Kristin grabs his shoulders caressing his muscles moaning in ectasy relishing in the pleasure. Arching her back she moans "ahh baby, so good" as she orgasms in delight. Mark kisses her tummy and her nipples and kisses her mouth and neck with a rock solid hard on. Kristin gently grabs his cock, stroking it while cupping his balls. She leans over and slides his dick in her mouth licking it and stroking him as he sighs in complete desire.

Mark can't wait anymore and climbs on top of Kristin entering her. He stares into her eyes French kissing her as he is moaning and makes love to her with a perfect rythum holding her. Kristin feeling him stroke her g spot moans and has mutliple orgasms over and over as Mark is about to climax turned on by her pure pleasure. Mark cums for at least two minutes in an explosion kissing her neck moaning louder than Kristin did. The couple hold each other stroking each other's bodies in complete satisfaction.

Mark kisses her and brushes his hand through her hair and whispers sweet nothings in her ear. They stare into each other's eyes and Kristin says "I am the luckiest girl in the world. That was beyond incredible darling. I am hopelessly in love with you Mark. You are my prince charming. Laying her head on his rock solid chest Mark replies "The passion and chemistry between us Kristin. I loved making love to you. And everything about you. I am still cuming doll. That is how much I loved it"

Kristin about to fall asleep sneaks into the bathroom, goes pee and uses a washcloth to wipe herself off. Washes her face with cleanser that she brought with her. Applies a tinted face cream, deoderant, eyebrow pencil and brushes her teeth. She walks back into Mark's bedroom drooling over his fit body. He hugs and kisses her and dissapears into his bathroom to pee and brush his teeth.

Kristin stares at the waves from the ocean rolling in on the sand as Mark puts his arm around her kissing her neck and says "I love you baby doll" takes her arm and leads her back to his bed. The couple hug and kiss caressing each other's bodies until Kristin falls asleep in Mark's arms feeling safe, loved and wanted. Mark completely relaxed holds Kristin like he never wants to let her go kissing her head and cheek holding her tight. Maybe he won't tell her that she is the best lover he has ever had; sure that she feels the same way and falls into a deep sleep.

Kristin and Mark sleep until 9:00am. Kristin kisses his face and rubs his body in complete lust over her lover. She freshens up in the bathroom and Mark does the same. Kristin watching the waves roll in feels Mark hug her from behind with a huge hard on he is sliding his cock in between her legs. Mark is hugging her caressing her nipples kissing the back of her neck. He picks her up and lays her in bed French kissing her rubbing her back and hips. He slides his hand in between her legs fingering her and feels her cum as she moans in two minutes. Kristin strokes his cock and licks the cum from it. Mark lays her on her side and slides his dick inside her resting his hand under her thigh. He picks up a rythum like making music. Kristin in ectasy has mutliple orgasims as Mark is fucking her kissing her neck in desire. He drives 'it home' moaning in pleasure hugging and kissing Kristin. Breathing in her ear "You are mine forever baby. I fucking loved that". The couple dozes off completely satisfied and sleeps until 11:11am.

Mark hugging and caressing Kristin's body whispers in her ear "Coffee baby doll?". Kristin climbs on top of him kissing him holding his hands staring into his eyes. "Of course darling" and goes into his bathroom to freshen up and put on her raspberry sundress. Licking the lip gloss on her lips admiring herself in the mirror finger combing her hair she heads to Mark's kitchen with Rex following her at her feet. Mark hugs her and pours her a cup of coffee and with a radiant manly smile on his face and asks "Cream and sugar doll?".

Kristin smiles at Mark giggling and says "Yes. Please darling. Again. And again. I am begging you for it. Mark your view is incredible. I love your kitchen and Rex" as she pet's the dogs head. Mark sits down at his kitchen bar and Kristin sits on his lap kissing him on the lips sipping her coffee.

Mark uses a remote control to stream last nights news on his plasma TV. Putting his arms around her kissing her as the news show plays. They show a video of Poindexter's bodyguard leading him and Julia in front of the camera and transitions to Mark and Scott with Kristin and Susan walking step by step arriving next to Poindexter. He makes his speech with the 'Fabulous Five' staring into the camera. Kristin flirts with the press and they follow them inside on the ship. The video continues with Poindexter's speech and zooms in on the architect's rendering of the restored Plantation. The camera pulls down to an aireal view of Eagle Point and then the group standing on the deck of the Buckaneer Pirate ship sailing by the Plantation.

Mark picks Kristin up and hugs her. He says twirling her around the room saying "Victory" kissing her on the lips. He fires up the griddle and cracks six eggs, and places six slices of bacon on the griddle. He says "Wheat toast doll?" and puts four slices of bread in the toaster. Grabing two plates as Kristin hugs him and kisses his shoulders he scrambles the eggs and turns over the bacon. Kristin is rubbing his ass kissing him on the neck while he cooks. Kristin butters the toast and sits down.

Mark serves her two eggs and the rest for himself with the bacon. He pours a glass of fresh squeezed orange juice to share kissing her cheek. The lovers eat breakfast smiling at each other thrilled with their intimacy, with Rex standing next to the table. The lovers finish their breakfast and Mark says "Can we go on a walk on the beach with Rex baby doll?" kissing her ear. Kristin says "I would really like that sweetheart".

Mark takes her hand and leads her out onto the sandy beach breathing in the warm salty air as Rex runs down the beach in front of them". Holding hands and stopping to hug and kiss watching the waves roll in. Kristin says "I didn't realize how much I missed the beach until now. Thanks darling" as she leans her head on his shoulder.

After their walk Mark takes Kristin back into his bedroom and pulls her dress down kissing her navel. He pulls off her dress and his shorts and leads Kristin into his shower kissing her on the lips. He turns on the hot water adjusting it perfectly. Grabs a washcloth and soaps Kristin's back, her arms and legs while he is kissing her. Kristin in absolute Heaven over the attention returns the favor to Mark admiring his fit body and muscles. The lovers step out of the shower and Mark hands her a bath towel and dries himself off and wraps the towel around his waist.

Laughing he says "I see you are pleased with my 'goods' darling". Smiling she kisses him and says "Mark how did you know? Ecstatic is a more appropriate word". She puts his hand over his heart and says "And this too handsome".

Kristin puts on her outfit. Does a quick makeup and clips her hair up the same way that she wore last night, brushes her teeth and puts on a berry colored lip gloss. Mark wears a pair of khaki pants and an indigo blue button up beach shirt with pictures of surfboards on it and a pair of brown loafers with a matching belt.

He smiles at Kristin's alluring feminity and says "I love the way your dress Kristin. And your hair up". He picks her up twirling her around hugging her and kissing her neck. He asks "Do you want to see my surfboard collection?". Kristin giggling stares into Mark's peircing baby blue eyes and replies "Show me the way darling. I love your shirt too".

Mark takes her hand and leads her to the living room which has floor to ceiling windows decorated with a brown leather couch, love seat and two pub chairs. A blue and cream striped room sized rattan rug with matching pillows on the couches. Several palm trees in sapphire blue pots on other side of the fireplace with a gas insert log. And picures of famous surfers and marine life on the walls. Kristin sees four surfboards standing upright against the wall.

She says "Mark they are absolutely beautiful. Which one is you favorite sweetie?". Mark rubs a blue, and white striped board and says "This one. She is an 8' Wavestorm Classic. I bought her in California. She is my trusty stead and cost me $7,500. And this neon orange one is called 'the Wingnut' and is meant for speed. And this cool wooden board is a 'Classic Waikiki'. This lime green one with a shark on it is a 'Channel Islands Rocket' which I use when the surf is rough. Rex sits on the beach and watches me surf and I usually grab a neighbor to go in the water with me too".

Kristin says "Do you want to honeymoon in Haleiwa and meet my dad? I am sure I can talk him into giving you one of his $22,000 hollow wooden surfboards as a wedding present. You two can go surfing at Waimea Bay if you have enough energy after screwing me all night and morning" grabbing his ass and kissing him flirtatiously.

Mark replies "Anything you want hot stuff. I have never been to Oahu. Do you want to see my office baby doll?" French kissing her, rubbing her hips and hugging her. Kristin embraces Mark never wanting to let go. She replies "Absolutely. I would love too. I used to fly to Oahu once a month on Hawaiian Airlines. Rountrip from LAX was only $200.00. I would spend two or three days there and miss my horse and come back to Los Angeles. The Turtle Bay Resort is beautiful. And the botanical gardens".

Mark leads her down a hallway holding her hand smiling affectionately at her. He opens his office door which has walnut paneling, built in walnut floor to ceiling file cabinets, four computer systems, a large screen TV, cream velour sofas, a huge built in walnut desk and bookcases. There are blown up pictures all over the walls of his projects. And a mini refrigerator.

Mark picks Kristin up and throws her on the couch and lies on top of her kissing her and hugging her. He whispers in her ear "You are so beautiful Kristin. I love your voice. And everything about you. I just can't get enough of you". Kristin smiles at him and says "You just made a slogan darling. 'I just can't get enough'. That is a good thing". Kissing him back and rubbing his muscular arms thinking she is going to have another orgasm.

After an hour of making out Mark clears his throat and takes her to his bookcases and pulls out dozens of folders showing her his accomplishments in deep pride. Kristin looks at the pictures of his work thoroughly impressed with admiration. She says "Mark you are truly gifted. And a workaholic. I can't tell you how impressed I am with your work. No wonder Poindexter is hot after you. You should be so proud of yourself darling. You must have an innate gift. Honestly my greatest ambition in life was to horse show and be a house wife. I perservered in the mortgage industry just to raise my kids and exposed them to as many enrichment activities as I could. I worked seven days a week and just pretty much got lucky. My clients gave me so many referrals I had to hire an assistant".

Mark shows her the file of the Castle in England. Kristin looks at the restoration and says "I hope you can take me there one day. I love the quaint churches in the British countryside and they have Indian restaurants to die for". Mark gently nibbles her ear lobe rubbing her ass.

Mark announces "Baby doll I have a business meeting at 9:30am in Roanoke tomorrow morning-it is a huge commercial historical project downtown for the City of Roanoke. I am so tempted to take you back to bed and make love to you again. I want to take you to this place called Simply Blues. It is a five star restaurant with live jazz music in a penthouse suite overlooking the ocean right after the Virginia Beach tunnel. I am going to do my best to have you spend every weekend with me for the mean time. I just need you Kristin. And want to be with you as much as I can". Kristin laying her head on his shoulder says "I feel the same way Mark. And I would very much love that sugar. Thank you for everything Mark".

He walks her to his bedroom with Rex following her in delight. She puts her things back in the overnight bag and the Tiffany diamond necklace back in the box. Petting Rex who is whimpering knowing that she is leaving. She freshens up, missing her horses but really does not want to leave. Taking a deep breath she stares into Mark's eyes like she is connecting with his soul. He kisses her on her head and she naughtily massages 'his package' and he walks her out to his Mercedes.

Mark opens her car door like a true gentlemen and fastens her seat belt for her. Closes her door and climbs in the driver's seat holding her thigh. He speeds off through the tunnel exiting on Ocean Drive and pulls up to a modern high rise building and stops at the valet parking.

He puts his arm around Kristin and walks her to the elevator kissing her cheek. The two enter the elevator and hug each other not wanting the weekend to end. Mark presses the penthouse button. As they arrive at the top and the doors open to a beautifully furnished red velvet wallpaper room with live jazz music playing. The hostess Ana eyes Kristin and Mark and leads them to a booth with a glass window overlooking the ocean smiling at the couple.

Mark puts his arm around her reading the menu sitting very close to her. Kristin with her hand on his thigh says "I love this place Mark. Reminds me of a special place that I used to frequent in Santa Monica. I have always enjoyed jazz music. Thank you darling" and kisses his cheek. She says "Order anything vegetarian for me sweetie. This is a real treat. And so are you".

Mark kisses her lovingly enjoying her company. A waiter shows up placing dinner rolls and butter on a plater in front of them and says "Hello. I am Francis your server. What can I get you to drink?". Mark looks at Kristin and replies "A bottle of chardonney. And two ice waters with lemon please".

Kristin butters two rolls and places one on Mark's plate and devours hers. Mark says "I love that Kristin. Lick it off of your lips. It just turns me on" sliding his hand up her thigh under her dinner napkin. Kristin smiles flirtatiously at him and says "Sex makes me hungry".

Francis returns with a bottle of wine and pours one sip in Mark's glass. Francis stands there as Mark takes a sip and nods his head. He fills both parties wine glasses and asks "Are you ready to order sir?" Mark eying Kristin replies "Yes. I will have the Thai curry chicken with pineapple. My lady will have the vegan pad Thai noodles with cashew sauce. And the vegetarian dim sum appetizer to start please. And a side of the ginger carrot salad to share. Thank you sir".

Mark picks up his wine glass and says "Here is to us baby doll. Kristin you are sophisticated, amazing and the hottest sex bunny I have ever come across. And I love you". Kristin replies "Mark. I am very much in love with you. You are my hero. I adore you in so may ways. Not just for your sucess and connections and the hot sex. Or your incredible body. It is just you. And me. And everthing about you" staring into his eyes. She starts laughing as Mark is rubbing her thighs deciding just to trust him and enjoy the ride.

Francis brings their salad and appetizer with two pairs of chop sticks. The couple hug and kiss and Kristin picks up her chopsticks and expertly pierces a dim sum and dips it in the sauce and places it in Mark's mouth. And another one for herself. She says "This is delicious. Excellent choice darling and serves them both another one as Mark is stroking her inner thigh.

The manager of the restaurant walks over to their table smiling and says "My name is David. I saw the two of you on the news last night. And again this morning. You also made the front page of The Virginia Times Newspaper. Congratulations and enjoy your dinner". Mark says "Thank you David. The food is excellent". David nods his head and walks off.

Kristin giggling says "We are officialy celebraties darling. We will have to stop and buy a dozen newspapers as collector's items". Mark smiles at her and says "Kristin I am going to have to buy you a diamond engagement ring to fend off all of the men out there who a drooling over you. Just wait until we hit the cover of Forbes and the other magazines. The press will go absolutely insane wanting to do more interviews. And talk shows". Kristin gives Mark her TV smile giggling and "If you are trying to sweep my of my feet darling you are doing an excellent job" and kisses him on the lips.

Francis returns with their dinner and salad. He refills their wine glasses and Mark says "Thank you Francis" now leave us alone. Kristin says "Ohh Mark this smells so good I love the smell of ginger". She picks up a some of the carrot ginger salad with her chopsticks and places it in Mark's mouth and another for herself.

Mark says "You are more than welcome to lick the ginger off of my lips doll". Kristin serves him another bite and kisses him and seductively licks his lips staring into his blue eyes. She giggles and starts on her pad thai. Kristin daintily places the chopsticks in her mount and moans out loud and says "Baby this is delicious. Do you want to try a bite?" and serves him a taste. Mark whispers in her ear "Kristin if you do that again I am going to have to take you home and give it to you again. That is really good". Kristin giggles and replies "Mark you are making me wet" and finishes off her entire dinner as does Mark.

Francis returns to take their plates and recites the dessert menu. Mark orders the apple tart with vanilla ice cream. Francis refills their wine glasses and asks "Would you care for coffee?". Mark says "We are good thank you" and sips his wine. Francis returns with their dessert and Mark and Kristin devour the tart and ice cream. Mark says "That was excellent. I really enjoy your company Kristin. I haven't had this in so long. I have been waiting for years for Poindexter to close the deal on Eagle Point. That is how long I have watching you Kristin".

Kristin replies "I have been waiting patiently for you too Mark. Call it one of those 'divine timing' things. I will have to learn to make apple tart from scratch for you honey. And I can't imagine life without you Mark". Mark hugs her and kisses her cheek. Francis arrives with the bill and Mark pulls out his credit card. The new found lovers romanticly watching the waves crash on the ocean listening to the jazz music stand up and Mark puts his arms around her swaying to the music. He signs the check and holds her by the hand leading her to the elevator.

Mark says "I am going to have to take you dancing Kristin. You are an incredibly sensual woman". Kristin says "Thank you Mark. I would love that. And thank you very much for dinner" as she grabs his firm ass smiling up at him. Mark responds as the elevator door opens "It is all my pleasure. Get used to it Kristin. And I am going to pleasure you over and over and over again". He kisses her gently on the lips as the valet pulls up Mark's Mercedes. Mark opens the door for her and says "My lady" helping her into the car brushing against her breasts as he fastens the seat belt for her.

Mark gets into the driver's seat tipping the valet a $20 and heads off to the freeway. Kristin says "I wonder how Susan fared with Scott this weekend" laughing out loud. Mark holding her thigh says "Kristin I have completely forgetton about everyone and everthing while you were with me this weekend. I bet they were naughty. Susan looked like she lightened up after the boat ride. I am going to pull over at 7-Eleven and buy some newspapers" and turns towards the Highway 17 exit towards Gloucester. Kristin looking up at Mark says "I know darling. Back to reality. Or better the unreality of Eagle Point Plantation. Susan and I are having coffee tomorrow. I will get the steamy details".

Mark pulls in front of the store, kisses Kristin and says "Stay here woman. Be right back". He walks into the store and buys every Virginia Times newspaper in the turn style and walks back to the car placing the stack of newspapers in the back seat, grabs one getting into the driver's seat and shows the front page to Kristin with the picture of the 'Fabulous Five' standing in front of the Pirate ship in front of the journalists and news reporters.

The headline reads "Eagle Point Plantation-Criss Cross Properties LLC and William Poindexter's latest acquisition". Kristin says "I am going to have to frame this one. You are drop dead georgous Mark. We are a hot couple". Mark says "Sizzling Kristin. Your composure in front of the camera is a natural. Frame one for me too doll to hang in my office".

Kristin lays her head on his shoulder as he pulls down the driveway to the kitchen entrance. Mark looks at the huge mansion and then at Kristin and says "Baby doll I worry about you here by yourself. Not only about the electrical problems and the hurricanes. All creeps have to do is Google this place and to find you. I am going to talk to Poindexter about installing an electric gate at the entrance with a keyed in passcode. And security cameras" cupping her face kissing her and rubbing the back of her neck.

Kristin says "Okay darling. I have help from above and am just used to living here in isolation. I have never locked the doors and worry more about my horses in that barn with an electrical fire. I am going to miss you sugar".

Guadalupe walks out to the car and says "Hi Mark and Kristin. We saw you on television last night and this morning. You both looked radiant. Ryan was very nice and I love your daughter Kristin. We spoiled the horses and cleaned the house. I am going to drive home before it gets too late. See you soon" and walks to her car and heads down the driveway.

Mark opens Kristin's door, carry's her bags and walks her inside the massive rambling mansion holding her hand. He pulls her in his arms holding her tight kissing her neck sighing. He takes his fingers under her chin and lifts her head up staring into her eyes "Kristin you are mine. All mine. Now and forever. You and me" and French kisses her. Kristin relaxing in his arms, intuitively knowing with all of her heart that Mark is genuine and a keeper.

Ashley and Danny walk into the kitchen. Ashley clears her throat and says "Hi Mom. And you must be Mark. Are you a GQ model? I love your dress mom. You look so happy. You two make a flaming hot couple. I loved watching you on the news last night. And noticed you were on the front page of the Virginia Times Newspaper today. Take good care of her Mark-my mom has been through living hell with a narcissist and deserves to be treated like a queen. Cool tattoo by the way".

Mark looks at Ashley and kisses her hand and shakes Danny's hand and says "I love your tattoo too Ashley. Is that a black widow protecting you from harm?. And I am going to give your mother everything she ever wanted in life. And more. And spoil her rotten. For the rest of her life. You will have to be a flower girl at our wedding. Your mom speaks very highly of you both. Very nice to meet you sweetie".

Ashley and Danny kiss Kristin on the cheek and Danny says "We have to run back to Richmond and close down the Grandin Road. The manager had to leave for an emergency. We adore Guadalupe too. You should do this more often Kristin. Nice to meet you Mark. See you guys soon" as the kids run out the door.

Kristin and Mark start laughing and embrace each other never wanting to let go. Mark rubbing Kristin's ass kisses her on top of her head wafting in her scent. And part of her soul within him. Bonding. Unconditionally. For eternity.

Mark says "Kristin you are a great mother. Both of your kids love you. I have to look at my schedule next week. I think Poindexter is going to have another press conference at Eagle Point after sending an army of gardners here this week. Just take Susan to town and get a pedicure and go shopping so you don't have to listen to the lawn mowers or smell the pollen. He may orchestrate another business luncheon. I am planning on picking you up on Saturday after I go surfing. I want you to spend the weekend with me again and take you out to dinner and spend more time with you".

Kristin teary eyed says "Mark I would love that. That is so sweet and protective of you. I haven't had this in ages. I will miss you terribly. You have no idea how grateful I am Mark for you and everything you do. And it just really fucking turns me on too". The couple hug for the longest time and Mark kisses her and rubs her shoulders and back as Kristin does the same to Mark.

Mark whispers in her ear "Anticipation darling. And I love everything about you Kristin and never stop thinking about you. I will call you tomorrow after I get off of work. If a news reporter shows up just say 'contact Mr. Poindexter's press secretary'. And do not let anyone in the house. And please lock the kitchen door tonight. And every night from now on. You are completely helpless here by yourself".

Kristin replies staring into his blue eyes "Yes master. And I am not helpless anymore. I have you. And I would love to spend the weekend with you. That really gives me something to look forward to Mark. Sorry I am just an emotional sentimental. And I need you. Maybe I can watch you surf one day soon. If you have enough energy after making love to me all day. Tell Rex I miss him too. Drive safe my darling. And thanks again for everthing Mark. Sweet dreams baby" as she hugs him and kisses him again.

Mark not wanting to let go or leave says "I will see you again before you know it. I will miss you too doll. Just get some rest and just relax and ride your horses this week and hang out with Susan". He kisses her again and takes a deep breath and walks to his Mercedes staring at Kristin on the kitchen landing watching her intently as she waves goodbye blowing him a kiss. Kristin retreats back into the silent lonely house grateful for Mark on cloud nine.

Kristin walks down the long hallway to the East Wing. Hangs up her evening gown and dress. Changes into a yellow romper and places the diamond necklace and tennis bracelet that Mark gave her on her vanity. Thinking is all real? Glad that Ryan is asleep. She walks to the barn to visit with her horses stargazing at the constellations. She says out loud "I love you Archangel Saint Michael. And you to my guides. All of the years of torture were worth it. Gratitude. Amen. Jesus".

The stable is as immaculate as the house. Guadalupe and the kids must have worked all day. She pets Zeus and Coconut feeding them peppermints and apples. Kristin gives them a scoop of oat cubes, turns off the lights and walks back home. Staring at the planet Arcturus above the Plantation in wonder of the Universe.

And the omnipresence and omniscience of God. In divine peace Kristin decides to just go to sleep wanting to smell Mark on her all night. She texts Susan "Whirlwind. Fairytale. Heaven. Hopelessly in love. See you tomorrow". Kristin climbs in bed and falls into a deep sleep in an instant.

Waking up to the smell of Mark still on her. Kristin actually smiles at what life is bringing her. Finally. Thinking about Mark. And how he makes her feel. And who he is inside. The blatent acts of kindness from him. The smiles he puts on her face. His protectiveness and nurturing. His fondness for her sexuality. Letting her be herself. His generosity. Understanding of her fucking life with a special kid. And Poindexter taking her under his wing.

With her long blonde hair tousled with no makeup on, Kristin walks to the bride's mirror in the foyer. She opens her short pink silk bathrobe. Poses seductively and snaps some photos. She sends the best one to Mark in a text with a note 'Enjoying the scent of you still all over me. And the part of your soul that is inside me. Thinking about you hot stuff".

Blushing as Kristin knows that Mark is at work and just read her message turns on the coffee pot. Throws her robe in the washer and puts on a pair of leggings and her Criss Cross Properties LLC windbreaker over a t shirt and the ball cap. Glad that Ryan is at work. She eats an entire pint of raspberries, a banana and a granola bar. With no agenda she slips on a pair of tennis shoes and walks down the path to the barn.

Zeus and Coconut whinny at her in delight. Kristin stares up 'Beyond the Veil' at the Heavens. And the many realms above planet Earth. Connecting with the divine energy. That she has been blessed with. Listening to 'A flock of sheep baaing' that does not exist in her 'Paradise City'.

At Eagle Point Plantation. In a small rural town called Gloucester. Thinking to herself 'Take me home to that very last city'. Where would that be? The Lost City of Atlantis? Hollywood with the pretty people?

Kristin listening to 'Sweet Child O'Mine" on YouTube watching herself in music video at the Troubador on Hollywood Boulevard with Guns and Roses before they were discovered just laughs. And the Angels will make it all right.

Her own personal 'Paradise' is here with Mark. With his love. And the synergy of the 'Fabulous Five'. Covers of magazines?. Cool. Love that. Bring it on. I see it all of the fucking time. Just enjoy it Kristin tells herself. Talk shows? Fuck yeah. I love that. With a sophisticated calm charm about herself, Kristin will take all of the press up to the 'Highway to Heaven". Letting them stay at the Hotel California. With the bright spirit lights encandesing them. With bottles of pink champagne on ice. Laughing to herself as she listens to Guns and Roses "Mother Fuckin Jive Talker" song about Warren Beaty.

'Harmony'

Kristin feeds the horses breakfast and turns them out in the pond field and does her chores. Listening to the songbirds, admiring the Blue Herons standing around the pond at peace with the horses with the crazy peacocks scattered around the pasture fanning their feathers still in mating season. Zeus and Coconut are 'tree hugging' itching their necks and rumps on the massive hundred year old Ash trees while watching the sailboats drift down the river in the breeze.

Susan arrives at the barn to chat with Kristin. Susan absolutely glowing says "Hi Kristin. Tell me everything. I know you were bad. You sure look happy. Scott is such an incredible man and lover. A true gentleman. Isn't that great that Mark's maid can stay here with Ryan? You really need that break Kristin. Do it as often as you can. I can always help with the horses. You need a break from all of that work too".

Kristin laughs and says "Yes I know. And I will Mark carried me through the threshold of his front door like 'Romeo and Juliet'. I love his house. It is contemporary style with floor to ceiling glass windows right on the beach. Obviously professionally decorated. He has a German Shepard named Rex. He carried me straight to the bedroom. We made out and did the oral sex thing and then we had wild passionate steamy sex. I had multiple orgasims. Mark is the best lover I have ever had. And so loving and kind. We did it again in the morning and it was even better than the night before. He made me breakfast. Afterwards he took me for a walk on the beach with Rex. Mark showed me his surfboard collection, his office and pictures of his work portfolio. He took me out to dinner at a fancy jazz club called Simply Blues at a penthouse high rise building on the beach".

Susan looks at Kristin laughing and says "That sounds lovely just like pure chivalry. We both got lucky Kristin. They are both so sophisticated and charming. I loved the newspaper article. I can't wait to see the magazine covers. Scott told me Poindexter loves press-he is going to play this thing with Eagle Point to the limit. One of the best things about it is that both Mark and Scott have us both by their sides in the photos from the press. That really means alot to me. Trust and integrity is very important to me in a relationship. Scott is taking me out again on Saturday night".

Kristin smiles at Susan replying "Yes Susan. We are both damaged goods scared for life from toxic relationships. Mark invited me over again on Saturday. He is going to pick me up and take me out to dinner. He also said that Poindexter may do another press thing at Eagle Point or a luncheon. His crew of landscapers should be here any minute. Spa treatment again on Friday? Can I come over later and go for a swim so I don't have to listen to the lawn mowers?".

Susan says "Of course you can. Here they come now. Looks like a dozen trucks with trailers full of equipment. Just text me when you are on your way. I will go for a swim with you. Scott and I went swimming after we came over and checked on the horses. I made him eggs benedict for breakfast. Scott grilled us Halibut for lunch. It's like we are already a couple. I am absolutely on cloud nine. Just text me when you are on your way. I will either be in my garden or in the chicken coop. Love you". Kristin gives Susan a hug goodbye.

Kristin opens the pasture gate and calls to the horses before the gardeners unload their equipment. The horses trot into the barn into their stalls. Kristin turns on all of the ceiling fans and sprays them with fly spray, brushing their hair coats. She waves at the army of landscapers in complete gratitude for Poindexter and walks back home before they start their zero turn lawnmowers and weedeaters. She makes it back home just in time as dozens of men start their equipment and chainsaws trimming the Holly Berry and Crype Myrtal trees.

Kristin scrambles two eggs, toasts an English muffin. Eats breakfast watching the crew who are all wearing Criss Cross Properties LLC t shirts and matching ball caps. Thinking to herself 'Well fucking I love this. Thanks be to you God'. She walks down to the East Wing, pulling out a hot pink one piece bathing suit. She puts on the bathing suit and then a floor length marine blue gauze cover up with hot pink Hibiscus flowers on it. Grabs a towel and a can of Hawaiian Tropics SPF 150 sunscreen, a pair of flip flops, grabs her purse and runs out the door.

She texts Susan "On my way. There is a literal army of gardners here".

Kristin drives down to Susan's and parks in front of her chicken coop. Susan is standing there feeding her beloved chickens mealy worms off in LaLa land. Kristin says 'Susan your chickens are obese. And so is your horse. Your vegetable garden looks like the Garden of Eden. I am really hot. Can I go dive in your pool?". Susan laughs and says "I am right behind you. There is literally zero ozone left on Earth. I just stay in the AC. Let's go!".

The ladies walk to Susan's pool. Throw their clothes on a lounge chair and dive into the pool. Kristin swims three laps back and forth at the bottom of the pool before coming up for air. Kristin says "Thanks sweetie. This feels so good. The gardner's that Poindexter sent are ripping the place to shreds. The pollen is horrifying. Swimming is really great for your inner thighs and stomach muscles. Where are you and Scott going for dinner Saturday?".

Susan smiling at Kristin replies "I love to swim too. Water is so soothing and therapeutic. I think I will ask Scott to take me to the Mobjack Tavern. They have a live band and really great seafood, and it's only ten minutes from us. I want to do a candle light dessert with champagne on my deck afterwards and just hold hands and talk. Before we retreat into my love chambers of course", laughing out loud.

Kristin giggling says "Why Susan. You have officially graduated to a sex kitten seducing your man. I love it!. I am going to let Mark plan everything. Maybe I will wear that beautiful floor length backless white lycra dress with sequins around the cowl neck that Alice gave me. He loves a submissive woman. Susan, this whole thing is so surreal. And erethral. I have this deepest soul connection with him. We are just at such ease with each other. He makes me laugh. And then I want to cry from his touch that makes me feel so beautiful. After all of that abuse I had. He adores you too".

Susan says "You deserve that Kristin. Plus he is a true gentlemen. I need to get out of the sun. The gardners are driving down your driveway. Ryan should be home from work soon. Call me tomorrow. I have another dentist appointment. I have this dire need to just call Scott tonight. I think I am going to turn on a movie and take a nap when I get home".

Kristin replies "Sounds good to me. Talk to you soon sweetie. Come over tomorrow if you want to go jumping with me" as she climbs out of the pool and wraps the towel around her drying off. Kristin puts her sundress back on to cover up her skin and drives back home.

Thrilled with a manicured farm, Kristin couldn't believe how much work the crew did today. Watching the Transit bus bring Ryan home from work she walks into the kitchen. Grabs a bag of coconut beer battered fried shrimp and curly fries from the freezer and places the food on a baking sheet and puts it in the oven for him. She walks into her bedroom and pulls off her wet bathing suit, changing into a dry cream colored cotton sweatsuit. Placing her clothes into the washer she pulls Ryan's dinner out of the oven and serves him dinner in the dining room. Ryan says "Thanks mom. I am so tired. I am going to bed early. Love you". Kristin smiles at him and returns to the kitchen.

Kristin sees the clock flashing 5:55 as Mark is calling her. She answers her cell projecting her voice "How art though Romeo? Your damsel in distress is so happy to hear from you". Mark starts laughing and says "Kristin. You are the light of my life. I loved your picture this morning. I have been thinking about you all day. I have officially made you my sex bunny". Kristin giggles and says "Mark. Are you courting me sweetheart? You drive me crazy with desire. In every way. And are a true gentlemen. How was your day?".

Mark replies "Happy. After spending the weekend with you and making love to you. Kristin you are mine. Now and forever. Always. Just us. The closeness we share I never imagined could be so good. I am going to have to sweep you off of your feet".

Kristin smiling says "You are doing an excellent job Mark. You are the best thing that ever happened in my life. I can't wait for you to hold me. And carry me into your bedroom and undress me. I absolutely adore you sugar. Keep pouring it on Mark. I already fell for you. I am just really enjoying everything. You are turning me on".

Mark in his stud voice says "Kristin that is my pleasure. You are all pleasure. I love everthing about you. I hear Poindexter is going to do a press conference this Wednesday at Eagle Point he just hasn't announced it yet. Get some rest baby doll. Dress very sophisticated with your hair up and with the diamonds I gave you. I will be by your side. Do nothing but rest and think about me Kristin. I have reports to do tonight. See you Wednesday".

Kristin says "I never stop thinking about you Mark ever. Your wish is my command Captain. I will have to seductively think of new ways to pleasure you. In every way. Love you too handsome. I can't wait to see you. Sweet dreams baby".

Kristin walks to the barn and feeds both horses carrots. Admiring thir natural beauty and gleaming gold hair coats. She says out loud "You are so beautiful. And sanctified by God. You have the most beautiful souls. I adore you babies". As the horses gleam at her pure unconditional love for them.

Craving attention from their 'Mom". Kristin stands in the doorway, listening to the 'Mission Bell'. She takes Zeus out first and grooms him in the cross ties. Leads him to the arena and walks around in figure eights singing as loud as she can soothing their minds. She walks Zeus back into the barn. Hoses him off with hot water and puts him to bed. She does the same to Coconut. Feeds them sweet feed and heads home to crash dreaming about seeing Mark again on Wednesday.

With Ryan asleep already Kristin watches a few Yellowstone reruns thinking about Mark. Reflecting when she worked at Warner Bros and went to Taco Bell with her co-worker Linda for lunch. They stood behind Kevin Costner in line. Poor Kevin was completely ambushed by fans wanting autographs and they had to shut the restaurant down. Completey relaxed and thrilled with the turn of events with her life heads to the foyer and sits at the piano playing the Beatles 'Live and let Die'. Metaphorically the old Kristin died and has been rebirthed. All of a sudden wondering what was up in the 'Divine World of the Universe' she planned on talking to Ryan about it tomorrow before he goes to his volunteer job and heads off to bed.

Par for the course Ryan is up at 7:00am blasting the Jetsons cartoons in the kitchen. Kristin getting dressed walks down the hallway and says "Ryan can you please turn that down" noticing two empty Dr Pepper cans sitting on the kitchen counter. Ryan replies "Oh. Sorry mom. You scared me". Kristin replies 'Let me guess. Pop Tarts for breakfast? Here at least eat a banana. No, have two. Are you going to Cook Out for lunch with your friends today? How are things going up in the

Universe?".

Ryan replies "Yeah Cook Out. Sounds good. The Artcturians found this really cool portal in the Milky Way that takes you ten million light years away faster than the speed of light. There are hundreds of parallel galaxies in the Universe. We have been busy exploring the different galaxies and planets".

Kristin hands Ryan a $20 bill and says "Sounds like just fucking out of this world Ryan. The hidden mysteries of the Creator of the Universe. Glory to you God. Amen. Here is the Transit bus. Have a great day. Love you. Take a video for me next time you go galaxy hopping". Ryan waves goodbye and runs out the door.

Wow Kristin thinks to herself. She pulls out her Cuisinart blender and makes herself a fresh fruit smoothie with bananas, strawberries, vanilla greek yogurt, adding two tablespoons of flax seed and chia. Pours it into a cup with a lid and heads off to the barn. Sipping her drink she tells herself do this more often. She feeds the horses breakfast and gets a text from Susan "Is 11:00am okay to come over to ride?". Kristin texts back "Perfect. See you then". She feeds the horses and turns them out in the field with the pond while she cleans the barn.

Noticing a call from April, Kristin answers the phone "Eagle Point Plantation. Kristin speaking. How may I help you?". April laughs and says "Kristin you are just a natural. Mr. Poindexter is sending a maid service to the Plantation at 1:00pm today along with a window cleaning service. He has scheduled a press conference tomorrow, Wednesday, at 11:00am. Then he is taking the entire group out to lunch at the Ivy afterwards. It is coat and tie. He wanted me to tell you that there will be a security guard at the main entrance of Eagle Point starting today. Should any of the press try to approach you before then contact me immediately". Kristin smiles and says "Wonderful. Thank you so much April. Very nice talking to you again. Take care". Kristin screams out loud "Yesss!" like a little kid.

Susan drives her ATV up to the barn smiling. She says "Kristin did you hear the news? We get to go to the Ivy for lunch tomorrow. I have always wanted to go there. And we get to see Scott and Mark again!". Kristin says "I just off the phone with April. Shit Poindexter is the master orchestrater of our love lives. Do you want to go through my clothes after we go riding? Poindexter sent a maid service and window washers that will be here at 1:00pm. Can you believe how great the place looks after the army of landscapers were here?".

Susan says "Yes. Please. I would love that". Susan walks over to the pasture gate. Zeus and Coconut are standing with there heads hanging over the gate looking forward to a ride. Kristin puts a halter on both horses and she leads Zeus as Susan leads Coconut into the cross ties. The ladies change into their Dehner show boots and Tailored Sportmans britches and grab their Nelson Pessoa jumping saddles, the horses bridles and saddle pads placing the equipment on the saddle racks. Kristin grooming Zeus says "Mark told me last night to dress very sophisticated tomorrow. And to wear the Tiffany diamonds that he gave me. This must be a big one coming up. I just can't get enough of this".

Susan laughing says "After all of these years in isolation and loneliness Kristin, we both deserve it. The place looks beautiful. You need a break from cleaning that mansion too. I think we both will get used to all the glamour. And Poindexter's parties. Maybe next week we can go on a double date. I want to see Scott's house. I don't think I can play basketball but I will try" as she saddles and bridles Coconut.

Kristin leads Zeus into the indoor arena with Susan following, pulls her stirrups down and vaults onto Zeus's back. Susan mounts Coconut petting his neck. Kristin says "Thanks Susan. I am so sick of cleaning that house by myself. You and Coconut are making a great team. One day we can switch horses. I haven't played basketball since elementary school. I am horrible at tennis too. Zero hand eye coordination. The guys will have a great time laughing at us I bet".

Kristin nudges Zeus into a trot posting around the arena. She halts him and switches directions collecting him into a sitting trot. Susan laughing says "I was awarded a tennis scholarship in high school that paid for my BA degree. It was a country club lifestyle, traveling around to tennis tournaments. Then I went to law school and had to work two jobs to pay just for law books. My parents paid for my rent. The fondness of memories".

Kristin laughs "Same with the horse show world" and nudges Zeus with her outside leg into a canter. She canters several laps and then steers him across the diagonal with a flying lead change. Kristin let's the horses walk a few laps to catch their breath.

Kristin says "Let's trot the gymnastic a few times. After that we will canter the gate, do a turn back to the stone wall, the outside line in five strides and end up over the liverpool. Okay?" Susan petting Coconut's neck picks up her reins and says "I will play follow the leader. We are ready". Kristin picks up the trot and jumps the double X with ground lines back and forth three times. She picks up the canter and heads towards the gate jump, turns back to the right on the rail steering Zeus to the stone wall, down the line and gallops towards the liverpool which Zeus jumps four feet high over, landing with a buck.

Kristin laughing pets him, looking over her shoulder to make sure Susan is still on. Susan giggling says "That was a blast. How can you stay on when he bucks like that? Coconut is so smooth and comfortable. I can tell the horses love watching each other too". The ladies cool the horses out at a walk chit chatting. Walk back into the show barn and dismount smiling at each other. They untack the horses, put their equipment away in the tack room admiring the manicured lawn. Susan hoses the horses off with hot water while Kristin fills up their feed buckets. The ladies put the horses away and change their clothes.

Kristin asks Susan watching a fleet of Criss Cross Properties LLC Mercedes van's heading down the driveway "Can you help me give the workers a quick tour? Then we can go clothes shopping in my dressing room".

Susan says "Yes. Let's go. I see a florist van too". Kristin laughing says "Follow me in your ATV. I am really going to get used to this. Thanks Sweetie". The ladies drive their Kabota ATV's back to the house as the workers park their Mercedes van's on the front lawn. Kristin and Susan noticing every person is wearing a Criss Cross Properties LLC uniform and baseball hat look at each other cracking up. Several of the vans have trailers with scissor lift's in them to wash the windows.

Kristin waits until the entire crew with their equipment are standing in front of the kitchen. Smiling at the crew she announces "Welcome to Eagle Point Plantation. My name is Kristin and this is my associate Susan. We will both take you on a tour of the mansion to show you the layout. Some of the plumbing and electrical outlets are non functional. Thank you for your help!". The leader of the group wearing a name plate 'Saul' says "Muchas gracias senorita". Kristin leads the group through the massive Plantation and says "Please let me know if you have any questions" and heads to the main entrance where the florist truck has parked.

Kristin opens the front door and says "My name is Kristin. Welcome to Eagle Point Plantation". The four stout men climb out of the florist van with the logo 'Flowers Equal Peace'. The head florist comes to shake her hand and says "My name is Jose. We are here to decorate the front of the house and main entrance with elaborate floral arrangements, red geraniums and 24 hanging baskets of Boston ferns along the front porch for Mr. Poindexter. Very nice to meet you. The mansion is beautiful, as well as the water view". Kristin replies "Thank you so much Jose. Let me know if you need anything. Have a blessed day".

Kristin and Susan, laughing, give each other that look like 'How did we ever survive our pathetic boring lives before this' smile at each other and walk down to the East Wing to Kristin's dressing room to check out her wardrobe. Susan goes through the wardrobe closets holding the dresses, evening gowns and business suits one after the other in front of the mirror.

Kristin says "The sleevless ivory linen dress with the the beaded pearls around the neck and on the trim looks great with your hair. Alice bought it at Saks Fifth Avenue in New York. The fucking price tag is $5,000". Susan holds up a pale pink, ankle length formal business dress with a delicate rhinestone pattern and ruffled cap sleeves in front of Kristin.

Susan takes a pair of ivory high heeled shoes and says "Do this one. With the diamond necklace and your hair up with a few blonde curls to highlight your cheecks. Very sopshisticated and demure. And professionally sexy. I am going to take the ivory linen dress. And wear my hair up too".

The girls giggling take the clothes and walk down the hallway watching the group of cleaners listening to their Iphones as they clean. Kristin hangs her outfit up in her bedroom and follows Susan to the kitchen.

Susan says "Look at all of those beautiful flowers. I wonder how many newscasters are going to be here tomorrow. I have to go home and take care of Goldilocks and my chickens. See you around 10:30am tomorrow. Love you sweetie". Kristin waves goodbye, grabs a container of hummus, sliced Cracker Barrel Wisconson cheese out of the fridge and some crackers. Snacking away Kristin sees Mark's caller ID pop up on her phone at approximately 5:55pm.

Kristin answers the phone "Darling. My hero. Where have you been all of my life? I am so excited to see you tomorrow!". Mark laughs loving Kristin's enthusiam says "Baby doll. It has only been two days too long. Poindexter is absolutely infatuated with Eagle Point. WSET, ABC 7, CNBC Channel 4 and dozens of magazines are going to be at the news conference tomorrow. I know you are absolutely eating this up. And I can't wait to eat you this weekend Kristin. You taste like honey. Just hearing your sweet innocent voice gives me a hard on".

Kristin smug with desire replies "That is my job darling. To whissper sweet nothings in your ear. And to put a smile on your face. I am pleased that Poindexter is going the mile. He sent an army of maids and window cleaners here today, along with a florist. Susan and I went jumping together. I have decided to wear pale pink tomorrow. It is the hottest innocent sexy color this year. I will do my best to behave myself. Poindexter also sent a security guard to man the front gate. I love you Mark".

Mark replies "Kristin you are all mine. Now and forever. I can't wait to be by your side tomorrow. You are the hottest sweet innocent sex kitten of the year in my eyes. I heard the Ivy has the best food in Tidewater Virginia. Only a few more days until I get to take you home with me. And have my way with you. Over and over again. I am sending Guadalupe again to stay with Ryan. Just smile and give the 'fuck you look' to the press and don't answer any of their questions. Until then my darling love". Kristin giggles and says "Mark you are a true gentlemen. Keep on courting me handsome. To your bedroom. Love you sugar. Sweet dreams".

Kristin feeling that warm fuzzy feeling makes herself a huge Mediteranean salad and sits in the kitchen relaxing reading The Book of Enoch 3 by Paul C. Schieders. The Book of Enoch is an old composition considered a pseudoepigraphal work. It is also considered an apocryphal work meaning it has a hidden or unknown origin or it is known only in private circles. Listening to U2's 'In the Name of Love', Kristin finishes her dinner and starts singing out loud thrilled that the house is as clean as it could be under the circumstances.

Wanting to look well rested for the big day tomorrow Kristin walks to the barn and feeds the boys dinner and extra Timothy hay. They both looked content and tired from all of the jumping they did today. Kristin shuts the lights off and walks back home admiring the stars and the waxing crescent moon listening to the thousands of frogs croak like a 'Divine Orchestra' watching swarms of fireflies in the fields. Reflecting on her first night in Virginia Kristin walked outside and saw a shooting star and swarms of fireflies in her backyard. Which was the making of her spiritual journey to Eagle Point Plantation.

She decides to do a facial treatment and mask on her face. And one on her hair too. Walking up and down the hallways plugging in lavender scented Renuzit air fresheners through out the first floor. She stops at the Library room and sits down on a leather pub chair and picks up her Ebenezer guitar strumming old Joni Mitchell songs. And then she plays a classical tune by Hildegard Von Bingen. Takes a steaming hot bath, puts on a black silk nightie and falls asleep instantly.

Enlightenment

Feeling especially resfreshed admiring the beautiful floral arrangements Poindexter had delivered and the manicured lawn. With the scent of lavender wafting through the house. Kristin brews a cappucino, eats three oatmeal cranberry cookies and drives to the barn in a hurry. She feeds the horses breakfast and locks them in the indoor arena while she cleans the barn. After putting Zeus and Coconut back in their stalls petting them as they are eating their grain she speeds back home to the house to jump in the shower.

With divine syncronicity Kristin puts on her pale pink dress, curls her hair and puts on the Tiffany diamond necklace and bracelet that Mark gave to her. Does her make up and pins her hair softly up with the rhinestone clips that Julia gave her. Glancing out the driveway from her office window under the attic Kristin sees a fleet of black Jeep security trucks with the Criss Cross Properties LLC emblem, and several brand new black Suburban SUV's that belong to Poindexter with body guards flanking the grounds.

Kristin sees Mark driving his Mercedes AMG to the kitchen entrance with Scott in the passenger seat followed by Susan's Mercedes. Kristin puts on her expensive high heeled shoes and walks to the servants entrance. Mark walks into the kitchen picking Kristin up hugging her and kissing her neck, rubbing her ass wearing a tailored black suit, black wing shoes and a pale pink tie.

Mark says "Kristin. You are breathtaking baby doll" breathing in her ear sweet seductive things. Kristin rubs his crotch moaning and says "I aim to please sugar. I absolutely adore you darling. Keep courting me Mark. You are so incredibly handsome. Here comes Susan and Scott".

Mark and Kristin gain their composure smiling at each other. Kristin says "Hi family. Welcome home. You two look georgous. Poindexter's Rolls Royce Limo is pulling up in front of the house. Take a deep breath. Think happy positive thoughts. Shit here comes dozens of news reporters and camera men. One, two, three flash that 'fuck you look'. Poindexter is coming inside with his body guards" laughing at the fun of Hollywood giving Mark the 'I have to have you seductive smile'.

Poindexter walks into the kitchen between his two bodyguards in a custom tailored black suit that must have been made at Harrods in London. Wearing a pale pink tie to match Kristin's outfit. With a huge smile on his face he hugs Kristin and Susan and shakes Mark and Scott's hands.

Poindexter stares into Kristin's eyes and says "I do believe that you are in love. And are enjoying Mark. You did a wonderful job with my worker's. Kristin I am very proud of you. Everyone is very comfortable with your professionalism and just loves to work here. Susan and Scott so nice to see you both together. I am going to do a statement for the press. And then short interviews with the magazines. And we will take off in my limo before they can ask any questions to the Ivy. Smile for the camera's family".

Poindexter's bodyguards lead him to the front door beyond the foyer, unlocks the door and leads Poindexter out onto the landing. Mark leads Kristin to his left standing next to Poindexter with his hand holding her elbow. Scott does the same thing with Susan on his right standing in their 'Fabulous Five' pose. Dozens of newscasters turn on their video recorders and the photographers are flashing their cameras. Kristin looking at the newscasters vans sees WSET, ABC, CNBC and CBS. Kristin with Mark's nurturing energy by her side smiles her big fucking TV persona to the press staring boldly into the cameras.

Kristin looks at the reporters from the Wall Street Journal and the Virginia Times Newspaper with a twinkle in her eyes notices name tags on the paparrazi from the magazines labeled Entrepeneur, Billionaire Magazine, Fortune, Bloomberg Business Week and Money Magazine. Poindexter thriving in his success admiring his acquisition clears his throat and puts his hands up to quiet the reporters.

Poindexter, an expert and regular news media persona announces "Welcome to Eagle Point Plantation, the most recent spectacular achievement of Criss Cross Properties LLC. Preserving historic homes and buildings act as learning tools not only for architects and builders, but students and communities as well. Think of all the tangible education and history in Virginia that would be lost if historic buildings were demolished instead of preserved or restored. As defined by the National Trust for Historic Act 'preservation is the act of identifying, protecting and enhancing buildings, places, and objects of historical and cultural significance'. It is with our greatest intention to bring Eagle Point Plantation back to life in all of her grandeur to her original condition with my team's expertise and proven track record. I will continue holding press conferences to keep the public enlightened through the process with our master plan of action through completion. Ladies and gentlemen thank you for joining us on this special adventure today. In Jesus name. Amen".

With the cameras still flashing Poindexter answers the magazine reporter's questions one after the other to their satisfaction leaving them with his press secretary Lisa. The body guards lead the 'Fabulous Five' to Poindexter's Rolls Royce Limosine, opens the door as the party climbs in. One of the body guards by the name of Bruce gives the signal to the limo driver to head on. The entire security group surrounds the Plantation and the stables as the press loads up their equipment and heads down the driveway.

Poindexter smiles at his group in smug satisfaction and says "I am going to make Eagle Point more famous than the Cumberland Plantation. Surely fascinated, the magazines are going to be very impressed with the results. He pats Kristin's and Susan's knees affectionately and says "Ladies you were wonderful! I can tell you are getting used to the notoriety. Wait until the magazines hit the shelves. I might have to hire a body guard for you both. All of the executives from Criss Cross will be joining us for lunch. Thank you Mark and Scott for taking care of the ladies" and picks up a call from his secretary April.

Kristin smiles up at Mark giggling rubbing her hip and thigh against his. Mark, Scott and Susan laugh with Kristin at the positively contageous energy flowing through the group. The chauffer pulls up in front of the Ivy Restaurant parking beside a red carpet lined walk way adorned with antique brass oil lanterns and beautiful hanging baskets full of fresh flowers and trailing ivy plants against the fancy red brick building with black french window baskets overflowing with foliage. A valet opens the door to the limo with Scott exiting first helps Susan out, then Poindexter and Mark holding Kristin's hand walk into the restaurant.

The owner of the Ivy, Francis Paul greets the group and shakes Mr. Poindexter's hand. Francis says "Thank you so much for your patronage. Welcome to the Ivy. I will show you to your table". The group follows Francis into a great room decorated with gold silk striped wallpaper, elegant crystal chandeliers and expensive antique Mahogony dining tables. Poindexter's enterauge are already seated, drinking champagne. Francis pulls the chairs out and seats the party and says "Enjoy your meal'. Kristin rubs Mark's thigh under the gold linen table cloth thinking to herself 'Halleleujah Jesus'.

A server shows up and announces "My name is Thomas. I will be your server today". He hands everyone a menu and pours Crystal champagne into their flutes". Another server brings appetizer trays with bacon wrapped shrimp, brie cheese with flatbread, grapes and crudite.

Poindexter stands and says "I would like to make a toast. Thank you for your outstanding participation and stellar performance on your reports for the future restoration of Eagle Point Plantation. The press conference was a huge sucess today. They may become a monthly occurance to keep the public informed on the process of historical restoration".

He raises his champagne flute and says "Here is to Eagle Point Plantation and the staff of Criss Cross Properties LLC. In Jesus name. Amen". The group clinks their champagne flutes saying "Amen. Cheers" and they give Poindexter a standing ovation clapping.

Kristin studying the menu says "Mr. Poindexter your speech was brilliant, instantaneously drawing the audience in so they feel involved. And the connection to the history of Virginia. I am very impressed".

Mark replies "Great comment Kristin. I agree with you 100%. The public will feel included and become obsessed with the finished project". Scott says "I agree" with Susan smiling and shaking her head yes. Poindexter smiles at Kristin and says "Excellent observation Kristin. I actually wrote the speech myself".

Kristin asks Mark "What appeals to you? I am going to have the Belgium Endive and watercress salad and homemade pumpkin ravioli with sage butter". Mark sliding his hand up her thigh says "the Farmer's market brussles sprouts with pancetta, shallots and vinegar and the fresh jumbo Florida stone crab claws". Scott and Susan say "Louisiana jumbo lump crab salad". Poindexter says "I am going to try the lobster club sandwich with the Belgium Endive salad".

Thomas comes to the table and Poindexter places his tables order. Thomas refills their champagne flutes and glasses of ice water. Kristin using a cheese knife spreading brie over the flatbread crackers, feeds one to Mark, hands another to Poindexter and takes a bite of another one that she made for herself. Popping a grape into her mouth she says "The brie is absolutely delicious. Mr. Poindexter I had an idea that we should create a Podcast. Starting with small historical architecture renovations. We can start with a solid oak cross door. And move on to lathe and plaster. I would love to do that for you. College students and architects will die for it".

Poindexter looks at Kristin smiling and says "Excellent idea. Draw an outline and email it to April. I will put it on the agenda at the next Board of Director's meeting" as he picks of a fork full of bacon wrapped shrimp sliding it into his mouth. "This is fantastic. This almost compares to the Ivy Restaurant in Beverly Hills". Kristin laughing says "My brother took me to dinner at the Ivy for my 21st Birthday. And then we went to London for a week. I would have starved if I had to live off the gourmet meals at Langons".

Kristin feeds Mark a shrimp off of her fork wrapping her calf around his leg smiling at everyone. Thomas serves the party their lunch and refills the champagne flutes. Kristin places a few slices of brie on the Endive from her salad plate relishing the taste. Mark eyes Kristin licking her lips with complete lust in his eyes and caresses her inner thigh.

Scott laughs and says "The only thing worth eating in London is fish and chips. Or Indian food out in the country side. This is absolutely delishes. Thank you Mr. Poindexter. You have excellent taste in restaurants. And historical Plantations".

Susan says "I couldn't have said that better myself. My parents sent me to London after I passed the Bar Test. I splurged and bought a London Fog raincoat at Harrods and lived off of biscuits and jam and chocolate bars. Even the airplane food tasted good after eating kidney pie".

Mark laughs and says "I agree with all of you. Last time I stayed in London I went to the market and bought block cheese, French bread and fresh fruit. The 'Free Range Quail' dishes didn't do much for me. I would have to eaten ten of them to satisfy my hunger". Poindexter laughs replying "Julia agrees with you. She only goes to London to shop at Harrods. Then we fly to France and Italy where they have outsdanding cuisine".

The 'Fabulous Five' polish off their lunch and all of the appetizers. The bus boys clear their plates and Francis brings two silver carafes filled with coffee, decaf and creamer. He hands the group dessert menus. Kristin is the first to say "Strawberry shortcake please". Susan says "I will have the same. Poindexter, Mark and Scott order the cherry cheesecake. Kristin asks "Coffee gentlemen?". She serves Poindexter and Mark coffee and decaf for herself.

Francis serves the group dessert. Kristin looking at the huge serving of strawberries with real whipped cream picks up her dessert fork, pierces a strawberry, dips it into the cream and feeds it to Mark. And another one for herself. Kristin says "Susan let's get this recipe. This is delicious", and places a serving on Poindexter's plate. Poindexter tastes the shortcake "Outstanding. The cheesecake is very good too. Don't you feel like you are in Beverly Hills Kristin?". Kristin laughs and replies "This is better that Beverly Hills. The company seated at this table is unbeatable. Thank you very much for lunch Mr. Poindexter". Mark rubs Kristin's thigh with a twinkle in his eyes.

Francis brings the tab and clears the dessert plates. Poindexter pulls out his credit card and says "Mark and Scott, would you be available for a conference call this Friday at 11:00am? I want to go over some details from your reports. April should be done with the Board of Director's meeting minutes by that time". Mark and Scott reply "Absolutely". Francis brings back the lunch ticket smiling looking forward to his tip and says "It was a pleasure serving you. Please visit us again soon".

Poindexter signs the bill replying "Thank you Francis. I am sure that we will", stands up and announces "Thank you everyone for joining us today for lunch. I am sure you will enjoy Eagle Point Plantation on prime time news tonight. Have a great day business partners". The group stands up and claps.

Mark stands up and pulls out Kristin's chair wanting to kiss her. Scott and Susan in deep conversation walking next to each other follow Poindexter to his limo, with Mark and Kristin walking behind giving each other that 'Lust. I want you look'. The group climb into Poindexter's Rolls Royce limo 'covered by His grace' in complete satisfaction. Poindexter immediately calls April listening to his agenda for the rest of his day.

The limo drives down the driveway to Eagle Point and parks in front of the kitchen entrance. The river behind the Plantation is filled with sailboats and several deep water yachts cruising in the breeze. Poindexter puts April on hold and says "Ladies, Mark and Scott. As always I thoroughly enjoyed our day. See you on TV tonight" chuckling at Kristin and Susan fondly, returning to his phone call with April. The men help the ladies out of the limo. Mark hugs and kisses Kristin enjoying her scent and her adoration of him. Scott and Susan hugging next to Mark's car are making weekend plans.

Mark says to Kristin "I will call you tonight after the 5 o'clock news. I can't wait to bring you home with me again this weekend. And hide you in my chambers. And have my way with you. Over and over again. Baby doll. Love you darling". Kristin rubbing her hips against his groin whispers "I am counting the seconds master. I love you too Mark" and kisses Mark on the lips. Mark and Scott take off in his Mercedes, with Susan waving at Kristin following them down the driveway.

Elated Kristin walks down to the East Wing and hangs up her dress, takes of her diamonds, slipping into a red cotton t shirt and yoga pants. Admiring the Plantation and things of yet to come. She hears Ryan run down the hallway who says "Hi mom. Did you have a good day? Do you love your new boyfriend? You finally look happy. I worked very hard today. Can you make me some pork chops, cornbread stuffing and mashed potatoes for dinner?".

Kristin smiles at Ryan and says "Yes. I had a great day and love Mark very much. Things are going divinely well. I am glad that you had a great day too. I will go start your dinner" as they both walk down to the kitchen.

Kristin takes two center cut pork chops, a sliced Vidalia onion and a minced clove of garlic and places the ingredients into a glass Pyrex pan, drizzling olive oil on top and places the dish into the oven. She dices four Yukon Gold potatoes and places them in a pot of water. Chops two stalks of celery, another diced onion and a cup full of dried cranberries and ads the cornbread stuffing mix with two cups of vegetable broth into a saucepan. Kristin walks out to her garden and picks a basket full of green beans snacking on a one enjoying the fresh sweet taste of home grown vegetables.

Relaxed and happy Kristin watches the 5:00 o'clock prime time news broadcasting the press interview at Eagle Point this afternoon. Kristin calls out to Ryan "Come see me on TV hurry". She laughs at the charisma and charm of the 'Fabulous Five', gushing over what a great couple her and Mark make. Kristin serves Ryan dinner in the dining room and serves herself a plate of mashed potatoes, stuffing and green beans, leaving it in the microwave to eat for dinner later.

The phone rings at 5:55pm with Mark's caller ID flashing on her phone. Kristin answers "Hello my darling. How did you know that I was just thinking about you? You are my knight in shinning armor. We looked so sophisticately elegant and in love on the news tonight. And the 'Fabulous Five' looks like we can conquer the world with our positive energy. You must have drove Scott so I couldn't seduce you into my bedroom. Just teasing you honey".

Mark laughing replies "Kristin it is called self discipline. You are outrageously georgous. I enjoyed being by your side and smelling your hot sweet scent. We are going to be on every prime time news channel in the State of Virginia at 6:00pm and again at 10:00pm. I am never going to let you out of my sight again. I am trying to catch up on work so I can spoil you rotten all weekend".

Kristin giggling says "Keep on courting me sweetheart. You are all that my heart desires and are my dream come true Mark. I will be dreaming all night about your hot sexy naked body on top of me. Among other naughty things. Thanks again Mark for just you. Sweet dreams honey. Love you".

Mark laughs and says "Kristin it is all my pleasure. You are my treasure. And I am going to do nothing but pleasure you all weekend and listen to you moan over and over again. And take you out to dinner. Cook you brunch and take you on a walk on the beach. Sleep tight my princess, love and adore you too. Goodnight".

Kristin in euphoria walks to the barn to tuck the horses in, feeding them sweet feed and hay for dinner petting their beautiful faces. She turns off the lights and walks back home under the constellations Virgo-who in spiritual context holds the wheat in her hand with Christ 'the Bread of Life' feeding us wisdom and understanding and Bootes- one of the largest constellations in the sky located in the northern celestial hemisphere dominated by 'the Kite', a diamond-shaped asterism formed by its brightest stars, with swarms of dragonflies and fireflies lighting up the path in front of her. After finishing her dinner and loading the dishwasher, she soaks in the tub for a long time and falls asleep instantly in 'Divine peace, love and light'.

In gratitude, Kristin wakes up well rested. She puts on a yellow thin cotton sweat suit, heads to the kitchen noticing that the Bayside Transit is heading down the driveway to take Ryan to work. Looking up Kristin says "Thank you Jesus. Amen". Kristin turns on the coffee pot, scrambles a few eggs and toasts a Thomas English Muffin listening to Aerosmith's 'I Don't Want to Miss a Thing' singing out loud dancing around the kitchen. Finishing her coffee after eating breakfast Kristin drives her ATV to take care of Zeus and Coconut. Smiling as she listens to them whinny, Kristin hangs there breakfast buckets in their stalls, throws the peacocks a scoop of scratch grains in deep inner peace. She turns the horses out in a field as a Gloucester Florist delivery truck pulls up in front of the barn.

A short blonde woman wearing a name tag 'Daisy' gets out of the van carrying a crystal vase filled with several dozen pink and lavender colored long stemmed roses. Daisy asks "Would you happen to be Kristin? This place is huge. I have lived in Gloucester my entire life and didn't know this place existed. I saw you on TV last night. Enjoy your flowers, there is a card attached".

Kristin smiles as she inhales the scent of the roses, takes the card and replies "Why thank you Daisy. Now you can say that you have been to

Eagle Point Plantation. Just wait until you see this month's magazine covers. Have a blessed day!".

Kristin walks to her office in the barn, turns on the AC and places the flowers on her desk. Sitting at her desk she opens the card, intuitively already knowing that the roses are from Mark. Kristin opens the card smiling with tears in her eyes after all of the years of abuse she has been through. Reading the card out loud "Stay lost in this moment with your love that I treasure. Love, Mark". Kristin looks up and says "Thank God that we are together Mark".

Kristin takes a picture of the flowers and texts it to Susan "Jumping lesson? I am in the barn". Kristin texts Mark "Every special moment with you Mark is priceless. And irreplacible. Counting the seconds until I see you Saturday. You make my heart sing sugar. Love you darling". Susan texts Kristin back "Give me an hour. I can't wait. Thanks sweetie". Kristin turns on the radio listening to Bon Jovi's 'Alejuia' singing along out loud. She finishes cleaning the barn as Susan pulls her ATV up at approximately 11:11am.

Susan smiling says "Kristin, Mark is a hopeless romantic. I am so glad that you two found each other. You really deserve that. What a true gentleman. Scott sent me three dozen red roses last night. I just want to pinch you. Is this for real?". Kristin says "I know Susan. And it is. Just fucking call it a 'fate accompli', 'God's calling', divine intervention, persuasion from the Universe or 'Intergalactic healing energy'. And all of the above".

The horses run up to the fence with excitement. Kristin grabs a lead rope and hands one to Susan. The ladies walk the horses into the cross ties, grooming them and brushing out their long blonde flowing tails. Kristin and Susan change into their boots and britches in her office, grabbing their saddles and bridles. They tack up the horses and lead them into the indoor arena. Kristin turns on the fans admiring the jumping course that she had Ryan help her set up. The ladies mount and walk side by side around the arena talking about Mark and Scott, true love and God.

Kristin picks up the posting trot loving the rythum keeping Zeus on the rail. After four laps she changes directions and does a collected sitting trot for three laps. Brings Zeus down to the walk looking at

Susan on Coconut. She says "You two are sure making a team. I actually never thought that I would share him with anyone. I am glad he loves you". Kristin nudges Zeus into the canter with her outside heel feeling '1900 pounds of power underneath her'. Kristin does a figure of eight, asks Zeus for a lead change and rises into the two point position for two laps.

Kristin slows Zeus down to a walk to let him and Coconut catch their breath in the heat. Susan says "I absolutely love riding with you. I have never felt so good in my life with our friendship Kristin. And Scott. Ofcourse Poindexter as well. I can't wait to see the magazine covers" as she pets Coconut's neck.

Kristin laughs and says "Amen. Let's trot the double X oxer with the ground lines back and fourth four times. Trot in over the gate, canter five strides out over the yellow oxer, turn left over the roll top oxer, canter the outside line with the peacock blue striped rails in three strides, cross the diagonal and finish over the triple bar with the flower boxes underneath. Ready? 'Come Follow Me'. Like Jesus says".

Kristin picks up the trot steering Zeus toward the double X exercise back and forth four times. Smiling she picks up the trot, expertly riding Zeus through her jumping course. When she is done she turns her head as Susan is laughing and petting Coconut's neck in sheer 'Divine joy'. The ladies walk the horses around cooling them out and head back into the show barn. They lead the horses into the cross ties, unbridle them and put their halters on giggling at each other. They ungirth the saddles and put them back into the tack room. Susan gives the horses bathes while Kristin fills up their feeders with Timothy hay and sweet feed. Susan puts both horses in their stalls elated. The girls head back to Kristin's office, put their boots and britches away and change back into their street clothes.

Susan says "Thanks Kristin. I really needed that. I love your company and this place. Scott is taking me out to the Kilmarnock Inn Bistro on Saturday. I am falling madly in love with him. Lunch, manicures and pedicures on Friday?".

Kristin laughs replying "I told Mark to orchestrate everything. I love suprises. I will pick you up around noon. You are really advancing in your riding skills. Just ride the wave Susan. To the highest vibration of the Universe. To that special place called 'Unconditional Love'. See you Friday sweetie". Kristin gives Susan a hug, walks to her ATV and drives back to the 'Notorious previously haunted Plantation who is going to make a come back in all of her glory'.

'To be continued'

About the Author

Kristin Osborne

Kristin is a real estate foreclosure prevention specialist, avid equestrian and mother of two children. Her deep love of historical homes and fascination with the spiritual world brought her from her native Los Angeles to Virginia in 2010 where she resides in Gloucester with her son, two horses and two cats.

www.ingramcontent.com/pod-product-compliance
Lightning Source LLC
LaVergne TN
LVHW091632070526
838199LV00044B/1039